In Search of
April Raintree

Critical Edition

In Search of
April Raintree

Beatrice Culleton Mosionier

Critical Edition
Edited by Cheryl Suzack

PORTAGE & MAIN PRESS

Winnipeg • Canada

The publisher acknowledges the financial support of the Government of Canada through the Book Publishing Industry Development Program (BPIDP) for our publishing activities.

Canadä

Canadian Cataloguing in Publication Data
Mosionier, Beatrice, 1949-
    In search of April Raintree
    ISBN 1-894110-43-9

1. Métis – Manitoba – Winnipeg – Fiction.
I. Suzack, Cheryl. II. Title.

PS8555.U475I5 1999   C813'.54   C99-920120-4
PR9199.3.C767I5 1999

Book and Cover Design: Suzanne Gallant
Printed and bound in Canada by Kromar Printing Ltd.

Portage & Main Press
(Peguis Publishers)
100-318 McDermot Avenue
Winnipeg, Manitoba, Canada   R3A 0A2
Toll Free: 1-800-667-9673

Contents

Introduction

In a letter to American poet Constance Webb, noted political activist, intellectual visionary, and Caribbean writer C.L.R. James captures the spirit and character of collaborative working relationships. He states, "One person writes but in the world in which we live all serious contributions have to be collective;... Although one mind may unify, the contributory material and ideas must come from all sources and types of mind...." (qtd. in Grimshaw 10). James' words could not more appropriately describe this project. From its inception, this new critical edition of Beatrice Culleton Mosionier's *In Search of April Raintree* has been collaborative in nature and ambitious in spirit.

The catalyst for this edition is the continuing relevance and value of *In Search of April Raintree* for contemporary Canadian readers. Mosionier's representation of the life stories of two Métis sisters, who suffer the breakdown of their family relations and the injustices of the social services system, offers a powerful examination of the effects of racism in society. The author's treatment of a harrowing rape trial in which the defendants justify their actions on the basis that the woman was Native and a prostitute reinforces the connections between material realities and social injustices. Yet, as many essays in the collection illustrate, *In Search of April Raintree* appeals to readers through its emotional as well as through its literary and political merits. Helen Hoy's "'Nothing but the Truth': Discursive Transparency in Beatrice Culleton" notes how one of her students felt "distraught" and "off-kilter" for 24 hours after reading the novel. In "'The Only Dirty Book': The Rape of *April Raintree*," Peter Cumming remarks that in anonymous surveys students consistently place *In Search of April Raintree* at the top of the list of books that have meant the most to them. The novel owes its success as much to its ability to emotionally engage readers as to its consideration of familiar themes, values, and ideas. As Heather Zwicker points out in "The Limits of Sisterhood," the novel works through the "simplicity of its literal story, the story of sisters."

The publishing history of *In Search of April Raintree* also attests to its continuing appeal and broad readership since its first publication by Pemmican in 1983. In its first nine years of circulation, the novel sold over 82,000 copies, and continues, on average, to sell 6,000 copies a year with Peguis (Hoy 182). To date, it has been translated into three languages (German, Dutch, and French), and anthologized in such wide-ranging collections as *Our Bit of Truth: An Anthology of Canadian Native Literature* (1990), *Kitchen Talk: Contemporary Women's Prose and Poetry* (1992), and *Sociology* (1996). It is a novel that crosses disciplinary boundaries to engage with issues of racism and the socialization of Native children, "truth-telling" and the representation of social discourse, and First Nations literary history and the quest for identity. The essays represented here cross cultures as the collection draws on the experience and expertise of contributing scholars from a variety of cultural backgrounds.[1] As the first critical edition of a Native Canadian text, the collection aims to engage current debates in literary criticism and to intervene in the field of Native Canadian literature.

In the collection's opening essay, "Deploying Identity in the Face of Racism," Margery Fee examines the relationship between the "discourse of race" and state-controlled definitions of Aboriginal identity. Fee's analysis of the implications of revisions to the Indian Act with Bill C-31 and the inclusion of Métis as a category of Aboriginal identity illustrates how state-controlled definitions of "Nativeness" rely on concepts of "ethnic purity" for their legitimacy. They thus retrench identity as a fixed, stable category and overlook the multiple connections of Native peoples across historical, social, and political boundaries. Claiming that Mosionier's novel "rejects whiteness or Nativeness as simple, clearcut identities," Fee proposes that the category "Native" be rethought as both a fluid and contested site of identification in order for these affiliations to be recognized. Her essay focuses attention on the author's attempts to theorize Native identity not as an inherent category, but as a tool to use in ever-changing social relationships.

Janice Acoose in "The Problem of 'Searching' For April Raintree" demonstrates how Mosionier's novel thematizes the absence of positive narratives of Métis culture and history in her exploration of the Raintree sisters' quests to recover a sense of self and community. Connecting Mosionier's construction of a "dis-eased narrative voice" with the exclusion of Métis nationalist writers like Emma LaRocque and Howard Adams from public discourse, Acoose argues that *In Search of April Raintree* resists readers' attempts to find within it representations of Métis culture and history. Instead of offering a vision of Métis cultural identity, the novel "opens a space for critical discourse about the formation of identity and the transmission of culture." Acoose argues that by resisting readers' expectations, the novel encourages readers to look beyond the text and to take responsibility for their education. In this manner, Acoose suggests, readers "may come to know something about Métis history and culture."

In "Abuse and Violence: April Raintree's Human Rights (if she had any)," Agnes Grant analyses *In Search of April Raintree* from a position that is seldom recognized, yet has emerged with increasing urgency in light of the history of Indian residential schools in Canada: the position that considers the rights of the child. Drawing attention to the plight of April Raintree as she is relocated from the poverty of her birth family to the racism of her foster family, Grant argues that "there is no movement in Canada today, nor has there ever been one, that examines the rights of children the way feminists have explored the abuse of women." Grant illustrates how Mosionier's novel documents the vulnerability of Aboriginal women and children to poverty and racism while simultaneously insisting on the theme of resistance and renewal.

Beatrice Culleton Mosionier's "The Special Time" explores the personal events that have shaped her continuing engagement with issues of racism and suicide. Speaking of her struggle to overcome the devastation of suicide within her family, Mosionier describes how her response to the problem was transformed by Jane Elliot's "Blue-eyed/Brown-eyed" exercise, a program in racism awareness that allows individuals and groups to experience negative stereotypes commonly assigned to "people of colour, women, and other 'outsiders' in society." In her affirmation of the need to provide respect and dignity to individuals and communities, Mosionier raises the question of the nature of our individual and collective responsibility to each other, a question that is explored by many of the papers in this collection.

In "What Constitutes a Meaningful Life?: Identity Quest(ion)s in *In Search of April Raintree*," Michael Creal explores the "narrative quests" of April and Cheryl Raintree to illustrate Mosionier's engagement with questions of social ethics and moral issues. Creal suggests that the central spiritual issue for contemporary society is the problem of what constitutes a meaningful life. He argues that Mosionier's depiction of the quests of the Raintree sisters for a sense of self and community critiques the values inherent in contemporary society that jeopardize April and Cheryl's ability to regain a meaningful sense of themselves and their community. His essay shows how Mosionier's novel prompts readers to scrutinize social values in order to begin questioning the society that we participate in making.

Identifying the need for a broader understanding of the interaction of material realities and the shaping of narrative, Jeanne Perreault's "In Search of Cheryl Raintree, and Her Mother" considers the social and physical realities facing many people of Native heritage. These include "illness, infant mortality, foster care, alcoholism, rape, domestic violence against women, prostitution, and suicide." As Perreault writes, "representing these violations against her characters is not only an aesthetic choice for Mosionier. It is essential to the informing discourse of the novel." The statistics she relates provide invaluable information about the effects of systemic poverty and racism. They also illustrate the strength and commitment of Native peoples to redefine identity and to restore community values. Interwoven with the realities of systemic racism and economic impoverishment, as Perreault's paper illustrates, is a commitment to cultural revitalization, holism, and community that affirms the spirituality and survival within Native communities.

In "'Nothing but the Truth': Discursive Transparency in Beatrice Culleton," Helen Hoy examines early critical responses to *In Search of April Raintree* to critique reviewers' assumptions that the novel offers "uncrafted testimony" and "artless" narrative. Hoy observes that "in a novel in which the telling of truths and half-truths proliferates both socially and personally, in which 'lies, secrets, and silence' are both inflicted upon April and her sister Cheryl by foster parents, social workers, and history books, and prove to be a destructive component of their interactions, honesty and truth seem to function as talismans." Hoy argues that readers need to be "wary" of the novel's appearance of "art-less craft." We need to attend to its layered discursive registers, to its simultaneous "craft" and "craft-iness," for, as Hoy suggests, "if novelty, authorial self-expression, and originality of execution give way in Culleton's aesthetic credo to instrumental and communal values, then her writing may require different methods of evaluation" and the commitment on the part of readers to recognize these as "artistic achievements."

Jo-Ann Thom, in "The Effect of Readers' Responses on the Development of Aboriginal Literature in Canada: A Study of Maria Campbell's *Halfbreed*, Beatrice Culleton's *In Search of April Raintree*, and Richard Wagamese's *Keeper'n Me*," also credits the artistic achievement of *In Search of April Raintree*. Noting its importance for many Canadian Aboriginal writers, Thom contends that *In Search of April Raintree* "showed would-be Aboriginal writers that they could work in the medium of fiction to create narratives that do not claim to tell a true story but that nevertheless reveal 'truths.'" Thom draws on students' responses and new voices in contemporary Aboriginal literature to illustrate how the "truths" of systemic racism and cultural dislocation that Maria Campbell and Beatrice Mosionier examined are reimagined by contemporary writers like Richard Wagamese as narratives of cultural healing. Thom suggests that contemporary authors not only recognize and extend the work of previous Aboriginal writers, they also transform racist discourse into narratives that affirm Aboriginal culture and identity.

In "'The Only Dirty Book': The Rape of *April Raintree*," Peter Cumming contends that the revised version of *In Search of April Raintree* represents a seriously flawed adaptation of the original novel. Cumming notes how the edited version "obsessively sanitizes the overt sexuality and violence and swearing" of the original, and thus compromises the elements of verisimilitude that give the unrevised text so much political force. Focusing on the pivotal rape scene in both novels, Cumming questions the principles of revision that would remove the passages signifying violence against women, yet retain the racist slurs directed against the protagonist's Native identity. Cumming argues that if the rape scene metaphorically represents relations between Native and non-Native people, then the effect of its revision is to seriously depoliticize Mosionier's indictment of a society that simultaneously disempowers April Raintree both as a Native and as a woman.

In the final essay in the collection, "The Limits of Sisterhood," Heather Zwicker considers the implications of sisterhood in *In Search of April Raintree* in order to examine how Mosionier's novel theorizes the following questions that are at issue within feminism: how might we conceptualize community among women without asserting similarities or identities where there are none, and how do we celebrate difference without giving up on the possibility of solidarity? As Zwicker suggests, "the novel resonates with the metaphoric implications of sisterhood, demonstrating that even within a relationship as close as literal sisters there exist irreducible differences between women that make community a vexed and difficult, but nonetheless crucial, venture." Through an analysis of the political views that the Raintree sisters adopt—April decides to assimilate and thus becomes a proponent of "liberal quiescence," Cheryl embraces her Métis inheritance and articulates a position defined by "identity politics"—Zwicker argues that "the disintegration of the relationship between April and Cheryl as the novel unfolds serves to demonstrate the inevitable disintegration of a feminism that fails to respond to the need for a community founded on mutual responsibility and recognition of difference." Zwicker's essay raises compelling questions for readers about the relationship between political commitments and constitutive realities.

The essays presented here initiate debate, contribute to critical perspectives on Native Canadian literature, and attest to the continuing strength of stories to inspire and move us. If, as Merle Hodge suggests, "the proper role of fiction in human societies includes allowing a people to 'read' itself—to decipher its own reality" (205), then Beatrice Culleton Mosionier's *In Search of April Raintree* provides readers with a compelling narrative whose complex perceptions and powerful illustrations represent its determined attempts to decipher reality. These essays affirm its complexity, celebrate its achievements, and gesture toward what Jeannette Armstrong calls "a new order of culturalism and relationship beyond colonial thought and practise" (8).

Cheryl Suzack
Editor

Acknowledgments

I would like to thank the contributors to this critical edition for the pleasure of working with them on this project. I would also like to thank the many people who provided invaluable advice and support along the way. I am indebted to Sue Hamilton, Stephen Slemon, Sujaya Dhanvantari, Mary Elizabeth Leighton, Susan Sheard, Bill Roszell, Heather Zwicker, Nima Naghibi, Jeanne Perreault, and especially, Catherine Lennox and Charmagne de Veer. I am grateful to the Social Sciences and Humanities Research Council of Canada for a doctoral fellowship which has supported my research.

Notes

[1] I have opted to retain the terms of naming that individual authors use in their essays. Readers will note that authors make reference to Native, Aboriginal, Indigenous, and First Nations in accordance with their individual preferences.

Works Cited

Alford, Edna, and Claire Harris, eds. *Kitchen Talk: Contemporary Women's Prose and Poetry*. Red Deer, AB: Red Deer College Press, 1992.

Armstrong, Jeannette. "Editor's Note." *Looking at the Words of our People: First Nations Analysis of Literature*. Ed. Jeannette Armstrong. Penticton, BC: Theytusu, 1993.

Grant, Agnes, ed. *Our Bit of Truth: An Anthology of Canadian Native Literature*. Winnipeg: MB, Pemmican, 1990.

Grimshaw, Anna, ed. *The C.L.R. James Reader*. Oxford: Blackwell Publishers, 1992.

Hodge, Merle. "Challenges of the Struggle for Sovereignty: Changing the World versus Writing Stories." *Caribbean Women Writers: Essays from the First International Conference*. Ed. Selwyn R. Cudjoe. Wellesley, MA: Calaloux Publications, 1990. 202–208.

Hoy, Helen. "'Nothing but the Truth': Discursive Transparency in Beatrice Culleton." *ARIEL:* 25.1 (1994): 155–84.

Macionis, John J., Juanne Nancarrow Clarke, and Linda M. Gerber. *Sociology: Second Edition*. Scarborough, ON: Prentice Hall, 1997.

In memory of my sisters,
Vivian and Kathy

Acknowledgments

I would like to give special thanks to Associate Chief Judge Murray C. Sinclair for his advice and assistance. And, of course, my appreciation goes out to all my families.

Beatrice Culleton Mosionier

A Note on the Text

For this new edition, corrections have been made to the text of *In Search for April Raintree* to improve legibility and style. They include corrections in spelling, punctuation, ellipsis, formatting, and style.

The numbers in the margins of the text are the corresponding page numbers of the 1983 and 1992 editions.

Chapter One

Memories. Some memories are elusive, fleeting, like a butterfly that touches down and is free until it is caught. Others are haunting. You'd rather forget them, but they won't be forgotten. And some are always there. No matter where you are, they are there, too. I always felt most of my memories were better avoided, but now I think it's best to go back in my life before I go forward. Last month, April 18th, I celebrated my twenty-fourth birthday. That's still young but I feel so old.

My father, Henry Raintree, was of mixed blood, a little of this, a little of that, and a whole lot of Indian. My sister, Cheryl, who was eighteen months younger than me, had inherited his looks: black hair, dark brown eyes which turned black when angry, and brown skin. There was no doubt they were both of Indian ancestry. My mother, Alice, on the other hand, was part Irish and part Ojibway. Like her, I had pale skin, not that it made any difference when we were living as a family. We lived in Norway House, a small northern Manitoba town, before my father contracted tuberculosis.

Then we moved to Winnipeg. I used to hear him talk about TB and how it had caused him to lose everything he had worked for. Both my Mom and Dad always took this medicine and I always thought it was because of TB. Although we moved from one rundown house to another, I remember only one, on Jarvis Avenue. And of course, we were always on welfare. I knew that from the way my Dad used to talk. Sometimes he would put himself down and sometimes he counted the days till he could walk down to the place where they gave out cheques and food stamps.

It seemed to me that after the welfare cheque days, came the medicine days. That was when my parents would take a lot of medicine and it always changed them. Mom, who was usually quiet and calm, would talk and laugh in a loud obnoxious way, and Dad, who already talked and laughed a lot, just got clumsier. The times they took the medicine the most were the times when many other grown-ups would come over and drink it with them. To avoid these people, I would take Cheryl into our tiny bedroom, close the door, and put my box of old rusted toys in front of the door. Besides the aunties and uncles out there, there were strange men and they would start yelling and sometimes they would fight, right in our small house. I would lie on my cot listening to them knocking things over and bumping into walls. Sometimes they would crash into our door and I would grow even more petrified, even though I knew Mom and Dad were out there with them. It always took a long time before I could get to sleep.

There were days when they came with their own children. I didn't much like these children either, for they were sullen and cranky and wouldn't talk or play with us or else they were aggressive bullies who only wanted to fight us. Usually, their faces were dirty, their noses were runny, and I was sure they had done "it" in their pants because they smelled terrible. If they had to stay the night, I remember I would put our blankets on the floor for them, stubbornly refusing to share our cot with them. Once Mom had let a little girl sleep with us and during the night she wet the bed. It had been a long time before the smell went away.

My mother didn't always drink that medicine, not as much as my father did. That's when she would clean the house, bake, and do the laundry and sewing. If she was really happy, she would sing us songs, and at night, she would rock Cheryl to sleep. But that was one kind of happiness that didn't come often enough for me. To prolong that mood in her, I would help her with everything, chattering away in desperation, lest my own silences would push her back into her normal remoteness. My first cause for vanity was that, out of all the houses of the people we knew, my mother kept the cleanest house. Except for those mornings after. She would tell her friends that it was because she was raised in a residential school and then worked as a housekeeper for the priest in her hometown.

Cheryl and I always woke up before our parents, so I would tend to Cheryl's needs. I would feed her whatever was available, then wash her, and dress her in clean clothes. Weather permitting, we would then go off to the park, which was a long walk, especially on hot summer days. Our daily routine was dictated by our hunger pangs and by daylight. Darkness brought out the boogeymen, and Dad told us what they did to little children. I liked all of Dad's stories, even the scary ones, because I knew that Cheryl and I were always safe in the house.

It was very rare when Mom would go downtown to the department stores where they had ride-on stairs. Mom didn't like going shopping. I guess it was because sometimes people were rude to her. When that happened, Mom would get a hurt look in her eyes and act apologetic. One day, I didn't notice any of that because that day I saw my first black person. I was sure he was a boogeyman and wondered how come he wandered around so easily as if nothing was wrong. I watched him, and he stopped at the watch counter. Since Mom and Cheryl were nearby and there were a lot of other people close enough, I went over to him. My voice was very shaky, but I asked, "Mr. Boogeyman, what do you do with the children you catch?"

"What's that?" his voice seemed to rumble from deep within him, and when he turned to look at me, I thought he had the kindest eyes I'd ever seen. Maybe, though, they changed at night. No, he couldn't be bad.

"Nothing," I said and walked back to my mother's side. When winter came, we didn't go to the park anymore. There was plenty to do with the snow around our house. Sometimes, Mom would come out and help us build our snowmen and our houses. One December, we all went downtown to watch the Santa Claus parade. That was such a thrilling, magical day for me. After that, we went to visit an aunt and uncle where Cheryl and I had a glorious old time feasting on cake, fruit, and hot chocolate. Then we walked home. Dad threw snowballs at Mom for a bit before he carried sleepy-eyed Cheryl in his arms. I was enchanted by all the coloured Christmas lights and the decorations in the store windows. I think that was the best day ever, because Mom and Dad laughed for real.

Not long after that, many people came to our house to drink the "medicine," and in the beginning, they all sounded cheerful and happy. But later, they started their yelling, and even the women were angrily shouting. One woman was loudly wailing, and it sounded like she'd gotten smacked a few times.

In the middle of the night when everything had been quiet for a while, I got up to go to the toilet. There were people sprawled all over the place, sleeping and snoring.

One man, though, who was half sitting up against a wall, grumbled and shifted and I saw that his pants were open. I knew that I should hurry, but I just stood there watching and he played around with his thing. Then he peed right in my direction. That made me move back out of the room. I went through the kitchen, and there was my Dad sleeping on the bare floor, still in his clothes. I wondered why, so I went to their bedroom. When I put the light switch on, I saw my mother. She was bare-naked and kissing a strange man. I guess she realized that someone was in the room, and she sat up while trying to hide her nakedness. She looked scared, but when she saw that it was only me, she hissed at me, "Get out of here!"

I forgot about having to go to the toilet and went back to my bed. I tried to figure everything out, but I couldn't.

A few days later, I was sitting on my Dad's lap, and Mom was doing the laundry. A woman came to visit, but then it became an argument. She was shouting terrible names, and she began to push my mother around. Meanwhile, Dad just watched them and laughed and even egged them on. To me this was all so confusing. I just knew that Mom shouldn't have kissed someone else; my Dad shouldn't have slept on the floor; that old man shouldn't have played with himself and then peed on the floor; and right now, Dad ought to be trying to protect Mom, not finding the whole thing amusing. I squirmed off Dad's lap, walked over to that woman, and kicked her as hard as I could, yelling for her to leave Mom alone. I heard Dad laughing even louder. But it worked because the strange woman left.

That winter, I noticed that my Mom was getting fatter and fatter. When winter was finished, my Mom got so sick from being fat she had to go away to the hospital. One of our aunties came to stay with us. She and Dad would sit around joking and drinking their medicine. I used to wonder how come they all drank this medicine, yet no one ever got better. Another thing, they couldn't all be sick like Mom and Dad, could they? So one evening while Dad and Auntie Eva were busy playing cards, I picked up his glass and took a quick swallow before he could stop me. Ugh! It burned my mouth and my throat and made me cough and choke. I spit it out as fast as I could. It was purely awful and I was even more puzzled as to why they all seemed to enjoy taking it. I felt so sorry for them and I was real glad I wasn't sick.

When my mother came back, she wasn't as fat as when she left. The snow was all gone, too. We celebrated my sixth birthday and one of my presents was a book. I took my book with me everywhere. There was talk of my going to school in the fall. I didn't know what reading and printing were like, but I was very curious about them. I looked forward to school. I promised Cheryl I would teach her reading and printing as soon as I knew how. But for the time being, I would pretend to read to Cheryl, and as I turned the pages of my book like Mom did, I would make up stories to match the pictures in the book.

A few weeks later, we came home from a day's ramblings to find a real live baby in Mom's arms. Mom was rocking it and singing a soft melody to it. I asked her, "Where did it come from?"

"The hospital. She was very sick. She's your new little sister, Anna."

"Will she have to take that medicine? It tastes awful," I said, pitying the baby for being sick.

"No, she drinks milk. The nurse came this morning and helped me prepare some," Mom answered. I knew from the way she talked that she hadn't taken any medicine so far. I hoped that from now on she wouldn't have to take it any more. I studied the baby for a while. It was so tiny and wrinkled. I decided I'd much rather play with Cheryl.

That summer, Cheryl and I spent whole days at the park. I would make us sandwiches of bread and lard so we wouldn't have to walk back home in the middle of the day. That's when it seemed the hottest. We played on the swings and slides and in the sandbox as long as they weren't being used by the other children. We would build sandcastles and install caterpillars and ladybugs in them. If the other children were there, we would stay apart from them and watch the man mow the park grass, enjoying the smell of the fresh-cut lawns and the sound from the motor of the lawnmower. Sometimes the droning noise lulled Cheryl to sleep, and I would sit by her to wait for her to wake up.

There were two different groups of children that went to the park. One group was the brown-skinned children who looked like Cheryl in most ways. Some of them even came over to our house with their parents. But they were dirty looking and they dressed in real raggedy clothes. I didn't care to play with them at all. The other group was white-skinned, and I used to envy them, especially the girls with blond hair and blue eyes. They seemed so clean and fresh and reminded me of flowers I had seen. Some of them were freckled, but they didn't seem to mind. To me, I imagined they were very rich and lived in big, beautiful houses, and there was so much that I wondered about them. But they didn't care to play with Cheryl and me. They called us names and bullied us.

We were ignored completely only when both groups were at the park. Then they were busy yelling names at each other. I always thought that the white-skinned group had the upper hand in name-calling. Of course, I didn't know what "Jew" or the other names meant. Cheryl was too young to realize anything, and she was usually happy-go-lucky.

Our free, idle days with our family came to an end one summer afternoon. We came home, and there were some cars in front of our house. One had flashing red lights on it, and I knew it was a police car. When we entered the house, Mom was sitting at the table, openly weeping, right in front of all these strange people. There were empty medicine bottles on the small counter and the table, but I couldn't figure out why the four people were there. A nice-smelling woman knelt down to talk to me.

"My name is Mrs. Grey. I bet you're April, aren't you? And this little girl must be Cheryl." She put her hand on Cheryl's head in a friendly gesture, but I didn't trust her.

I nodded that we were April and Cheryl, but I kept my eyes on my mother. Finally I asked, "Why is Mom crying? Did you hurt her?"

"No, dear, your mother is ill and she won't be able to take care of you anymore. Would you like to go for a car ride?" the woman asked.

My eyes lit up with interest. We'd been in a taxi a few times, and it had been a lot of fun. But then I thought of Baby Anna. I looked around for her. "Where's Anna?"

"Anna's sick," the woman answered. "She's gone to the hospital. Don't worry, we'll take you for a ride to a nice clean place. You and Cheryl, okay?"

That was not okay. I wanted to stay. "We can stay with Daddy. He will take care of us. You can go away now," I said. It was all settled.

But Mrs. Grey said in a gentle voice, "I'm afraid not, honey. We have to take you and Cheryl with us. Maybe if your Mommy and Daddy get well enough, you can come to live with them again."

The man who was with Mrs. Grey had gone to our bedroom to get all our things. He came back with a box. I was more worried, and I looked from the woman to the man, then over to one policeman who was looking around, then to the other who was writing in a notepad. I finally looked back at my Mom for reassurance. She didn't look at me, but I said in a very definite manner, "No, we'd better stay here."

I was hoping Dad would walk in, and he would make them all go away. He would make everything right.

The man with the box leaned over and whispered something to my mother. She forced herself to stop sobbing, slowly got up, and came over to us. I could see that she was struggling to maintain control.

"April, I want you and Cheryl to go with these people. It will only be for a little while. Right now, Daddy and me, well, we can't take care of you. You'll be all right. You be good girls, for me. I'm sorry... "

She couldn't say anymore because she started crying again. I didn't like to see her this way, especially in front of these people. She hugged us, and that's when I started crying, too. I kind of knew that she was really saying goodbye to us, but I was determined that we were not going to be taken away. I clung to my Mom as tight as I could. They wouldn't be able to pull me away from her, and then they would leave. I expected Mom to do the same. But she didn't. She pushed me away. Into their grasping hands. I couldn't believe it. Frantically, I screamed, "Mommy, please don't make us go. Please, Mommy. We want to stay with you. Please don't make us go. Oh, Mom, don't!"

I tried hard to put everything into my voice, sure that they would all come to their senses and leave us be. There were a lot of grown-up things I didn't understand that day. My mother should have fought with her life to keep us with her. Instead, she handed us over. It didn't make any sense to me.

The car door slammed shut on us.

"Please, don't make us go," I said in a subdued, quiet voice, knowing at the same time that I was wasting my time. I gripped Cheryl's hand, and we set off into the unknown. We were both crying and ignored the soothing voices from the strangers in front.

How could Mom do this to us? What was going to happen to us? Well, at least I still had Cheryl. I thought this to myself over and over again. Cheryl kept crying, although I'm not sure she really knew why. She loved car rides, but if I was crying, I'm sure she felt she ought to be crying too.

We were taken to an orphanage. When we got there, Cheryl and I were hungry and exhausted. Inside the largo building, all the walls were painted a dismal green. The sounds we made echoed down the long, high-ceilinged corridors. Then this person came out of a room to greet us.

She was dressed in black from head to foot, except for some stiff white cardboard around her neck and face. She had chains dangling around her waist, and she said her name was Mother Superior and she had been expecting us. My eyes widened in fear. It was even worse than I had imagined. We were being handed over to the boogeyman for sure! When Mrs. Grey and the man said goodbye and turned to leave, I wanted to go with them, but I was too scared to ask. Mother Superior took us into another room at the far end of the corridor. Here, another woman dressed the same way undressed us and bathed us. She looked through our hair for bugs, she told us. I thought that was pretty silly, because I knew that bugs lived in trees and grass, not in people's hair. Of course, I didn't say anything, even when she started cutting off my long hair.

I was thinking that this was like the hen my mother had gotten once. She plucked it clean, and later we ate it. I sat there, wondering if that was now to be our fate, wondering how I could put a stop to this. Then the woman told me she was finished, and I was relieved to find that I still had some hair left. I watched her cut Cheryl's hair, and reasoned that if she was taking the trouble to cut straight, then we had nothing to fear. Between yawns, Cheryl complained that she was hungry, so afterward, we were taken to a large kitchen and fed some of the day's leftovers. When we finished eating, we were taken to the infirmary and put to bed. It felt as if we were all alone in that pitch black space. During the night, Cheryl groped her way to my bed and crawled in with me.

That was the last night we'd share the same bed, or be really close, for a long time. The next day, Cheryl was placed with a group of four year olds and under. I found out from the other children that the women were called nuns and that they were very strict, at least the ones who tended to my group. I'd

seen the ones who looked after the younger children smile and
laugh, but whenever I saw Mother Superior, she always
seemed so unruffled, always dignified and emotionless. But
the ones who took turns looking after us gave us constant
orders, and that made my head spin. One would want us to
hurry with this and that, and another would scold us for
hurrying. Like at mealtime I was told, "Don't gulp your food
down like a little animal."

Eventually, I figured out what the different nuns wanted
and avoided many scoldings. My parents had never strapped
us, and I never had to think about whether I was bad or good.
I feared being ridiculed in front of the other children; I feared
getting the strap; I feared even a harsh word. When I was
quietly playing with some toy, and somebody else wanted it,
I simply handed it over. I longed to go over to Cheryl and talk
and play with her, but I never dared cross that invisible
boundary.

Most of my misery, however, was caused by the separation
from my parents. I was positive that they would come for
Cheryl and me. I constantly watched the doorways and looked
out front room windows, always watching, always waiting, in
expectation of their appearance. Sure enough, one day I saw
my Dad out there, looking up at the building. I waved to him
and wondered why he didn't come to the door, why he just
stood there, looking sad. I turned from the window and saw
that the attending nun was busy scolding a boy, so I left the
room and went to look for Cheryl. I found her down the hall
in another room. I looked in to see where the nun was and saw
that her back was turned to Cheryl and the door. I tiptoed in
and took hold of Cheryl's hand, whispering for her to stay
quiet. I led Cheryl down to the front doors, but we couldn't
open them. They were locked. I didn't know of any other doors
except for the ones which led to the play yard at the back, but
it was all fenced in. I left Cheryl there and raced back to the
nearest empty room facing the front. I tried to call to Dad, but
he couldn't hear me through the thick windows. He couldn't
even see me. He was looking down at the ground, and he was
turning away.

"No, no, Daddy, don't go away! Please don't leave us here! Please, Daddy!" I pounded the window with my fists, trying desperately to get his attention, but he kept walking further and further away. When I couldn't see him anymore, I just sank to the floor in defeat, warm tears blurring my vision. I sat there and sobbed, for we had been so close to going home again.

"WHAT ARE YOU DOING IN HERE?" the nun from my room asked, making me jump. "Don't you know what a fright you gave me, disappearing like that? You get back into the playroom. And quit that snivelling." Then she asked why Cheryl was at the front and what did I intend on doing. I wouldn't tell her anything, so she gave me the strap and some warnings. That strap didn't hurt nearly as much as watching helplessly as my Dad walked away.

A few days later, I woke up feeling ill. My head hurt, my body ached, and I felt dizzy. When I sat at the breakfast table and saw the already unappetizing porridge, I knew that I wouldn't be able to eat it. I tried to explain to the nun at our table, but she merely looked down at me and said in a crisp voice, "You will eat your breakfast."

I made the attempt, but every swallow I forced down pushed its way back up. Tears had come to my eyes, and I finally begged, "Could I please be excused?"

The nun responded in exasperation. "You will stay right there until you are finished. Do you understand?"

To my horror, I threw up just then. Instead of getting heck, though, I was taken to the infirmary room. I was bathed and put to bed, and by then, I was feverish. When I slept, I dreamt I was somewhere near home, but I couldn't find our house. I was very hot, and I walked and walked, but our house was no longer where it should have been. I woke up and called for Mom and Dad.

The next time I went to sleep, I dreamt my parents were on the other side of a large, bottomless hole, and I had to edge my way slowly and carefully around the hole to get over to them. But when I got there, they were back over where I had started from. At last, I dreamt that I was finally running towards them, and there was nothing around that could stop me. They even had Cheryl with them. I felt such relief, such happiness! Just as I was about to jump into their outstretched arms, I glanced up at their faces again. The faces had changed. They weren't my parents. They were the two social workers who had taken us away in the first place. Meanwhile, my temperature was rising, and the nurse decided I'd better be taken to the hospital.

My dreams continued in the hospital. I was always on the verge of reuniting with my parents, but that was always thwarted by something beyond my control. When I was awake, a new kind of terror came to me. I guess it was delirious imaginings, but I would see this huge, white, doughy thing, kind of like a dumpling, and it would come at me, nearer and nearer and nearer. It would always stop just in front of me, and I felt that if it ever touched me it would engulf me, and that would be the end of me. Sometimes, its huge bulk would whiz around my head, back and forth in front of me. I was always scared it would bang into me, but I couldn't duck it or anything. It didn't matter if my eyes were open or closed, I could see it there, and it seemed to know I was scared of it. I remained in the hospital for about a week before the fever broke, and the dreams became less intense.

Chapter Two

I was glad to get back to the orphanage because I was looking forward to seeing Cheryl. A new social worker had been assigned to me. Her name was Mrs. Semple. She told me she would find a home for Cheryl and me together. Maybe she said she would try but I didn't understand that. When I found Cheryl was no longer at the orphanage, I thought she had already gone to our new home. I wondered how come I wasn't sent there too. But the day soon arrived when Mrs. Semple came for me. I was really excited but I pretended nonchalance. I figured if they knew how much I wanted to move with Cheryl, they might take me to another place or else leave me at the orphanage. So Mrs. Semple was now taking me to the Dion family.

When we arrived, I jumped out of the car, looking for Cheryl and wondering why she wasn't outside waiting for me. The front door was opened to us by a pleasant-looking lady.

I walked in, looked around, and asked, "Where's Cheryl?"

Mrs. Semple realized then that I had misunderstood her, and she tried her best to explain to me, but I wouldn't hear her. She assured me, "Don't worry about Cheryl. She'll be well taken care of in her new home."

"But I can take care of Cheryl," I said indignantly. "I want my sister."

"April, you'll be going to school now. So, don't make a fuss." Mrs. Semple had a hint of exasperation in her voice.

"Why don't you come into the kitchen, April? I've got some milk and cookies waiting for you," Mrs. Dion, my new foster mother, spoke up. For some reason, she reminded me of my mother. Obediently, I followed her and sat at the table. The two women went back into the living room, leaving me there, alone. My eyes were stinging as I took a bite of an oatmeal cookie. The tears spilled over and rolled down my cheeks. I was so sad, so lonely, so confused. Why was all this happening?

St. Albert was a small French Catholic town south of Winnipeg. The Dions lived on the outskirts, not far from the Red River. It was September 9, 1955 when I moved there, and the three Dion children were into their fourth day at school. Usually, they came home for lunch, but on this day, it had been raining quite heavily, and they had been allowed to take their lunches to school. It was midmorning when I arrived, and I spent most of that day moping around the house, fretting over Cheryl.

In the afternoon, Mrs. Dion turned the television set on for me. I'd never seen one before, and I sat in front of it transfixed. I was still sitting there when the Dion children came home. The oldest was Guy who was twelve. Then there was Nicole, whose room I would be sharing. She was ten, and the youngest was seven-year-old Pierre. They were all friendly and polite, and only Pierre asked about my hair which was still ridiculously short. Of course, I was very shy, and I couldn't look them in the eye. They reminded me of the rich white kids in the park, so I was amazed at their friendliness.

I had come on Friday. So the next day, I got up at eight with everybody else, had breakfast, then waited for Nicole to finish her Saturday chores. Meanwhile, Guy swept out the garage, washed the car, and collected all the garbage. When they were finished, we all went to the vegetable garden to do some weeding. Pierre and I carried the boxes of weeds over to a pile which was to be burned. We stopped for lunch, which Mrs. Dion brought outside for us. When we finished, some other kids came over, and we all played dodge ball. By the end of that day, I had forgotten how lonely I was.

The next day, when we got up, Mrs. Dion came into our bedroom and got out a real nice dress for me from the closet. She told me it had been Nicole's. I saw that there were some more nice clothes for me, and I was very happy. I thought now I was rich, too, just like those other white kids.

We went to Mass that morning. I didn't like it. I was fidgety from having to stay still for so long. But after Mass, we had a nice, big Sunday dinner. When the dishes were done, we all piled into the car to go on one of Mr. Dion's excursions to find plants to bring back to his gardens. On these trips, Mr. Dion would tell us about the trees and the plants and the wildlife that lived in the forests. Of course, I didn't learn much on that first trip. I was excited about the venture and explored things by myself.

Monday was my first day of school. Mrs. Dion came with me that day while the others rode on their bikes. I was scared and excited at the same time. When I was introduced to the rest of the class, I was so shy, I couldn't look at any of the other children. All I knew was that there must have been at least a hundred kids in that classroom. By the end of that first week, a few of the girls had deemed me acceptable enough to take possession of me. That is, they made it clear to the others that they were going to show me the ropes. At recess times, I played jump rope with them, along with hopscotch and other such games. Although I found them bossy, even haughty, I was very grateful for their acceptance.

I learned that I had been baptized a Roman Catholic when I was a baby. Therefore, I had to study catechism to prepare for my First Communion in the springtime. Since the majority of the students were also Catholics, we had catechism classes every day at school. Every evening, I was obliged to learn my prayers in French, so when they were said at church, I would be able to say them, too. I memorized all the Acts, and there were a lot of them: the Act of Love, the Act of Charity, the Act of Faith, the Act of Penance. I was allowed to learn the prayer for the confession in English, because later, I would be telling the priest my sins in English. I also learned the answers to all the questions in my manual, and there were a lot of things in it which puzzled me. My parents had done a lot of mortal sins because they had never gone to Mass on Sundays. That meant they were going to hell. I didn't think that I'd want to go to heaven so much, after all. Another thing was that the Church was infallible, never to be questioned. Yet, I couldn't help it, nor could I ask anyone else about it, or they would know that I, April Raintree, had sinned!

By October, all the vegetables and crabapples had been canned, and Mr. Dion had made his last trips to get transplants for his gardens. I had settled in at school, and I had found that this home could be as safe and secure as the tiny one on Jarvis Avenue. Sometimes, when it was windy, cold and grey outside, I even enjoyed the cozy feeling of being with a family. At the same time yearning to be with my own.

Back then, there were a lot of good shows on television. It made one wish for adventure. And also for pets just like the ones on TV. First there was Tornado, Zorro's black stallion. Then there was Rin Tin Tin, a big German shepherd. And, of course, Lassie. I wanted them all. When I grew up, I would have German shepherds and collies, black stallions and white stallions and palominos too! I spent many church hours thinking what it was going to be like.

By November, my hair had grown long enough that the other children in school who had teased me stopped. Mrs. Dion told me I could grow it long if I wanted to. But even better than that, she told me that I would be going to visit Cheryl and my parents at the Children's Aid office. I circled the date on the calendar, then waited with impatience and excitement. When the day finally came, and Mrs. Semple came to pick me up, I suddenly remembered those horrible dreams. I was very quiet on the trip to Winnipeg. What if something happened? What if Mom and Dad got too sick and couldn't come? What if Cheryl couldn't come?

"Why the glum face, April? Aren't you glad you'll be seeing your parents and sister again?" Mrs. Semple asked me.

"Oh yes!" I almost shouted, fearful that Mrs. Semple would turn the car around, and it would end up being me who didn't make it.

I was the first one there, and I was taken to one of the small sitting rooms down the hall. Mrs. Semple showed me some books and toys with which I could occupy myself while I waited. Then she left, shutting the door behind her. I chose to sit on the edge of the chair and stared real hard at the closed door, wishing with all my might that the next time it opened, there would be Dad, Mom, and Cheryl. I could see movements going back and forth through the thick-frosted windows. What if they all went to the wrong room? Maybe I should wait in the front waiting room. Better yet, maybe I should wait downstairs at the front entrance. I settled for opening the door a crack and peering out. When I saw someone approaching, I shut the door quickly and went back to the chair. The door opened, and in walked Cheryl, followed by her worker, Miss Turner. When Cheryl saw me, her face lit up, and she screamed, "Apple! Apple!"

26

I was just as happy to see her and, for a moment, forgot my fears that Mom and Dad might not make it.

"Hi Cheryl. I got a present for you. Mrs. Dion gave it to me to give to you." I presented the gift to her, and she tore off all the wrapping and held up a black-and-white teddy bear.

"Has he got a name, Apple?"

I nodded and said, "Andy Pandy. Do you like that name?"

"Uh-huh. I like Andy Pandy. I don't got a present for you, Apple. But you could have this." Cheryl put her hand in her pocket and pulled it out, her chubby little fist clutching something. She opened up her hand and, offered me a brass button which had obviously come off her coat.

Miss Turner and I both laughed, then I said, "It's not my birthday, Cheryl. Don't you remember having a cake for your birthday?"

"I had lots of cake," Cheryl answered, moving the arms of Andy Pandy.

"Why don't you girls take off your coats. I'll be back as soon as your mother and father come." I helped Cheryl take her coat off, then took my own off. While I asked Cheryl questions, I kept my eyes on the door.

"What's your new home like? Mrs. Semple told me you live with the MacAdams. Are they nice?"

"Oh, yes. We have lots of good things to eat. There's lots of other boys and girls there. And I got my own bed. At night, Mrs. MacAdams reads us stories. But no one reads good stories like you, Apple. Cindy always reads the same story. You used to read me lots of different stories."

27   "I'm going to school now and I'm learning to read and print for real. Pretty soon, I'm going to have a confirmation. Right now, I have to learn a lot of prayers in French."

"What's French?"

"French is, well, it's not English. We talk in English. And the Dions talk in English a lot, but they probably think in French. Do you go to Mass on Sundays, Cheryl?"

"Yes. I don't like going to Mass, Apple. We got to behave and not play. Mrs. MacAdams said so. Cindy was bad in church, so Mrs. MacAdams made her sit in a corner, and she couldn't have dessert. But I took her some cake to eat when she was sitting there."

I was laughing when the door opened again, and this time Mom and Dad entered. I was into my mother's arms while Dad picked Cheryl up and twirled her around the room. Then I noticed the tears in Mom's eyes.

"Oh, Mommy, did I hurt you?" I remembered that she was sick.

"No, April, I'm just so happy to see you again."

"See what we brought you?" Dad said, after he had hugged me. He had brought some doughnuts and milk and some candies for us to take home.

"See what Apple got me?" Cheryl said, holding up her teddy bear. "His name is Andy Pandy. He's going to be my friend now."

"So you're five years old. Happy Birthday, Cheryl. My baby girl is growing up fast. And we brought you a present, too," Dad said to her. He nudged Mom to open her purse and brought out a tiny leather purse with beadwork on it. Cheryl was delighted. Then she asked, "Could we come home now?"

We all became suddenly silent, and I looked at each one of them, hopefully. But Mom said very softly, "I'm sorry my babies, but we can't take you back yet. Soon maybe."

28   To change the subject, Dad said to me, "So, April, you're in Grade One now, eh? How do you like your school?"

I realized he wasn't all that interested, but I told him anyways. I didn't tell him how much I liked the Dions and I liked living there because I felt that would hurt their feelings. Besides, going back home with them was my first choice. We had our snack and talked some more. Cheryl talked the most because she liked to talk. Too soon, though, Cheryl's worker returned to say it was time to leave. As I was getting my coat on, I felt total despair. I didn't want to leave Mom, Dad, and Cheryl again. I kissed and hugged my Mom, then my Dad. I pleaded with him. "Please take us home with you. Please, Daddy?"

"April, we just can't do that. We want to but we can't."

"Why not, Daddy?"

"Look, you're making your mother cry, and you're going to make Cheryl cry. If it was up to us, you would never have left home. But this isn't up to us, and you can't come home with us. I'm sorry."

I felt defeated. My shoulders slumped inside my heavy coat. I walked out of the room, my head down. I didn't want anyone to see that my eyes were wet. Then I remembered I hadn't even said goodbye to Cheryl. I ran back and kissed and hugged her, and shot one last pleading glance at our parents. I knew it was of no use. I had to wait a bit for Mrs. Semple. By then, the rest of my family had left. As we were going down to the road, I saw my parents up ahead. Dad had his arm around Mom's shoulders. I wondered if they still lived in the house on Jarvis. They looked so much like they loved each other. It gave me a good feeling to see them like that. At least they were together. They had each other. As we passed them, I waved to them, excited that I was seeing them in such a short time. They both smiled and waved back to me.

As we drove further and further away from them, and I could no longer see them from the rear window, I became sad again. I just wanted to cry, but I couldn't, not in front of Mrs. Semple. I figured that if I did cry, she wouldn't let me see them again. I answered "yes" or "no" whenever Mrs. Semple asked me something because I knew my voice would give me away. When we got to the Dions, Mrs. Semple explained to Mrs. Dion that I would be moody for a while because of the family visit, but not to coddle me or I would carry on like this

after every family visit. I didn't much like Mrs. Semple for
saying that. How would she feel? I went off to my bedroom
and was glad that Nicole wasn't there. I felt the same as when
I first came there.

A little later, Mrs. Dion came into my room and asked me
in a gentle, coddling voice, "April, do you want to come out for
supper? It'll be ready in a few minutes."

"I'm not hungry," I said listlessly.

"I know how you must feel. But if you eat something,
you'll feel much better. How about if I brought a plate in for
you? Nicole can do her homework in the kitchen tonight."
Mrs. Dion patted me on the arm and left.

I ate all the food on my plate that night, knowing it would
make Mrs. Dion happy. When I finished, I took my plate and
glass into the kitchen. The Dions were all sitting at the
table having their meal. I felt shy and timid again. I felt
like an outsider. I felt that I didn't belong to this family. They
were being nice to me, that's all. And I did have my own real
family. I wondered again how long it would be before I could
go home.

"Are you feeling any better, April?" Mrs. Dion later came
in to ask me.

"Yes," I replied. I had been half lying and sitting, so I sat
up properly on the edge of the bed. Mrs. Dion sat next to me.
I asked, "Mrs. Dion, why can't I be with my Mom and Dad?"

"You poor angel. It must be so hard on you." Mrs. Dion put
her arm around my shoulders.

"I want to be with my Mom and Dad. I want to be with
Cheryl." I tried hard not to cry, but I felt so sorry for myself
that the sobs and tears broke loose. Mrs. Dion hugged me to
her and rocked me back and forth. She tried to explain.
"Honey, sometimes we can't have everything we want. Believe
me, living here with us is what's best for you right now. I know
it's hard to understand that. You just have to trust God's
wisdom."

"Mom and Dad say they're sick. They say that when
they're better, then we can go home to them. But they used to
take a lot of medicine before, and it never made them any

better. So, will they ever get better, will they? They never will take us home with them, will they?"

"Honey, that medicine that your Mom and Dad take does make them feel better but not for long and not in the right way. Someday you'll understand that. For now, just keep loving them and praying for them. And try to be happy with us. We all care for you very much, April."

"I know. It's just that... I belong to my Mom and Dad."

"That's true, April." Mrs. Dion gave me a big hug and then stood up. "Come and join us for the rosary now. Tonight we'll say it for your family."

I did feel a whole lot better, but I wondered about the mysterious medicine.

My first Christmas with the Dions was the most memorable because it was celebrated so differently than when I was with my family. We went to bed right after supper, but of course, we couldn't sleep for a long time. Then Mrs. Dion came to wake us up so we could go to the Midnight Mass. As we walked to church, it was snowing, but it wasn't cold. The snow shone like a million sparkling diamonds. The Mass seemed endless that night, but relief was provided by the choir singing Christmas hymns. After it was over, we went back home and gathered in the living room to open all the presents. That's what stood out for me, all those presents. I got a set of books, puzzles, games, a doll, and I couldn't decide which present to play with first. In the kitchen, Mrs. Dion had set out the best dishes, and all the baking she had been doing was displayed. By the time we had eaten, it was almost four in the morning.

It wasn't that long after Christmas that I received the very first letter from Cheryl. I was amazed that she could print, and she wasn't even in school or anything. There were spelling mistakes, and some of the letters were reversed, but I could make out exactly what she meant.

January 5, 1956

Dear Apple,

How ar you? Mrs. Madams tole me to ast that. I got lots a presnts. A dol and sum books of my very own an sum puzles

an gams to play with Cindy an Jeff an Fern an some craons
an a colring book. Wen they is at scool I colr an lok at my boks.
I am lerning to reed an print an count an Mrs. Madams says
I is fast lerner. I wish I was going to scool. Jeff is bad boy. I is
good. I is good girl like Dady tole me. I mis you, Apple. I mis
Momy an Dady.

luv,
Cheryl Raintree

p.s. I had to ast how to spel sum werds.

I had never written a letter, but I sure learned how to write
one that day! Nicole helped me write it, and I made sure that
my letter was a little bit longer than hers.

Our next family visit came in February. Until then, I had
begun to get the feel of being part of the Dion family. Like all
our future visits with our parents, the pattern would be the
same. From the day I was told about the coming visits, I
would become excited, and the excitement would mount until
the day of the visit. Then, when I actually saw our parents
and Cheryl, it was a constant high for those few hours. As
soon as a social worker came to tell either Cheryl or me it was
time to go, I turned instantly despondent, and I would stay
that way for maybe a week or more. But for those few hours,
I was with my real Mom and Dad, and I was with my real
sister. I loved them and they loved me. And there were no
questions of ties or loyalties. Just family.

32

I loved the Dions because they took care of me and they
were nice to me. They were deserving of my love because I had
nothing else to give them. But Mom and Dad were different.
It didn't matter that they were sick and couldn't give us
anything. I thought then that I would always love them, no
matter what. Cheryl and I did ask them when we would go
back with them—we would always ask them that—and they
would promise us that as soon as they got better, we would all
be together again. So, I had hope, and I knew it wouldn't be
long before we once again had our own home.

The next big event for me was my birthday. Mrs. Dion
gave a small birthday party, and some of the girls in my class

came to it. I got a present and a card from Cheryl. After that was my First Communion. I felt more grown-up because from then on I was able to receive Communion. I bragged about this to my parents at our summer visit, but they didn't seem at all interested. Then I remembered they had never gone to Mass and realized they probably knew they would go to hell. I wanted to tell them that if they went to confession and then went to Mass every Sunday, they too would go to heaven, but I felt awkward about the whole thing, so I didn't say any more on religion. Cheryl had been going to kindergarten, and she told us that she could read and print while most of her classmates were still learning their ABCs. She was still very funny, and she always made Mom, Dad, and me laugh. Most of the time, she had no intention of being comical. I sure did a lot of wishing, once I was back with the Dions.

It was after that family visit when I received another letter from Cheryl.

August 20, 1956

Dear Apple,

How ar you? Mrs. Madams got our scool thins. I is so cited to go to scool for reel. I wil be in Grad 1. Apple on Sunday I wuz bad. I did not meen to be. I wanted to see the litle peeple who lives in the radio. I culd see the lits on. The radio fel on the flor. The lites wont even werk an thos peeple is ded. I am skared. Mr. Madams is mad. He ast who brok it. I wuz to skared. I didnt say nothin. Dont tell Momy and Dady. Pleese Apple. I am so skared.

luv,

Cheryl

I felt so sorry for Cheryl. I used to feel scared like that at the orphanage. I knew what it felt like. I also knew that there weren't any people who lived in radios. I'd seen Mr. Dion fix their radio. Poor Cheryl. She was scared she'd killed some people, and she was scared she'd get heck. Mrs. Dion had told us that telling the truth was always easier and better than telling lies. I wrote to Cheryl and told her to go to Mr. MacAdams and explain how she broke the radio. I told her to

write me and tell me what happened afterward. Her response
came on August 30th.

Dear Apple,

How ar you? Mr. Madams sed you wuz good to tel me what
to do. He even laft after I tole him. He sed to me the peeples
werds cum frum waves in the air or sumthin. I dont no. Now
I is cited agin bout going to scool. 1 week to wat. I try to be
good. I promis.

luv,
Cheryl

I felt warm and happy that I had been able to help Cheryl. I
was glad that Mr. MacAdams was the kind who could laugh
at something like that. Not that I knew of any other kind
because Mr. Dion was just as understanding, and my Dad,
well, I really couldn't remember when we had broken
anything in the house. Of course, we never had much to
break. One of the good things about having nothing, I guess.

I don't remember the exact day when I began to call my
foster parents "Maman" and "Papa." I just copied their
children, and nobody made any comments about it. I was still
very shy, and if anyone had made note, I would have stopped.
It did make me feel more comfortable in their home.

At the beginning of the winter, when I was in Grade Two,
my classroom was overcrowded. I was among six students
who were placed in the Grade Three class. With Nicole's help
and patience, I was able to adapt very quickly to the higher
grade. When I passed with a good average, all the Dions were
very proud of me and they made a little celebration. For an
eight year old, I had a very large head for a while.

That summer and the following summer, we all went to a
Catholic camp at Albert Beach on Lake Winnipeg. Those two
weeks were filled with wonderment for me. At home, all the
neighbourhood kids would gather to play baseball, mostly in
the evenings. When there weren't many kids around, we'd
play badminton. If it were raining, we'd find something to do
indoors. There was always lots to do.

In winter, we'd go tobogganing down the slopes of the Red River. Sometimes, a man from a farm on the outskirts would come with a team of horses and hayrack and give the kids of the town a hayride. At the end, Mrs. Dion, or some other mother, would give us all cookies and hot chocolate. At Christmas time, we would go around carolling, even those of us who couldn't sing. And for me, there were my regular family visits. They always made me happy and sad at the same time.

Mrs. Dion had always been a happy, cheerful person, and as long as I had been there, she had never been sick in bed. I must have been the last to sense the change in her. Mostly, I was told that Maman was very tired, and Nicole urged me to help with the chores a little more. When Maman took to her bed, I offered to do as much as I could. At the end of November, Papa coaxed her to see a doctor. She was supposed to be going to the hospital for a week to have some tests done, but her stay was prolonged to another week, then another.

I remember that Christmas was my saddest. Maman came home and stayed for New Year's. Everyone was very sad but made a pretense of being happy. When I saw Maman, I wanted to cry. She looked so different. She used to joke about being too fat. She wasn't really—just pleasantly plump—but now... she was skinny, and to me she looked grey. Any movement, even breathing, seemed to be such a strain for her. Yet, she led us all in forced cheerfulness.

I'd lie in bed at night, worrying about her. I'd say my prayers over and over, pleading with God to make her better. I must have overheard Papa and Grandmère Dion saying in French that Maman was dying because my prayers to God changed to "please don't let Maman die." I would think of Nicole, Guy, and Pierre. It would be so awful for them not to have a real mother. Finally, I would cry myself to sleep.

One night, I sat up in bed and was wondering what had woken me. After a while, I put my robe on and went to the kitchen for a glass of milk. I was on my way back to my bedroom when I heard a noise in the living room. Because of the bright moonlight, I could see everything clearly. There in his rocker was Papa, with his arms on the armrests, and his

35

back very straight. I knew he wasn't sleeping, that he was very, very sad. I went in without turning on any lights and sat on the stool beside him. I wanted to comfort him, but I didn't know what to say. I put my hand on his and said softly, "Maman says it's okay to cry sometimes. Maman says it makes you feel better."

I saw tears, glistening in the moonlight, run down his face.

"Maman says we have to trust in God's wisdom."

I heard him restrain a sob and felt him patting me on my hand. I knew then I should leave him alone. I returned to my room and said another prayer for Papa.

In January, Mrs. Semple told me that I would be moving. At first, I thought I was finally going home. I was both happy and excited to be going home at last and very sad that I was going there only because Maman Dion was so sick and maybe dying. But my happiness was short-lived because Mrs. Semple began telling me about the farm which would be my new foster home. I was permitted a last visit with Maman in the hospital. She smiled when I walked into her hospital room, and after asking me about school and other things, she said, "April, I wanted to say goodbye to you. We're all very sorry to see you go, but the final decision was theirs. You understand that, don't you?"

I nodded slowly, trying hard to smile courageously. I couldn't talk because of the lump in my throat.

She continued, "I wanted to say some things to you before you... Papa told me how you gave him comfort. We all love you very much, April. When life seems unbearable, remember there's always a reason. April, you're a very special person. Always remember that. Mrs. Semple says that the home you're going to is a fine home. I'm sure you'll be happy there."

"I love you, Maman." It was the first time I had ever said those words. To me, they were precious words to be used on very special people. When I saw how much she appreciated hearing those words, I was glad I had said them.

There were tears all around when I said goodbye to the rest of the Dion family. I had promised to write and always keep in touch with them. I left them with the hope of either coming back to live with them or returning to my own home.

Chapter Three

I was taken to a small farming community further south of Winnipeg, on the outskirts of Aubigny, to the DeRosier farm. It was a Friday afternoon when we arrived. While Mrs. Semple talked with Mrs. DeRosier, I studied my new foster mother with great disappointment. She was a tall woman with lots of makeup and badly-dyed hair. If she had been a beauty once, the only thing left of it now was the vanity. Her voice was harsh and grating. The more I watched her, the more positive I became that she was putting on an act for Mrs. Semple's benefit. I wondered why Mrs. Semple couldn't figure that out, but then I thought it was okay as long as Mrs. DeRosier gave me a good home.

After my social worker's departure, Mrs. DeRosier turned to me. I looked up at her with curiosity. She went to the kitchen drawer, took out a strap, and laid it on the table near me. She told me the routine I would be following but in such a way that it made me think she had made this speech many times before.

"The school bus comes at eight. You will get up at six, go to the hen house, and bring back the eggs. While I prepare breakfast, you will wash the eggs. After breakfast, you will do the dishes. After school, you'll have more chores to do, then you will help me prepare supper. After you do the supper dishes, you will go to your room and stay there. You'll also keep yourself and your room clean. I know you half-breeds, you love to wallow in filth. You step out of line once, only once, and that strap will do the rest of the talking. You don't get any second chances. And if you don't believe that I'll use it, ask Raymond and Gilbert. And on that subject, you will only talk to them in front of us. I won't stand for any hanky-panky

going on behind our backs. Is that clear? Also, you are not
permitted the use of the phone. If you want letters mailed, I'll
see to it. You do any complaining to your worker, watch out.
Now, I'll show you where your room is."

I was left alone in a small room at the back of the house.
It was cold, smelled mouldy, and felt damp. There wasn't even
a closet, just nails sticking out all over the walls. The Dions
had given me a new set of suitcases, and I opened one up and
started hanging a few things on the nails. I stopped and sat on
the bed. The mattress was soft and warped. Self-pity was not
good for one's spirits, Maman Dion had told me, but right now,
I felt sorry for myself. Mrs. DeRosier had said "you half-
breeds." I wasn't a half-breed, just a foster child, that's all. To
me, half-breed was almost the same as Indian. No, this wasn't
going to be a home like the Dions'. Maybe if there were other
children, they might be nice. Most people I'd met when I had
stayed at the Dions had been nice enough. With this thought, I
finished hanging up my clothes, looking forward to the arrival
of Raymond and Gilbert, who I thought must be at school.

I was waiting at the kitchen table in order to meet them.
Mrs. DeRosier was in the kitchen too, but she only glared at
me as if to warn me to stay quiet. I saw the school bus from
the kitchen window and thought how nice it would be taking
a bus from now on. Four kids got off: two older boys around
thirteen or fourteen, and a girl and a younger boy. I was
hoping that they would like me. They all walked in, but the
two older boys walked by without looking at me, and I heard
them going up the stairs. The younger boy and the girl eyed
me contemptuously. The boy said to Mrs. DeRosier, "Is that
the half-breed girl we're getting? She doesn't look like the last
squaw we had."

The girl giggled at his comment.

"April, you may as well start earning your keep right now.
Here, I want you to peel these potatoes." Mrs. DeRosier got
out a large basket of potatoes and put them down in front of
me. I was sure that the two children must be Mrs. DeRosier's
very own. They made themselves sandwiches, making an
unnecessary mess in the process. When I finished peeling the

potatoes, Mrs. DeRosier told me to clean up their mess. Mr. DeRosier came in at suppertime, and it became apparent to me that Mrs. DeRosier towered over him, not only in size, but also in forcefulness of personality. He and the two boys, who had changed into work clothes, sat on one side; Mrs. DeRosier was at the head; and Maggie and Ricky and I sat on the other side. The only talking at the table was done by the mother and her two children. I had finished my milk and reached for the pitcher to pour myself another glass.

"You're not allowed more than one glass," Maggie said in a whiny voice. I froze, my hand still on the handle, waiting for Mrs. DeRosier to confirm that statement or say it was all right. I wondered if I should give in to this girl, then realized I had no choice because Mrs. DeRosier simply remained silent. Slowly, I withdrew my hand from the pitcher and looked over at the mother and daughter. Maggie had a smug look on her face. I wanted to take that pitcher of milk and dump it all over her head. At other meals, she would make a show of having two glasses of milk herself.

When Ricky finished eating, he burped and left the table without excusing himself either way. The other two boys had also finished eating but remained seated until Mr. DeRosier got up to leave. Then they followed him outside. Mrs. DeRosier put the leftovers away and indicated I was to start on the dishes. While I washed and wiped them, Maggie sat at the table and watched. I wondered why this family was so different from the Dions, especially those three. So much malice, so much tension. It seemed to me that it was a lot easier being nice, after all, the DeRosiers were Catholics, too. How I wished that my own parents would rescue me, and right this minute would be a good time. I finished wiping the last pot and put it away. I started for my bedroom, relieved to get away from Maggie's watchful eyes.

"You're not finished," Maggie said in a bossy tone. "You didn't even sweep the floor. I heard you half-breeds were dirty but now I can see that it's true."

"You didn't do anything yet. Why don't you sweep the floor?"

"Because it's not my job. My job is only to see that you do yours. So get the broom!" Maggie hissed at me.

I stood there for a minute, looking down at Maggie. She was still sitting, very composed, very sure of how far she could go. Helpless fury built up inside of me, but I was alone here, unsure of what my rights were, if I even had any. So I went to get the broom. After sweeping the floor, I went to my room. I had nothing to do but think. Was it only this morning I had felt loved and cherished? Now, I had been told I would have to earn my keep. I knew that Children's Aid paid for my keep. And I didn't like that word "half-breed" one bit! It took me a while to get over all these new things I didn't like so I could get ready for bed and say my prayers.

Praying could bring me comfort, Maman Dion had told me. I had memorized the Lord's Prayer in French and English, but I had never really thought about the meaning of each sentence. Now, I said it slowly.

"Our Father, who art in heaven, hallowed be thy name. Thy kingdom come, thy will be done, on earth as it is in heaven. Give us this day our daily bread. Forgive us our trespasses, as we forgive those who trespass against us. And lead us not into temptation, but deliver us from evil, Amen."

I would have to forgive these people their trespasses and no doubt there would be many. "But, hold on there, God," I thought. "I don't have any trespasses for them to forgive. So how come I'm going to have to forgive theirs?" I looked for the answers in the talks and the Bible readings at the Dions, I remembered the saints and the martyrs. They had been tested. Maybe I was being tested. Maybe what I had to do while I was here was turn the other cheek. When I went to sleep, I was feeling very saintly.

Saturday morning, Mr. DeRosier rapped at my door, telling me I was supposed to go for the eggs. It had been windy all night, and I had not slept well in my chilly room. I sleepily got dressed and went to the kitchen. No one was there, but I saw a pail by the doorway and supposed I was to use that. It was still dark outside, and it took me a while to find the chicken house. There were deep drifts of snow which had been

whipped up by the wind overnight. Another thing I decided
was that I didn't like winter anymore. Not as long as I lived
on this farm. I gathered the eggs and got nasty pecks from the
hens that were too stubborn or too protective. As I floundered
through the snowdrifts, my mouth watered at the thought of
breakfast, but when I entered the house, no one seemed to be
up. I was still cold and very hungry, but I didn't dare touch
anything. I washed the eggs and found that a few had broken,
and many were cracked. I worried while I waited for Mrs.
DeRosier. A few hours later, she came down in her housecoat,
and she looked a whole lot worse without her makeup.

She started to put some coffee on to perk and noticed the
eggs still drying in the trays.

"What the hell did you do with these eggs? They're all
cracked. I can't sell them that way!" I jumped up when she
screamed. She picked up a few of them and threw them down
on the floor in front of where I was sitting. She went on
ranting and raving, not wanting my explanations. Finally, she
told me to clean up the mess, and she started breakfast.

When everyone had eaten, she and her two children got
ready to go to town. She left me instructions to wash the floors
and clean the bathroom after I finished the breakfast dishes.
I thought to myself that if Ricky had been a girl, I would have
been just like Cinderella. When I finished my assigned chores,
I washed out my own room, trying to rid it of the musty smell.
I had a few hours to myself before they came back, but when
they did, Maggie, with her boots on, walked all over the
kitchen floor, and I had to wash it over again.

On Sunday morning, we all went to Mass. After the
services, while Mr. DeRosier and the two older boys waited in
the car, Mrs. DeRosier chatted with some neighbours. I was by
her side and she explained my presence, adding that I was a
lovely little child, and we all got along very well. She wallowed
in their compliments on what a generous, good-hearted woman
she was to take poor, unfortunate children like myself into her
home. I just stood there meekly, too scared to say different.

I had looked forward to Monday because I would be going
to school on a bus. There were a lot of kids on the bus already,

and being too shy to walk further, I took the first empty seat near the front. I could hear the DeRosier kids tell their friends that I was a half-breed and that they had to clean me up when I came to their house. They said I even had lice in my hair, and told the others that they should keep away from me. They whispered and giggled, and once in a while, they would call me names. I sat all alone in that seat, all the way to school, staring straight ahead, my face burning with humiliation. Fortunately for me, no one on the school bus was in my classroom. By the end of the first day, I had made one friend, Jennifer. Unfortunately for me, I had to board that school bus again to go back to the farm. I had decided that I wasn't going to let them see that their taunts really hurt me.

The months went by very slowly. The kids on the bus tired of picking on me, mostly, I guess, because I wouldn't react. My tenth birthday passed without celebration. One evening in May, Mrs. DeRosier told me I wouldn't be going to school the next day because of a family visit. That was my first happy moment since I had arrived. She drove me in to Winnipeg, complaining all the way that these visits would disrupt the routine she had set for me.

I was waiting, alone, in the reception area when Cheryl came in, bubbling with enthusiasm.

"Hi April, I got a present for you. Can we go to a visiting room now Miss Turner?" she asked her worker. After we were left alone in one of the small cubicle-sized rooms, Cheryl turned to me and handed me a gift-wrapped package.

"Happy Birthday, April. It's a book."

"You're not supposed to tell me what it is, Cheryl. Half the fun is trying to guess what it is while I unwrap it." I grinned at her and shook my head.

"A book about Louis Riel?" I said and crinkled my nose in distaste. I knew all about Riel. He was a rebel who had been hanged for treason. Worse, he had been a crazy half-breed. I had learned about his folly in history. Also, I had read about the Indians and the various methods of tortures they had put the missionaries through. No wonder they were known as savages. So, anything to do with Indians, I despised. And

here, I was supposed to be part Indian. I remember how 44
relieved I was that no one in my class knew of my heritage
when we were going through that period in Canadian history.

"He's a Métis, like us," Cheryl said proudly. "Mrs.
MacAdams says we should be proud of our heritage. You know
what that means? It means we're part Indian and part white.
I wish we were whole Indians."

I just about fell off my chair when I heard that. There
were a few Indians or part-Indian kids in my class who
couldn't hide what they were like I did. They knew their
places. But here was my very own sister, with brilliant grades,
saying such idiotic things. Well, I didn't want to argue with
her so, I didn't voice my opinion. She continued talking, which
was usual for her.

"Mrs. MacAdams is a Métis you know, but Mr. MacAdams
isn't. He teaches somewhere. Not at my school. They got a lot
of books on Indian tribes and how they used to live a long time
ago." Cheryl paused for a breather, then continued in a
sombre tone.

"Mrs. MacAdams gave them to me to read because no one
at school would talk to me or play with me. They call me
names and things, or else they make like I'm not there at all.
This one girl and her friends would follow me home and make
fun of me, so I slapped that girl. So her Mom called Mrs.
MacAdams. And Mrs. MacAdams says that all the bad stuff
was 'cause I'm different from them. She told me I would have
to earn their respect. How come they don't have to go around
earning respect? Anyways, I don't even know what respect is,
exactly. I just wanted to be friends with them."

I knew what Cheryl was talking about from my own
experience on the school bus. Yet, I couldn't share that with
her. I suppose it was my vanity. She had admitted to me that
some people didn't like her because she was different, but I
simply couldn't return that kind of honesty. So, I told her 45
about the DeRosiers, and how much I missed the Dions.
Telling her how the DeRosiers were mean to me was easy
because they probably didn't like anyone and it wasn't
only me.

"Why don't you give those two kids a good whack?"
Cheryl asked.

"Are you kidding? Mrs. DeRosier would kill me," I replied
as I leafed through the pages of my new book. "Besides, you
can't go around whacking people you don't like."

"Well, that's what I do," Cheryl retorted offhandedly.

"And what if the kids are bigger and stronger than you?"

"Then I pretend not to hear them," Cheryl answered with
a mischievous smile. We both laughed over that, and then we
talked of more light-hearted things.

I got to wondering about the present my Mom and Dad
would be bringing me. Those precious hours together slipped
away, and Cheryl's good mood faded, too.

"Maybe they're not going to come," she said as she paced
back and forth. She was puzzled and hurt, and she was
fighting back tears.

Miss Turner came in to tell me Mrs. DeRosier was there
to pick me up. Cheryl begged for just a little more time. I sat
back down, and Cheryl came to me and knelt before me.
She looked up at me with her large, questioning eyes,
now glistening.

"They're not coming?" she asked softly.

"Maybe they got mixed up on the days or something." I
knelt down to face her on the same level. "Cheryl, no matter
what, we'll always have each other." I hugged her close,
knowing that what I said was small comfort to her. She
started to cry, and that made me cry, too. Miss Turner came
and poked her head in, saying I really had to go. Cheryl and I
started putting on our jackets. She looked so pitiful when I
left her alone in the visiting room.

Mrs. DeRosier had been told that my parents had not
come for the visit. That evening, at suppertime, she told her
own children they were fortunate in having a parent like her
as my parents were too busy boozing it up to even come to
visit me. I sat silently, not believing a word of what she said
and pretending the insult of my parents didn't even bother
me. She was forever putting my parents down, so I was
getting used to her remarks. But inside, I despised her more

than I would despise my own parents, even if all the things she said about them were true.

Later that night, I lay in my bed, unable to go to sleep and unable to say my prayers. I couldn't forget that look on Cheryl's face when I had to leave her. I felt anger towards my mother and father because they were responsible. They were responsible for me being in this foster home. While I was at it, I turned on our Holy Father in heaven.

"Oh God, why did you let me be born? Why? Why was I ever born? Why do you let these bad things happen to Cheryl and me? You're supposed to be loving, protective, and just. But you're full of crap, God! You're just full of crap and I hate you. You hear me? I hate you!" That's how angry I was. I started crying, and when I had cried my heart out, I then felt sorry for saying those things. At last, I was able to say my prayers and ask God to help me be strong and good.

For the rest of that month, the DeRosier kids taunted me about having drunkards for parents. It was new ammunition for them to use against me, and it bothered me a lot. One Saturday morning, they started in on me again, and finally I made my feeble defence. "They're not drunkards! They're sick. That's all. Sick."

"Sick? Boy, what a dummy you are. But then half-breeds and Indians are pretty stupid, aren't they?" Maggie said maliciously.

"Yeah. Your parents didn't know how to take care of you. They just know how to booze it up," Rick added. And then they started mimicking drunken people and talking to each other with slurred speech, laughing at intervals.

"NO!" I screamed.

I ran out of the house, across the grain fields, running as hard and as fast as I could. They had acted and sounded just like my parents and their friends, I remembered. I could run all I wanted, but I couldn't run away from the truth. When I reached the edge of the woods, my side was aching. I stopped and sat down, my back against a pine tree. I was panting and sobbing very hard. By the time I caught my breath, I could picture my parents.

47

"So. That's why you never got any better. Liars! That's what you are! All those promises of getting well. All those lies about taking medicine. Liars! You told us, 'Soon, April; soon, Cheryl. We'll take you back home as soon as we get better.' Well, you lied to us. You never intended to get better. You never cared about us. You made Cheryl cry and you don't even care. And because of you, I'm stuck here. I hate you both for lying to us. I hope I never see you again."

I got up and started walking back to the house because I still had floors to wash. I stopped and thought, "No. Why should I? They can beat me if they want to. I don't care. I just don't care anymore. To hell with them! To hell with my parents! To hell with everyone, except Cheryl. Even the Dions didn't answer my letters. They lied too. They didn't really care for me. But that's okay because I don't care either!"

I turned back into the woods and made my way through the heavy underbrush. I don't know how far I walked before I came upon a small clearing which bordered the Red River. The sunlight filtered through the towering trees, warming even the shady spots. The area was alive with the sounds of birds, squirrels, and bugs. But I felt at peace, the tensions from the past months were lifted. I knew I felt this way because I was all cried out, and I had decided that for now, I didn't care about anything.

I wasn't really thinking about anything when I noticed my arms and hands. They were tanned a deep, golden brown. A lot of pure white people tanned just like this. Poor Cheryl. She would never be able to disguise her brown skin as just a tan.

People would always know that she was part Indian. It seemed to me that what I'd read and what I'd heard indicated that Métis and Indians were inclined to be alcoholics. That's because they were a weak people. Oh, they were put down more than anyone else, but then, didn't they deserve it? Anyways, I could pass for a pure white person. I could say I was part French and part Irish. If I had to, I could even change the spelling of my name. Raintree looked like one of those Indian names, but if I changed the spelling to Raintry, that could pass for Irish. And when I grew up, I wouldn't be

poor; I'd be rich. Being a half-breed meant being poor and 44
dirty. It meant being weak and having to drink. It meant
being ugly and stupid. It meant living off white people. And
giving your children to white people to look after. It meant
having to take all the crap white people gave. Well, I wasn't
going to live like a half-breed. When I got free of this place,
when I got free from being a foster child, then I would live just
like a real white person.

Then the question came to my mind. What about Cheryl?
How was I going to pass for a white person when I had a Métis
sister? Especially when she was so proud of what she was? I
loved her. I could never cut myself off from her completely.
And she wouldn't go along with what I planned. I would never
even be able to tell her what I planned. I sat there thinking
for a long time, but the problem wouldn't be resolved. Well, I
had a long time to figure that one out. For sure, she would
never turn out to be like the rest of the Métis people. She and
maybe Mrs. MacAdams were special people. Cheryl was
already a whole lot smarter than all the rest of the kids in her
class. I sighed, stood up, and stretched. I felt I was ready to
face whatever the DeRosiers had in store for me. One day I
would be free of them. One day... 49

Over the summer holidays, Maggie was going to
Vancouver to visit her grandmother. I looked forward to the
day when she would be leaving because she, more than Ricky,
made my life miserable. She had started coming into my room
whenever she felt like it, saying it was her house and she
could go wherever she pleased. One night, she was looking at
my suitcases thoughtfully, and then she said, "I'm going to
borrow your suitcases for my trip."

I looked up at her and said, "You can't take them with you.
What if I had to move while you're gone?"

"Move? My mother's not going to let you move from here.
C'mon Ape, I've got to start packing tonight," she said, in what
was supposed to be a sweet coaxing voice. I knew very well that
her mother would let her have her way, but I still felt stubborn.

"Look, you owe it to me. You live in my house and eat our
food. You're just lucky I don't tell Mother about your

selfishness." With that, she dumped all the things in my suitcases on the floor and took them with her.

When she came back from the trip, she kept my suitcases. I asked to have them back several times, but she would ignore me. One day, I entered my bedroom, and my suitcases were there. They had been scratched up as if Maggie had deliberately tried to cut into them with a knife. Inside, there was dried red fingernail polish poured to form the words, "Ape, the bitch." I was angry but there was nothing I could do about it. I couldn't even show them to my social worker because it would be her word against mine. I thought that would be the end of it, but it wasn't.

That same night, during supper, Maggie said, "Mother, Ape let me use her suitcases, and I forgot to give them back right away. So you know what she did today? She went up to my room, threw my stuff around, and stole some of my money and my jewellery. I wasn't going to say anything about it, but it makes me mad that she can just come into my room and do that."

I couldn't believe what she'd said, and I looked over at her with complete astonishment. I practically growled at her, "You bloody liar!"

Mrs. DeRosier slammed her fork and knife onto the table, stood up, and came over to where I was sitting. She slapped me across the side of the head, took a vise-grip of my arms, and yanked me out of my chair to shake me, seemingly all at the same time. And she was screaming.

"Don't you ever talk to my daughter in that tone of voice again! Who the hell do you think you are? We take you in because your parents don't want you, we give you food and shelter, and this is how you pay us back?"

Then she asked Maggie, "Is your room still in the same condition that April left it in?"

"Yes, it is, Mother," said Maggie in an injured tone of voice.

"April, you march up there right now. We're going to see what you did. And then you're going to get the strapping of your life."

I'd never seen Maggie's room before because the upstairs was off limits to me. Her room was beautiful. The fancy furniture all matched and was white with gold trimming. Her bed even had a canopy over it. The wallpaper was of pink and yellow roses. But right now, books, papers, and clothing littered the deep pile rug.

"You must be a sick girl, April, to do this kind of thing. What did Maggie ever do to you?" Mrs. DeRosier asked.

All the while, I was being shaken about like a rag doll. She marched me back down to my room and started to look through my things. In one of the pockets of my coat, she found some money and some earrings. Maggie was standing at the doorway with a smug look of satisfaction on her face. While Mrs. DeRosier went for the strap, Maggie said softly, "That's what you get for bugging me, April Raintree."

The beating I got that night was one of the worst, but I wouldn't cry. That seemed to infuriate Mrs. DeRosier all the more. I was sure that after that, Mrs. DeRosier would have me moved. I thought the beating would have been worth it, after all. I waited for things to start happening, but over the next few weeks, nothing more was said about the incident.

At the end of the summer, Cheryl and I had another visit. When we got to the Children's Aid office, we were told that our parents were not expected to come. I felt guilty about the resolutions I had made a few months back. To make up for it, I told Cheryl how our family life had been when we were all together. That is, I told her the good things. I told her how Mom used to rock her to sleep and sing songs to us; how Dad always laughed and joked and played with us for hours, telling us lots of stories; how we would all go out to visit our aunts and uncles or that they would come over to our house; how Dad would bring out his fiddle and play while everyone danced jigs. I wondered if it was right to tell her only the good things. Maybe I was lying by not telling her about the drinking and the fights and the dirty children. But then, Cheryl didn't need to know that just yet. I wanted Cheryl to be happy.

At our next family visit in October, only Dad came. He explained that he had been up north and couldn't get back for our visits. Mom, he said, was sick. Cheryl accepted the explanations with ease. She was, as usual, affectionate with him. But I knew the truth about them. I was aloof but polite. I had thought once of telling him about what a bad place the DeRosier farm was. But now I didn't bother. He wouldn't care. He'd pretend to care, but he wouldn't do anything about it. I didn't have much to say to him. As children, that would be the last time Cheryl and I would see him.

Winter and spring passed. Life with the DeRosiers was the same: miserable. I had become bitterly passive, and I now said fewer prayers. I was sure that God had heard me say I hated him and he never heard me ask for his forgiveness. Three more visits were arranged, but our parents never showed up. Each time, Cheryl would end up crying. She was beginning to change. Before she had been outgoing, always talking, and normally cheerful. At the last two visits, I tried my hardest to bring out her laughter but was rewarded only with sad smiles.

By the end of June, I had passed Grade Six with a low B average, and that was because English, French, and Math were easy for me. I felt torn in different directions and often changed my mind regarding my parents. Sometimes, I would think of the life I would have been leading if we were all together. So what if we were poor and lived in slums. Being together would be a million times better than living on this horrible farm. Other times, I would remind myself that my parents were weak alcoholics who had made their choice. And then I would loathe them. Or I would think of the Dions and all their religious teachings. What was the sense of praying to a God who didn't care about me either? On Cheryl, it was still the question of how I was going to live as a white person with her around. I had seven more years of probably being stuck with the DeRosiers, and if not, then in some other foster home. Seven years of not having control of my own life.

Most of the kids in my class were excited about the summer holidays. Some were going away on trips. Me, I was just going to be alone, unloved, with nothing to look forward to. For seven more years... Did I ever feel sorry for myself.

Chapter Four

In July, Mrs. DeRosier had her husband move an old, musty-smelling dresser from one of the outbuildings into my room. It had a cracked, spotted mirror on it, and the thing looked like it was about to fall apart. But I was grateful to have something to put my things in and wondered why the small kindness. Later, Mrs. DeRosier went out and bought an old cot from an auction and had it put in my room. Since it was in worse condition than the one I already had, my curiosity was really piqued. I suspected that Maggie knew the reason, but I knew better than to ask her. She and Ricky had stopped calling my parents drunkards. I knew it was my lack of reaction which made them ignore me for the most part. Now, they were constantly at each other to their mother's mortification. And to my amusement.

I was weeding in the garden the morning the car drove into the farmyard. I glanced at it, not really caring who it was. I glanced again, surprised to see Miss Turner get out. My face had a grin from ear to ear when I saw Cheryl getting out on the other side. I dropped my garden tool and ran over to her.

"Cheryl, what are you doing here? Oh, I'm so happy to see you."

Mrs. DeRosier had her phony smile showing, and she said to me in a pleasant tone, "I wanted this to be a surprise for you, April. Your sister has come to live with us. We all thought this would be a good idea because your parents haven't come to see you." She then took Miss Turner into the house for a cup of coffee.

I turned to Cheryl and asked her why she had moved from the MacAdams. I knew that she had liked them a lot, and that they were real nice people.

"They asked me last month if I would like to move with you. I asked why you couldn't move there because you didn't like it here, but they just said they didn't have the room. I told them that I liked them, but that I'd rather be with you. So here I am." Cheryl shrugged and grinned, as if she had pulled off a brilliant plan.

From the day she arrived, I changed. I was more alert and openly defiant towards the DeRosiers, sending them silent warnings to leave my sister alone. We did all the chores together, and while we did them, we talked and joked around. While we did the outside work, Maggie would put her bathing suit on to tan herself. She would lie on a blanket wherever we happened to be working. The first time she tried to order Cheryl to go in and get her a glass of lemonade, Cheryl said, "Get it yourself."

We were weeding in the garden, and I was further away from Maggie and behind Cheryl. I stood up and eyed Maggie with such loathing that Maggie got up and went off to get her own drink.

"You lazy half-breeds," was her comment as she stalked off.

I bent down to resume my weeding, and Cheryl turned to me and said, "See? That's all there is to it. They got no guts."

Before Cheryl had come, the DeRosier's dog, Rebel, had always followed the foster boys around, down to the barns or out to the fields. Now, he stuck close to Cheryl's side. When I took Cheryl down to my favorite spot by the river, the big yellow mongrel came with us. Cheryl told me the MacAdams had taken her to see this movie, *Old Yeller*, and Rebel looked like Yeller. She'd tell me all about the television shows that she'd seen. Since I'd moved to the DeRosiers', I wasn't even allowed to go into the living room, except to clean it. Our privacy at the river was protected for us by nature. A few times, the DeRosier kids had tried to follow me before. Maggie found the underbrush too scratchy and too difficult, and she had given up. Ricky had come down with a bad case of poison ivy the first time. The second time, there had been too many mosquitoes for his liking.

When school started in September, the DeRosier kids had the other kids on the bus picking on Cheryl and me. Cheryl was easy to goad, and she'd get into verbal exchanges of insults. It was impossible for me to get it across to her that that was exactly what they wanted from her. At home, there was a constant testing of wills between the DeRosiers and Cheryl and me. I grew tired of feeling I always had to be on guard. I preferred the passive state I'd been in before Cheryl had come. I was worried that Cheryl would get into physical fights when I wasn't around. Fist fights were for people who couldn't keep their self-control. Furthermore, they were undignified. Because Cheryl hadn't made any friends in her own class, she often sat with Jennifer and me at lunchtimes. We had different recess periods. I guess she managed to keep out of fights because I never heard of any.

When our report cards came out before Christmas, Cheryl had maintained her high grades, despite the DeRosiers. My own average jumped considerably. Knowing the DeRosier kids had done poorly by their mother's reaction, Cheryl and I were both vain about our marks. It was about the only thing we could rib them about, especially Maggie, and we took full advantage. We'd say things like, "Hey Maggie, you told us that half-breeds were stupid. Well, if we're stupid, you must lack brains altogether." It was the only time I'd refer to myself as a half-breed—to spite them.

It was after Christmas that Cheryl got into trouble at school. She told me all about it at lunchtime. That morning, her teacher had been reading to the class how the Indians scalped, tortured, and massacred brave white explorers and missionaries. Cheryl's anger began to build. All of a sudden, she had loudly exclaimed, "This is all a bunch of lies!"

"I'm going to pretend I didn't hear that," the teacher had said calmly.

"Then I'll say it again. I'm not going to learn this garbage about the Indian people," Cheryl had said louder, feeling she couldn't back down.

Everyone else had looked at her as the teacher came and stood by her desk. "They're not lies; this is history. These things happened whether you like it or not."

56

"If this is history, how come so many Indian tribes were wiped out? How come they haven't got their land anymore? How come their food supplies were wiped out? Lies! Lies! Lies! Your history books don't say how the white people destroyed the Indian way of life. That's all you white people can do is teach a bunch of lies to cover your own tracks!"

The teacher had marched her down to the principal's office. Cheryl had been scared, but she was also stubborn. She believed she was right, and she intended to stand up for her beliefs, no matter what they dished out.

57

Her teacher had explained Cheryl's disruptive attitude and then left the principal's office.

"So what's this business of upsetting your history class? Learned men wrote these books, and you have the gall to say they're wrong?" the principal had boomed in his loudest voice.

"They are wrong. Because it was written by white men who had a lot to cover up. And I'm not going to learn a bunch of lies," Cheryl had said, more scared than ever before.

The man then pulled a strap from his drawer and said, "Now, I don't want to have to strap you, but I will. You'll go back to your classroom, apologize to your teacher and to the class, and there will be no more of this nonsense. All right?"

Cheryl had shaken her head defiantly. "No. I won't apologize to anyone because I'm right." Then she had put out her hand, knowing he would give her the strap. He did. Each time he hit her, her resolve had grown stronger and stronger. When he stopped to ask if she was going to come to her senses, she had answered, "Giving me the strap isn't going to change the fact that your history books are full of lies."

Seeing he wasn't going to get anywhere, he put his strap away and phoned Mrs. DeRosier. She had arrived in about half an hour and was angry. She told the principal she had nothing but trouble with Cheryl. He left her alone with Cheryl in his office.

"You're going to do exactly as they wish or else I'll call your worker, have you moved, and then I'll make sure you never see April again. Now, are you going to co-operate?"

Cheryl nodded meekly. The fight had gone out of her.

Before Mrs. DeRosier left, she had turned and warned Cheryl, "I'm not through with you yet, Cheryl Raintree."

When Cheryl told me all this, I swelled with pride. My kid sister was spunky. She had guts. More than I would ever have. But Mrs. DeRosier's warning bothered me. No doubt, Cheryl was in for a beating, and somehow I had to do something. For the rest of the day, I was nervous, but Cheryl didn't seem worried at all.

That night, when we sat down to supper, Mrs. DeRosier said, "Cheryl, since you already got the strap at school, I'm not going to give you another strapping. Instead, you won't have supper tonight, and when we're finished, you will do the dishes all alone. Now, go to your room and wait till we finish eating."

I was surprised to find that was going to be Cheryl's only punishment. I told Mrs. DeRosier that I wasn't hungry, since Cheryl had to miss supper.

"Very well, you can go to your room and stay there for the rest of the night."

With that, she followed me to my room and commanded Cheryl to follow her to the kitchen. When Cheryl came back a few hours later, I looked up and was shocked. Cheryl's long hair had been her pride and glory. *Had* been her pride and glory. There was hardly any left, and it was cut in stubbles. As she told me what happened, my anger mounted.

After she had finished telling me about it, Cheryl added, "And she made me sweep all my hair from the floor and then do the dishes. But I didn't cry, April. Not once."

Still, I wasn't going to let that old hag get away with that without voicing my opinion! My fury outweighed my normal fear of Mrs. DeRosier. I stormed into the kitchen, saw Mrs. DeRosier there, and demanded, "Why did you scalp my sister?"

Instead of answering me, Mrs. DeRosier slapped me.

I ignored the sting from the slap and yelled, "You had no right to do that!"

"No two-bit little half-breed is going to yell at me like that!" Mrs. DeRosier screamed back. Out came the scissors, again. I actually pushed her hand away from my hair. I think we would have had a fight except that she used the threat of separating Cheryl and me for good. So, in the end, I, also, went back to our room minus my own crowning glory. I was still breathing hard when I walked in. Cheryl looked at me and did a double take. Her eyes, like saucers, remained on my hair. Her mouth opened and closed a few times, but she remained speechless. She had heard the commotion in the kitchen, but Mrs. DeRosier's threat had kept her back. I looked in the mirror. My new hairdo looked worse than Cheryl's. There I was, the big, protective sister going out to avenge the humiliation of my little sister, and I came back, myself properly humbled. It all seemed ridiculously funny, and I started to laugh. Cheryl joined in. It was good to be able to laugh defeat in the face. Heck, our hair would grow back.

The next morning, though, the DeRosier kids told the others that we had tried to dye our hair, and that's why our hair had been cut. We were jeered and laughed at. At lunchtime, I confided in Jennifer, and she went to the Home Economics room and got some scissors. In the washroom, she cut Cheryl's hair and mine, so that it looked better. The aggravation over this incident gradually died down. The DeRosier kids were back to fighting with each other, although I sometimes had the feeling they were conspiring against Cheryl and me.

Left to ourselves in our room, Cheryl and I did our homework and read a lot. Sometimes, she would read my geography book and daydream. But mostly, she'd read about animals and adventure stories. I was into Nancy Drew books and other mystery books, and occasionally I would read some of Cheryl's animal books. So far, I had not read the book on Louis Riel. Whenever Cheryl wanted to talk about him, I would change the subject. I guess she got the hint because she began staying away from such topics.

On Saturdays, Mrs. DeRosier would take her eggs in, do her visiting and her shopping, and usually her kids would go with her. Mr. DeRosier, Raymond and Gilbert went to work at the barns, or in the springtime, they would work the fields all day. Cheryl and I would have Saturdays to ourselves. Since I was good at doing the floors, I'd let Cheryl go rambling outside with Rebel. One Saturday morning, in the springtime, Ricky and Maggie didn't go to town with their mother. Later that day, Cheryl and I knew why.

Cheryl was outside looking for Rebel. I was cleaning the kitchen. Ricky had already gotten a hold of Rebel and he brought the dog close to the house for Maggie to watch. Then, making sure Cheryl didn't see him, he slipped out to the pasture where the bull was kept. When he saw Cheryl nearing the pasture, he climbed back through the fence as if he had just come through the pasture. He yelled to Cheryl that Rebel had been hurt and that the dog was on the other side of the pasture. He said he was going for help.

Thinking that Ricky had just come across the pasture, Cheryl climbed through the fence and started running. She didn't notice the bull raising its head to watch her. She didn't see it start moving towards her. Her mind was only on Rebel.

As I saw this through the kitchen window, I flew out the door, saw Maggie giggling to herself, and ran horrified towards the pasture. The bull was now charging across the field, straight at Cheryl. I called Rebel and raced towards Cheryl. I climbed though the fence and yelled to Cheryl to run.

Cheryl heard the pounding of the bull's hoofbeats, and at the same time, she heard me. She stopped to look around and when she saw the bull, she froze in terror. I was screaming all the while for her to run, and at the last minute, she did move. The bull narrowly missed her. It slowed to stop and turned around. Cheryl heard Rebel barking, but she didn't know that he had streaked behind her and was now preoccupying the bull. I was running towards her, and when I reached her, I grabbed her hand and we ran back to the safety of the fence. We turned to see how Rebel was doing. The dog was prancing around the bull, easily avoiding the short charges. Cheryl called him, and he came happily loping back to her.

Ricky and Maggie had stopped laughing, and they glared defiantly at me as I walked up to them. Without saying a thing, I hauled back and punched Maggie right in the face. Her nose started bleeding as she landed on the ground. Ricky jumped on me from behind, and his weight knocked me off balance. Cheryl, who was still shaking, walked over to him and kicked him hard. I motioned for Cheryl to leave things to me. Ricky and Maggie fought back and screamed bloody murder. I was silent as I ploughed into them. The fury in me wouldn't let their punches and their scratches hurt me. When my anger had evaporated, I stepped back and looked at them with contempt. They were bloody and crying. As I turned to ask Cheryl if she was all right, I noticed Mr. DeRosier and the two foster boys in the distance. The boys, who were standing just behind him, had big grins on their faces, the first time I had ever seen that. The expression on Mr. DeRosier's face was unreadable. He didn't say or do anything. He just turned and continued towards the garage.

At suppertime, Ricky and Maggie came down after everyone else was seated. Maggie wore a sleeveless dress to show off all the bruises and scratches she had received. Ricky had also dressed for the occasion. As they expected, their mother noticed their appearances right away.

"What happened? Did you two get into a fight?"

Maggie turned the tears on, so Ricky explained. "April and Cheryl were teasing the bull this morning, and we tried to make them stop, so they beat us up."

Before Mrs. DeRosier could turn on us, Mr. DeRosier spoke up in a quiet voice. "Now try telling the truth for a change. The tractor broke down this morning. I came back for some parts. You didn't see me, did you, Maggie and Ricky? But I saw you. And what you tried to do. You're both darn lucky I didn't have time to get to you first."

"Are you calling my children liars?" Mrs. DeRosier asked him, angrily.

"They're worse than liars! What they did this morning could have gotten Cheryl killed. What the hell's the matter with you? You three make me sick!" He slammed his fist on the table and silenced Mrs. DeRosier from saying any more. After a minute, he got up and stormed out of the house. Raymond and Gilbert looked lost. Even though they had barely begun to eat, they got up and left after him.

The rest of us finished our meal in silence. Mrs. DeRosier told Cheryl and me to go to our room when we finished the dishes. I know she wasn't going to let this go by without doing something, but I kept this worry to myself.

On Monday, Mrs. DeRosier kept Maggie home from school. When we got off the bus that evening, Maggie was in her good clothes, and it looked as if they had gone somewhere. She looked gleeful and triumphant. She whispered to Ricky, and they went into the living room, laughing.

At the beginning of the summer holidays, about a month after the incident, I was in the house one morning when I noticed a car enter the driveway and saw that it was Miss Turner. Then it hit me. Miss Turner was here to take Cheryl away. Of course, that's what their secret had been. That's why we had never been punished. I panicked. I couldn't be separated from Cheryl again! I just couldn't! But what could I do to stop it? Nothing! Nothing, except run away with Cheryl! But where could we go? Cheryl was outside somewhere. I didn't stop to think what we would take. I just ran out the kitchen door and looked around the farmyard. I saw Cheryl coming towards the house. Ricky and Maggie were still upstairs, sleeping. I heard Mrs. DeRosier calling for Cheryl from the other side of the house. I ran towards Cheryl and urged her to duck behind a building.

"Cheryl, Miss Turner is here. I'm sure she's come to take you away." I was shaking. I was glad to see that Cheryl had her jacket on.

"April, I don't want to go away from you. They told me I'd never see you again."

"I know, Cheryl. We are going to run away. Right now."

I looked around the corner of the building. There was nobody in sight. We ran across the open grain field as fast as we could, trying to keep low. When we were into the safety of the woods, I said, "We're going to Winnipeg. I'm sure I know the way there. We'll just follow along the roads through the fields. When we get there, I'll try to find the Dions. I'm sure they'll help us. I know Mrs. Semple. She'll just believe whatever DeRosier tells her. Okay?"

Cheryl nodded, and we started on our journey. I had no idea how far it was, or how long it would take. We followed alongside Highway 200, the same way we went to Winnipeg by car. We walked all that day, ducking low in the tall grasses in the ditch whenever we saw or heard a car. Sometimes, we walked through nearby woods. Once, we saw a car moving slowly, and when it came closer, we saw that it was an RCMP car. I knew they were looking for us, and that we'd have to be more careful. It grew dark, and the darker it got, the harder it was for us to walk through the weeds. We waited until it was pitch black and returned to the road. Cheryl began complaining that she was hungry and tired and wanted to stop and rest.

I urged her on, saying that we had a better chance to make it if we continued through the night. In the middle of the night, Cheryl insisted she just couldn't go on anymore. I knew how she felt because I was dead tired myself. We left the road and found ourselves in a field. Cheryl fell asleep, her head resting on my lap. I sat for a while to guard her, but I soon lay back and fell asleep, too.

I was awakened by somebody who prodded at me. The sun was shining down on us, and when I remembered where we were, I felt exposed. I blinked and was dismayed to find a police officer standing over me. Cheryl was already sitting up, and she was still rubbing her eyes.

We were told to get into the car, and I sat there, glumly. The Mountie talked to us, but we ignored him and didn't say anything. I was so disappointed that I couldn't think of anything except that we had been caught. I wondered if running away was a crime. We couldn't possibly go to jail, just because we wanted to stay together. I was surprised when we got to Winnipeg, after all. But we were taken straight to a police station. We were told to sit in the waiting area. After awhile, the officer came back and gave us milk and cinnamon buns. I was wondering why we were waiting there.

"We almost made it, didn't we?" Cheryl said. "If I hadn't gone to sleep, we would have made it."

"I went to sleep, too, Cheryl. Don't worry, we'll explain everything to them." I had read about the RCMP. I knew they were good guys and that they would listen to us. I began to wish that I had talked to the Mountie in the car, after all.

We never did get another chance to talk to the Mounties. Mrs. Semple came in first, and she gave us a disapproving look.

"I never expected this of you, April. Mrs. DeRosier is worried sick. Don't you know how much she cares for you? You girls put a scare into all of us. You should be ashamed of yourselves. Do you know what could happen when you hitchhike? Why you... could have been hurt."

"We didn't hitchhike. We walked," Cheryl said, sullenly.

"Don't try to tell me that you walked all that way. You girls have had a very bad influence on each other." She turned to stare at Cheryl. "And you, young lady, I won't be surprised if you land in reform school."

"Why should she land in reform school?" I said, bitterly. "I'm the one who talked her into running away. I didn't want us to be separated again."

"And I suppose you're the one who attacked Maggie?" Mrs. Semple asked.

"I beat her up. And Ricky, too. They tried to kill Cheryl."

After I said it, I realized it must have sounded ridiculous. Nothing was coming out right. I had wanted to explain everything out in a very sensible manner. Instead, here I was sounding almost hysterical.

"You have too much imagination and not enough common sense," Mrs. Semple said. "Mrs. DeRosier brought her poor daughter in and showed us what happened. Now they have no reason to lie about who did what. It was a very vicious act, Cheryl. Especially when Maggie refused to defend herself. Furthermore, Mrs. DeRosier brought a report from school to back her claim that you are a troublemaker. April, it's touching that you want to cover up for your sister. But if we don't do something now, she'll end up in a reform school."

"I'm not covering up! I'm telling the truth!" I shook my head in disbelief. How come they couldn't see through Mrs. DeRosier and Maggie? How could I convince them of our honesty? Then I remembered Mr. DeRosier and the boys. He had spoken up for us once. If he knew about this, surely he would speak up again.

"Did you talk to Mr. DeRosier and Raymond and Gilbert?" I asked excitedly.

Mrs. Semple eyed me suspiciously and said, "April, you're a beautiful girl. I advise you to keep your charms to yourself. Mrs. DeRosier told us that you've been flirting with them."

Of course. The old hag had that covered too. After that, I just didn't know what to say. Then Mrs. Semple gave us a little speech about what she called the "native girl" syndrome.

". . . and you girls are headed in that direction. It starts out with the fighting, the running away, the lies. Next come the accusations that everyone in the world is against you. There are the sullen, uncooperative silences, the feeling sorry for yourselves. And when you go on your own, you get pregnant right away, or you can't find or keep jobs. So you'll start with alcohol and drugs. From there, you get into shoplifting and prostitution, and in and out of jails. You'll live with men who abuse you. And on it goes. You'll end up like your parents, living off society. In both your cases, it would be a pity because Miss Turner and I knew you both when you were little. And you both were remarkable youngsters. Now, you're going the same route as many other native girls. If you don't smarten up, you'll end up in the same place they do. Skid row!"

I thought if those other native girls had the same kind of people surrounding them as we did, I wouldn't blame them one bit. Much of the speech didn't make sense to me anyway. I'd never heard the terms shoplifting, prostitution, and I didn't even know what drugs were. I'd been into drug stores and they sold all sorts of useful things. So far, I hadn't had a crush on a boy, well, not a major crush. And what the heck was skid row? All I knew for sure was that somewhere in that speech, she had insulted our parents, and I could see that it rankled Cheryl. I held her hand.

I thought of once more trying to reason with Mrs. Semple, but then Miss Turner walked in. Mrs. Semple went over to her and they talked for a few minutes. Then they came to us and told us we were going to the Children's Aid office.

There we sat alone in one room, while they discussed our futures in another. I was still angry and felt like a criminal. We hadn't done anything wrong. Well, maybe I shouldn't have laid such a beating on those two brats. But it was Cheryl who was getting all the blame. Between the two of us, she was the more innocent. It was unjust.

"Cheryl?" I said quietly.

"What?"

"I'm sorry."

"You're not the one who should be sorry. All of them are the ones who are doing wrong. They're the ones who ought to be sorry," Cheryl said, vehemently. After a few minutes, she said, "I guess I'm going that syndrome route, huh?"

"Of course not. Why do you say that?"

Cheryl smiled. "I just kind of accused everyone of being against us, didn't I?" We both laughed.

It was a while before Mrs. Semple and Miss Turner came back into the room. Mrs. Semple said to me, "April, we've decided it's in your best interest for you to return to the DeRosiers. You never got into any trouble until Cheryl came to live with you."

"No, don't send her back there. They're mean people. Mrs. DeRosier said we'd never see each other again," Cheryl shouted.

"Cheryl, we've arranged for you to go to the Steindalls. If you give them a chance, you'll be happy there. And don't you worry. There'll be visits between you and April," Miss Turner said.

"Please don't send April back to the DeRosiers. They'll do something bad to her. I just know it. Why can't she come with me?"

"Because you're not good for each other. Now, I don't want any more nonsense, Cheryl. April, if you can talk any sense into your sister, you'd better try," Miss Turner said to me.

"I want to talk to Cheryl alone," I said. The two women looked at each other, shrugged, and left the room.

I knelt before Cheryl and said, "Cheryl, we can't fight them. I know I'll be okay with the DeRosiers. I don't want you to worry about me, okay? And I don't want to have to worry about you. I want you to be good at the Steindalls. I want you to keep your grades up. This won't last forever. When we're old enough, we'll be free. We'll live together. We're going to make it. Do you understand me? *We are going to make it.* We are not going to become what they expect of us." I sat back on my heels and looked her in the eyes. She nodded and smiled through her tears.

"Okay, April, I'll try to be good."

Chapter Five

In the ride back to the DeRosier farm, I went over what I had said to Cheryl. Those were big words said on the spur of the moment. I had this idea that anyone who went to reform school was doomed for life so I didn't want Cheryl to end up in one. I could let the DeRosier's suck out my dignity for now, and I could pretend they had me where they wanted me. But my future would belong to me. I had said to Cheryl that we would live together, but that was a long way off. Maybe things would change, and I wouldn't have to live up to that statement. Or maybe if I became so rich and important, people wouldn't care that I had a proud Métis for a sister. As we approached Aubigny, my thoughts returned to my present predicament. Just what was in store for me? It was easy to think to myself that I didn't care, but living it was different.

I'd often thought to myself that those three DeRosiers were crazy. That night, when I did the dishes and they all sat behind me, silently staring at me, I was sure of it. Earlier that day, when I had returned with Mrs. Semple, Mrs. DeRosier had made a big fuss over me. It had made me sick, and I hadn't been able to hide my hostility towards her. For that whole summer, they wouldn't talk to me except to give me curt orders. Ricky and Maggie made no comments about Cheryl, and I thought this plan of theirs of giving me the silent treatment must be hardest on Maggie because she was such a verbal person.

The only companion I had was Rebel, who had now adopted me as his new friend. When I could sneak off, I'd go down to my spot at the riverbank, taking Rebel with me.

By the end of the summer, I didn't have anything good to tell him. "You know, Rebel, I think you're going to be my only friend around here for a long, long time. When I first came here, I hated you because you were their dog. Now I think of you as Cheryl's dog. You saved her life, you know. You must miss her as much as I do. But now, I don't have to worry about protecting her from them any more. Doesn't help me from being jumpy, though. If it's not the hot stuffy air in my room keeping me from sleep, it's staying awake, listening for sounds. I'm so scared they'll do something during the nights. They're crazy, Rebel. I don't trust them one bit. I wish you could sleep in my room."

Rebel would give a low whine and wag his tail to indicate he was still listening whenever I had one of these talks with him.

"You want to hear the latest? That old hag gave me a box of school clothes. You should see them, Rebel. All 'gramma' stuff. And she told me that from now on I won't be able to use the sewing stuff. I'm going to look worse than a Hutterite. I guess I shouldn't say that. They look all right to each other. But me, I'm going to have to go to school in those things. I don't know what I'm going to do. I'm glad they built that new high school. That means Ricky and Maggie won't be in my school. And I hope Ricky doesn't fail, or he could end up being in my class next year. This year, I'm going to ask Jennifer if she can mail my letters for me, and if I can have letters for me mailed to her place. I'm positive that old DeRosier has been throwing all my letters away. Cheryl said she wrote to me, and I wrote to her, but neither of us got any letters at all. I sure hate it here, Rebel. Except for you. Oh yeah, and you want to know what else that old hag came up with? Now, if I want my clothes washed, I'll have to do all the laundry and ironing. But if she thinks that's going to keep me from doing good in school, she's wrong. You know, Rebel, you and me, we talk the same language. We both whine." I smiled and scratched him behind the ears. Cheryl had said he liked that. Then I got up to walk back.

I started Grade Eight as the laughing stock of the school, and from the first day on the bus, I was often called, "Gramma Squaw." I renewed my friendship with Jennifer, but I could see that even she was embarrassed to be seen with me. One day, we were in the washroom, and she made fun of the way I was dressed. I expected that from the others, although when they would call me "Gramma Squaw," it was more painful than I'd expected, and each time a lump would come to my throat. But when Jennifer teased me, I did start crying. She immediately became contrite and sympathetic, and that made me cry even more.

"April, don't cry," she said. "I'm sorry. I didn't mean it. Hey listen, I'll bring you some of my stuff and you could keep it in your locker, okay?"

I was wiping my eyes when our Home Economics teacher walked in to see what was taking us so long.

"What's going on? What's the matter, April?"

Jennifer explained, "Mrs. DeRosier's making her wear these kinds of clothes, and she won't let April use the sewing things at home to make them look better."

"Would it help if I transferred you from the cooking class to the sewing class right now?" the teacher asked me.

Her kindness made me want to cry all over again, but I kept my self-control and simply nodded.

Between the chores I was assigned and all my homework, there wasn't much time to alter my clothing. Whenever I could, the first things I'd do would be to shorten my skirts as they hung down almost to my ankles. I'd still have to wear the black, ugly shoes to school, but once I'd get to school, I would change into a pair that Jennifer had brought from home. I told her about my postal problems, and she checked with her mother, and they agreed to be my go-between. The first letter I wrote was to the Dions. It would have been to Cheryl, but I still didn't know where she was. In November, my letter to the Dions was returned. They had moved from St. Albert.

Before Christmas, I had a visit with Cheryl. She was full of enthusiasm about her new foster home. Mostly, it was because the Steindalls had horses.

"Mr. Steindall gives lessons most nights, and when he's not busy, he's been teaching me how to ride. We went on a sleigh ride last week. Oh, April, it's so much fun. It's easy being good there. The kids at school are all right. They don't make fun of me or anything. And some of the girls who like horses made friends with me, but that's only 'cause they figure I'll invite them over and they'll get to ride. Mr. Steindall gave me my own horse to ride. His name is Fastbuck. I got to help clean their stalls and feed them, but I like doing all that."

She went on telling me all the good things that were now happening to her, and I hardly said anything. What could I say? That I was lonely and miserable and my foster mother dressed me funny? I envied Cheryl. I envied her having her own horse to ride. I envied that she could feel so much excitement. I knew I should have been so happy for her, but comparing our lives, I simply envied her. I even envied the fact that she was so smart at school. Before we parted company, I got her address and told her Jennifer's.

In early February, I received my first letter through this new courier system. I had sent her a letter in January.

Dear April,

How are you? Mrs. Steindall says we will have our next visit in April or May. I can't wait. We had to make speeches in front of the class, and I made mine on buffalo hunting. Mr. Darnell, my teacher, said I was an exceptional Métis, 'cause most would have avoided such subjects. That made me so proud that I just had to send you what I wrote. Tell me what you think of it.

Have a Happy Valentine's Day. I've enclosed a home-made card. Do you like it? I'm going to ask Mrs. Steindall if you could at least come to see me here for the summer holidays. I want to show you my horse. (Not really mine.) Would you like that? I told them about the DeRosiers, but I don't think they believed me. That's the only thing I don't like about them. I got your letter. I feel so sorry for you, April. I wish there was something I could do to help you. I'm glad you got a friend like Jennifer. I'm glad too that Rebel's keeping you company. I sure do miss him. He was a good ol' dog. They have an Irish red setter here. Nice looking, but what a nervous wreck. She follows me all over the place. I thought of all these funny things to tell you so you would laugh when you read this letter, but once I started writing, all those funny things disappeared. Sorry about that.

Well, I'll close off for now and I'll be seeing you in the springtime. Write back soon.

Love,

Cheryl

Buffalo hunting! That was almost as bad as giving me a book on Riel. I looked at the card. Cheryl had drawn a picture of a horse, a girl, and a red setter. Meant to be her setting. How lucky could one get.

Then I chided myself, "Now, April, you should be happy for her. Isn't that what you wanted? Didn't you want her to be safe and sound? Yeah, sure, but can't I even be a little bit jealous?"

Great, now I was talking to myself. Dutifully, I started reading her speech. I had to be impressed, it was so well written, and it was so obvious she had pride because she was writing about her people.

. . . The Métis hunters, equipped with buffalo guns, used one method known as "running the buffalo." This was perhaps the most dangerous way but definitely the most exciting. Men on horseback would ride through the stampeding herd, shooting prime animals. Once a shot was fired, the hunter had to pour some more powder from his buffalo horn into the muzzle of the gun, spit in one of the lead balls which he carried in his mouth, hit the gun butt on his saddle to shake down the powder and ball. All this was done as he raced his horse among the stampeding buffalo. If a horse stepped into a gopher hole or if the rider became dismounted for any other reasons, his hours as a buffalo hunter were probably numbered to mere seconds. Perhaps a bull would turn on him, or a stray shot could bring

*him down. Or he may have loaded his rifle too fast or not
properly enough, and it could explode and blow his hand off.
The hunt required steady nerves, much skill and expertise in
horsemanship and marksmanship. . . .*

For a very brief moment, I was caught up in her excitement.
Then I wondered how she ever had the courage to stand up in
front of her class and give the speech. I would never have
the courage.

Grade Nine became the very worst school year I'd ever
have. A lot of the kids in my class had started pairing off and
going steady. I'd never been interested in boys, except as
friends. When I was younger, I had thought different ones
were cute, but that was the end of it. As long as I lived with
the DeRosiers, I knew that I would have to give up any ideas
about special friendships with boys, and the easiest thing to
do was simply not to look.

But then a new family moved into Aubigny, and with it
came a boy who was in Grade Eleven, the same class Maggie
was in. While I secretly worshipped him from afar, Maggie
talked about him every night at the supper table. Mrs.
DeRosier even went so far as to invite his family over for a
Sunday dinner. The boy was named Peter. I guess he liked me
because after that Sunday dinner, he would stop and talk to
me at school. Being seen with him brought me more friends. I
loved school.

Until the other kids' attitudes changed, Maggie had not
been openly hostile towards me. I knew she felt that way
because of Peter's friendship with me, and not with her. It had
even made me smug and more sure of myself. As soon as the
whispering started behind my back, I knew that she and
Ricky were behind it. Whatever they were saying spread
throughout the school quickly. Kids were looking at me and
snickering. I'd pass by a group of boys and they'd whistle. I
started getting notes on my desk that said things like, "If you
want a really good time, meet me at such and such a place."
Some of the notes had obscenities in them, and the comments
I got from the boys were also obscene.

First Peter stopped talking to me, and then Jennifer began avoiding me. This confused me even more. Jennifer was the kind of girl who would stick by a friend no matter what. I asked her, "What is going on, Jenny?"

Jennifer had looked around quickly because there were other kids watching us and obviously talking about me. "April, I have to go."

She slipped me a note that said she'd still post my letters for me, but that was all. I became so angry and hurt, my first impulse was to tell her to just forget it. But she was my only connection with Cheryl, and I had to accept things the way they were. Again I was a loner, and now, I didn't have a single friend at school.

I was glad I still had Jennifer as a go-between on letters because in January I got another fat envelope from Cheryl. At lunchtime, I looked around to make sure Maggie and Ricky weren't around. If they ever found out that Cheryl and I were exchanging letters, I felt sure they would put an end to it. I was rather disappointed when I opened the letter and found most of it was a speech on the Métis.

January 26, 1964

Dear April,

How are you? I just know you're waiting for my next speech with anticipation. Well, here it is. Actually, it's not really a speech. I'm just caught up in this stuff. I don't think... Scratch that, it's a silly expression. I think my fellow classmates might not be able to hack another speech on Métis people. I was going to deliver this speech, but now I've decided I will keep it among my papers on the history of the Métis people. I think it's important that we know our own history. It's rather a short history compared to other races but it's interesting, as I've already stated, and I wouldn't have minded one bit living in those days. Mrs. MacAdams used to have so many good books on the subject of natives. I've been babysitting lately, and next time we go to Winnipeg, I'm going to spend all I've got on books. I wish I could afford to buy every book there is. Sally says I'm soon going to need glasses. I doubt it. I'd hate to have to wear glasses. Wouldn't you? It's un-Indian.

Oh, I made the volleyball team. We'll be going around to different places and playing other schools. Rita, one of the girls in my class, says it's not fair that I'm so smart and athletic, too. Of course, I'm not the only one. It's too bad you couldn't try out for after-school sports. I know you'd be good. Come spring, I won't join any outdoor stuff because I'd rather practice riding.

Write back to me, April. And tell me what you think of my project. I'm going to work on something about Riel. I need a few more books, though. Well, I'll sign off for now. Got a load of homework to do.

Love,
Cheryl

Again, I dutifully read through her essay. Again, she wrote about the Métis with such pride.

. . . The two armed parties met at Seven Oaks. Grant sent an emissary to Semple, demanding his surrender. An argument ensued and a settler fired. The sound of gunfire brought a nearby group of fifty more Métis to the scene. The battle-experienced Métis fired their round of shots and then fell to the ground to reload. The settlers, thinking they had shot these men down, began to cheer. The Métis, with their guns reloaded, charged the settlers. Terrified, most of the settlers turned and ran. The horsemen took over as if running buffalo. They overtook the settlers and shot them. Within fifteen minutes, twenty settlers and two of Grant's men were dead. . . .

I thought it just made the Métis look like blood-thirsty savages, but Cheryl went into great detail pointing out all of the "grievances" of the Métis and why they had fought some of their battles. But when I finished reading, I didn't feel much happier. I hated dates and company names. And how come all this mattered to Cheryl so much? She was going to keep it among her papers. Did it help her accept the colouring of her skin? Was that why we thought so differently? That and her superior intelligence? One had to be intelligent to find this kind of thing exciting. Skin colouring didn't matter in this school. Everyone treated me like a full-blooded Indian. "Gramma Squaw!" I hated those DeRosier kids so much. I sure wished I knew what they had been up to this time.

A few months later, I did find out. The guidance counsellor, Mrs. Wartzman, was waiting for me in the hall one day at lunchtime. She said she wanted to see me in her office. As Mrs. Semple had done, the Counsellor came right out and made her speech. I suppose the speech would have been okay if I had been guilty of any wrongdoing.

"April, I've heard some disturbing things, and I feel I should talk this over with you. I know that you're a foster girl, and perhaps that's the reason. You feel a psychological need to be loved. Well, what I'm really trying to say is that you shouldn't be letting Raymond and Gilbert fondle you. From what I understand, you've also been trying to flirt with Mr. DeRosier."

I sat in the chair with my mouth open. I felt such humiliation. I was sure my face was red. I thought later that Mrs. Wartzman probably assumed I was embarrassed because the truth was coming out.

"Perhaps it's not my place to be talking to you. But it's such a sensitive issue. I know that you're doing well in your grades, and I want to warn you that a pregnancy would disrupt your life. Let's see if we can't get your life on the right track again. And if Mrs. DeRosier has taken this up with your social worker, I can say that we had this little talk. Okay?" Mrs. Wartzman finished it with a smile.

I walked out of her office in a daze. It was a warm spring day so I went outside to eat my lunch. I really wanted to avoid the lunchroom and have some privacy to myself, but there were kids outside. When they saw me, some of them snickered. I wanted to die, crawl away into some hole, and never be seen again. Instead, I sat and nibbled my sandwich. If it had been Peter I was accused of fooling with, I would have been embarrassed. But Raymond and Gilbert? Both? At the same time? Not only were they ugly and pimply, but they passed their grades only because of their age and their size. I didn't have anything against them, but I'd have to be plumb out of my head to even look at them in "that" way. Well, it was no wonder Jennifer and Peter stayed away from me. But then, how could Jennifer believe that of me? And had Raymond and Gilbert gotten that same kind of speech? Probably not. Only girls got pregnant.

For the rest of that week, I walked around thinking of this. On Saturday, I found myself at the riverbank, talking to my old friend Rebel.

"I know I shouldn't feel so sorry for myself. I know that other kids go through much worse than me. But knowing that doesn't help very much. At least Gilbert and Raymond are getting out of this rathole. I wonder who they're going to accuse me of doing things with next. And if they don't get some other boys, I'll probably have to take the bales off the fields all by myself. How could Jenny believe all those things about me? How could she? I thought she was such a good friend. Maybe she doesn't believe them. Maybe she's just scared to be seen with me. Boy! I'm going to get even with those DeRosiers. I don't know how, but somehow, some way, I'm going to get them. And when I get through with them, they're never going to get another foster kid. Never!"

Chapter Six

I had no idea how I was going to get even with the DeRosiers for those horrible rumours. It just made me feel a little better to think I could. I would entertain different ideas, but I discarded them all. Talking to my social worker was futile because she'd already proven to me that she was on Mrs. DeRosier's side. And the same thing went for the teachers at school.

Since I never saw Jennifer over the summer months, Cheryl and I didn't write to each other. It was when I went into Grade Ten that my opportunity presented itself to do something about the DeRosiers. I didn't recognize it as such. Jennifer came to me with a letter from Cheryl in September. I expected her to walk away, but she stayed and finally talked to me.

"April, about last year... I guess I should have told you what was going on when I first heard about it. But there are these sayings, you know, about being judged by the company you keep. Well, I didn't want to get the same hassles you were getting. I'm chicken. I couldn't take that kind of thing."

I looked at her and said, "Did you believe any of that?"

"No. I knew you. I knew you wouldn't do anything like what they said. I'd like for us to be friends again."

"I'd like that, too," I said, gratefully.

In October, Mrs. Gauthier, our English teacher, told us that the Southern Journal was holding a competition for Christmas stories and we'd have two weeks in which to submit entries. At lunchtime, Jennifer and I talked about the competition. English was my strongest subject, and compositions were easy for me. It was mostly just a matter of choosing a topic that would attract attention.

"Why don't you write about your life with the DeRosiers?"
Jennifer asked with a grin.

I thought it was a great idea. But then I said, "It has to be
a Christmas story, and they have a way of destroying
Christmas for me."

For a week I pondered over how I could work my life at the
DeRosiers into a Christmas story. Finally, the idea came to me,
and I worked on my story at lunchtimes. The title was "What I
Want For Christmas," and I ended the story with the sentence,
"What I want for Christmas is for somebody to listen to me and
to believe in me." I handed it in to Mrs. Gauthier.

The next day, Mrs. Gauthier asked me to stay at lunch. I
waited and was surprised when Mrs. Wartzman came into the
room with my story in her hand. Mrs. Wartzman said to me,
"This is an incredible story, April. Is this really what's been
going on?"

I nodded, unable to speak because that lump in my throat
was back. I was sure they were going to throw my story in the
garbage after giving me a good scolding. Maybe they would
even show it to Mrs. DeRosier. Mrs. Gauthier's next words
gave me hope. "I believe the story. I've heard the rumours
about April, and she's never done anything to indicate that
they were true. She's a very good student."

"Oh, I'm sure she is. I've checked with Cheryl's former
Grade Five teacher and she confirmed what you wrote, April.
I can't believe that workers would place children in this kind
of home."

"Why didn't you ever tell your social worker or one of us?"
Mrs. Gauthier asked.

"We tried. We tried to tell our workers but they would only
believe what Mrs. DeRosier told them. And when you said
those things to me last year... " I looked at Mrs. Wartzman.

"I owe you an apology, April. I'm sorry I jumped to
conclusions," Mrs. Wartzman said.

It was decided that my story would not be entered in the
competition, and they urged me to write another one in its
place. From what I understood, Mrs. Wartzman was going to
call my social worker herself. That was good enough for me.

I waited impatiently, and in November 1963, something happened in the United States which made me forget my impatience temporarily. The President of the United States, John F. Kennedy, was shot. I was just coming back from lunch when I heard the news. The whole class was subdued, and I was shocked. Cheryl and I had talked about him a few times. She admired him for many reasons. In the weeks which followed, I saved clippings from the newspaper on his funeral and his family. I wasn't allowed to watch television, so I missed an awful lot, including the death of Lee Harvey Oswald. I planned on giving my clippings to Cheryl. We were supposed to have a visit, but for some reason it was put off.

I returned to my impatient waiting. Had the wheels of motion begun, or was nothing going to come of my story, after all? Christmas passed and then it was 1964. The only consolation I had until then was that two grown-ups were aware of my predicament. Then, in January, I got a letter from Cheryl.

January 16, 1964

Dear April,

How are you? I got your letter, and obviously, you didn't know you missed a visit with me. I waited at the Children's Aid office all afternoon December 23rd, then Miss Turner came and told me that Mrs. DeRosier called to say she wasn't able to make it to town because she'd gotten stuck. Did you know about that? Anyways, I'm glad you've gotten through to your teachers. Have you heard anything further? We are getting a new social worker, did you know that? I sure hope she's going to be good for us.

Wasn't it terrible about President Kennedy being assassinated? I wanted to see you so much to talk about it. I cried that night when I was alone. I read a lot of history. All the Kennedys were so interesting and young and vital. I used to collect items on them. I'm sure that Robert Kennedy will get in as President, though. I hope he keeps the same speech writers. Kennedy's speeches were really good.

Anyways, I've enclosed my historical piece on Riel at the Red River Insurrection. You ought to see this load of crap we have to take in History. I don't know if you took the same textbook. It's *Canada: the New Nation*. It makes me mad the way they portray native people. It makes me wish those white men had never come here. But then we would not have been born. At least the Indians would have been left in peace. Nothing those tribes ever did to each other matches what the whites have done to them. Whoa, there, Cheryl. You probably don't agree with me, do you, April? But history should be an unbiased representation of the facts. And if they show one side, they ought to show the other side equally. Anyways, that's why I'm writing the Métis side of things. I don't know what I'm going to do with it, but it makes me feel good.

Well, I hope you like my essay. I'll sign off for now. Let me know what happens. Sure is taking a long time.

Love,

Cheryl

When I finished reading her letter, I felt awful about the fact I had missed a visit and had not even known about it. Did Mrs. DeRosier do that because she knew about my own essay? All of a sudden I felt scared. She did know. She had put a stop to everything. I was going to be stuck here until... until when? It wasn't fair. It just wasn't fair.

To preoccupy my mind, I read Cheryl's essay on Riel and the Red River Insurrection. But reading her essay didn't help. Knowing the other side, the Métis side, didn't make me feel any better. It just reinforced my belief that if I could assimilate myself into white society, I wouldn't have to live like this for the rest of my life.

That afternoon, I didn't pay much attention to classwork. My mind was on my present problem. I believed Mrs. DeRosier knew about my essay. I felt I had been betrayed. What could I do about it? I could think of only one thing. Come summer, I'd take off. But then, I had wanted to finish school so bad. I had wanted to be able to get a good job. I wanted to be rich. Oh, to heck with being rich. I'd run away anyway. Maybe to some other city so they wouldn't find me. I'd lie about my age if I had to, and I'd get a job. For the moment, being free was more important than anything else in the world.

That night, I lay in bed still thinking about my soon-to-be future. Another problem came up. I had no money at all to even start out. I'd have to get some. But how? Steal it? I'd been accused of stealing already, so why not? That would be justice of a sort. Oh, sure, April, and when you run out of money in the city, you can just sell your body. And what else do native girls do? By now, I knew what skid row meant. I bet all those girls who ended up on skid row just wanted freedom and peace in the first place. Just like me. I'd had good intentions about my life. But here I was, forced to go out into that world, unprepared and alone. With only a Grade Ten and no money. No matter, I'd still run away. I felt so, so sorry for myself and what I'd end up being, I started to cry. My life would be hard. But staying here would be harder. I felt I had no choice.

My running away plans were discarded when rescue did come at the beginning of our spring break. It came in the form of Mr. Wendell, my new social worker. When I saw him enter the house and introduce himself, I was downright disappointed. He was a short little man with a meek demeanor. Glasses and balding. Really! He was no match for Mrs. DeRosier. I studied him as he exchanged preliminaries with the old hag. Suddenly, he said, "I'd like to see where the boys slept."

"The boys?" Mrs. DeRosier asked. She was obviously flustered by his unexpected question. I could tell, and I was glad she was off-balance. But the thought that she was going to get more boys must have hit her the same time it hit me. She recovered and my face grew long.

"Oh, yes, Raymond and Gilbert. How are they doing now that they're on their own? I hope they're not getting into any trouble. They were such good boys when they were with us. And such hard workers. You couldn't get any better workers. I believe that hard work is good for the soul, don't you?"

I thought to myself, "So that's why she doesn't make her kids work; they have no souls." Mrs. DeRosier led the way into the living room towards the stairs, saying, "They used to share my son's room. We moved their bunks into the storage closet for now."

When we were upstairs, Mr. Wendell had a look but didn't say anything. He asked where my room was. Mrs. DeRosier took him down the hall to Maggie's room. I followed them everywhere, and when she could, Mrs. DeRosier scowled at me as if trying to tell me to get back downstairs.

"I can only see one bed, Mrs. DeRosier. I understand you have a daughter. Isn't this her room?" Mr. Wendell said.

"The girls share it. The other bed was old, so I've ordered a new one. It should have been here by now." She smiled at him.

This was my chance to prove what a liar Mrs. DeRosier was. I said, "My bedroom's really downstairs, at the back."

Mrs. DeRosier said quickly, "Well, the girls have been having trouble, so I moved April there but only temporarily." She glared at me when Mr. Wendell turned to start back down.

"I've been in that room since I first came here. And so was Cheryl." I was beyond caring about the later consequences.

"How about if you show me where your room is, April?" Mr. Wendell said to me when we were back in the kitchen. Mrs. DeRosier said nothing as Mr. Wendell looked at my belongings.

"Well, Mrs. DeRosier, I think that under the circumstances, I can only recommend that April be moved as soon as we find a new foster home for her." He was about to say more, but Mrs. DeRosier cut him off.

"And I think you can take her and get out of my house right now," she bellowed.

"Mrs. Semple has had a very heavy case-load, otherwise I'm sure you wouldn't have been able to fool her for so long," Mr. Wendell said to her.

He told me to get my things ready. When we started for the car, Rebel came to me. I stopped to pet him one last time. "Poor old Reb. I wish I could take you with me. Thank you for being my friend here. Bye, Rebel." Rebel wagged his tail, and as we drove off, I saw him lie down by the roadside, probably waiting for me to come back.

Chapter
Seven

Once we arrived at the Children's Aid office, arrangements were quickly made for me to attend St. Bernadette's Academy, but they were now on their spring break. I waited that whole morning in the waiting area, not quite sure I wasn't dreaming all this. I would actually be going to an Academy. Rich girls went to Academies. When Mr. Wendell came back late in the afternoon, he brought back news that topped my excitement. I was going to the Steindalls to be with Cheryl until the spring break was over. All of this excitement was inside me. Outwardly, I might have smiled slightly, but I was now used to keeping my feelings to myself.

When we arrived at the Steindall's place, in Birds Hill, 88 Cheryl was waiting for me on the veranda. When she saw our car pull into the driveway, she bounded off the steps and came running up to greet me. She was practically jumping up and down. I greeted her in a cool, reserved manner, and that put an injured look on her face. At the time, only Cheryl and Mrs. Steindall were home. Their own daughter was away in the city for the holidays, visiting an older sister. After Mr. Wendell made sure I was settled in, he left. I had lunch while Cheryl chattered away. Mrs. Steindall seemed nice enough, but she didn't attempt to join in Cheryl's questions. Cheryl seemed used to her being quiet because she wasn't the least bit self-conscious about what she said.

After lunch, she was anxious to show me her horse.

"You know what I used to think about doing all the time?" Cheryl asked me as I admired the horse.

"What?"

"I used to think of riding him to the DeRosiers and rescuing you from them. But then I probably would have gotten lost, and I couldn't figure out how to feed and water the horse. Anyways, Mr. Steindall only gave me the horse to ride, not for keeps. If I'd taken him, I'd have been a horse thief." While I smiled, Cheryl seemed to ponder for a minute before she spoke again. "April, how come you didn't seem very glad to see me?"

"I was Cheryl, really. It's just that I'm used to keeping the way I feel inside of me. I've been doing that for practically five years now. Maybe even longer. I don't know. It just seems it's safer not to show your feelings. Like, if the Steindalls were mean people, or even Mr. Wendell, and they saw that we liked being together, they might try and keep us apart. Remember, DeRosier did that."

"Yeah, I guess you're right."

After that, Cheryl and I talked every minute that we could, catching up on things we didn't say in letters. I must have made up for all the laughing I didn't do while I was living at the DeRosiers. But, too soon, I had to leave for school.

I finished my Grade Ten at St. Bernadette's Academy. When I'd been living at the Dions, I had known nuns and they were okay people. I was able to relax at the convent. A daily routine was followed. I made friends with a lot of the boarders. The only thing was that they spoke of their friends and families back home, and I had no one to speak of, except Cheryl. It wasn't until June that I came up with an outright lie, an excuse for being with the Children's Aid. I told my friends that my parents died in a plane crash. I didn't plan on that lie. It just came out on the spur of the moment, when I was being asked about my family. They were so sympathetic towards me that I knew I would never be able to take those words back. I credited my ability to make friends easily to the fact that none of them knew I was part Indian.

My summer holidays that year were simply wonderful. The Steindalls had agreed to take me for the two months. Mr. Steindall taught me how to ride. Sometimes, we would all go out riding, even Mrs. Steindall, who looked out of place in her pair of jeans and cowboy boots. When I became a good enough rider, Cheryl and I were allowed to go camping overnight by a small creek about four miles away. The first time, Mr Steindall rode over in the evening and helped us set up the tent.

One night, when we were sitting in front of our small fire, Cheryl told me the things she had dreamt of when we lived together at the DeRosiers.

"Remember how I used to look at your Geography book?"

"Yeah, and daydream."

"Well, I used to think that when Mom and Dad got better and took us back, we could move to the B.C. Rockies and live like olden-day Indians. We'd live near a lake, and we'd build our own log cabin with a big fireplace. And we wouldn't have electricity, probably. We'd have lots and lots of books. We'd have dogs and horses, and we'd make friends with the wild animals. We'd go fishing and hunting, grow our own garden, and chop our wood for winter. And we wouldn't meet people who were always trying to put us down. We'd be so happy. Do you think that would ever be possible, April?"

"It's a beautiful dream, Cheryl." She was watching me, and I didn't want her to know then that I had my own plans. I wanted to be with people, not isolated in the wilderness.

"But do you think it's possible that it could happen?"

"Maybe. Maybe our parents might start coming to see us again. But it all depends on them." I realized that moment that I had stopped thinking of our parents as Mom and Dad and it was hard for me to refer to them as Mom and Dad now.

"I wanted to ask our social workers about them, but I was too scared. I don't know why. I still think about us living out there together. When I'm feeling down, that picks me up. Mom and Dad would become real healthy again. I always think of Dad as a strong man. He would have been a chief or a warrior in the olden days, if he had been pure Indian. I'd sure like to know what kind of Indians we are. And Mom was so beautiful to me, she was like an Indian princess. The only thing that I couldn't be realistic about in my daydreams was that Rebel would be with us." Cheryl's eyes sparkled. I could tell that this fantasy had meant a lot to her. It had probably helped her get over her loneliness. So I didn't tell her the truth about our parents. I felt that by not telling her I was also betraying her, letting her hang on to impossible dreams. If only Cheryl would forget about them, forget that she was Métis. She was so smart that she could have made it in the white world. White people have a great respect for high intelligence. Again, I wished my parents were dead.

When I first came for the summer, I'd tell Cheryl how great it was to be at the Academy. But by the end of it, when she started talking about going there, too, I changed my tune. I then told her, "You wouldn't want to leave this place and Fastbuck to go to a Convent, would you? I'm sure you wouldn't like it there. There are hours and hours of praying in the chapel and then there's also the hours of study periods. There's hardly any sports activity. You'd be bored to death." I didn't want Cheryl at the Academy because of the lie I had told about my parents, and because I was white as far as the other girls were concerned. I wanted to keep it that way as long as I could.

"Sounds to me as if you don't want me there," Cheryl said, tilting her head to one side.

"You know it's not that. You have it so good here. And I could probably come and visit you for holidays. Besides, I'll be finished school in two years, and you still have four years to go. What would you do if you didn't like it? When I graduate, you'd be alone. If you left there, they might put you in another home like the DeRosiers'." Cheryl shrugged and accepted my reasoning. I was very relieved.

Going to St. Bernadette's was good for me. I had many friends, and it was easy to study and do well in my school work. On weekends, I was invited to go to other girls' homes, with Mr. Wendell's okay. I never told Cheryl about those weekends, knowing she'd probably feel slighted. Long weekends, I always went to the Steindalls. I'd often wish that I had been placed as a boarder at this school long before.

There were no hassles about belonging to a family all the time. There was no one who made fun of my parents. Of course, that was due to the lie I had told. I might not have known a family life as I had at the Dions, but I would not have known the cruelty of the DeRosiers either. I spent Christmas with the Steindalls. Perhaps Cheryl had put her family fantasy aside, I thought, because when I went there, she had something new to tell me.

"You know, April, I think that since we have made it, or we're going to make it, we ought to help other kids like us make it, too. You know what I've been thinking? I'm going to become a social worker when I finish school. And I'm going to be a good social worker, just like Mr. Wendell. What about you? What are you going to be when you grow up?"

"I haven't got a clue what I'm going to be. I used to think of being a lawyer, but I'm too shy. All I know for sure is that I don't want to be in anything medical, I don't want to be a teacher or a social worker. I just don't know."

"Well, geez, April, you better start thinking about it because you only got a year and a half to go."

True, I did have only a year and a half to go before I would graduate. But even so, I'd only be seventeen. What I wanted to do was start working and making money.

At the end of my Grade Eleven school year, Mr. Wendell gave me the option of returning to the Steindalls for the summer or going to Winnipeg and finding myself a summer job. He said my room and board would be provided. Not another foster home, but room and board. I opted for the city. To ease the guilt I felt for not choosing Cheryl's company, I told myself that I had to start making my life, for me, and that both of us should have friends of our own, not always relying on each other. I wrote Cheryl a hurried letter to tell her all this.

I moved to Spence Street, just off Portage Avenue, near the heart of the city. It didn't take me long to find a job as a waitress, and I made new friends among the other boarders. Some of them were natives from northern communities and were there to go to the University of

Winnipeg. Others were former foster children who were
working at steady jobs, on the verge of going into the world
on their own, but who still required the security of the
Children's Aid to fall back on. I would work from eight in
the morning to four-thirty. After supper, I would go with
the other girls, down to a coffee shop where a lot of other
kids hung out. On Fridays and Saturdays, we would all
go to the Hungry Eye, a discotheque on Portage Avenue,
near Carlton.

The people I met at the discotheque were fascinating to
me; from the musicians who played in the bands to the
individuals with whom I made friends. I liked the way they
dressed, and I liked the way they danced. They were good and
bad at the same time. Good in that native girls I saw were
beautiful and sure of themselves. Good in that natives could
go with whites and no one laughed. Good in their open
acceptance of others. Bad in that they went shoplifting, drank
liquor even though they were under-aged, and had easy
sexual relationships with each other. When the discotheques
closed, all-night parties followed. I always went back to my
place, though. I felt at home with these new friends, but a lot
of times, I imagined myself much better than they were. The
girls made me think of Mrs. Semple's speech on the syndrome.
So, I enjoyed the good things they offered but stayed away
from the bad.

I worked hard all that summer and put all my earnings in
a savings account. I hadn't bothered to write to Cheryl
because I had kept putting it off. When I returned to do my
Grade Twelve at St. Bernadette's, I was more aware of what
was happening in the world. I was there less than a week
when I got a letter from Cheryl.

September 7, 1965

Dear April,

How are you? In case you forgot, it's me, Cheryl, your
sister. How come you never came to see me once this past
summer, and you never even wrote to me? Your last letter
made me very sad. It's like you don't want to have anything to
do with me anymore. Your pretense about not caring seems to

be turning into reality. I was looking forward to our spending the summer holidays together again. Instead, all I get is a short letter. I know we each have to have our own friends and make our own lives. But it was you who said all we've got is each other. We're family, not just friends. Are you coming for Christmas? I hope so.

94

I finally got another essay done on Riel. I didn't have much time in school with sports and other things going on. I did have a lot of rainy days when I was alone this past summer, though. I'll probably grow up to be a nag, huh? You're so lucky to be in Grade Twelve. They really should have let me skip a grade too. Well, I'm going to sign off now. This was just going to be a short note to let you know how much you hurt my feelings. Hope you like Riel at Batoche.

Your loving sister,
Cheryl

I felt guilty all over again after I had read the letter. She was right. I should have written to her and given her my address in the city. I should have made a special effort to go and see her. I tried to imagine myself in her place. Yes, she must have felt abandoned by me. More than she showed in her letter. I had to write her a long letter to make up for it. I even sent her lavish compliments on her essay. It was quite extraordinary for someone her age. But it had no big effect on me. Riel and Dumont, they were men of the past. Why dwell on it? What concerned me was my future. And this essay proved my point once again. White superiority had conquered in the end.

By Christmas, I had decided what I was going to do. Some of the girls had talked of becoming secretaries. That sounded good enough for me. I would take a secretarial course after I graduated. Over the Christmas holidays, I told Cheryl my plans. She was disappointed. She was sure I could do something better, like become a psychologist or something. She figured I would be wasting my life away. I told her she was beginning to sound like one of those ambitious white mothers she scorned so much. We teased each other back and forth, but I knew she was serious. She really did want me to

attend university. And, of course, she was still set on becoming
a social worker.

95   After my graduation, I got my old job as a waitress for the
summer months. It was arranged that I would go to the Red
River Community College in September. I lived once again on
Spence Street, expecting everything to be the same as the
previous summer. It wasn't. The Hungry Eye had been closed.
I ran into a few of the old crowd. They told me that some of
the others had gone to other cities, or they were doing time at
Headingley Jail. Another discotheque had opened on Graham
Avenue. I went along with them to check it out. One of the
girls I had met the last summer now had a baby at home and
was living on welfare. That bothered me a lot and somehow
the magic of that kind of nightlife was gone for me.

By September, I had over eight hundred dollars in the
bank. I thought I was quite wealthy. My first boyfriend wasn't
really a boyfriend. He spent most of his time pining away over
his old girlfriend. We went to the school dances together, but
in private, we never got real close to each other. If he had tried
to kiss me, I would have ended it right there. The thing I liked
most about Ted was that he was safe to be with. I turned
eighteen two months before I finished my course. When I
finished the course, I knew I would never see Ted again,
except by accident.

Children's Aid assured me they would support me until I
found a job. About three weeks later, I became employed as a
legal secretary at the law firm of Harbison and Associates. I
was thrilled when I found out I'd be making over four times
the amount I had as a waitress.

When I had my last talk with Mr. Wendell on what I
called my Independence Day, I showed no outward reactions.
He gave me the accumulation of my family allowances, along
with reassurances that if I needed assistance of any kind, I
could always come to him. Then I heard myself asking about
my parents, and what were the chances of finding them. He
went off and came back with a list of names and addresses. I
thanked him and said goodbye. I'd probably see him again,
96   but I would no longer be a foster child. I was free, *free! FREE!*

Chapter Eight

I found freedom rather boring, once I'd settled into my new routine. I'd found an apartment on Cumberland Avenue, which was within walking distance of where I worked. Then I furnished it with used furniture. Working was easy, that is after the first couple of weeks when I got over my nervousness. I worked for Mr. Lord, a young lawyer who did real estate work. I was nervous about making mistakes when I typed up all the legal forms; I was nervous answering the phone; I was nervous each time I handed in the letter I had typed for his signature in case I hadn't got my shorthand right. Mr. Lord was generous with his compliments, though, and that soon put me at ease. The other girls in the office were pleasant, several were my age, and when I got to know them better, we would go to movies or shopping together.

Evenings and weekends, I spent on the search for my parents. I'd take the list and a map of the city and go to the addresses on the list. Sometimes the addresses would lead to a parking lot or a new building. The house where we had lived on Jarvis had been torn down and replaced by a government building. I would feel a vague relief when this kind of thing happened, because I didn't like the people I'd meet who once knew Henry and Alice Raintree "a long time ago." I found out that both of them had relatives in the North. I wasn't going to go to the northern towns on the slim chance I might find them because I considered it unlikely.

At one address on Charles Street, I was practically dragged into the house by a rather large, squat woman. When I asked if she knew the whereabouts of Henry or Alice Raintree and told her who I was, a grin spread on her face from ear to ear. All happy and smiling, she took me by the arm

and led me into the house. She hadn't seen my parents for the
last couple of years but maybe Jacques had. I figured Jacques
to be her husband. I didn't want to stay there but I could think
of no polite way of leaving. Besides, she assured me that
Jacques would be home in a short while. Meanwhile, she
offered me some tea, then a beer, but I refused both. She'd
been cooking and she resumed her position at the old stove. I
sat at the kitchen table, looking around.

What a horrible place. The linoleum was coming apart at
the seams, and here and there pieces were missing. I could see
why it hadn't been washed. The cupboards had been painted
white, maybe twenty years ago. The plaster was also coming
off the walls, and the ceiling was warped and water-stained.
Flies! They were everywhere and reminded me of the book
Lord of the Flies. One fly landed on the rim of an uncovered
lard can which sat on the table with some bread. It rubbed its
legs together, as if with glee. How could anyone eat that food
and not be sick? Suddenly, it was very important to me that
those flies not touch me, and I waved them away. Of course,
the windows couldn't be closed, but hadn't they ever heard of
screens? I wondered what they did in wintertime, when the
smell of the place must be raunchy. They were probably
immune to all the germs in the house, but me, I feared going
home, getting sick, and missing work.

I stared over at the old woman, her back to me, probably
unaware of my presence. From our initial encounter, I
thought she would have been the talkative type, but no, she
was silently busy filling up a pot with cut-up vegetables. I
thought she probably used the flies for meat, and then I
scolded myself for being so merciless. I couldn't help it,
though. I looked down at her feet, stockingless, and stuck into
a pair of men's backless slippers. Her legs were lumpy with
varicose veins or some other disease. Her heels were dried
and scaly. Ugly! Her, this house, this kind of existence. I
finally cleared my throat, mostly to remind her that I was still
sitting behind her.

"I really have to go now. I'm supposed to meet someone. I
could come back another time," I said.

"Oh, I'm sorry, I was sure Jacques would have been back by now," she said, turning to me. "Are you sure you really have to go? You could stay for supper."

"Well, thank you, but I really have to go." I turned to leave, knowing I would not return.

Later, as I sat in the bathtub, washing off all those germs I'd probably picked up, I thought about the scene I had witnessed. If I hadn't been brought up in foster homes, I would most likely have been brought up in those slums. I would have been brought up with flies, with mice and rats and lice and germs. I would have been brought up by alcoholic parents, and what would I be like now? Would I have any ambitions? Or would I come to live just for today, glad when each day would end? I would not go back to that house on Charles Street. I would not go out of my way for a long, long time to try and find the parents who had abandoned Cheryl and me—all for a bottle of booze! When I finished my bath, I put all the papers Mr. Wendell had given me, along with the new addresses I had been given, into a box and stuck the box in the back of the closet, out of sight and out of mind. If I did find my parents, there would be emotional pain for Cheryl and me. It would probably tear me apart, once again. That part of my life was now finished for good. I had a plan to follow, and from now on, I would stick with it, whether Cheryl agreed with it or not. It was my only way to survive.

Mr. Steindall usually came to get me for long weekends so I could spend them with Cheryl. Otherwise, I usually stayed home, watched TV, read books or magazines, and if I wanted to go out and do something, I would go to the movies.

I'd buy magazines that featured beautiful homes and study how they were decorated. Then I would lie back and daydream of myself being in one of those homes, giving lavish parties, and I'd have a lot of friends surrounding me. I also studied fashion magazines, and I'd spend hours shopping for just the right thing. I had no idea how I was going to become rich. All I knew was that one day I would have a beautiful home, a big fancy car, and the most gorgeous clothing ever. Yes, when fortune kissed me with wealth, I'd be well prepared.

I had been working at Harbison's law firm for almost six months when another lawyer was added to the eleven already there. When I first saw Roger Maddison, I thought to myself, "Now there's a man I wouldn't mind spending the rest of my life with." It wasn't that I was a sucker for all handsome men, just that his rugged kind of handsomeness was the kind I could look at forever. Since some of the other girls openly swooned over him, I figured I'd be cool about my infatuation with him. But then I had to do some work for him because he didn't have his own secretary. My infatuation quickly wore off. He was a perfectionist, and when I made my first small mistake, he tore into me. I was so angry that he would criticize me. Or maybe it was that I was hurt that our feelings weren't mutual. I practically yelled right back at him. From then on, we were sarcastic towards each other, made snide remarks, always trying to outdo the other. Even when he did get his own secretary, and she began to do all of his work, we still glared at each other whenever it was appropriate. Or, he would smile and greet everyone, excluding me. The thing I couldn't figure out was that he seemed to study me an awful lot. I'd be working away, then I'd feel his eyes on me. I'd look up and there he was. But he'd give me a dirty look and turn away.

While I worked, Cheryl was finishing her Grade Twelve. In June, she graduated at the top of her class and even won a scholarship to go to the University of Winnipeg. If she hadn't, Children's Aid would have paid for her education, anyway. There were some advantages in being a ward of the C.A.S.

In July, Cheryl moved in with me, even though she wouldn't be eighteen until October. Children's Aid agreed to pay all her expenses. The day Cheryl moved in with me, July 6, 1968, was like the real honest Independence Day. The Steindalls brought Cheryl and her belongings to my place that Saturday morning, had lunch with us, and then left. Cheryl and I went shopping for a sofa that opened into a bed.

Then we went on to other stores. We dropped our purchases off back at the apartment, then went out for supper. That evening, we sat around talking and thinking about the wonderful feeling of being together with no one to control our destinies but us.

I went to work on Monday, and Cheryl went to the Winnipeg Native Friendship Centre. She volunteered her services for the rest of July and August, believing the experience would help her in her future career as a social worker.

Cheryl began her first year of university in September. I began to meet her for lunch in the university cafeteria. She quickly accumulated a number of friends, both white and native. To my biggest surprise, she started going out quite steadily with a white student, Garth Tyndall. I was amazed because the way she had talked in the past, she didn't like anything white. I wasn't surprised she could attract the opposite sex because she was very beautiful. She was also outgoing in her new crowd, and stubborn when she made up her mind about anything. When she was home, she'd usually have her friends around. And when she was over at Garth's place in the evenings, I would be alone.

101

I gave a party for her eighteenth birthday. I could see that night how close she and Garth had become. He seemed to care about her more than she did about him. I was very pleased. If anyone could change a woman's mind about things, it was a man.

But my hopes were dashed when, a month later, they split up. At first, Cheryl wouldn't tell me what happened. One night, she was supposed to have been going to dinner with him and then to a movie. They had gone out together, but later in the evening, Garth had called for her. When she came in a few minutes later, I said to her, "I thought you two were going out tonight."

"No. Something more important came up. If he calls again, tell him I'm not in. I'm going to take a bath and go to bed." She seemed very depressed.

"Hey, Cheryl, did you two have a fight?"

"No, not a fight. More of an insight." With that she stalked off to the bathroom.

Garth called again, and I was tempted to ask him what had happened, but I felt I should hear it from Cheryl. The next day was Saturday, and Cheryl was still in a state of depression. Finally, I asked her again what had happened. After hesitating, she finally told me.

"We were walking down Portage, and Garth saw some of his friends coming toward us. He told me to keep walking, and he'd catch up. I pretended that I was window shopping so I could listen to them. You know what he did? You know what that creep did? He left me there and went for a beer with them. He didn't want them to know about me. That goddamned hypocrite. He's ashamed of me."

I didn't say anything. I didn't say anything because I was guilty of that, too. I had never invited Cheryl to come and meet me for lunch because I didn't want anyone at work to see her, to know she was my sister. Even now, I knew this wouldn't change me. I would continue to walk the five blocks or so at lunchtime, so I could meet her where she was already accepted. That night, Cheryl decided she was going to keep a journal. I smiled and told her she shouldn't start a journal with an unhappy opening.

"Wait until something good happens to you, something special."

"Well, I haven't got a lifetime. I want to start this thing right now. I have a feeling there will be a lot more of this kind of thing."

I thought to myself, "Oh, no, I could be in there one day."

Not long after Cheryl's breakup with Garth, I met someone I thought was very special. I was waiting for Cheryl outside one of her classrooms, when another of Cheryl's professors approached me. We talked until Cheryl came out. His name was Jerry McCallister, and whenever he saw me alone after that, he'd stop to chat. One day, he asked me to go out with him. I guess he thought I shared some of the same ideals as Cheryl because he talked about native subjects, like their housing and education. Having heard Cheryl speak about such things often enabled me to carry a reasonable conversation with him. When he dropped me off at my apartment, he asked me to go out with him again, but he didn't try to kiss me. I had gone out with some of the students to plays and concerts, but they had only one thing on their minds at the end of the evening. So Jerry's behavior was refreshing to me. We'd go out together frequently after that, even during the week. He was always a perfect gentleman. The more I saw of him, the more I appreciated him.

103

Finally one night, when we stayed at my place for dinner and some conversation, he made his first advance. I held back. Good girls didn't do that kind of thing. Furthermore, and more importantly, if things got out of hand and we went all the way, there was the risk of getting pregnant. Maybe that was my worst fear because when Jerry tried to get too close, I would always back off. Jerry's initial amusement and patience waned, and one night he was trying to coax me again. Finally, he said, "April, what are you scared of? Are y ou scared of getting involved with another human being? Or is it sex you're afraid of?"

"I don't know. I never... well, I never... so how would I know? I can't. That's all." I hadn't wanted to reveal that I was of the stone age. It made me feel so immature.

Jerry smiled and said, "April, if you feel the same way that I feel, then making love is the most natural thing in the world. And if it's respect you're worried about, I'll certainly not respect you any less. We're not teenagers anymore. We're man and woman. Adults, with adult feelings and adult needs." He pulled me close to him and I tensed up.

"I can't."

"Why not? There's nothing wrong with it. Now stop acting so childish." He took his arms from around me and sat up.

"No, I'm sorry, Jerry. I want to, but I just can't." I looked to him for some understanding.

He stood up and went to the closet and got his coat. As he put it on, he said, "I don't like playing silly little games, April. Either you want me or you don't. When you make up your mind which it is, I'll be at the university."

In the following weeks, I agonized over Jerry's absence. I
had really liked the intimate suppers, long talks, and having
104   a steady friend to go out with. I had planned to ask him to our
social and show him off, especially to Roger Maddison. I didn't
attend the law firm's Christmas social, after all. I went with
Cheryl to spend Christmas with the Steindalls and returned
alone because of work. I was so lonely during the holidays
that my resolve broke down, and I decided to call him. I had
never been out to his home, and I looked up his name in the
phone book. As I dialed the number, I thought of being
flippant about the whole thing. I'd say something like, "Hi,
Jerry. I was wrong and you were right, so I'm yours for the
taking." No, that wasn't my style. I'd just play it by ear.

"Hello?" a small child's voice answered.

"Uh, hello. Is Jerry McCallister there, please?"

"No, Daddy's not home. Do you want to talk to my
Mommy?" and before I could say no, I heard the child calling
to his mother.

"Hello," came the voice of a woman. I tried to picture what
she looked like.

"Oh, hello, Mrs. McCallister? I'm a student from the
university, and I was working on a project over the holidays,
but I needed Mr. McCallister's advice on something. I'm sorry
to be bothering him at home." My cheeks were flaming hot.

"Oh, that's all right. He should be back any minute now.
Could I have him call you back? Oh, just a minute. I think he's
at the door now. Hold on."

I thought of hanging up, but if I did that, it might arouse
his wife's suspicions.

"Hello," Jerry's voice came on.

"It's me, April. I guess I made a terrible mistake. I'm
sorry." I hung up before he could say anything. I felt incredibly
stupid. I had been going around with a married man. Not only
that, he had a child, maybe more than one. And I was about
to go to bed with him! I shook my head and sat there for a long
time.

He came to see me one evening in the new year. "April, I'd
105   like to explain."

"There's nothing to explain. You're married! You wanted me to... to... well, you know. And all the time, you were married. And YOU don't like playing games?" I said, sarcastically.

"My wife and I have been talking about getting a divorce. Then I met you, and I wanted to get to know you right away. I'm sorry I didn't wait until it was all proper and legal."

"And I'm sorry, too. But I don't go out with married men. That is when I know they're married. It's finished. Over. Just leave me alone." I opened the door for him to go, and then stood back waiting.

"But April, you know how I feel about you. We could have a good future together," Jerry said, stalling.

I gave him the coldest, hardest look I could muster. He had no choice but to give up and leave. He looked dejected, and I felt sorry for him. For a second I almost said, "It's okay, we could still be friends, at least." I didn't. I closed the door on my almost first lover.

For the next few months, I didn't go out on dates. I just stayed in and moped. When Cheryl brought home another of her strays for supper, I didn't even mind. That's what I called the Métis and Indian girls she befriended from the Friendship Centre. Nancy was a dark-skinned native girl with long, limp black hair. The story of her family life was similar to that of other native girls Cheryl met. Drinking always seemed to be behind it. Nancy had been raped by her drunken father. Cheryl remarked that people called that incest, but Nancy insisted it was rape. Everyone in Nancy's family drank, even the younger kids. Or the new rage was sniffing glue. Both Nancy and her mother had prostituted themselves. Sometimes for money, sometimes for a cheap bottle of wine. Nancy was like a wilted flower. She even had a defeatist look to her. What a life to have led. I supposed she had stayed at home because there was nowhere else to go. I was shocked when Cheryl told me Nancy was only seventeen. She looked at least twenty-five.

How Cheryl could stand to hear those kinds of stories all the time was beyond me. That she wanted to make a lifetime career out of it was impossible for me to understand. It was depressing, especially when I knew that Nancy and the other strays came from the same places that we came from.

I'd go out with Cheryl and Nancy to nice restaurants and treat them to suppers. I began to notice what being native was like in middle-class surroundings. Sometimes, service was deliberately slow. Sometimes, I'd overhear comments like, "Who let the Indians off the reservation?" Or we'd be walking home, and guys would make comments to us, as if we were easy pickups. None of us would say anything, not even Cheryl, who had always been sharp-tongued. Cheryl and I never talked about these things, either. Instead of feeling angry at these mouthy people, I just felt embarrassed to be seen with natives, Cheryl included. I gradually began to go out with them less and less. Anyhow, Cheryl was starting to spend more evenings at the Friendship Centre, leaving me alone with my magazines and my daydreams. I was even reading books on proper etiquette, preparing myself for my promising future in white society. If Cheryl had known I was reading that kind of material, she would have laughed or criticized me. It wouldn't have mattered, because I began to think I would be dreaming such dreams right into my senility. Oh, well, Cheryl once had a fantasy which comforted her, and now I had mine.

The other thing I thought about a great deal was the kind of man I would marry. If my future were to be successful and happy, I'd have to give the man in my life much consideration. I would not be able to afford to let my heart rule my head. I couldn't marry for money or I'd be rich but I wouldn't be happy. So I'd have to find someone who was handsome, witty, and charming. He'd be a good, honest person with a strong character, but he'd also have a fine sense of humour. He'd be perfection personified. "Oh, yeah? Dream on, April Raintree. If such a man existed, he'd be surrounded by females. What makes you think you could ever compete?" With all my planning and everything, I'd probably end up falling in love with a poor farmer or something. And I'd have to work for the rest of my life.

But that spring, my Prince Charming did come into my life. I was typing a mortgage agreement when he walked into the office. He was to see Mr. Lord, and the receptionist sent him to my desk. I let him stand there, without even looking at him, while I finished typing. Then I looked up into his merry, blue eyes. He was one of the smoothly handsome men, the kind I didn't like, the kind that was so polished he just had to be conceited.

He smiled at me as he asked to see Mr. Lord. I told him Mr. Lord had a dentist's appointment that morning and had been delayed. I asked him to return at one o'clock.

"Well, I suppose I could be induced to return by your having lunch with me."

I thought of saying, "I'm sorry, I'm busy," because it was obvious he was the conceited type I had thought he was. Instead, I asked, "How do you know I'm not married?"

"I looked for a wedding ring. There's none." He spread his fingers before me to show that he was not wearing a ring, either.

I looked closely at his finger and saw that there were no tell-tale marks. At the same time, I figured he couldn't be so conceited, after all, since he didn't wear any flashy rings. I realized some of the other secretaries had stopped to watch. I smiled self-consciously and said, "Well, I don't take lunch until twelve."

"I'll wait."

For the next half hour, I felt him watching me from where he sat. My fingers felt too stiff to do any typing at all, but I made a show of being efficient by finishing page after page, all filled with mistakes.

Over lunch, he introduced himself as Bob Radcliff from Toronto. He had his own wholesale furniture business which he ran with his mother. His father had died when he was in university, and he and his mother had taken over the business. He was in Winnipeg to purchase land for expansion. Since I knew his home was in Toronto, I had no intention of becoming further involved with him. Just this lunch and that would be it. But then on our way back, he asked me out again

108

that evening. Okay, so he must be lonely. But after this one night, that would be it.

It wasn't. For the next month we spent nearly every evening together. He met Cheryl and had shown no negative reaction. They got along quite well, considering Cheryl had resumed her anti-white role. I found Bob was gentle, good-natured, and very considerate. He was everything I thought a good husband should be. It was just too bad he had to go back to Toronto.

The events of the next several weeks are a blur in my memory. Bob proposed. He asked me, April Raintree, to be his wife. He wanted to get married in a small civil ceremony in Winnipeg. My dreams were coming true, and I ecstatically floated on cloud nine. Everything happened so quickly.

The only discord came when I told Cheryl that Bob had proposed to me. I expected her to be as excited and happy as I was.

"What do you want to go and marry this dude for? You're asking for trouble. You don't know anything about him, really."

"I know all I need to know. You're just saying this because of Garth, aren't you?"

"Maybe I am. Even if Bob isn't prejudiced, maybe his friends are. And what will they think when they find out he has married a half-breed? If he had to choose, do you really believe he'd stick with you?"

"Cheryl," I said in a warning, angry tone.

"Or what if you had children and they looked like Indians? Do you want them to go through what we went through? It would be better for you to stick to your own kind. I've always felt so out of place, living with white families, surrounded by whites. You really want that for your children? Oh, of course, you're going to pass yourself off as white, aren't you? You're not going to tell anyone there who and what you are, are you?"

"Well, I'm certainly not going to go around saying, 'Hi, I'm April Radcliff, and I'm a half-breed.' So just knock it off, Cheryl."

I stormed into the bathroom, cutting our discussion short. I was angry. Not so much by Cheryl's telling me I shouldn't marry Bob, but by her throwing shame and guilt, or whatever it was, into my face. We'd never talked about it before. I was sure she had not suspected how I felt. But all this time, she knew. She knew I was ashamed of being a half-breed.

We were married on July 25, 1969, on a Friday afternoon with only Cheryl and a "not anyone special" male friend of Bob's to witness our exchange of vows. I wondered why he hadn't even wanted to invite his mother, but he had just said that was the way he wanted it. I accepted it, I was so happy. From that moment, I wouldn't have to worry about changing the spelling of my name because it was now legally April Radcliff.

Cheryl came with us to the airport on the Saturday afternoon when we were to fly to Toronto. I guess Bob knew I wanted some time alone with her because he left to do some last minute things. At first, Cheryl and I let some of our precious minutes slip by, just looking at each other and not saying anything.

Cheryl spoke first. "April, in spite of what I said the other day, I do hope you'll be happy. I really do. I was just mouthing off, you know. I'm sorry."

"Don't be, Cheryl. I guess I got on the defensive because some of the things you said were true. And I've never wanted to admit them. You didn't come right out and say it, but I am ashamed. I can't accept... I can't accept being a Métis. That's the hardest thing I've ever said to you, Cheryl. And I'm glad you don't feel the same way I do. I'm so proud of what you're trying to do. But to me, being Métis means I'm one of the have-nots. And I want so much. I'm selfish. I know it, but that's the way I am. I want what white society can give me. Oh, Cheryl, I really believe that's the only way for me to find happiness. I'm different from you. I wish I wasn't but I am. I'm me. You have to do what you believe is right for you, and I have to go my way. Remember, though, I'll always be there if you need me."

Cheryl was smiling, but sadly. Finally she said, "April, I have known how you felt for a long time. And I decided that I was going to do what I could to turn the native image around so that one day you could be proud of being Métis." To lighten the mood, she added, "Of course, you may be old and gray when the day does come, but it will come. I guarantee it."

Bob came back, and it was time for us to board the plane. And for me to say my goodbye to Cheryl. We hugged each other and said goodbye. I felt good, I felt there was a new kind of honesty between us. I was moving into a new phase of my life with a man I loved and who loved me. And I had just had a good honest talk with the other most important person in my life.

But once we were airborne, I was still thinking of Cheryl. I missed her so much already. For a younger sister, she was a lot wiser than me in some ways. So, she had known about my shame for a long time. And she had never said anything. She had just accepted me the way I was, in silence. I wished I could do that whole part of my life over again. She was such a giving, unselfish person. What was it that made her like she was and me like I was?

Chapter Nine

I was totally unprepared when we arrived at Bob's home, and now mine. When he had spoken of his business, I assumed it was a small-time operation. There had been the land deal in Winnipeg. I had worked on that, but I had assumed there would be a large mortgage on it. But from the moment I saw their house, excuse me, mansion, I knew I had badly underestimated the wealth I had married into. The house was huge and was located on a sprawling estate.

I felt Barbara Radcliff's disapproval of me from the very start. I couldn't blame her, though. She had missed out on her son's wedding, and that's when I realized why she hadn't been invited. He had, in effect, eloped. She was, however, very polite to me and extended a gracious welcome to their home. Somehow, I had the feeling I had landed in another foster home. I was even subtly ordered to call her "Mother Radcliff," although at times I thought of her as "Mother Superior," and religion had nothing to do with it.

We entertained a great deal, and in turn, we were invited to social events and theatres and concerts and dinners and clubs. Because it was all new to me, it was quite thrilling. I had plenty of moments of being nervous and tongue-tied, committing social gaucheries, and I was forever wondering what the other women thought of me. In all fairness to Mother Radcliff, I must say she taught me all I hadn't learned from my long-ago books. She took me on shopping excursions and on twice-a-week appointments to hair salons, always giving me advice in a detached way. Although we spent a good deal of time in each other's company, we never did become close, never joking and laughing together. Her laughter seemed reserved only for those on her social level. I used to wonder what Bob's father had been like. He must have been a good-humoured man because Bob was so easygoing.

As for Bob, we got along very well. We had none of the problems which face most newlyweds. No hassles over finances or work or even in-laws. I suppose because of my childhood, it was easy enough for me to play second fiddle to a woman like Mother Radcliff, even to the point of allowing her to run our lives.

By November, it occurred to me that it would be nice if Cheryl could see how right I had been in my decision to marry Bob. I checked with Bob to see if it would be okay for her to come for the Christmas holidays. He thought it would be a great idea, and urged me to phone her. I did and was surprised that she accepted, just like that. I found out on the phone that Nancy had moved in with her. I thought once again that Cheryl didn't belong with a bunch of native people. Then the other thought struck me. Not once had nativeness been discussed in this household.

Mother Radcliff had resented me simply because Bob had married me without her approval. What would she think once Cheryl came? And Christmas times were for gatherings. What would all the others think?

I should have thought twice about inviting Cheryl to visit. I wanted to show off to her so much that I had forgotten that, in turn, I would have to show her off to these people. I looked over at Bob, who was smiling at me. Well, if it didn't matter to him, why should it matter to me? Still, I felt that perhaps Cheryl's predictions would come true. If Bob were ever forced to make a choice, what would it be? In his mother's hands he was like putty. I was beginning to realize that my Prince Charming had a flaw.

Cheryl came on the Saturday before Christmas. Bob and I went to pick her up at the airport, and when we arrived home, I was dismayed to find that Mother Radcliff had some of her friends over for dinner. I watched her face for a reaction when Cheryl was introduced, but there wasn't any. It was the same as when I had been introduced five months earlier, gracious but cool. I showed Cheryl around the "mansion" after dinner, and although she was complimentary, I could tell she wasn't all that impressed. I was piqued. She was so religiously Metis!

Every minute we were alone, she would talk about the Friendship Centre and the program she and some other counsellors had started for teenaged native girls. She loved what she was doing, though, and that was great. It was when she criticized my lifestyle that I got on the offensive.

"What you aim to do is very commendable, Cheryl, but I can't see you changing a whole lot of people. You may turn a few lives around, but they're not the ones who are going to make an impression on the rest of the population. It's the ones who are dirty and unkempt and look like they've just gotten out of bed with a hangover and who go to your neighbourhood department store, they're the ones who make a lasting impression."

"Well, there are just as many white people out there who are in the same state," Cheryl shot back.

"It's not the same. I don't remember the white ones, I only remember the drunk natives. It seems to me that the majority of natives are gutter-creatures, and only a minority of whites are like that. I think that's the difference."

"I still think our project with the native girls is worthwhile. Damn it, April, why do you have to be so prejudiced?" she exclaimed.

"I'm not prejudiced, Cheryl. I'm simply trying to point out to you how I see things."

"Through white man's eyes."

"Maybe so, but that should be an advantage to you. How many white people would honestly tell you what they think? I don't want to discourage you completely. Helping some of the teenage girls avoid the native girl syndrome thing is certainly worth the effort. Remember Mrs. Semple telling us about that? First, you do this and then you do that, and next you do this and next you do that, and she had our whole lives laid out for us. Well, we fooled her. But the thing is, you'll never change the image of the native people. It would take some kind of miracle," I said, attempting to lighten our conversation.

That's how our private talks went, and I was grateful that
Cheryl kept the native subject private. As I expected, we had
a full social calendar over the Christmas holidays, and I tried
to coax Cheryl, unsuccessfully, to go shopping with me for
evening gowns I was sure she would need. She could not see
the sense in spending money on clothing she would never
wear again. So, I insisted she wear some of my dresses, since
we were the same size. As a matter of fact, we could have been
almost identical twins, except for our skin-colouring. No
wonder I had always found her so beautiful. My pretentious
way of admitting my own beauty.

I had taken it for granted that Cheryl would be able to
attend the dinners to which we had been invited, but
Mother Radcliff took me aside, actually she summoned me
to her study, and informed me that it would cause upsets to
have an uninvited guest. She also stated that Cheryl would
feel out of place, and although I agreed and understood, it
was unthinkable that I would leave Cheryl alone. Mother
Radcliff pointed out that we were giving a New Year's party
so Cheryl would not be left out of all the festivities. I left her
study wondering how much of this I was going to tell
Cheryl. At the same time, I was relieved that Cheryl's debut
into my society was to be delayed. When I made my
explanations to Cheryl, she made it easier by saying it was
all right because she hadn't really wanted to go to the big
fancy gatherings anyhow, and she was relieved to be able to
avoid them.

On New Year's Eve, all the important people I had met
over the past months, and many I had never met, gathered in
our living room and the adjoining family room. To me, it was
the biggest sign of how wealthy and important we Radcliffs
were. I guess I was the only one who was so greatly
impressed, because when I took Cheryl around to introduce
her to some of the women I already knew, I got a few
surprises. It was worse than I had expected. After praising all
these people to Cheryl, some came out with the most
patronizing remarks.

"Oh, I've read about Indians. Beautiful people they are. But you're not exactly Indians are you? What is the proper word for people like you?" one asked.

"Women," Cheryl replied instantly.

"No, no, I mean nationality?"

"Oh, I'm sorry. We're Canadians," Cheryl smiled sweetly.

Another woman, after being introduced to Cheryl, said, "Oh, we used to have a very good Indian maid. Such a nice quiet girl and a hard worker, too."

I suppose she meant it as a compliment, but I felt like crawling into a hole, I was so embarrassed for Cheryl.

Then two men came over, and one asked Cheryl what it was like being an Indian. Before she could reply, the other man voiced his opinion, and the two soon walked away, discussing their concepts of native life, without having allowed Cheryl to say one thing.

Cheryl and I shrugged to each other, and I was wondering how she was taking it. It was the questioning stares that bothered me the most.

About an hour later, my discomforting thoughts of what people must be thinking were interrupted when I noticed the entrance of an actress we had seen recently at a theatre production. As I watched Mother Radcliff greeting her, I remembered her name. Heather Langdon. She seemed to know Mother Radcliff quite well. I saw Heather look around the room in anticipation, and I noticed the satisfied look on her face when Bob appeared and kissed her on the cheek. They looked like they knew each other even better. And I felt this twinge of jealousy and worry. Mother Radcliff spotted me just then, and indicated I was to come over.

When I reached them, Mother Radcliff said, "April, I would like you to meet Heather Langdon. We saw her play the other night, remember?"

"Yes, I do. I enjoyed your performance," I said as I shook her hand. What was the right thing to say to an actress?

"April, go find your sister. I am sure she would like to be introduced to Heather." I was ordered. I obeyed.

Strange, I thought, that Mother Radcliff would want Cheryl to be introduced to an actress. I found Cheryl and brought her back to be introduced and noticed the exchange of looks between Mother Radcliff and Heather. I couldn't read any meaning into the looks and shrugged it off. Heather seemed to make a point of socializing with me for the rest of that evening, and my initial worry and jealousy disappeared.

On Friday, Bob went to his office, so Cheryl and I had the whole day to ourselves. It was supposed to be a pleasant day, but Cheryl had to get her two cents worth in on what she thought about my lifestyle. I think the only thing that really aroused me in those days was when someone criticized me. So I tore right back into Cheryl, openly angry.

"Cheryl, get off my case, will you? I don't ask you to live my kind of life. I know why you're doing this. You want me to take up your glorious cause. Well, I'm happy here. I love the parties, and I love the kind of people I meet. I love this kind of life, and I have no intention of changing it. So, go home. And live by what you believe in. But stop preaching at me. I admire your devotion and your confidence in native people, but to me, they're a lost cause. I can't see what anyone can do for them, except the people themselves. If they want to live in their rundown shacks that are overridden with flies, and who knows what other kinds of bugs, and that stink of filth, and soiled clothing and mattresses, and if they want to drink their lives away while their children go hungry and unclothed, then there's not much that can be done for them, except to give them handouts and more handouts. So don't ask me... "

"How the hell would you know how they live? You wouldn't go near them if your life depended on it. Who are you to sit around up here in your fancy surroundings and judge a people you don't even know?" Cheryl cut in, even angrier than I was.

"I know because I looked for our parents in those kinds of places. So, don't tell me that I don't know what I'm talking about. I went... " I stopped abruptly as I realized I had just let out my secret search.

Cheryl and I looked at each other for a few silent seconds and our tempers were forgotten. Then she said in a quiet, accusing voice, "You went to look for Mom and Dad? How come you never told me, April?"

I sighed and wondered which way to go. "There was nothing to tell. I never found them. I came to a dead end. And later, when I thought it over, I figured it was probably just as well. Finding them would most likely have opened old wounds for them and for us."

"What do you mean? It wasn't their fault. The Children's Aid had to take us because they were sick. You told me that. You told me Dad had tuberculosis, and Mom just had poor health all the time. Anyhow, you should have told me. How did you know where to start? I thought of looking for them. That's one reason why I spend so much time down at the Friendship Centre and listen for names."

"Cheryl, I still think it's best to leave it alone. Just pretend that we never had parents. Leave all that behind us." I thought that now was the time I should tell Cheryl what I already knew about our parents. They were liars, weaklings, and drunkards. That all the time we were growing up, there was a more important reason for them to live, and that was their booze. But no. I couldn't do that to Cheryl. I couldn't tell her that alcohol was more important to our parents than their own daughters. I had given her cherished memories of them. I couldn't take that away now. They were too important for her. Those memories and her too idealistic outlook for the future of native people. Those things helped her and gave her something to live for. I added, "Pretend that we're orphans."

"No! They're our parents, April! And we're not orphans," Cheryl's eyes blazed. "I want to see them again. Please, April. I have the right to make that decision for myself. You have to tell me where to begin. How do I find them? You have to tell me, April."

I silently argued with myself. The information I had was dated. Even the notations I had added were now dated.

118

Chances of Cheryl finding our parents were so slim that I felt
she wouldn't find them. And because I felt that way, I
relented.

"Okay, I guess you're right. Mr. Wendell is the one who gave
me the old addresses and names. I guess they were places
where our parents used to stay. A lot of the places have been
torn down, and I've marked that down so you won't have to go
there. But Cheryl, when I went to those places and saw the
living conditions, well, I would hold my breath so I wouldn't
smell the stink or breathe in the germs. I'd try not to touch
anything, everything was so dirty. And if they offered me
anything to eat or drink, I'd refuse because I was sure their
cupboards were infested with bugs. I'd back away from people
so I wouldn't get their lice. I didn't feel sorry for them Cheryl.
All I felt was contempt. They are a disgusting people. And
maybe, just maybe, our parents are part of that. And if that's
where we came from, I sure don't want to go back. That's why
I'm happy with my life here. Happiness to those people was a
bottle of beer in their hands. I vowed to myself then that no way
was I ever going to end up like them or live in places like theirs.
So, Cheryl, if you want to criticize me for my lifestyle, then go
ahead, because if I can help it, I'm not ever going to change it."

"Oh, April, I didn't know why you felt the way you did. I
didn't mean to criticize you. I just wanted to rouse you out of
your passive state. I just wanted you to be aware of who we
are, what we are, and what's been happening to us."

"If you're referring to all the negative aspects of native
life, I think it's because they allow it to happen to them. Life
is what you make it. We made our lives good. It wasn't
always easy, but we did make it. And they are responsible
for their lives."

"I don't agree with you. We had a lot of luck in our lives.
We've had opportunities which other native people never had.
Just knowing what being independent is like is an
opportunity. But that's not the point right now. I still want to
look for our parents, okay?"

"I doubt that you'll find them after all this time, but okay,"
I sighed and went over to one of my dressers. As I looked

through the dresser drawers, I said, "They usually move from town to town from what I understand. I think it's going to be   120
a waste of your time."

"Well, I've got to give it a try. Need some help looking? What do you need all these clothes for? I bet you don't wear half of them."

"You're criticizing again. Here we are. My shoe box. Now this is classy, isn't it?" I held up an old shoe box where I had hidden my past away.

Cheryl looked through the papers and asked, "How come you kept all this stuff if you weren't planning to ever look for them again?"

"I don't know. Some deep, profound motive, I guess. Maybe my last link with my parents. Who knows?"

We copied the names and addresses down, and Cheryl said, confidently, "When I find them, I'll let you know. Wouldn't it be great to have a family reunion?"

I smiled. Nothing could be worse.

This time, when Cheryl and I parted at the airport, I knew it was more realistic to acknowledge there would never be complete honesty between us. And then again, as long as my mouth kept running over, I just might reveal everything I had tried to protect her from. But knowing Cheryl had not hidden any aspects of her life from me made me feel inferior to her, in that way. She was so fearless. Me, I was a coward, and I knew it. Cheryl never worried about what other people thought about her. Only what she thought about them mattered. Cheryl was that stalk in the field of grain which never bent to the mighty winds of authority. At the same time, that stalk could bend to the gentle breezes of compassion. That was Cheryl.   121

Chapter Ten

I watched her plane taxi down the runway and gather speed, until its wheels no longer touched the ground. I watched until I could see it no more. Suddenly, I felt so empty. So alone.

Funny I should have felt that way when Bob was right there beside me. On the drive back home, he was as preoccupied with his thoughts as I was with mine, so we didn't say much. Sunday dinner that evening was eaten in silence, and not even Bob and his mother made any conversation. The atmosphere reinforced my feeling of loneliness. As usual, Bob and his mother retired to his office to plan the coming week's business strategy. I went upstairs to our room. I was restless and didn't know why. I turned the television set on, but there were no programs that interested me. I left it on just for the voices. I looked at a book, then another. That was no good either. It wasn't the first time I had felt this way, but it was the worst. This bored restlessness which usually came after big parties or large gatherings. Maybe if I had something of my own to do, something which involved... what? Useless. That's what I was. Bob had his business. Mother Radcliff had her social calendar, plus the business. Cheryl had her great cause. I had nothing. I had everything I ever wanted, yet I had nothing.

Mother Radcliff and, therefore, I were on different charitable organizations, but none of them grabbed my heart or loyalty. Bob and I had our group of friends, but I felt I had access to them only as long as Bob was with me. But I did find our own age group much more interesting than the older ladies with whom Mother Radcliff surrounded herself. Especially after Heather Langdon joined us. I wanted to fashion myself after her so much because she so enjoyed living. She lived by her own approval, not that of others. Just like Cheryl.

Cheryl and I wrote monthly letters to each other, but the chasm between us had grown wider, and there was less to say in our letters. The only thing she told me that was of great interest was her ongoing search for our parents. Where I had spent about a month of weekends and quit, Cheryl wouldn't quit. I worried. Then in May, I got a letter in which she indicated she had finally given up. I was relieved. I didn't know what she would have done if she had found our parents. I hadn't even wanted to think about that possibility. Now that she had ended her search, I no longer worried about how shocked and disillusioned she would have been. My conclusion about alcoholism was that once an alcoholic, always an alcoholic. And if one's own children weren't enough reason for one to recover, then there could be no reason at all.

Her letters started to arrive less and less often. She wrote about her education and her work at the Friendship Centre. I found myself again in the position of envying her. She had a reason for being. She was her own person. I merely existed. Comfortable and surrounded by socially prominent people. But I felt that I really didn't belong. That feeling grew worse as the months went by. I didn't belong because I didn't care. Not the way the others did. I was quite content to let Mother Radcliff and Bob run my social life. I performed all my duties as expected.

That September, I picked out a very expensive IBM Selectric typewriter for Cheryl's birthday. That was something she could appreciate. I even thought it might be nice to go back to Winnipeg to spend some time with Cheryl. I tried phoning but found that the service had been disconnected. I wrote Cheryl immediately, offering financial aid if she needed it. She wrote back that she was hardly ever home and didn't need a phone. As if to emphasize her point, she also told me that she had been invited to Brandon over the Christmas holidays. I felt as if she were abandoning me, because I read between the lines that she didn't want me in Winnipeg.

Christmas passed, New Year's 1971 came, and I still couldn't shake my feeling blue. Actually, I don't know why they say "blue" when it's more like gray. The year of 1971 was to be a year of many changes for me. My feelings of inadequacy and boredom turned to resentment and jealousy. I came to hate how Heather and Bob could laugh so easily and suspicions set in and I began nagging Bob in private. Meaningful conversation between us had all but disappeared. I guess all he could see was my totally negative side, and he couldn't see any reason for it. I couldn't have explained it to him at the time anyway, since I didn't quite know what was going on inside of me. Mother Radcliff even showed an open disgust for me, because on different occasions, I had rebelled and refused to perform my social duties. But that was okay, because I was just as disgusted with her and her snobbish friends and her card games and her charitable works, done only so she would be identified as a philanthropist. All these people lived for one of two things: money or power. They were hypocrites, all of them. Charming to each other when they were face to face, but get them into separate rooms and their tongues could cut like knives. They were such superficial people.

I became quite good at it, seeing all the negative sides and criticizing them to high heaven to myself. It came to me that I had criticized the native people, and here I was doing the same thing to white people. Maybe that's what being a half-breed was all about, being a critic-at-large.

I suppose things could have continued like that for a long time, but in August, I overheard a conversation between Mother Radcliff and Heather that roused me out of my passive state and got me fighting mad. Our bedroom had a closed-in balcony which overlooked a private garden. A few days earlier, Bob and I had had a big fight. To make up for it, Bob had decided to take the day off work and take me out for the day. We had planned to start out right after breakfast. I was amused at Mother Radcliff's obvious chagrin. But then

Bob and I had another difference of opinion in our bedroom that morning, and he left in his car without me. I was so embarrassed that I hid myself in my room and planned to stay there until Bob got back.

It was about noon when I heard a car drive up. I looked out and saw Heather walking up to the front door. I wondered what on earth she was doing there. I knew she and Mother Radcliff didn't have that close a friendship that they would have lunch together. I went back to the balcony to return to my book, wondering all the time what was going on downstairs. I didn't have long to wait. They came out into the garden below, presumably to have their lunch there. Their voices drifted up to me, and I could hear everything they were saying clearly.

Mother Radcliff was saying, "I'd like to get straight to the point. Is this affair you're having with Bob serious, or are you just toying around with him?"

An affair? With Bob? Serious? I couldn't believe I was hearing right. Not Heather. She was my friend. Bob was my husband.

"Of course it's serious. You knew how we felt about each other when you broke us up. And don't deny it. I'm not as naive as I used to be. No, it won't be long before Bob asks April for a divorce."

"Well, it doesn't appear it will be all that soon when he starts taking time off work to spend with her," Mother Radcliff responded.

I heard Heather scoff at that and say, "Well, he's taken a lot more time off for me, I'm sure. But I can't help wondering how come, now that he's married, you approve of Bob and me? I know you purposely went out of your way to have me at your New Year's party. What do you have against April? She makes a nice, obedient wife. Why don't you want her for a daughter-in-law?"

"Didn't you notice her sister? They're Indians, Heather. Well, not Indians but half-breeds, which is almost the same thing. And they're not half-sisters. They have the same father and the same mother. That's the trouble with mixed races,

125

you never know how they're going to turn out. And I would simply dread being grandmother to a bunch of little half-breeds! The only reason I can think of why Bob married her after knowing what she was, was simply to get back at me. Well, I had my doubts as to how serious he was with you because of days like today."

Heather shrugged it off. "Don't worry. Bob's a husband with a guilty conscience. He'll realize the best thing for April is a divorce."

"Yes, I suppose you're right. Of course, we'll give her a nice large settlement."

"You are so bloody right," I almost shouted. Perhaps they said more about me, I don't know. With my face burning hotly and my heart thumping like a war drum, I headed downstairs to confront them. They were both surprised and off-balance when I stepped out on the terrace to face them.

I had always treated Heather with a certain amount of awe and respect, and I had also given Mother Radcliff her due respect. But in that moment, I eyed them contemptuously and they realized their secrets were out.

"What are you doing here?" Mother Radcliff asked.

I was still breathing hard. Ignoring her question, I said, "You two make me sick!"

I looked at Heather. "You, you pretended friendship all this time, and I gave you my trust. Oh sure, I suspected. I'm not blind. But I really thought it was only my imagination. Maybe I hoped it was my imagination. That Bob's mother would rather have a person like you, a hypocrite, an adulteress, as her daughter-in-law, rather than risk a few grandchildren who would have Indian blood in them, well, that's beyond my comprehension."

Mother Radcliff started to cut in, but I turned on her and cut her off. "And you! You make everyone that comes within your reach into puppets. But thank you very much for cutting my strings. And thank God I didn't become pregnant by your son. I wouldn't want the seed of your blood passed on to my children." With that, I turned my back on them in a deliberate gesture and walked out.

A little while later, when I was up in my room, I heard
Heather's car start up, and she drove away. My heavy
breathing returned to normal. My trembling rage subsided. I
had to figure out what to do. Only one thing was certain. They
were going to give me a large settlement. A very large
settlement!

Well, so I had seen through them, yet didn't even know it.
All my criticisms were justified. My big fight with Bob had
been about Heather. Turned out, he was a liar, too. Just like
my parents had been. Married me only to get back at his
mother. Heather, deceiving me with friendship, while all the
time she only wanted Bob. Mother Radcliff, making me call   127
her "mother" when she so detested what I was. And then there
was Cheryl. She had told me how it would be, but I hadn't
believed her. And although I had the same thoughts as
Barbara Radcliff about children, it was unforgivable for her to
tell them to my rival. I did have a fear of producing brown-
skinned babies. How could I give my loving to such children
when I still felt self-conscious about Cheryl? Well, this wasn't
the real issue. I had to plan a course of action. First thing I'd
have to do would be to see a lawyer.

I called Ronald Feldman, who I knew was a divorce
lawyer from the conversations at parties. I phoned him, and
he said he couldn't see me for two weeks, but he suggested
that if I were serious about getting a divorce on the grounds
of adultery that I should cease living with Bob. I thought that
meant I had to move out immediately.

Next, I phoned Bob at work. I wasn't surprised to find him
there, nor that he sounded cold and distant with me. I
demanded that he come home at once as an urgent matter
had come up. While I waited for him, I looked through the
newspapers and phoned to inquire about different
apartments for rent. The thought of living in a huge empty
place was depressing. I didn't know anyone who would go out
of their way to come and visit me. What I also needed was a
job to keep me occupied. Still, I knew from past experience
that evenings could be long and lonely. Maybe I would get so
lonely, I'd join the ranks of women who frequented singles

bars. I spotted a column under the heading of "Shared Accommodation." That would be better than living alone. I phoned and was able to make some appointments for the following day. For now, I could stay in a hotel. I looked forward to a new life where I wouldn't be controlled by anyone else. I felt as if the sun were coming out from behind the clouds, and it was a wonderful relief that there was still a sun. "Oh, I know you didn't mean to, 'Mother' Radcliff, but you've made me a happy woman."

128

When Bob finally came home, I must have sparkled with excitement, because he said, "I thought something was wrong, the way you sounded on the phone. But you look like the cat that swallowed a mouse."

"Well, Bob, I understand you're about to ask me for a divorce. I'll save you the trouble of having to ask."

"Oh, not that crap about Heather again. Is that what this is all about?"

"Well, sweetheart, if you like, I could call a meeting of all those involved. 'We are gathered here today to establish whether there is, or there is not, an affair going on between my loving husband, Bob, and my good friend, Heather.' I was planning to be very bitter about it, but I've changed my mind. I'm going to be sarcastic." I smiled as I watched Bob sit down, and the look on his face acknowledged the affair.

"How did you find out? Did Heather tell you?"

"In a manner of speaking, yes. And your mother told me. And in a lot of different ways, you told me, too," I said. "I'd appreciate it if you took me to a hotel for now. I'll look for an apartment or something and then I'll send for my things."

"Don't you even want to make any explanations to Mother before you leave?"

"I'm sure your mother knows I'm leaving. I've packed a few things and I'd like to go. Now."

In less than a week, I had found a place to my liking. It wasn't far from the subway on Woodbine Avenue, so I had easy access to the downtown area where I planned to find a job. The rooms were in a large three-storey house, and the kitchen and dining rooms were shared by all the tenants.

Most of the men and women who lived there were artistic types, and they provided me with long overdue companionship, right from the first day I moved in. Once I was settled, I turned my thoughts to getting myself a job. Money wasn't a problem because Bob had given me more than I'd ever need and that was just for one month. One of the other boarders, Sheila, suggested I do temporary work like she did. I signed up with her agency and was sent to different locations, filling in for absent secretaries. Mr. Feldman, my lawyer, told me in December that the court hearing was to be held on January 26th. He assured me that everything was going extremely well. We were both pleased with the settlement Bob had offered. I remembered the time I was starting at Red River Community College and I had eight hundred dollars in the bank. I had thought then that I was rich. Now, I knew without doubt that I was rich. And independent.

That same day, when the mail came, I found that the letter I had sent to Cheryl in November had been returned. On it was marked, "Moved—no forwarding address." That was funny. Why hadn't she written to me to let me know? Or she could have called. I had given her my new number, my new address, and had told her about my new situation. She should have written or called. After all her thinly-disguised refusals and excuses why she couldn't come, or why I couldn't visit her, I began to feel like my own sister was giving me the cold shoulder. Did she think I was such a failure? On the other hand, I had always said she ought to go her own way and I'd go mine. Maybe that's what was wrong.

Since Cheryl didn't write to me about any Christmas plans, I spent it with those other boarders who also lacked families to go home to. On Christmas Day, we all went to this old folk's home where Sheila's grandmother was living. That's when I got my first understanding of how Cheryl must have felt when she made somebody's day a little brighter.

One Saturday morning, in early January, I received a phone call at eight o'clock. Thinking it was probably the agency looking for last minute secretarial help, I was tempted to let it ring. But I wasn't one who could ignore a ringing telephone. In a second, I was wide awake. It was a nurse calling from the Health Sciences Centre in Winnipeg, asking if I were related to a Cheryl Raintree. Then she said that Cheryl had been brought in during the night. I immediately asked how serious it was, and the nurse said she was still unconscious, so they couldn't be positive. Serious or not, I felt I had to at least be by her side. That afternoon, I was on a flight back to Winnipeg.

Chapter Eleven

As soon as I arrived at the Winnipeg airport, I rented a car and drove straight to the hospital on William Avenue. There, the staff doctors informed me that Cheryl had been found in the early hours of the morning suffering from hypothermia and possible concussion. They were holding her for observation. I thought immediately that she must have been assaulted, and I became resentful when the doctor asked me if Cheryl had a drinking problem.

"Why, because she's part Indian?"

"No, Miss, but when she came in, she was highly intoxicated."

"What about the concussion you mentioned?" I demanded.

"It does appear she may have been beaten," he admitted.

I nodded and stalked off towards Cheryl's room. Drinking problem! I was sure it was said because she was part Indian. I entered the room and Cheryl was at the far end. At first, I wasn't sure it was Cheryl. I mean, I knew it was Cheryl but it didn't look like Cheryl. Her beautiful, strong face was now puffy and bruised, and her cheeks were hollow. She had lost so much weight. Under the fluorescent lights, her skin was yellowish. He arms, resting on the white covers, were thin. She really had lost too much weight. And aged! I stared. It had been two years since I had last seen her. Two years. It hadn't seemed that long. It looked to me as if Cheryl had been possessed. A cold chill ran down my back. "...highly intoxicated." Oh, God, please don't let her be an alcoholic.

I pulled a chair closer to her bed and sat down. Maybe Cheryl had some kind of disease, and she hadn't wanted me to find out about it, and that was why she had refused to come to Toronto, or had put off my coming to Winnipeg. People did that. They would find out they had a terminal illness, and they didn't want to tell anyone until the very end. Knowing Cheryl, that's the kind of thing she would do. She'd try to protect me from that kind of truth. Cheryl stirred and woke up briefly.

"Cheryl, it's me, April. Everything is all right. I love you, Cheryl."

She gave my hand a squeeze and dozed off again. I left when the visiting hours were over and took a room in a hotel on Notre Dame, within easy walking distance of the hospital.

I returned the next day and found Cheryl fully awake. She didn't seem to want to talk about what had happened, so I didn't push her for answers. I sat there for the longest time, in silence. My mind was on what had happened to her and everything else that might have been said was blanked out. It was Cheryl who started talking.

"I'm sorry your marriage didn't work out, April."

"Well, I've been thinking that maybe it's for the best. Bob and I were never passionately in love or anything. And now I've gotten... well, used to the idea." I was almost going to tell her I would be getting a very large settlement, but for some unknown reason, I decided not to.

"Did you get a full-time job yet?" Cheryl asked.

"No, I decided to work for a temporary agency. I'm not at all sure what I want to do once the divorce goes through. I'm changing my name back to Raintree. I was thinking of returning to Winnipeg for good, though."

Actually, the thought had just come to me. It looked like Cheryl could use any support I could give her by staying. If I missed Toronto, I could always go back once Cheryl got a job as a social worker. In June, she'd be finished university. It wouldn't be that long.

"Well, you're almost finished university, huh? And pretty soon, you're going to be a professional. And then I can brag to everyone, 'My sister's a professional'." I smiled but she didn't smile back.

"April, I quit university. I've got a lot more to tell you, but let's not get into it now, okay? I'm tired."

"Sure, okay, we'll talk about it, maybe tomorrow, if you feel like it."

I was shocked by what I had just learned, but I tried to cover it up. I left with a faked understanding smile on my face.

All the way back to the hotel, I thought about Cheryl quitting. Why did she quit? Had she failed or given up? All the letters she had sent me, they were all about her courses and her work at the Friendship Centre. Were they lies? When I got to my hotel room, I took a bath, then got into bed with the television set turned on. But all I could think about was Cheryl. I speculated on different reasons why she may have quit and what other things she had, or hadn't, done so that when she would tell me, I'd be at least partially prepared. As long as she didn't tell me she was dying of some incurable disease, then I could accept anything. I turned the television off and got back into bed. What if she were an alcoholic? How could I accept that? That was an incurable disease. And one was as good as dead if that were the case.

The next day, as Cheryl and I talked, we both avoided the issue. When evening came, I figured it might help if we discussed my marriage failure first.

Afterward, Cheryl said to me, "Well, at least you've experienced what you always longed for, and now you know that's not for you."

"I know. I could treat the marriage as if it were one long holiday, especially since I haven't been hurt by breaking up with Bob. It's funny that I don't feel more pain. I really thought I loved him when I married him."

"Well, everything happened so fast that you never had time to find out for sure. And maybe you convinced yourself that you loved him."

After she said this, Cheryl became thoughtful, and I wondered if she had been similarly involved with a man.

"Cheryl, have you ever been in love?"

She looked at me and smiled. She didn't say anything for a few minutes, and then she sighed and said, "I lived with a man. I thought in the beginning that I loved him. I know that

I wanted him. Before I actually met him, there was this great
physical attraction between us. So, we moved in together. His
name's Mark DeSoto. I was living with him right up until I
landed here. He doesn't even know where I am."

"Do you want him to know where you are? Do you want
me to tell him?" I asked.

"Oh, no, I should have left him a long time ago, but I
didn't. I should have," she seemed to be talking more to
herself. "Are you serious about staying in Winnipeg? You're
not going to come back on account of me, are you?"

135   "Well, I haven't any close ties in Toronto. And this is my
home town. If you wanted to come to Toronto, then I would go
back. But I'm not staying here only because of you. Should I
try what I've just said in a different way?"

Cheryl laughed and said no, she got the general idea.
Since she was in a better mood, I figured it would be as good
a time as any to bring up the past. "About those things you
didn't want to discuss last night, you feel like talking about
them now?"

"I was... I wanted to tell you that I've been living with a
man who wasn't good for me."

"Oh."

"Well, what did you think I was going to tell you? That I
was dying or something?"

"As a matter of fact, yes."

Cheryl started to laugh, and I sat there watching her
closely, trying to determine whether she was being honest
with me. When she realized I wasn't going to join in the
laughing, she asked, "What's wrong?"

"It's the letters you've been sending me for the past two
years. Why didn't you tell the truth?" I asked, as tactfully as
I could.

"Oh, the letters. Sorry about them. I just didn't want you
to worry about me. You seemed happy enough out there."

"But why did you quit university? How come?"

"It wasn't going very well," Cheryl shrugged. "And the
stuff I was doing at the Friendship Centre, well, I believed I
was accomplishing something at first, but then a lot of girls

we were trying to help just kept getting in trouble. In different ways, it all boiled down to one thing: as a social worker I don't think I would have made the grade. So I quit and got a job instead.

"That was two years ago. It's funny, you know, I was right about it not working out for you in Toronto, and you were right when you said the native people have to be willing to help themselves. It's like trying to swim against a strong current. It's impossible."

"I thought if anyone could do it, you could."

"You're disappointed that I've given up?"

"After all the griping I did against it, yeah, I suppose I am. I used to envy you for having something so meaningful in your life. I mean, I couldn't do it because I didn't believe it was possible—making a better way of life for native people, giving them a better image. So what kind of job did you get?"

Cheryl made a face and said, "Oh, it doesn't matter because I lost it. Mark and I used to party a lot, and I started drinking a bit. Anyway, the day I got fired, I had a big row with Mark, and then I went out and got all tanked up. So that's how I ended up here. I feel so stupid."

"Well, anyone who drinks goes overboard once in awhile. I remember I got fuzzy once at a party, and then Bob's mother poured a pot of coffee into me and... I bet she thought I was getting to be an alcoholic. Just because she knew I had Indian blood. When I think of it now, a lot of things make sense in the way Mother Radcliff treated me."

Visiting hours ended then, so I had to say goodnight to Cheryl. On Tuesday morning, the doctor told Cheryl she would most likely be discharged on Wednesday. When she told me, I asked, "What are you planning to do when you get out?"

"You make it sound like I'm in jail or something. I don't know. I don't want to go back with Mark. I don't even want to go back there to get my things."

"Are you scared or something?"

"Oh, no, it's not that. He might want me to stay and then there'd be a scene, maybe."

"I could go and get your things for you. Just tell me the address, and I could go tonight. Then you could come and stay at the hotel for now, until you get a permanent place."

"Are you sure you wouldn't mind? It's in a rather rundown section of the city."

"If Mark is there, will he give me any problems?"

"No, just explain that I'm in the hospital, and you're going to look after me for awhile. He looks tough, but he's okay. When he laid into me, he was drunk, and I pretty well asked for it. Besides, I'm sure he'll be out. Oh, April... " Cheryl's face had a guilty look on it.

"What?"

"You know all the things you left me? Well, I sold them. I'm sorry."

"That's okay, Cheryl. If you needed money, though, you should have asked me. I would have sent you some."

"No, I couldn't do that. You see, I was kind of supporting Mark. He's out of a job. Anyway, it would have just gone to him."

Cheryl was looking down at her hands and nervously twisting her fingers together. "Two suitcases should do it. All I've got is clothing. Our room is right at the top of the stairs to the left. And there's two boxes under the bed with my papers and books in them. You can just take them."

That night, I had supper before looking for the address on Elgin Avenue. I had a lot to digest about Cheryl's past. I had thought mine was full of turmoil and dark secrets. By the time I got to the address, I was thinking of the future. With the money from Bob, I could buy a house in Winnipeg. Maybe we could even rent out some rooms, and that way, we'd have an income every month. On second thought, Cheryl would probably insist on taking native boarders. Besides, people make up creepy stories about two sisters renting out rooms. That wasn't very classy. Heck, with the money I had now, I could buy two houses and rent one out. No, then I'd be responsible for the taxes and repairs, and what if someone couldn't pay their rent? I'd end up letting people stay for free all the time.

I spotted a parking spot not too far from the house. It was too bad I couldn't get a spot right in front of the house. I got out of the car, and a cold gust of wind struck me. I shivered. The temperature seemed to have fallen. I looked around. Cheryl hadn't been kidding when she said it was in a rundown section. It was spooky. And dark. I got to the gate and wondered why on earth they would have a gate that closed when most of the fence was down anyway. At the same time, I was wondering if Mark would be home. And what was he like? I had to take my glove off to fiddle with the latch.

Suddenly, a male voice close to me said, "Can I help you with that, baby?"

I jumped. Where had he come from so suddenly? I looked up at him and he seemed to be leering at me. This couldn't be Mark. Maybe I should get back to the car.

Before I had a chance to move, an arm came from behind and grabbed me by the front of the neck. There were two men! I stepped back into the man as hard as I could, ramming my elbow into his side. He released his grip. The other man was now grinning.

"You bitch. Oh, no, you're not going to get away from us."

He grabbed my arm but I twisted loose and pushed against him. We were on a patch of ice and he slipped, lost his balance, and fell backward, all the while swearing. This all happened in a couple of seconds, and I was able to run back towards my car. I didn't know what their intentions were, but it was my intention not to find out. I opened the car door and was about to jump in when one of them reached for me and got a hold of me. They were yelling to someone to bring the car up. Headlights were turned on and I saw the two men clearly. I struggled desperately to free myself. The other man who had fallen reached our side, and when the car was beside us, he opened the door and shoved me in the back seat and got in beside me. The other one closed the door on my rented car and got in beside the driver.

Like a helpless animal, I was trapped and terrified. They meant to kill. I was sure of it. Otherwise, they would have disguised themselves or something. They whooped it up and

congratulated each other on their "catch." I figured if I was
going to die, I was going to go down fighting. But then I
thought I'd have a better chance if I watched for a police car. I
watched for one at the same time as I kept an eye on the man
beside me. They were crazy men and now they were probably
aroused from chasing me. Crazy men with crazy grins. The one
beside me put his hand on my breast. I hit it away. He hit back
much harder, as if he had a right to do whatever he pleased.

"So, you're a real fighting squaw, huh? That's good 'cause
I like my fucking rough." He laughed at that.

The driver said, "Hey, we're only supposed to give her a
scare. You're talking rape, man."

"Shut up, dummy. And slow down. We don't want to get
stopped now. You're in this as much as us," growled the man
beside me. So he was the leader, I thought.

The other man in the front snickered and turned to eye
me. I wondered how he knew I was part-Indian. Just because
I had long black hair? I didn't pay too much attention to what
the driver had said about just giving me a scare. I figured that
this had started as a lark to scare women, and now the leader
and his accomplice wanted to rape me. Maybe I could count on
the driver to help somehow. And maybe they weren't out to do
any killing. I just didn't know. I hadn't been in Winnipeg long
enough to know whether there had been a rash of rapes and
strangulations going on. Maybe that's what was going to
happen to me. And if they had knives, it would be a whole lot
worse. They could torture me to death, cut me to pieces, or beat
me up and leave me to die in the cold somewhere, all bloody
and broken. "Oh, God, I want to live. This isn't the way I want
to die. This isn't my moment to die." I couldn't help trembling
with fear. Horrible thoughts rushed through my mind.

The night ahead could only be shameful, humiliating, and
even if they didn't physically wound me, it would be torturous.
I braced myself mentally and physically, so I would be able to
face up to anything they did. I knew I wouldn't be able to stop
them from abusing me physically, so I'd try to be like a rag
doll. I'd close my emotions and mind off. Maybe it wouldn't
affect me so much.

The leader was groping at me and he grabbed my breast roughly. I gritted my teeth and sat rigidly, trying hard to ignore his hand, trying hard to show no reaction. I smelled the liquor on his breath as he leaned toward me. Then his hand slid to the crotch of my jeans and I had to pull his hand away. I was pressed against the side of the car. He was saying vulgar things to me, watching my face at the same time. I guess he wanted to reduce me to nothingness.

"Hey, you guys, we're going to have to teach this little Indian some manners. I'm trying to make her feel good and she pulls away. The ungrateful bitch."

As they laughed, the leader grabbed a handful of my hair and pulled my head back. One minute he was laughing, the next he was saying in a low, frightening voice, "Listen, you little cunt, I know you want it, so quit pretending to fight it, okay? Or I'm really going to give it to you."

The man beside the driver was watching and he asked, "Hey, man, could I have a turn with her?"

"Don't worry, you'll get your turn soon enough," the leader said, ominously.

We were out in the countryside somewhere. I didn't know where, because I had lost all sense of direction. They had turned the interior lights on. The leader moved in on me, trying to take off my jacket. I pushed his hands away, and for a few minutes, my anger overcame my fear.

"You filthy, rotten freaks!" I threw myself at the leader, trying to scratch and bite him.

"You keep your filthy, rotten hands off me!" I was panting from a mixture of my anger and exertion.

I could hear them laughing like lunatics. The leader held me away from him with ease but I managed to scratch his face, drawing blood.

"You goddamned cunt!" he yelled in rage. Then he followed that with a hard punch to my midriff. That knocked the wind out of me and sent me flying back against the left side of the car again. My head hit the window. The leader then grabbed the front of my blouse and ripped it open, tearing the buttons off. I tore back into him.

"Why you fucking little savage. You're asking for it."

He gave me a backhand across the side of my head, which made my ears ring. He resumed trying to take my clothes off and I tried my hardest to stop him. That's when he systematically started hammering into me. I could hear the driver making weak protests.

After his merciless onslaught, I was too weak to try to defend myself anymore. I felt him taking off the rest of my clothing and feebly I tried to put my arms across my breasts to cover myself. He shoved them aside.

"All right, you guys, mission accomplished. Hey, dummy, you gonna drive all night? Park this damn thing someplace. Maybe we'll let you join the party," he laughed as he turned his attention back to me.

"Yeah, you little savages like it rough, eh?"

He undid his zipper and pulled down his jeans. Then he forced me to lay the full length of the car seat. When he prepared to come down on me, I shifted myself to the side, blocking him with my leg. Without saying a word, he slammed his fist into my ribs, which I already thought had been broken.

Then he said very softly, "You do that again, you slut, and I'm going to lay you wide open. You understand?"

Defeated, I lay there listlessly, my eyes half-closed because I didn't want to see his face, but at the same time, I didn't trust him to close my eyes completely.

Suddenly, he shoved his penis into me so violently that when I felt the pain of his thrust tear into my body, my eyes opened wide with terror. I struggled again to get away from him. Again, he grabbed my hair and yanked my head to the side. "You want me to lay you open?" He could see the terror in my eyes. I think that was what he enjoyed the most.

"What's the matter, she giving you trouble?" the man in the front seat with the driver asked.

"Shut up! I can handle this little whore."

He thrust into me again as if he were stabbing me with a deadly purpose. It was pure agony. Inside my head, I screamed long and loud, trying to block everything out.

"Hey, she likes this, boys. These squaws really dig this kind of action. They play hard to get and all the time they love it. You love this, don't you, you little cocksucker?"

After what seemed an eternity, he withdrew, only to exchange places with the man beside the driver.

I don't think I could have fought anymore, even if my life had depended on it. Besides, I thought, the worst was over. I allowed myself to be handled like a rag doll. The second rapist made me turn on my stomach, but I was beyond caring. He inflicted a whole new pain but of the same intensity. My moans were muffled into the car seat. Every driving movement of his sent new pain searing through my body. And all the while, he giggled wildly.

When he finally withdrew, he said to the driver, "It's your turn, dummy."

"Naw, I don't think so. I don't feel like it," the driver said, and I knew he was scared. And the others knew it, too.

"You're going to fuck this bitch, dummy, whether you like it or not. You're in this with us, all the way. Now get back there and do it," the leader ordered.

The driver came back, made me turn on my back again, and tried. I don't know if he had no intention of raping me, but he pretended to, and then he told them he was finished.

"You sure?" the leader asked, suspiciously.

143

"Yeah, I'm sure," the driver answered.

I lay there, not daring to move, lest it drive them back into more activity. But now that they had finished, what would they do with me? Would they kill me or let me go?

To my great dismay, the leader came back into the back seat and pulled his pants down again. He made me sit on the floor of the car and then he shoved his penis in front of my face and ordered, "Suck on it, cocksucker. And don't get any funny ideas about biting it or you'll be sorry. You'll be real sorry."

I didn't move so he yanked my head and pulled me closer. "I said suck!"

My whole face was sore, and my lips were cut. He pressed his penis against my mouth. Sluggishly, I turned my head away and opened my mouth a bit to avoid the pressure against my lips. Suddenly, he moved my head back and brought it to him so fast that I almost choked on his penis, which now filled my mouth. I opened my mouth as wide as I could in an attempt to avoid touching his penis. It touched the back of my mouth and I gagged.

"Suck on it, you little bitch!" he threatened again.

Then he turned to his two companions and said, "Boy, do I ever feel like taking a piss right now."

I heard the driver say, "You wouldn't, would you? Not right in her mouth? Well, for christsake, don't get the car dirty."

I heard them saying this, but my sense of reasoning was numbed, and by the time the meaning of it filtered through to me, it was too late. Just at that moment, the leader tightened his grip on me and started peeing. Right into my mouth. I started retching violently, and I struggled but couldn't move my head because of the vise-like grip he had on me. I felt the urine run down my chin, soiling the rest of me as well as him. Thinking I was going to vomit all over him, he let go of me.

The driver was yelling, "You're getting the car all dirty and she's going to fucking puke all over the place. Get her the fuck out of here."

The leader jumped out of the car, and he began putting on what clothing he had taken off. The driver jumped out of the car and reached in the back and dragged me out. Then he grabbed all my clothing and my purse and threw them out after me. I kept retching, although the intense need to vomit had passed.

When the three of them had straightened their clothing, the man from the front seat beside the driver yelled, "Fucking squaw!" I heard the leader laughing as the car doors slammed. I pretended I was still trying to vomit. When the lights came on, I was able to make out the licence number, just before the car sped off.

Chapter Twelve

I was free and I was alive! As I put on my clothes, I kept looking in every direction, fearful they might return. I would run for safety into the fields, even in the deep snow in my bare feet if I had to. Tears ran down my face, but I didn't sob. I was finally dressed and started down the road in the opposite direction from which they had taken, praying I wouldn't run into them again. As I walked I repeated the licence number. Out in the open, with no obstruction to impede it, the winds shrieked with icy glee. But they didn't touch me. It must have been thirty below, but I didn't even feel the cold. I was numb and beyond feeling. I strained for any sounds of an approaching vehicle and often turned to look behind me. I had no idea where I was.

Finally, I saw a light in the distance. I felt fear and hope at the same time. When I neared the light, I saw that it was a farm yardlight. Then I heard a dog barking. As I walked down the driveway, a large German shepherd came out to inspect me. It continued its thunderous barking, all the way to the porch door. A porch light was turned on, and a man looked out cautiously. From the way he looked at me, I'm sure he at first thought I was some drunken squaw who had gotten into a fight and had been thrown out of a car. Begrudgingly, he asked me in, only after I told him I had just been raped and would he please call the police. His wife had come out, and she offered me a cup of coffee. I asked her where the washroom was, while he called the police.

After I washed my mouth out, and came out of the washroom, they asked me what had happened. The chill that hadn't touched me outside caught up with me in the warmth of their kitchen, and I began to tremble so violently that the

woman went and got a blanket off their bed. Tears streamed
down my face and my teeth were chattering, although I still
didn't sob.

When the RCMP came, I expected that they would
insinuate I had somehow provoked the rape. But the two
officers were soft-spoken and kind. They wanted me to show
them where the car had been parked, and on the drive
there, I had the unreasonable fear that they, too, might turn
on me. We soon came to the place where I had walked into
the deeper snow to get my purse. When they finished
examining the tire tracks and the area, they drove me to
the hospital back in Winnipeg. I sat in the back seat, my
teeth still clicking together from a coldness that just
wouldn't leave me.

They took me to the Emergency of the Health Sciences
Centre, where Cheryl had been taken just a few days earlier.
The doctor on duty examined me and took all the samples
that would be required for court purposes if they ever caught
those rapists. As he was preparing to swab my mouth, I told
him I had washed it out. He chided me for doing so, saying
they needed all the evidence. I couldn't believe his words. I
was supposed to go around with the residue of piss in my
mouth for the sake of evidence?! I figured he had enough
evidence. Before he sent me for x-rays, he asked me if I was
related to Cheryl Raintree. When I told him I was, he
informed me that he had been on duty when she came
through. The x-rays showed no fractures or broken bones, so
the police took me to their headquarters to take my
statement. They told me to recount everything, exactly as I
remembered it. The whole thing took a long time, and it was
taxing. While I talked, tears rolled down my face, but again I
didn't do any sobbing. It seemed to me my voice droned on and
on and on, but at last I was finished. They told me they would
be talking to Cheryl in the morning to see if she had any ideas
on possible motives, since I was initially picked up at her door.
As they drove me back to the hotel, they informed me that
they would later have me look at some pictures to see if I could
make any identifications. They also said they would have to

take all my clothing for purposes of evidence. They waited outside in the hall while I changed into a nightgown and robe.

Once they had gone, I took a long bath. My whole body felt sore and I seemed to ache all over. Although I stayed in the bath for a long, long time, thinking about the rapists, I couldn't get rid of their smell. I tried to fathom why they would do such a thing, but I couldn't. It was beyond reason. Later on, in bed, every once in awhile I'd give a shudder when the visions of the night became too clearly realistic. It was a long time before my tensions eased off. I stopped shivering and I finally drifted into sleep.

I was awakened by the sound of someone knocking on my door. It was Cheryl and two officers, although not the same ones as the night before. Apparently, they had picked up Cheryl and brought her to the hotel. Cheryl at first was going to throw her arms around me, but as she saw me brace for the pain, she stopped.

"Oh, April, I'm so sorry. It's all my fault you came here in the first place. I'm sorry."

"It's all right, Cheryl. I'm okay. Really."

I looked at the two officers. One of them said they would like me to go with them to look at a car. They said they'd wait for me in the lobby while I got ready.

After they left, Cheryl again said, "This is all my fault."

I was dead tired and I snapped, "Oh, Cheryl, stop it, it's not your fault. It just happened." I felt awful for using such a tone of voice, so I added in a lighter tone, "Come, help me get dressed. I can barely move."

She did so in silence.

Before I left, I asked her to wait for me, and we would go together to get her things and the rented car. As we were on our way to the Public Safety Building, the RCMP officer told me they had seized the car and arrested the owner. I would have to identify both the car and its owner. Some of my buttons had been found in the car, so my identification was merely routine. But a little while later, I identified the owner as one of the rapists from a lineup. He looked very scared, almost like a little boy. Even though he had taken

part in the heinous crime against me, I couldn't help feeling
sorry for him. All I really wanted to do was hate him. I
remembered that he, Stephen Gurnan, had done nothing to
try to stop what had happened. My feeling of sympathy
disappeared.

When I returned to the hotel, Cheryl was waiting for me.

"April, you look exhausted. Maybe you should try and get
some sleep and I'll go and get the car and that. Do you want
something to eat?"

"Yes, I'm starved. And I need some coffee. Are you sure you
want to go back alone?"

"Oh, sure. After this, I don't care if Mark does make
a scene."

After we had eaten, and she made sure I was comfortable,
Cheryl left. I got out of bed and ran some water into the tub.
I got in and then ran the rest of the water as hot as I could
stand it. I lathered myself with lots of soap. I had to get rid of
that awful smell on me. I could smell it as if they were in the
same room as me. Their dirty, stinking bodies. I could feel
their hands all over me. I had to get rid of that feeling, too. I
scrubbed wherever I wasn't sore or bruised, sometimes hitting
a sore area that brought back new pain. But no matter how
much I scrubbed and lathered, I still felt dirty and used. It
was no use. I cried, my tears rolling down my cheeks into the
water, because it was no use. I couldn't get myself clean. I
would never be clean again, free from the awful smells, free
from the filthy feelings, free from the awful visions.

In bed, I realized just how much I had learned to hate. It
wasn't a natural emotion. I had known deep resentments, but
if I had been given choices, I would rather have been friends
with people like the DeRosiers, Mother Radcliff, and Heather.
But a real, cold, deep hatred had crept into me, and I knew
that I wouldn't want to let go of it, not for the rest of my life.
I wanted those two men, in particular, dead. By my hand. Yes,
I wished with all my might that I could be the one to kill them
and make their deaths prolonged and painful. I knew what I'd
do. I'd castrate them. Then I'd watch them bleed to death, in
agony. Oh, I wanted them dead! I had been touched by evil,

and from now on, it would always be a part of me. Wanting three men dead was evil in itself, but, nonetheless, I wanted them dead.

Finally, I fell asleep. When I woke up, I saw the suitcases and the keys to the car, but Cheryl wasn't there. She must have gone to get something to eat. I got dressed and went to the restaurant. She wasn't there, but I had something to eat, anyway. It was almost eleven p.m. When I got back to my room, Cheryl still wasn't there. Maybe she had gone for a drink. I looked in the mirror and hoped that most of the bruises would disappear within the week.

Cheryl came back about fifteen minutes later. 150

"You're awake. How long have you been up?"

"Almost an hour. How did it go?" I asked, purposely not asking where she had just been.

"Mark wasn't even there. He moved out, I guess. I was just down in the lounge. Are you hungry?"

"No, I just had something to eat down in the restaurant. I had a good sleep and I feel much better. I bought a newspaper, and I was going to look through it, but I wanted to talk to you first."

"About what?" Cheryl asked, in a guarded tone, as if she had read my thoughts.

"Well, I'm supposed to get some money from Bob once the divorce goes through. We could buy ourselves a house. What do you think?"

"You mean you'll get enough money from Bob to buy a house?" she asked, incredulously.

"Well, I'm not exactly sure how much it's going to be, but I'm sure there'll be enough for a down payment." I retreated to half-truths. I didn't know yet exactly how much I would be receiving, but I was sure I'd be able to afford two average-sized homes.

"Why not? Beats renting," Cheryl shrugged.

"Good, we can start looking tomorrow."

I started looking through the ad section of the newspaper while Cheryl turned the television on.

"Do I get a say on where we'll live?" she asked.

"Of course. I haven't any strong preferences. I only know where I don't want to live." I was glad she was interested.

Two weeks later I was en route to Toronto, a day before my divorce hearing. I went to my place on Woodbine and settled everything with the landlord, telling him that, after the twenty-seventh, I would no longer be needing the place.

On Wednesday morning, plastered with makeup to cover my bruises, I met with my lawyer, Mr. Feldman, and we went to the courthouse together. Bob, Heather, and Barbara Radcliff were all waiting outside the courtroom, so I made a special effort to be busy talking to Mr. Feldman to justify my ignoring them. Inside the courtroom, everything went smoothly, although I was nervous when I was on the stand. I also experienced feelings of hurt and regret when a former "friend" testified about the relationship in which Bob and Heather were involved during our marriage. But when it was over, I felt almost smug, since I was more independent, money-wise, than I had ever been before in my life. I wasn't quite as smug as Heather, though. She had a possessive hold on Bob's arm as we left. Remembering the rage I had felt on that day of revelation, I was tempted to go up to them all and say something terribly sarcastic, but since I couldn't think of anything, I left quietly with Mr. Feldman. He told me that his fee could come out of the settlement, as we had agreed, and then I would receive the balance of the money through my bank within three weeks, at the latest. Later that evening, I was on a flight back to Winnipeg.

Cheryl had continued looking for a house while I was gone for the few days, and when I got back, she found a house she liked on Poplar Avenue. It was close to Henderson Highway, Watt Street, and the Red River. Come summer, we would be able to take walks and watch the boats. Ever since I had spent those long hours by the river when I was with the DeRosiers, I had found areas by water had a soothing kind of feeling. Sometimes, if I watched the water long enough, I got the feeling that it was I who was moving. I also loved to watch the birds circle overhead, swooping down, now and then, for a morsel of food. I thought Cheryl's choice was a very good one, and I asked the salcalady what the earliest date of possession would be. Unfortunately, she said it wouldn't be until March 1st. That meant another month of living in a hotel room.

That same evening, Cheryl and I both settled in our room to watch television. Things were shaping up.

152

"I can't wait for March 1st, eh? We'll have to go shopping for furniture and make sure they can deliver it by March 1st. Let's see, that's a Wednesday. Yeah, there shouldn't be any problems. Are you sure you want to take an upstairs bedroom?"

"I'm sure. That way, you'll be close enough to the kitchen, and when I come down in the morning you'll have coffee and breakfast all ready for me."

"Oh, yeah? Thanks a lot," I said as I threw a pillow at her.

Then she looked at her watch and said, "Hey, April, you want to go down to the lounge with me and have a few drinks? To celebrate finding ourselves a new home?"

I had noticed that she had grown fidgety, and only then did I suspect why. An instant decision was required.

"Sure, sounds like a good idea."

Later that night, when we were both in bed, I was unable to go to sleep. I had no idea on how to deal with Cheryl. It appeared she really needed those drinks. Maybe she was an alcoholic. And what would have happened if I had refused to go along with her? She'd been like a child asking me for a favour. Would she have reacted like a child and thrown a tantrum if I had not gone along? I thought that, from now on, I would have to be careful with my words and reactions, and that was the only way I knew how to deal with Cheryl.

I was also caught up in my own problem and spent hours thinking over the rape and its consequences. What would I and other "squaws" get out of my going to court? Maybe two years of safety from those particular rapists. Probably less, because hardly any criminal ever served a full sentence anymore. Rehabilitation, today, meant coddling the prisoners to the point of giving them every down-home comfort. Cheryl

had told me of a lot of native men who did something illegal
so they would land in jail for the winter months. So what was
the big deal about going to prison? I sighed at the hopelessness of so-called justice. Mostly, because there was nothing
for the victim. Nothing, especially for victims of sexual
assaults, except humiliation in and out of the courtrooms.
Nothing but more taxes to put more luxuries into the penal
institutions. To keep a single prisoner for a year cost more
than what a security guard earned in that year. So where was
the justice of it? The only consolation I could derive was from
killing them over and over again in my mind.

I had an appointment to see Mr. Lord, who was handling
the real estate transaction for me, on February 8th. He was
very happy to see me, and despite my fears that I would be
embarrassed because of my divorce, everything went
smoothly. When I came out of his office, it was almost noon.
Roger Maddison came out of his office just then, and he
seemed not at all surprised to see me. I was wondering if he
remembered me, his old verbal fencing partner, when he said
in a pleasant voice, "Hello, April, how are you?"

"Hello, Mr. Maddison. I'm fine, thank you. What about you?"

"Fine. Alex told me you were coming in today."

"Oh."

"I was looking forward to seeing you again," he smiled and
then asked, "How about lunch?"

"Okay, I'd like that."

I did most of the talking over lunch. He listened and drew
more out of me with appropriate questions. He asked me if I
would go out with him sometime. This gentle, concerned side
of Roger, I hadn't seen before. I wondered why he had never
gotten married. Then I wondered if he had gotten married.

"Have you ever been married?" I asked.

"No. I never found the girl I wanted to spend the rest of
my life with. Once, I thought I had found her." By the
reflective way he looked at me when he said that, I wondered
if I could have been that girl. But I didn't have the gumption
to ask that question.

"Well, I guess I'd better let you get back to the office. Thank you for the lunch. You can reach me at the Maryland Hotel. That's where I'll be staying until we move into our house."

Before I headed back to the hotel, I bought several books for Cheryl and me. There wasn't much that one could do in a hotel room. I picked up a book called *Bury My Heart at Wounded Knee* by Dee Brown. Cheryl would like that. Maybe it would keep her from going down to the lounge. Like that morning, she said she was going over to visit Nancy, but then Nancy was supposed to have a steady job, so how come Cheryl was visiting her during the day? Maybe Nancy worked nights. Or maybe Cheryl was out drinking somewhere. No. Although Cheryl had a drink almost every day, she'd never been drunk or even appeared to be close to being drunk. Maybe drinks to her were what coffee was to me. I couldn't get a day started without at least two cups of coffee.

On Thursday, Roger phoned in the morning to ask if Cheryl and I would like to have dinner at his place Friday evening. I told Cheryl about it, excited that he really had called.

"I really didn't think he'd call me."

"Isn't this the same guy whose guts you used to hate when you worked at the law firm?"

"The same one. Oh, you're not going to tell him that tomorrow night?"

"Don't worry. I'm not even going to be there tomorrow night."

"Oh, you have to."

"Oh, but I don't. He really wants you there. I've got things to do. Besides, you don't need me to hold your hand." I tried to change her mind, but she wouldn't budge.

Friday evening started out with both Roger and I trying to make polite conversation. I guess he was as uncomfortable as I was. After the meal, I was sipping coffee when I asked him, "Roger, how come you were so nasty to me when I worked there?"

"I liked you," he smiled.

155 "Well, that was no way to treat someone you liked."

"Well, I got your attention, didn't I? Until that man came along."

"I did like you, you know," I said. "I hated you, too. I hated liking you. Of course, if I had known you liked me, then maybe things would have been different."

"Well, that's what I get for playing games. I've decided not to play games anymore. So, why didn't Cheryl come tonight? Has she no faith in a man's cooking?"

"No, she just figured we ought to be alone, I guess. It was a very good meal. Where did you learn to cook?"

"I've been a bachelor for a long time. You were telling me about your marriage, care to tell me about why the divorce?"

"Well, I divorced Bob on grounds of adultery. But now when I think about it, that's not what bothered me most. My mother-in-law, she was some lady. She didn't want to be grandmother to a 'bunch of little half-breeds' as she put it."

"Why would she say a thing like that? You're not Indian, are you?"

"No. I'm... a Métis." I had to force those words out.

"And from the way you say that, I gather you're not too proud of it." Roger had a hint of an understanding smile on his face, but his eyes were serious.

"I'm not. It would be better to be a full-blooded Indian or full-blooded Caucasian. But being a half-breed, well, there's just nothing there. You can admire Indian people for what they once were. They had a distinct heritage, or is it culture? Anyway, you can see how much was taken from them. And white people, well, they've convinced each other they are the superior race, and you can see they are responsible for the progress we have today. Cheryl once said, 'The meek shall inherit the Earth. Big deal, because who's going to want it once the whites are through with it?' So the progress is questionable. Even so, what was a luxury yesterday is a

156 necessity today, and I enjoy all the necessities. But what have the Métis people got? Nothing. Being a half-breed, you feel only the shortcomings of both sides. You feel you're a part of

the drunken Indians you see on Main Street. And if you inherit brown skin like Cheryl did, you identify with the Indian people more. In today's society, there isn't anything positive about them that I've seen. And when people say offhandedly, 'Oh, you shouldn't be ashamed of being Métis,' well, generally they haven't a clue as to what it's like being a native person. Oh, I'm sorry. I didn't mean it. I meant the words, I didn't mean for them to come out all at once."

I was really embarrassed. I had held those words in for such a long time, and then I lay them on Roger of all people.

"Well, believe it or not, I understand. There will always be some form of discrimination, whether it is someone discriminating against an Indian on Main Street, or your Church telling you you have to teach your children its beliefs because theirs is the only right one. I've got a brother, an adopted brother who's an Ojibway. Joe thinks it's not important what others think of him. It's what he thinks of himself that counts."

"Well, Cheryl lives pretty much by that philosophy, and even so, she's come down with a drinking problem, I think. I'm not really sure. Anyway, only she has the right to tell me I ought to be proud of what I am because she's worked so hard to do something about the native image."

"Your sister sounds remarkable. Maybe something is bothering her. It could be she's impatient to see the changes, or it could be almost anything."

"I think my being back in Winnipeg will help a lot. It's funny, you're the last person I thought I'd be able to talk to about these things. Thanks for listening."

"I found it interesting. I find you interesting. I'm not going to tell you to be proud of what you are. Just don't be so ashamed."

Chapter Thirteen

On March 1st, Cheryl and I moved into our very own home. By March 2nd, most of our furniture and appliances had been delivered. The following Saturday, I gave a housewarming party, but only Roger came. Cheryl refused to invite Nancy or any of her other friends.

Next, Cheryl and I went looking for a car. It was wonderful to have money to be able to pay cash for a car. The salesman really catered to us, even offered us a two-car deal. But Cheryl absolutely refused my offer to buy her her own car. I really wanted a big expensive luxury car, but because of Cheryl, I bought a little Datsun, which I never did like very much, not after the Radcliff automobiles. Cheryl asked me again in that accusing manner just how much money I did have. I counter-attacked by saying, enough to send her back to finish her university courses if she liked, adding that was about it. Of course, I had no idea how much that would have cost. But it was convincing and made Cheryl change the subject. She insisted she had no intention of being a social worker.

It was the middle of March, and I was half watching the evening news as usual, when a news story came on which made me sit up and take notice. Actually, it was a picture of a man who'd been shot to death by the police earlier that afternoon. It had something to do with a bank robbery. I wasn't sure, because I had also been reading the newspaper. If I hadn't glanced up at that moment, I wouldn't have seen the picture of one of the men who had raped me. It wasn't the leader, and it wasn't Stephen Gurnan. It was the one who had helped grab me and had sat beside the driver. I was positive. My heart was beating fast, and I paced back and forth in the living room, wondering if I should wait for the late news to come on again, or whether I should call the police immediately. Since I was positive, I called the police right away.

I was told someone would be sent down to see me, so while I waited, I thought things over. If only it had been the leader. Maybe the leader had been with him. Maybe they've got the leader. I looked through the paper again, but the story wasn't in the paper. I was sure that if they had arrested the other man, I would be asked to go down to police headquarters to identify him. I was sure that those two would hang around together.

Then I hoped Cheryl wouldn't return while the police were there. I had never talked about the rape to her in detail because she had initially blamed herself. So far, I hadn't even told her about Stephen Gurnan. For that matter, she had never told me what questions the police had asked her. I had wished those men dead, and now that one was dead, I was glad. But it should have been the other one.

Almost two-and-a-half hours passed before two officers showed up. They had brought some pictures for me to look at, and I picked out the dead rapist immediately. They asked if the other rapist was among any of the other pictures, but he wasn't. None even looked like the third man.

On March 23rd, I got a call from the police asking if I could come down to the Public Safety Building immediately. It was in the afternoon, and Cheryl was out job hunting. There could only be one reason why they'd want me there. They must have arrested the third man. After I got there, I had to wait for at least forty-five minutes. Then, there in the lineup was the leader! He looked arrogant and unafraid. He looked evil! It gave me great pleasure to be able to pick him out so easily, without any fear of being mistaken. At the same time, that cold chill came over me again. From the minute I saw him, I began to tremble, just as I had that night. Not being able to control myself scared me. I really feared the possibility of losing my mind. Going crazy. In that way, rape was a double assault. Rapists abused their victims both physically and

159

mentally. Some victims' minds really did snap after a brutal sexual assault. Maybe it had something to do with what I had tried during the assault. Separate my mind from my body. I didn't know. I wasn't a psychologist. I just knew how I felt. I was driven home in a police car and I was grateful for that. To be out alone, especially in the dark, was just too terrifying for me.

Cheryl hadn't yet returned, so I again went through my ritual of trying to exorcise the evil within me by bathing. I poured half a bottle of perfumed oil into the hot water and then spent the next hour scrubbing vigorously. When the water would get cold, I would just add more hot water. All the while, I thought of the rapists, laughing crazily, pawing at me, coming down on me, putting their smell on me, putting their dirt on me. And no matter how hard I scrubbed, I couldn't get rid of the smell of their awful slimy bodies, the awful memories. I wanted to scream aloud, that long silent scream I kept in my head that night. I wanted them to feel my anguish. I wanted to gouge their eyes out. I wanted to whip the life out of them. Mutilate them. Kill them. Because bathing never worked.

I always got worked up like that whenever I would take a bath, although it had never been with such intensity before. Back in the bedroom, I paced the floor back and forth, cursing Fate for having placed them on Elgin Street that night, cursing the judicial system because those two, if they went to jail, they would get out again to rape again. When I had cooled down somewhat, I began wondering for the hundredth time why they had kept on calling me squaw. Was it obvious? That really puzzled me. Except for my long black hair, I really didn't think I could be mistaken as a native person. Mistaken? There's that shame again. Okay, identified.

When Cheryl got home, I hadn't even started supper yet. We decided to order pizza and have it delivered. Cheryl had news that she was quite sure she was going to be hired at a downtown factory, where she had put in an application that afternoon. She had to phone back the following Monday. I asked her what she would be doing because I couldn't see her

160

working on an assembly line. She said she'd be doing a lot of different things but wouldn't specify. What a waste, I thought to myself.

That started me thinking of opening our own business, maybe a fashion boutique, like the ones I used to visit on Yonge Street and in the Yorkville area of Toronto. From my shopping experiences with Mrs. Radcliff, I'd learned a lot. Could have learned more if I would have paid more attention. But Cheryl was what discouraged me. She would insist on drawing in native women, which would drive others away. Moreover, Cheryl's heart wouldn't be in it. She dressed well enough for one of her crowd, but that certainly wasn't the world of high fashion. In the end, I thought it would be best not to mention it.

For the time being, I decided that I would go back to temporary secretarial work because I didn't want to be tied to a job until the whole rape trial ordeal was over.

161

In April, Roger, Cheryl, and I went out to celebrate my birthday. It was only rarely we did anything together. Cheryl still hadn't brought over a single friend to our place. She went out a great deal. She would come home from work, have supper, change, and go out again. I spent more and more time with Roger.

In May, I was cleaning the house on a Friday because I didn't have a job for that day. It was when I was collecting the garbage from Cheryl's room that I came across an empty whisky bottle in her garbage container. I was so shocked to see it, the implication of it rushing into my head. Cheryl wouldn't do that. Sneak drinks. So why the bottle? I tried to think of a number of reasons why she'd have a bottle in her room. I had never seen her even slightly drunk. Of course, we hadn't seen much of each other over the past few months. I decided I was making too much of it. We were getting along all right, and I didn't want to change that. Cheryl never did say anything to me, although she must have realized I had found the empty bottle when I had done the cleaning.

A few weeks after this, I spotted a promotional piece in the newspaper about an Indian powwow to be held on the July 1st

long weekend at Roseau River. It would be good if Cheryl
and I attended the festival, I thought. Especially good for
Cheryl. Perhaps it would renew an interest in her native
cause.

That evening, as soon as Cheryl came home from work,
I asked, "Hey, Cheryl, what's an Indian powwow?"

"Oh, it's mostly a dancing competition among different
tribes who come from all over the place."

"Are they interesting?"

"Oh sure, I've been to several of them. I like going to
them."

"Well, there's going to be one in Roseau on the July 1st
weekend. I'd like to go to it and see what it's like. How about
it? We could buy some camping stuff and make like we were
teenagers again. Remember?"

"You really want to go?"

"Yeah, I said I did, didn't I?"

"Okay, I'm glad you want to go. You'll finally rub shoulders
with real Indians," Cheryl said, and I wasn't sure if she was
happy or just being sarcastic.

I was quite anxious to go, and then I thought of Roger's
brother, Joe. Funny that so many Indian boys were called
Joe. Probably Catholic mothers naming their sons after
Joseph, the foster father of Jesus. I wondered if Joe was
married. Roger hadn't said. I thought maybe I should invite
Roger to bring his brother and join us for the powwow. I'd
have to ask him.

I never did ask him, though. I had supper at his place not
long after, and I was wondering about how to broach the
subject, but Roger had picked that night to decide it was
high time we showed our affection for each other. During
the past weeks of seeing each other, I had subtly dissuaded
him from giving me even a simple goodnight kiss. As far as
I knew, Roger was most likely seeing other women, which
was fine with me. Men, to my knowledge, did not tend to be
celibate for long periods. And Roger and I were just good
friends. But on this particular night, he kept getting
uncomfortably close. At one point, I went over to look out

the window, but he followed me. He made me turn to face him and was about to kiss me.

"Don't touch me," I heard myself say in a cold, icy voice that stopped him dead. He looked at me for a long time before he released me.

"I'm sorry. I wanted for us to be just good friends, that's all, just good friends," I said in a whispery voice.

"Well, I wasn't going to rape you, April. I can't figure you out. I thought we had more than just a friendship going for us." His voice was neutral, and I couldn't tell whether he was angry or hurt. After that, he served me coffee, but our conversation was stifled. He saw me out to my car, but this time he didn't say he would call me. He just said goodnight.

163

I had an appointment on June 1st to see the Crown attorney, Mr. Scott. I had already received a subpoena from an RCMP officer for the preliminary hearing. Mr. Scott's office was in the basement of the Legislative Building. The police had explained some of the general court procedures, but Mr. Scott explained things in more detail. For instance, as we went over my statement, he told me I was allowed to say things like "I smelled liquor on his breath," but not "he was drunk." It had to do with hearsay evidence. One could testify to what was directly known. Anyways, it was quite complicated to me, and I worried about messing up my testimony. I also worried about the defense counsel misconstruing whatever I would say.

On the day of the hearing, I went early to Mr. Scott's office as we were to meet there. As we went to Stonewall, I reread my statement which Mr. Scott handed me. He reminded me of a few things, and before I knew it, we were at the Community Hall in Stonewall where the judicial process was carried out. Mr. Scott showed me to a small room where I was to wait for my turn to testify. By lunchtime, I still hadn't been called and I was both bored and apprehensive.

After lunch, I went over my statement again, although I loathed going over those words that told the story of that night. I was finally called to give my testimony and I started shaking as soon as I heard my name. My stomach had been tied up in knots all day, but it tightened up even more by the time I was in the witness stand.

Mr. Scott asked me to recount the events of January 11, 1972. I did, but minimized the dirty details as much as I could. On occasion he'd have me go into some of those details, like the rape itself. I couldn't just say I had been raped. I had to describe the act itself. I tried at all times to look only at his eyes, or his lips as they moved, pretending I was talking only to him and that no one else was there.

Of course, I could feel their eyes burning into me. I knew darn well there were others in that room, listening to what I was saying. When that thought would overwhelm me, my voice would fade out and the court stenographer would ask me to repeat myself. I wondered what those other people were thinking. It wasn't just a simple matter that a horrible degradation had happened to me. The thing was *I had been part of it.* I'm sure that's what they all thought, even if unwillingly. I had been part of that depraved sexual activity. I had known in advance that I would have to use explicit words when referring to private parts of the anatomy. And I had come across those words as well as the slang words in the past. But to me, to say them out loud, in front of all those people, well, I faltered every time I had to say them. In the future I would better understand why some women chose not to seek justice in the courtrooms.

And then I was questioned by the defence counsel, Mr. Schneider. He sounded very skeptical, at times even sarcastic. He tried different insinuations, which made me feel defensive. I felt like it was me who was on trial by the time he was through with me. He persisted in making me go into depth about some incidents, and I really believed it was just to make me say those words I had stuttered on. I understood full well that it was his job to defend his client in any way he could, but I also felt what he did to me was morally wrong.

A recess was called after I was allowed off the stand, and I headed straight for the washroom. Once there, I threw up. One woman had been in there when I walked in, and she glanced at me. I couldn't interpret what was in her glance, but when she expressed sympathy, I broke down and began crying. I wished for the moment that I could stay in the washroom until everyone was gone, but I had to go out to Mr. Scott's car. I fixed my makeup and braced myself and returned to the courtroom, very grateful that at least one person sympathized with me.

165

The court ruled that there was sufficient evidence to proceed with a trial. That's what the preliminary hearing was for. The court also ordered a ban on the publication of evidence, for which I was extremely grateful. On our way back to Winnipeg, Mr. Scott was in good spirits because he had been successful. I was just relieved that this portion was over and done with. There was still the trial ahead.

Cheryl and I left early Saturday morning for the Roseau Reservation. There was a camping area set aside for the likes of us. As we made our way to the main area, we noticed licence plates from Montana, the Dakotas, Minnesota, and even Arizona. Men, women, and children were in traditional tribal costumes. Somewhere in the background, drums could be heard, sounding the heartbeat of the people. Teepees had been set up, and Indian women in buckskin dresses now tended to fires, making bannock for curious onlookers.

The main event, as Cheryl had said, was the dancing competition. During the intervals, everyone was invited to participate in the dancing. Cheryl joined in, but I stayed on the sidelines. That night, we sat, Indian-style, around a bonfire, listening to the chanting and tales of Indian singers. Cheryl told me that was probably how it had felt on those long-ago buffalo hunts. I was impressed by all the sights and sounds. It went deeper than just hearing and seeing. I felt good. I felt alive. There were stirrings of pride, regret, and even an inner peace. For the first time in my life, I felt as if all of that was part of me, as if I was a part of it. It was curious to feel that way. I had gone expecting to feel embarrassment, maybe even contempt. I looked over at Cheryl. She, too, seemed so relaxed.

She was deep in conversation with some people on the other side of her. I didn't attempt to join their conversation. I was occupied with enjoying my own realizations. I also noted with satisfaction the old animation on Cheryl's face as she gestured and talked with her companions. Earlier that evening, an Indian family had set up their tent next to ours and had come over to offer help. At the end of the ceremonies, Cheryl and I returned to our tent.

"Well, did you enjoy yourself?" Cheryl asked.

"Oh, I don't know. In this atmosphere everything is staged. It's romanticized. On Monday, we'll all go home, and to what? I'll go back to see the drunken Indians on Main Street, and I'll feel the same old shame. It's like having two worlds in my life that can't be mixed. And I've made my choice on how I want to live my everyday life."

"Yeah, but the Indian blood runs through your veins, April. To deny that, you deny a basic part of yourself. You'll never be satisfied until you can accept that fact."

"How do you do it, Cheryl? How is it that you're so proud when there's so much against being a native person?"

"For one thing, I don't see it that way. Maybe I have put too much faith in my dreams. But if alcohol didn't have such a destructive force on us, we'd be a fabulous people. And that's what I see. I see all the possibilities that we have. Nancy, for instance, you never did think much of her when I was attending university, did you? Well, she does drink and does other things that you would never dream of doing. But she also holds a steady job, and she's been at the minimum wage for a long time. They use her and she knows it. And she gets depressed about it. But with her education and the way things are, she knows she doesn't have many choices. She helps support her mother and her sister and a brother. The reason why she left home in the first place was her father. He was an alcoholic who beat her mother up and raped Nancy. Okay, she doesn't have much, maybe she never will have much, but what she's got she shares with her family. And she's not an exception."

"I didn't know that," I said. We sat for a time in silence before I spoke again.

"When we lived with our parents, I used to take you to the park. The white kids would call the native kids all sorts of names. If they had let us, I would have played with the white kids. Never the native kids. To me, the white kids were the winners all the way. I guess what I feel today started back then. It would take an awful lot for me to be able to change what I've felt for a lifetime. Shame doesn't dissolve overnight."

167

"I can understand that. Me, I've been identifying with the Indian people ever since I was a kid. The Métis people share more of the same problems with the Indian people. I guess that's why Riel was leader to both. I wrote this one piece in university, but they wouldn't publish it because they said it was too controversial. I still know it by heart. Want to hear it?"

"Sure," I said. There was little in our conversation we hadn't discussed before, but sitting there in our tent, surrounded by proud Indians, everything seemed different.

"White Man, to you my voice is like the unheard call in the wilderness. It is there, though you do not hear. But, this once, take the time to listen to what I have to say.

"Your history is highlighted by your wars. Why is it all right for your nations to conquer each other in your attempts at dominion? When you sailed to our lands, you came with your advanced weapons. You claimed you were a progressive, civilized people. And today, White Man, you have the ultimate weapons. Warfare which could destroy all men, all creation. And you allow such power to be in the hands of those few who have such little value in true wisdom.

"White Man, when you first came, most of our tribes began with peace and trust in dealing with you, strange white intruders. We showed you how to survive in our homelands. We were willing to share with you our vast wealth. Instead of repaying us with gratitude, you, White Man, turned on us, your friends. You turned on us with your advanced weapons and your cunning trickery.

"When we, the Indian people, realized your intentions, we rose to do battle, to defend our nations, our homes, our food,

168

our lives. And for our efforts, we are labelled savages, and our battles are called massacres.

"And when our primitive weapons could not match those which you had perfected through centuries of wars, we realized that peace could not be won, unless our mass destruction took place. And so we turned to treaties. And this time, we ran into your cunning trickery. And we lost our lands, our freedom, and were confined to reservations. And we are held in contempt.

"'As long as the Sun shall rise... ' For you, White Man, these are words without meaning.

"White Man, there is much in the deep, simple wisdom of our forefathers. We were here for centuries. We kept the land, the waters, the air clean and pure, for our children and for our children's children.

"Now that you are here, White Man, the rivers bleed with contamination. The winds moan with the heavy weight of pollution in the air. The land vomits up the poisons which have been fed into it. Our Mother Earth is no longer clean and healthy. She is dying.

"White Man, in your greedy rush for money and power, you are destroying. Why must you have power over everything? Why can't you live in peace and harmony? Why can't you share the beauty and the wealth which Mother Earth has given us?

"You do not stop at confining us to small pieces of rock and muskeg. Where are the animals of the wilderness to go when there is no more wilderness? Why are the birds of the skies falling to their extinction? Is there joy for you when you bring down the mighty trees of our forests? No living thing seems sacred to you. In the name of progress, everything is cut down. And progress means only profits.

"White Man, you say that we are a people without dignity. But when we are sick, weak, hungry, poor, when there is nothing for us but death, what are we to do? We cannot accept a life which has been imposed on us.

"You say that we are drunkards, that we live for drinking. But drinking is a way of dying. Dying without enjoying life. You have given us many diseases. It is true that you have found

immunizations for many of these diseases. But this was done
more for your own benefit. The worst disease, for which there
is no immunity, is the disease of alcoholism. And you condemn
us for being its easy victims. And those who do not condemn us
weep for us and pity us.

"So, we the Indian people, we are still dying. The land we
lost is dying, too.

"White Man, you have our land now.
Respect it. As we once did.
Take care of it. As we once did.
Love it. As we once did.

"White Man, our wisdom is dying. As we are. But take
heed, if Indian wisdom dies, you, White Man, will not be
far behind.

"So weep not for us.
Weep for yourselves.
And for your children.
And for their children.
Because you are taking everything today.
And tomorrow, there will be nothing left for them."

Cheryl had become more and more emotional as she went on.
When she finished, we sat in silence. The only sounds were
those of the crickets. Somewhere in the distance, a child was
crying.

Finally I said, "I can see why they said it was controversial.
I think it's powerful." We sat in silence for a few more
minutes. "At the same time, though, I think you put too much
blame on white men for everything. The Indian people did
allow themselves to be treated like children. They should
have stood up for their rights instead of letting themselves be
walked on. You know what I mean?"

"Yeah?" Cheryl shot back in a challenging voice. "Where
did it get the Métis?"

"But what exactly is it the Métis want? To live like Indians
on reservations? To be dependent on the governments and,
therefore, the white people? You once said the Métis people
were an independent breed, freedom lovers."

"I still maintain that. But we don't have that kind of life."
Cheryl added as an afterthought, "Because we don't have very
many choices.

"Besides, that piece was mostly to warn those in control
that they are going too fast. I'd like them to slow down. Let's
enjoy life, give our children hope for tomorrow and get rid of
171   those bloody clouds of bombs hanging over us all."

Chapter Fourteen

After that long weekend, I tried to keep the feeling I had alive, even though I was back in the city. I noticed Cheryl had gotten some good out of it, too, because she made more appearances around the house. She also seemed more relaxed, more willing to discuss events concerning native people which appeared in the newspaper and on television. No matter what the issues were, she always found some way to defend the native side of the question. Now when she began telling me that she was going to the Friendship Centre, I knew, without doubt, that she was indeed going there. The old fire had been rekindled. Cheryl began tearing clippings out of the paper, presumably to act on them, if possible. For Cheryl, I knew it was probable.

I returned to working part time, but the scenes I saw on my way to and from work on Main Street gradually made that weekend's emotions disappear. I remembered my original evaluation of these people. Everyone always said, "Those Indians on Main Street," but there were a lot of Métis there, too. No, I felt no affection towards any of the native peoples there. But for Cheryl, I faked interest. So, when Cheryl asked me to go down to the Friendship Centre with her one evening, I agreed.

We decided to walk, or rather, Cheryl decided to walk. Walking was Cheryl's chief mode of transportation, even in winter. I suspected she was also snubbing my little car. However, it was a beautiful evening to be out, the kind where you could breathe deeply and smell the delicious night air. It made one feel giddy, as in giddy-up-go, the kind of evening that if I were a horse, I'd be kicking up my heels and running like crazy.

Cheryl and I talked about the Steindalls kind of longingly. We admitted that we both felt too embarrassed to go back and see them, having been out of touch with them for so long. And perhaps our main desire would have been just to see and ride the horses. Cheryl and I decided we would go horseback riding a lot more often than we had been doing. It was one way for me of getting her into my car. Our car.

When we got to the Friendship Centre, we entered a large recreation room. I saw a lot of elderly native people, and Cheryl mixed among them immediately, with me tagging along behind her. While she conversed with them, I could only smile patronizingly, and nod when it was expected. I knew that Cheryl saw their quiet beauty, their simple wisdom. All I could see were watery eyes, leathery brown skin—uneducated natives.

Cheryl explained that many of the people were in the city for either medical reasons, or they were visiting relatives. When they returned north to their homes, they would resume fishing, trapping, and committing themselves to crafts.

"One thing you wouldn't like is the way they live in winter," Cheryl said to me. "Some of them have to walk miles and miles just for their water. They roll up newspapers inside their jackets for extra warmth. Cardboard and plastic replace broken window panes. Their furniture is wooden crates and blankets on the floor. Well, you've seen the pictures in some of the books I've given you."

"Sure, but I thought that was in the olden days. I thought they had new houses now."

"New houses, yeah, but cheaply made, no plumbing, no sewer system. Besides, those housing programs were thought up by Indian Affairs, which means only Treaty Indians get any of the supposed benefit out of them. Non-status Indians and Métis get welfare and that's it."

I didn't know what to say. I felt it was good that they didn't have the federal government to rely on, that it would help them be independent, to a certain point. But I also knew what Cheryl said was true about non-status Indians and Métis, and employment was hard for them to come by.

Just then, an older woman came up to Cheryl. Thinking that she wanted a private word with Cheryl, I moved away a bit and occupied myself by studying some Indian art hanging on the wall. Then Cheryl and the old woman approached me. The old woman suddenly reached towards me and put her hand on mine. I glanced down at her hand. It looked rusted and old. Her fingers were swollen at the joints, disfigured, the veins stood out, and it took everything I had not to move my hand away from hers.

Her hand felt so warm, so dry, so old. I'm sure my smile froze and then faded. I waited for her to take her hand away. I looked at her questioningly, but she didn't say anything. Her gaze held mine, for I saw in her eyes that deep simple wisdom of which Cheryl had spoken. And I no longer found her touch distasteful. Without speaking a word to me, the woman imparted her message with her eyes. She had seen something in me that was special, something that was deserving of her respect. I wondered what she could possibly have found in me that could have warranted her respect. I just stood there, humbled. At the same time, I had this overwhelming feeling that a mystical spiritual occurrence had just taken place.

Sheepishly, I told Cheryl how I had felt as we walked home. Cheryl smiled and said, "Well, you should be honoured. White Thunderbird Woman is an Elder. I told her that you were my sister but in blood only. I told her your vision was clouded, but that when your vision cleared, you would be a good person for the Métis people."

"You do have a unique way of putting things."

"Comes from reading so many Indian books. Actually, most Indians today don't talk like that at all."

"It's a pity. It sounds so poetic."

When my vision cleared... Would it ever? And would it mean that someday I would come to accept those Main Street people?

I gave that incident a lot of thought over the following weeks. If I'd had such a grandmother when I was growing up, maybe I wouldn't have been so mixed-up. My emotions were getting the better of me. Finally, I put it all down to the fact that it was a very emotional time of my life with the divorce and rape and all. Still, I continued to waver back and forth as to just how I felt about being a Métis. It was a part of me. I was part Indian. But so what?

In September, Roger came over to my place on a Saturday morning. It had been two months since I had last seen him. I had missed him, of course, and I had found it lonely without his company. But then, I had Cheryl's company, and that made up for it, a little. I had consoled myself by thinking that with me, no deep relationship would ever be possible, and therefore, it was better for Roger to stay away. When the doorbell sounded, I wondered who it could be because Cheryl and I had virtually no one to call on us.

Even though she had returned to her former self, Cheryl still had invited no one to our house. It was probably an Avon lady.

"Hello, April."

"Roger! What are you doing here?" I was surprised and pleased to see him, and a smile came to my face, instantly.

"Oh, I was in the neighbourhood, thought I'd drop by for a cup of coffee, and see how you were," he smiled.

"In the neighbourhood, huh?" I smiled back, and led him into the kitchen. When I had gotten the coffee, we sat at the table, but didn't say anything.

Finally, he said, "Look before... "

At the same time, I said, "I missed you."

"Well, I missed you, too. I was hoping and waiting for you to call me. But then, that's like playing a game, isn't it? And I said I wasn't going to play games anymore. If you don't want to see me, then I want you to tell me now, and I want you to tell me why. Is it because of your marriage? Did you get hurt by it? Is that why you've always held me at arm's length?"

"No. No, it has nothing to do with my marriage. I do like you, Roger. I just don't want you wasting your time with me, especially if you want more than just being friends. I can't give you more than that. And I can't tell you why. I won't tell you why." I sighed and put my cup down, emphasizing how hopeless the situation was.

Roger looked at me. I didn't look at him, but I knew he was looking at me. I could feel it. After a while he said, "Well, I'd rather for us to be friends than nothing at all. So, we'll continue seeing each other, all right? And if you ever feel like telling me exactly what is bothering you, then don't hold back, okay?" He reached out and put his hand under my chin and made me look at him.

"Okay. But just don't count on it."

Roger had some things to do, but we made plans to go out later that evening. When Cheryl came down later, I told her Roger had been there. Then I wondered if my going out with him again would have an adverse effect on her.

"You don't mind me going out with him, do you, Cheryl?" I asked after much hesitation.

"Of course not. I think he's a heck of a lot better than Bob. I'm glad. You need a strong man to take care of you. You know what I mean? I'm the kind of woman who might feel smothered by a man after awhile. But you, well, it's not that I think you're weak or anything. Just that I see you with a husband and kids and still doing what you have to."

I liked Cheryl telling me that. It wasn't quite the way things were between Roger and me but if I hadn't been deranged by those rapists, that's probably how things would have been.

In the middle of September, a police officer came to my place to serve me with a subpoena to appear in court in the trial of *The Queen v. Donnelly* on October 10, 1972.

On October 3rd, I had to return to that basement office in the Legislative Building to see Mr. Scott, the Crown attorney. He explained that Oliver Donnelly was going on trial only for the charges of unlawful confinement and rape. If a verdict of "Not Guilty" were reached, then he would proceed with the other charges of indecent assault, gross indecency, and assault causing bodily harm. If the verdict was "Guilty," then the lesser charges would be stayed. When I left, I was well aware that the trial was less than a week away.

I told Cheryl about the trial, and she said she was going to attend. I told her I'd rather she didn't, but she was insistent.

"Look, April, you've changed a lot, and I want to know why. You've never told me exactly what happened. You smile, you laugh, but I can see in your eyes there's no joy. I want to help you in any way I can."

"Cheryl, you blamed yourself in the first place, and it's not your fault. What happened to me was Fate. But I know you, you're going to start blaming yourself when you had absolutely nothing to do with it. Some terrible things did happen to me, and I don't want you to know about them. So please stay away, okay?"

"I won't make any promises," Cheryl said. "If I can take time off work, I still might come."

On Tuesday morning, I was at Mr. Scott's office by nine a.m., in case I had to go over any last-minute details. Then I was secluded in a witness room while the jury selection took place, and the professionals, like the doctors, had their turns to testify first, so they could get back to their jobs. Lunch came and went, and it was two-thirty before I was called.

I could feel everybody's eyes on me as I walked to the witness stand. My insides were twisted into a knot. Nervously, I listened to the clerk ask me if I would swear to tell the truth, the whole truth, nothing but the truth, so help me God. I said, "I do."

I was already trembling, and I hadn't said but those two words. While the Crown attorney shuffled through some papers on his table, I looked around, not moving my head. On my left were the jurists. On my right and higher up was the Honourable Mr. Justice Saul. There in front of me, enclosed in the prison dock, was Oliver Donnelly, staring up at me. I quickly averted my eyes.

Mr. Scott was quite different in his role before the jurists. He was very sympathetic and seemed thoroughly offended by what he knew had happened to me. Again, I had to tell of the night of the rape. I answered in as much detail as I thought he wanted. I faltered at times, turned red, looked at the floor. It was a horrible experience saying in front of all those people what had actually happened to me. I had to fight to control my trembling and shaky voice. I had to pretend it wasn't as bad as all that. I was asked to describe the man who had raped me. I did so.

"Is that person whom you are describing present in the courtroom today?"

178

"Yes, he is."

"Could you point that person out?"

"He's over there," I said, pointing at Donnelly, as I had been previously instructed to do.

Mr. Scott said, "Let the record show that the accused, Oliver Donnelly, has been identified by April Raintree, the complainant."

When Mr. Scott finished with me, it was Mr. Schneider's turn. He was the defendant's lawyer. I expected him to be aggressive, as he had been at the preliminary hearing, but he wasn't.

After going over my identification of Oliver Donnelly, he asked, "All right, you were in the car. What did you do while you were still in the city limits?"

"I sat in the corner of the back seat."

"Did you fight or plead with them to let you go?"

"No, I was... "

"So, you didn't do anything at all?"

"No."

"Now, would you say the defendant was intoxicated?"

"I don't know."

"Didn't you state that you smelled liquor on his breath?"

"Yes, I did."

"You did what, Miss Raintree?"

"I did smell liquor on his breath."

"You stated that you were going to your sister's place to pick up her effects. Is that correct, Miss Raintree?"

"Yes."

"Do you know how your sister earned her living at that time?"

I answered "No" at the same moment Mr. Scott raised his
voice, objecting that the question wasn't relevant to the case.
The judge intervened to say he didn't have to make a ruling,
because I had already answered.

179   After I had completed my testimony, the Crown attorney
called Stephen Gurnan to the stand. He was sworn in, but the
judge called a recess until the following day.

That night, I wondered why the defense counsel had
asked me what Cheryl did for a living. She seemed distracted,
but I didn't think it was important enough to ask her. She said
she was going to go out for awhile. I took the opportunity to
take my ritual bath. Maybe tonight, I would be able to get rid
of that awful stench, forever. But instead, everything was
more intensified. The smell became stronger, as if the
perfumed oil had somehow turned into their bodily scents. I
again had the visions of their lunatic faces, laughing,
sneering. I hadn't been able to say that in court! Frantically, I
scrubbed and lathered and scrubbed some more. Finally, I
broke down and started crying. I dried myself off, roughly.
Then I put my nightgown on and, methodically, began to
brush my hair.

Suddenly, I could stand it no longer. I threw the brush
down and it hit the bath tub with a resounding clang. Then I
snatched the bar of soap and the bath brush and threw them
on the floor. With my arm, I swept all the perfume jars and
other containers off the vanity. All I felt was a frenzied
frustration. My sobbing had grown louder and louder and I
finally screamed.

"You bastards! You lousy dirty bastards. I wish you were
all dead! Do you hear me? I wish you goddamned bastards
were dead!"

I slumped to the floor and pounded the ceramic tiling as
hard as I could. I wanted to transfer the pain from inside to
my fist. I cried until I had no more tears.

I stayed there for a while, not thinking of anything.
Gradually, some of my humour returned, and I chided myself
for making such a mess, because it was me who had to clean it
up in the end. But first I'd have a coffee. I went to the kitchen,

made myself a cup, and sat down at the table to smoke a cigarette. It sure felt good after all the crying I'd just done.

The second day of the trial started with the Crown   180 attorney having Stephen Gurnan tell everything that had occurred that night, and they went over the identification of the rapist. There was no doubt that the Crown attorney had the identification area well covered. As far as I was concerned, the defendant didn't have a leg to stand on, in the way of defence.

The defence counsel then got up to question Gurnan. As expected, he asked him what he had originally been charged with. He noted to the jury that Gurnan had gotten the charge reduced to forcible confinement. Mr. Schneider's tone when he questioned Stephen Gurnan showed his open contempt. The defense counsel brought out the fact that Stephen Gurnan had told Donnelly that the intended victim was a known prostitute.

"How did you know that this certain girl you were supposed to scare was a prostitute?"

"Objection! That's hearsay evidence. Mr. Gurnan could not know that for a fact, since he didn't know the complainant."

"It is hearsay evidence, My Lord, but we believe this evidence is important, not to prove that the girl was a prostitute, but that the witness believed her to be a prostitute."

Mr. Justice Saul said to Mr. Scott, "He does appear to have a point. Overruled."

The defence lawyer repeated his question, to which Stephen Gurnan answered, "My sister told me."

"And what is your sister's name?"

"Sylvia. Sylvia Gurnan."

I was indignant that I could be mistaken as a prostitute. If Mr. Schneider intended to prove that I was, or had ever been, a prostitute, he'd better forget it. I could prove beyond a doubt that I was a decent citizen.

It was after the lunch recess when Cheryl showed up.

"I lied at work and told them I was sick. I would have come a lot earlier, but I was stuck at something I had to finish. Anyways, how's it going? And how do you feel?"

181   "Well, I'd like to say I'm happy you see you, but you
shouldn't have bothered coming."

"That's gratitude. How's the case going?"

"I think it's almost over, but I'm not sure. I think, too, that
the defence counsel is trying to prove I behaved like a
prostitute or something. They'll try anything."

Cheryl and I entered the courtroom together and sat near
the front. A little later in the afternoon, Sylvia Gurnan was
called to the stand. She testified that she had asked her
brother, Stephen, to scare a certain prostitute. I presumed her
testimony was to corroborate what Stephen Gurnan had said,
thus making him a credible witness in the eyes of the jurists.

"You specifically told your brother, Stephen Gurnan, that this
certain girl was a prostitute?" Mr. Schneider asked.

"Yes. We all knew she was a prostitute. It wasn't a secret,"
Sylvia replied.

"Did you know this girl's name?"

"Yes. Her name's Cheryl Raintree."

Shock waves went through me. I looked sideways at
Cheryl. She didn't move at all. It was as if she had been
expecting it. I sat there shivering. My own sister? Champion
of native causes. A whore?

"Cheryl, say this isn't so," I whispered to her in a hoarse
whisper, begging her to deny it. But she didn't. She just sat
there looking at the floor.

What happened after that I'm not really sure. My mind
was in a whirl. I know the jurists left the room, but it didn't
have anything to do with this recent exposé. A police officer
testified as to how Oliver Donnelly's statement had been
obtained. Then I remembered that Mr. Scott had told me
about this *voir-dire*. When the judge was satisfied that the
statement had been given voluntarily, he ruled that the
evidence could be submitted, and the jury was called back.
Then Oliver Donnelly's statement was read to the court.

He said he had been first approached by Jason Steeps to
help Stephen Gurnan put a scare into some hooker. "Jason
182   and I had been drinking heavily, most of the afternoon prior
to that evening. We sat in Stephen Gurnan's car, which was

parked where the hooker was supposed to be living. When the girl came, Stephen Gurnan told us she was the one, so we grabbed her and got her into the car. We drove around for a while, and the girl never said anything, so I figured it would be all right to have sex with her. I believed she was a prostitute. When she did object, I thought it was because I hadn't paid her. I had never paid before, and I wasn't going to start then. The liquor made me lose control, and I hit her a few times. If I hadn't been drunk, I wouldn't have hit her. I believed at the time when I had sex with her, it was with her consent."

There were no further witnesses, so court was adjourned until the next day for the summations by the lawyers. Because it seemed Cheryl wasn't going to budge from her chair, even though the courtroom was almost empty, I said, "We'd better go now." My voice sounded cold, even harsh.

Cheryl stood up then and looked right at me. I saw her face in that split second before I looked away from her. I just couldn't look her straight in the face, not at that moment. I didn't even know how I felt towards her. She followed me to the bus stop. All the way home, we were silent. I then understood that she really had been to blame. I blamed her. At the same time, I didn't blame her. Or didn't I want to hold her responsible? I waited for her explanations, her excuses, but she didn't make any. When we had eaten supper, she went out.

I again checked the newspaper and was relieved to find they hadn't printed my name. I was simply referred to as the complainant. What a way to get into the papers, as a victim. A victim of my own sister's folly. A victim of Sylvia's revenge. Another victim of being native. No matter how hard I tried, I would always be forced into the silly petty things that concerned native life. All because Cheryl insisted in going out of her way to screw up her own life. And thus, screwing up mine.

For some reason, I didn't feel the urgent need for the ritual bath that night. I turned on the television to get my mind off Cheryl. It didn't help much. I kept thinking of the look she had given me that afternoon. The look I had so coldly turned away from. As if I had judged her guilty. Still, she was my sister, my flesh and blood, and when she returned, I would tell her everything was okay. It really wouldn't be okay, but I decided I would try my best to forgive and forget. The late show came on, and Cheryl still hadn't come home. I fell asleep and woke up about three-thirty. The movie was over, and there was still no sign that Cheryl had returned. I went up to her room to make sure. Afterward, I went to bed disappointed and worried.

The next morning I went to the trial alone. The Crown attorney made his summation to the jury. He went over all the testimony of the witnesses, emphasizing that the element of corroboration and legal principle had been met by both my testimony and that of Stephen Gurnan. Then he pointed me out and said, "Ladies and gentlemen of the jury, look at the poor victim, the victim of this deplorable crime. How she has suffered, not only from the physical and mental anguish, but also the emotional pain of the whole onslaught. Whether she was a prostitute or not, and I stress to you that she is not and never has been, is not the question at hand. The fact is, ladies and gentlemen of the jury, that she suffered at the hands of Oliver Donnelly. She will never forget the torment of that winter night. Remember how she gave her account of what happened that night of January 11, 1972? Trembling, but honest. Not once did she change any of her testimony. Not once did she waver between truth and fiction. Ladies and gentlemen of the jury, there is one thing we can do on behalf of the girl, April Raintree. That is to find this man, the defendant, Oliver Donnelly, guilty of rape. To give her justice."

I had to squirm under everyone's scrutiny. I objected to being pointed out like that, and being called that "poor girl." It sounded overly dramatic. It sounded like he wanted them to say the defendant was guilty on the grounds that I was such a pitiful creature. I wanted him found guilty because of what he had done. I was glad when he concluded his summation. I took the opportunity to look behind me to see if Cheryl had come. All I saw were strange faces, staring at me.

184

Next, Mr. Schneider, the defence counsel, went to work on the jury to try and convince them that his client was innocent. He emphasized that Donnelly had been drinking heavily, that Donnelly honestly believed that the girl was a prostitute, but more importantly, had consented by her own silence to have sexual intercourse. The accused further believed that the objections by the complainant were made only because she had not received compensation for her services. I sat there thinking of only one thing. That man, the accused, that bastard, Donnelly, had raped me. He had done more than rape me. He deserved to be found guilty and nothing else. By the end of the defence counsel's speech, I began to worry that there was a possibility that the jurists would find him innocent. The judge called a lunch recess.

I walked down the corridor, then the stairs, wondering why Cheryl hadn't come and feeling lonely for her company. I also wondered if Donnelly was going to get off, scott-free. But then how could he get off when Gurnan had already pleaded guilty to one charge? Wouldn't that be ironic?

I was on my way out the front doors when I heard Roger's voice.

"April, what are you doing here?"

I looked at him, dismayed. I thought of lying, but I couldn't think of any good lies. "I'm attending a trial."

"Oh? What trial? You didn't tell me about it"

"It's *The Queen v. Donnelly*. It's a rape trial. I'm a witness. Or is complainant the proper word?" I said, looking straight at him.

Roger looked at me for a minute, a long minute. "You should have told me about it. I'm sorry. It must be rough on you. How is it going?"

"It's almost over, I think. I don't know how it's going to end. What are you doing here?"

"Oh, I had a few things to do, and I was going to do some searches at Land Titles for Alex. But it can wait. How about I take you for lunch right now? Is Cheryl here?" he asked, looking around.

"No. She didn't come today. She was with me Tuesday and yesterday," I answered, not mentioning her involvement.

We had lunch, and afterwards, he said that he'd come back to the courtroom, later in the afternoon, when he had finished his work. I talked with Mr. Scott in the hall, and he took time to explain what was going to be happening next. He also assured me that things looked good.

I felt slightly better when I took my seat back in the courtroom. The Honourable Mr. Justice Saul gave his charge to the jury, summarizing once again the evidence given, explaining the law pertaining to the charges. It strained my patience to have to listen to him. I began thinking of what I should tell Roger. No doubt, if he hadn't read last evening's paper, he would read about the trial now. So far I had been able to talk to him on just about anything. He had listened and given me good advice, on occasion, and all in all, he had been comforting. It was almost three-thirty when the jury filed out of the courtroom to consider its verdict.

The courtroom emptied, and I walked out into the corridor, hoping to find Roger. He was coming towards me from the other end of the hallway. We waited together, not saying anything about the trial. He asked me again about Cheryl.

"I'd rather not talk about Cheryl right now, Roger. I just hope she's fine, but I'm worried because she didn't come home last night. But I'll tell you about it later. Right now, I'm just waiting to see what the jury decides."

It was a little over an hour later when we were summoned back to the courtroom. I was impatient because it took everyone such a long time to get back in their places, especially the judge. I sat there, scarcely breathing, waiting for that one word: Guilty. The jury filed back into the courtroom, and there was more legal footwork as I waited for that word. I looked at a distant point in front of me, not daring to look at the faces of the members of the jury. I heard the Foreman of the jury respond affirmatively to the question of whether they had reached a verdict. And then I heard it: "We find the defendant guilty as charged." I sighed with relief. Justice, to a certain point, had been done.

Chapter Fifteen

Before Roger and I returned to my place, we went out for supper. When we did get home, I looked for signs of Cheryl, but it appeared she hadn't bothered eating or anything, if she had been home. Cheryl usually piled her coffee cups and dishes in the sink, and there were none. I made coffee, knowing Roger was waiting for me to talk. As we were drinking coffee, I did.

"Well, you found out what my big secret was. Do you understand why I felt the way I did?"

"Of course. I don't know why you didn't say something, though."

"Rape isn't something you talk about, Roger. I never even discussed it with Cheryl. Cheryl... she blamed herself, you know. She blamed herself because she was in the hospital and I came to Winnipeg to be with her. It was when I was going to her place that I was raped. That was why she had blamed herself. And then in court, we both found out that those men were after her. It wasn't just my bad luck. She caused them to be there at that time. She apparently had angered some woman, and that woman wanted her to pay for it. And instead, I paid for it."

"How do you feel about Cheryl?"

"I don't know. They said she was a prostitute. I can't resolve how I feel about her. I just don't know. One minute, I want to hug her and tell her it doesn't matter. And the next, I just want to give her hell. I feel like her babysitter. As soon as I leave her alone, she goes out and does all these incredibly stupid things. And I always thought she had it all together, more so than me. What is the matter with her?"

"Maybe you feel that way about her because what you went through is a very traumatic experience."

"You're right. It's not as if she made me lose all my money. Funny, that doesn't even seem so important any more. Once, all I wanted was money, lots of it. And now, what I did lose was much more precious than money. I'll never be the same as I once was. You know, when I was married, I didn't want children because I thought they might turn out looking a little native. Lately, now that I can't have children, I would really like to be able to. Settle down and raise a dozen kids."

"Why can't you have any children?"

I looked at him. Couldn't he figure that out?

"Because I was raped. I'd be scared to... to ever let a man get close to me."

"And how long are you going to feel that way, April?"

"I don't know. I suppose I'll always feel that way."

"Do you like feeling sorry for yourself?"

"I don't feel sorry for myself," I said, indignantly. "I just know how I feel inside. I feel dirty and rotten and used. I'll never be what I was before. I'll never be the same. Can't you understand that?"

"From what I understand, you're keeping what you feel inside of you alive. You're not even trying to let go. Now that the trial is over, let it go, April. Let time do its healing. The big tragedy now is not that you've been raped. It's that you refuse to let yourself heal."

"You men! You haven't a clue as to what rape does to a woman. It kills something inside. That's what it does."

I was angry with Roger. Perhaps what he was saying had some truth in it, but I felt he was being very insensitive to my feelings on that day.

In my anger, perhaps because of the emotional roller coaster I'd been on, I ordered him to get out of my house. I wanted someone to comfort me, not make me feel that I was wrong in my reaction.

"I'm sorry, April. Maybe I shouldn't have said what I did, but I really believe you're going to have to let go of your hatred and resentment sooner or later. I'll call you tomorrow."

My anger continued to burn after he left. Who was he to tell me my reactions were wrong? What did he know about rape? I stormed into the bathroom and began to run the water for my ritual bath. Then I realized Roger would think I was just wallowing in my self-pity, so I shut off the tap and stormed back into the kitchen and poured myself another cup of coffee. It was cold, and I slammed the cup back down on the table and sat there, staring at nothing in particular. What could any man ever understand about rape? They just had no comprehension!

But as I sat there, I began to think about what he had said. It was true that I had come to look forward to those ritual baths. I enjoyed killing them over and over again in my mind. But, really, who was I hurting by it? I had wanted Roger to comfort me, but maybe what I really wanted was his sympathy, maybe even pity. It was something he hadn't given me, and I resented it. How was I supposed to just "let go," as he said? It simply wasn't possible.

When I finally tired of waiting for Cheryl, I went to bed, my mind still in a muddle about my feelings. I was still full of hatred, but I was also beginning to realize that probably Roger was right and I should try and let go. The same feelings were with me when I awoke the next morning. I spent the day wandering aimlessly around the house, trying to read a book or watch television. I was making supper when Cheryl walked in.

"Cheryl, where have you been?"

"That's none of your bloody business."

I was taken aback by the bluntness of her answer.

"Sorry. I was just worried. There's no need to snap at me."

"Oh? You think things should return to normal, do you? Well, good luck! I've got to go up and change." With that she quickly went upstairs, not giving me a chance to say more.

I walked back to the kitchen. Then I went back to the foot of the stairs and called up, "Hey, Cheryl, supper's almost ready. Are you going to come down soon?"

"I'm not hungry," she called back.

While I was washing the dishes, I heard Cheryl coming down the stairs. I was glad. Maybe we could talk. But she called, "I'm going out. See you later."

"Cheryl, wait... "

But the front door slammed. It was no use. I could just see myself scurrying down the street, pleading for her to come back so we could talk.

Roger called a little later and asked if I wanted to go out to a movie or something. I agreed, thinking it would take my mind off Cheryl.

I didn't go to court the day Donnelly was sentenced, but I learned on the news that he had been sentenced to five years at Stony Mountain. I wondered if those five years—he'd probably be out on parole after three—would leave as deep a mark on his life as he had left on mine?

In the following weeks, Cheryl absolutely refused to talk to me unless it was in little biting sentences. At first I was patient, but then I started losing my patience with her and my sympathy. Sometimes I'd come home from a date with Roger and she'd go upstairs, leaving me in mid-sentence. Sometimes she'd come home, drunk. That really upset me. Then she'd say all kinds of nasty things about me that weren't true or were only half-true. Those things would hurt me the most, and once she saw the hurt in my eyes, she'd seem satisfied and would leave me alone.

One Saturday afternoon, she came in the front door. She looked in pretty rough shape, her hair was dishevelled and her eyes were reddish, dopey looking. She immediately went upstairs as I expected. But a few minutes later, she came down, carrying one of her whiskey bottles.

"Thought I'd keep you company today. I haven't seen my big sister in such a long time. I'll watch you clean up the place. It's like an Indian having a white maid. Well, go ahead, don't let me stop you. I'll just go and get me a glass. I can drink this stuff straight, you know. Want to see?" She took a swig from the bottle, then smacked her lips.

"Well, I'm sorry to disappoint you Cheryl, but I've already done the cleaning. And while you're getting a glass, get me one, too, will you? There's Coke in the fridge. I'm not up to drinking it straight."

Cheryl looked at me suspiciously. "Oh, I get it, if you can't beat 'em, join 'em, eh? And what is poor, sweet Roger going to think?"

"Doesn't matter. Once I told you that we were going to make it. Well, if you're not going to try, then why should I?"

"Oh, no. Don't lay that crap on me, big sister. You turned your back on me a long time ago. You think I don't know why you married Bob? It was to get away from me, that's why. I'll bet you wished you were an only child. I bet you wished I was dead." 192

"You know that's not true!"

"And now you're back here, right in there, with another white man. Half-breeds aren't good enough for you. You're a bigot against your own people. You want to know something else, April? I'm ashamed of you. Yeah, ashamed. You're not my sister. You're my keeper, buying this house, paying for my keep. That's all you are, just my keeper. You're disgusting. And you have the nerve to look down on me?"

"I've never looked down on you, Cheryl. Never. Just on what you do. What you're doing to yourself. I don't understand why."

"Don't give me that bull. You heard what they said in court, and I saw what you felt when you avoided looking me in the eye. You think you're better than me. You've always thought you were better than me. And you'll never understand me. You'll never understand me." Cheryl repeated the last line more to herself than to me. Then in a louder, more aggressive tone, she said, "You know, April, you sure have lied to me a lot. You tell me one thing when you know it's a bloody lie. It's pretty bad in this stinking world when you can't even trust your own sister."

Cheryl never did pour me a drink. She went back upstairs, I assumed, to sleep it off. I felt as if I had been in a physical fight with her. I was breathing hard. I lit up a cigarette. It was unreasonable of Cheryl to accuse me of all she accused me. She wasn't faultless. So why, why, why, did she tear into me all the time? I thought of Alcoholics Anonymous. Cheryl would never go there, not in a hundred years. Cheryl was an out-and-out drunkard. In the previous several months, I hadn't seen her sober, because when she was sober, she avoided me like I was the plague.

In December, Roger invited me to go to Killarney with him to meet his parents. They lived on a farm, and Roger went out to visit them as often as he could. I felt I couldn't leave Cheryl alone, and Roger said I was to invite her, too. I knew Cheryl wouldn't go, and in the end, Roger decided he would remain in the city for Christmas and spend it with me. I protested, of course, but he remained firm in his decision.

We waited most of Christmas Day for Cheryl to return so we could open our presents together. Cheryl didn't come. I was embarrassed. Roger had forsaken Christmas with his family to be with Cheryl and me. I had forsaken a Christmas with his family for Cheryl. And Cheryl didn't even do us the honour of staying home.

We spent New Year's with his parents. I also met his brother, Joe, who wasn't Indian at all. When we were by ourselves, I said, "You lied to me, Roger Maddison. You said your brother Joe was an Ojibway."

"Well, I figured that would help you open up a little," Roger grinned. "I thought it would make you feel like we had something in common. Actually, the guy I was talking about was a good friend in school. Heck, for that matter, I was going to tell you I had a sister who had been raped. So I could say I did understand how you felt, even though I was a man."

"Were you really? You don't have any scruples, do you? And here I was going to ask if Cheryl could meet Joe and you know, maybe get together," I squeezed his arm and shook it, pretending anger. It was the first time I had voluntarily touched him...

It was almost a full year after the rape. Roger had succeeded in making me feel good about myself again. I'd have moments when I'd remember but they weren't all-consuming. It would take a long time before I would heal completely. But Roger was right. Time was the best medicine.

Still, I couldn't get through to Cheryl. There was no communication between us. I had resumed my part-time job, but one day at the end of February, I didn't have anywhere to go. I sat around for most of the day, bored.

194

Late in the afternoon, I decided to do some baking. It was already dark by the time I put the muffins in the oven. That's when Cheryl came home. I heard her as she came down the hall and into the kitchen. She still had her jacket on, but she took it off and placed it over the seat behind her.

"Aren't we domestic today," she said in sneering voice. "Practicing up, are you?"

"No, I just thought it would be nice to have some home baking. It's a little early, but do you want supper?"

"If I wanted something to eat, I'd fix it myself. After all, I do live here, don't I?" Cheryl said.

"Well, excuse me, I was just offering."

Cheryl got up and went upstairs. I figured tonight if she wanted to grind away at me, I was going to give her some of her own medicine. Sure enough, a few minutes later, she came downstairs again with a full bottle of whiskey. She set it on the counter, got herself a glass, poured some Coke in after the whiskey. It was about half and half.

I watched her do all this and then I said, "Is this private property or can I have some, too?"

"Go ahead, help yourself. Don't expect me to serve you." She went back to sit at the dining room table.

I decided to join her with my drink.

"So, are the three of us going to have a nice cozy little chat?" Cheryl asked, looking at me. Her eyes were glassy, and she had to focus to look straight at me.

"What do you mean, the three of us?" I said, looking at her stomach area, avoiding her eyes.

Cheryl laughed and said, "You, me, and my good friend there," she said pointing back at the bottle of whiskey. "He's going to keep us company. Yes, sir, the family that drinks together, stays together," Cheryl laughed again.

"Well, do take off your boots and stay awhile," I said, sarcastically. I had washed and waxed the floor the day before, and I noticed then that Cheryl had tracked watery marks on it. Cheryl ignored me and took a long sip of her drink.

"Cheryl, I wish you'd tell me what's been bugging you these past months. Ever since that day in court you've been treating me as if I'd done something wrong."

Cheryl looked at me but didn't say anything.

"I wish we could get everything out in the open. I wish there were no secrets between us. I want to help you, Cheryl, that's all I want to do. Put that away for tonight. Go to bed and tomorrow we can have a really frank discussion, okay?"

"Quit it, April. All you ever do is nag at me. Nag, nag, nag. Is that how you drove Bob away? And how long is this new one going to last, eh? How long is Roger going to last before you try to run his life? Ex-Mrs. Radcliff. Socialite of the East. Big shot. You're such a phony. Couldn't manage her own life, but she wants to manage mine." Cheryl finished her drink and got up to pour herself another one. She brought the bottle with her and set it down beside her glass.

I sighed and said, "Cheryl, don't."

Cheryl cut me off and mimicked my plea, "Cheryl, don't, Cheryl, don't. Don't do this, don't do that. You're only hurting yourself, poor, dear Cheryl. Well, I know damn well what I'm hurting. Because of me you don't bring any of your white friends here, do you? And with Roger, you had to explain all about your poor, drunken sister, didn't you? So he would understand about me. And pity me. Same way you pity me. Well, I don't need your goddamned pity."

I studied Cheryl. This was far worse than it had ever been before. I didn't know what to do. Should I try to appease her or provoke her into talking to me about what was making her say these things?

"You're ashamed of me," she continued. "You're ashamed of what I do. If you were ever proud of me, you'd be proud to be a half-breed. Proud, I tell you." Cheryl glared at me, daring me to say differently. She was swaying from side to side as she again refilled her glass. 196

I said in a quiet voice, "Go look in the mirror and tell me what I've got to be proud of."

"Oh, so the truth comes out. As long as I act like a proper whitey, I'm something, eh? But a few drinks and I'm a stinking, drunken Indian."

"You're doing all this to hurt me, right? Why? Do you hate me, Cheryl?"

"Hate you? No, I don't hate you. I hate a lot of things about you. You're a snob. You have double standards. You were so shocked when they said I was a hooker. Well, look at you. How did you buy this house, April? How did you buy that car out there? How, April? You prostituted yourself when you took Bob's money, that's how. You never loved that man. You loved his money. You figured you were going to be Miss High Society. But you figured wrong. But you still came out of it with your pay. A nice big fat roll for a high-class call girl. Yeah, your kind makes me sick. Big white snobs who think they're the superior race. Your white governments, your white churches, sitting back in idle, rich comfort, preaching what ought to be, but making sure it isn't. Well, Miss Know-It-All, I know something you don't. And you won't feel so goddamned superior once I tell you what I know."

Cheryl put her finger across her lips as if to warn herself to keep silent.

"Shh, I'm not supposed to tell her," she said to herself.

She smiled a silly, secretive smile, then frowned to herself, questioningly. It looked as if she were wondering why she had to keep this secret.

I was waiting, hoping she would continue. I felt that what she was on the verge of saying would help solve the mystery of what had made her give up on everything. I felt it wasn't just that she blamed herself for the rape. Something had happened before that. She had started drinking before that. 197 Maybe it was something I had done. Whatever it was, I wanted to know. To goad her into more angry outbursts, I said in a cold voice, "Cheryl, you've had enough. Come on, I'll help you to bed."

I got up and put my hands on her arm to help her.

Cheryl shook them off, viciously. "You take your bloody hands off me. I'm gonna have another drink and no one's gonna stop me. Especially not a superior white bitch. I can take care of myself. I don't need anyone. Not anyone."

I recoiled at her loud outburst and sat down again. I watched the liquid in Cheryl's glass go down once again. The bottle beside her was half-empty.

"I don't need anyone," Cheryl repeated to herself. Then she looked at me and said, maliciously, "Especially not you. I couldn't give a shit about your fancy ways. You're just a social climber who didn't make it."

Cheryl was slurring her words badly, and when she saw that I winced every time she used a vulgar word, I could see that she was delighted.

"So, April Raintree, you think you got all the answers, eh? But you can't tell me a goddamned thing, can you? Because in reality, you know fuck all. I'm the one who knows what life is really all about. Me. That's who. I got the answers. I found the answers all by myself. You lied to me and I lied to you. I did find our precious dear ol' Dad. He's a gutter-creature, April. A gutter-creature! All the tricks I turned, well, that helped him, you know? That kept him in booze. Not only that, I joined him, too. Ah, but that's not all. The best part is still to come."

She smiled a lopsided smile, as if she had lost control of her facial muscles.

"Mother, you know what happened to our poor, dear Mother? She jumped off the Louise Bridge, is what she did. Committed suicide. You know why she stopped seeing us? Because she couldn't bear the pain. Yup, she committed suicide. They were bums, you know. Both of them. Bums. Boozers. Gutter-creatures. Dad took all that money from me. He didn't know where it came from. He didn't care where it came from. Mark DeSoto. Jack of all trades. Drug pusher, bootlegger, stealing, breaking and entering, pimping; if it was illegal, he was in it. And guess who was right there in it with him? Your little sister, Cheryl Raintree. Your baby sister. Pardon me. There was another one after me. Baby Anna. Did you know about her? Well, she died when she was still a baby. She was the luckiest one of us."

Cheryl leaned her head on her arms which were crossed in front of her on the table. She was weeping to herself, repeating the last sentence, "She was the luckiest one."

I was shocked by her revelations. I didn't believe them. Cheryl was only trying to shock me. Except, she wasn't watching me for the desired effect. She wasn't lying. I stood up, taking the bottle with me to the kitchen sink. I was going to make coffee for us. Then I was going to see Cheryl to her bed. Tomorrow we were going to talk together. Now that I knew the reason behind her actions, I knew I could do something about it. I was also relieved that it wasn't because of me that Cheryl had given up. Absent-mindedly, I began pouring the liquid from the whiskey bottle down the sink.

"WHAT THE HELL DO YOU THINK YOU'RE DOING?" Cheryl screamed at the top of her lungs. She startled me so much that I dropped the bottle into the sink as I jumped. For all of Cheryl's drunkenness, she moved as swiftly as a mother cat coming to the rescue of her endangered kittens.

"Give me that, that's mine, you bitch!"

I had a hold of the bottle again, and Cheryl lunged for it. We both struggled for control of it. I guess all Cheryl could see was that her precious liquid was seeping down the drain. All I wanted was for her to quit drinking for the night. When the last drop was gone, I let go of the bottle. I started turning towards Cheryl. She was enraged. She glared at me furiously, and before I could speak to her, she brought her hand up and struck me as hard as she could across the face. I was already off-balance, and the blow sent me reeling backward across the kitchen. I hit the refrigerator hard with my back and shoulders. I put my hand to my head where Cheryl had struck me and looked at her unbelievingly.

199

Cheryl, momentarily horrified by what she had just done to me, seemed to come out of her drunken stupor.

"Well, you shouldn't have done that." Then she grabbed her jacket and I heard her go down the hall. The front door slammed.

200

Chapter Sixteen

I shook my head to clear it. This was all too much. I returned to the sink and put the empty bottle into the garbage container. My mind started activating again and I realized I should have gone after Cheryl. I went to get my jacket and boots and then I had to look for the house keys. They weren't in my purse and I couldn't remember where I had put them. It was stupid to think of such things but my mind was still in a muddle. The closest bus stop was at Watt Street so I walked in that direction. I reached the bus stop but there was no sign of Cheryl. I went back towards Henderson. I was sure that if Cheryl had intended to take a bus, she would have gotten one by now. Just in case, I waited at the bus stop for the next Downtown bus and got on. I tried looking out both sides of the window, but with it being dark outside and lighted inside, plus the condensation on the windows, I couldn't see the sidewalks very well. I got off in front of City Hall and decided to walk back home, over the Disraeli Bridge and all.

That meant the Main Street strip. I walked on the west side because there were more people on that side. If Cheryl were among these people, I could spot her. But I walked all the way home without running into her.

I couldn't sleep at all that night. The wind had picked up outside, and I was sure there was a blizzard going on out there. Mixed in were the noises of the house, all those creakings one doesn't notice during the day. I listened to them, deciphering what made them, and several times, I thought Cheryl had returned. I got up more than once and went upstairs to check her room. The next morning, I got up, tired. I thought perhaps I had made too big a deal the night before when I worried about never seeing Cheryl again. Nonetheless,

I called where she worked and found out that she had quit a few months back. I called the Friendship Centre, but the person who answered didn't know Cheryl. I made coffee. I spent most of the day waiting and worrying. When my employer from the agency called asking if I wanted to start a job Monday, I said no, that I'd be taking some time off again.

At four-thirty, Roger phoned to say he was going to pick me up in an hour. We were supposed to go out for supper, but I had forgotten.

"Oh, Roger, I can't go. Cheryl left last night. I don't know where she is. She's not going to come back."

"Well, April, Cheryl has been away overnight before. Why are you so worried?"

"We quarrelled. She was drinking heavily. She told me everything, Roger, all the things that have been bothering her. I have to find her."

"Okay. We'll have supper, and then we'll go and look for her, all right?"

"You don't have to come with me. I don't even know where to begin."

"I'll come with you. Don't worry, April, we'll find her."

While I waited for Roger, I decided we could go down to the Friendship Centre and talk to anyone who might know where Cheryl would be. I tried to remember places Cheryl had mentioned in the past. Was it Carlos or was that the name of a beer? I got my coat and boots on and waited for Roger. I went back to the kitchen and looked in the phone book. There was a place called DeCarlos. That was it. I noted the address. Since it was a Friday night, I thought we might even find Nancy. I cursed myself for not taking more interest in Cheryl's friends. I didn't even know Nancy's last name.

After we had a quick supper, we went to the Centre. A few people said they knew Cheryl but that they hadn't seen her for the past couple of months. From there we drove down Main Street over to DeCarlos, which was on Carlton. There was a lineup of people waiting to get in, different types of people, and it reminded me of the Hungry Eye. My crowd once. When Roger and I got in, we looked over the crowd.

202

Already there was a smoky haze hanging over everyone's heads. Music was blasting from the amplifiers. The way we were dressed, Roger and I were obviously out of place. We ordered a drink but were barely able to talk because of the noise. I looked for Cheryl or Nancy. I even felt I'd be able to tell who Mark was if I saw him. I wondered if this was where they all still hung out. On the other side of the room, there was a girl who reminded me of Sylvia Gurnan. I couldn't see clearly because of the dimly-lit, smoky atmosphere. People kept passing between us, and sometimes, I was sure it was Sylvia, and then I wasn't sure. I studied the other people at her table. They were all white. Mark, as far as I knew, was Métis. When the band took a break, Roger asked me if I recognized any of Cheryl's friends. I said I didn't, and we might as well leave.

203

We drove around for a while, up and down the downtown streets, as we searched the faces for Cheryl's. We were unsuccessful. We returned to my place, and I went upstairs to see if she had returned, but she hadn't. We took our coffee into the living room, and I turned the television set on.

"You know, Roger, I'm to blame. No, I'm not going into a self-blaming thing. It's just that I wanted her to have all these good memories of our parents. I always told her only the good things that happened when we lived with them. I knew that they had drinking problems. That's why we were taken away. I should have told her when I gave her those names. I should have told her then that our parents were alcoholics. But I didn't. I just gave her the stuff and hoped that her search would come to an end. And she went out and found our father and found that he was an old drunk. I'm sure she never told me all of the things she discovered because she felt she had to protect me from the truth. She carried that around with her all alone, not wanting to share her problems. And I knew about it! Well, not the part about our mother committing suicide. So many lies to protect. And in the end, they destroy anyway. I just can't understand why all that would have such an adverse effect on her. Unless... "

"Unless what?"

"Well, maybe she just used these things as an excuse to start drinking. Maybe she was an alcoholic all along and she just needed some real good reason to start into it. Do you think that's possible?"

"I guess anything is possible, but Cheryl doesn't sound like the type of person who would use that as an excuse. The reasons for drinking can be very complicated."

"Sometimes, I think if we really were white, we wouldn't have all these complications in our lives. I'd just be a wife, maybe a working mother, just an ordinary person. You know what I mean? There probably wouldn't be any problem with alcoholism. Our lives would be so different. But as it is, I lie to protect her and she lies to protect me, and we both lose out. I don't know. If I was more like her or she was more like me, maybe we wouldn't have pulled apart."

204

"Maybe that's what's been wrong. You've both pulled in different directions. Cheryl has identified with the Indian people and all the wrongs that have been done to them. And you, having identified with the white people, well, she's taken everything she's felt out on you. Earlier when you told me the things she used to say when she was drunk, well, she wouldn't believe them herself when she was sober. Being drunk gives one false courage."

"Cheryl never needed false courage. She was always spunky enough. She had courage."

"I think, from what you've told me, Cheryl saw you in a superior white role. You supplied her with all her needs. You stayed in Winnipeg to help her, to be by her side. You've stressed that she can depend on you, right?"

"Well, I am her big sister."

"Maybe you could have told her that you needed help from her. Or at least, not have made it so clear that you were in charge. People need to feel that they are needed and worthwhile. I'd say Cheryl has a very low self-image right now. Drinking helps wipe out that image. And she can't let herself become sober because it hurts when she's sober. So she drinks again."

"I kind of figured something like that. I wanted her to go to bed and sleep off the alcohol. I wanted for us to really talk when she was completely sober."

The weeks passed and Roger and I continued to look for Cheryl. She had never come back to the house. Every day when I'd get home, I'd look in her room, and everything was always just as it had been that first night. We returned to DeCarlos regularly but always without any luck. Sometimes, we'd drive around and I'd spot someone who I was sure was Cheryl. I'd get Roger to park the car, and I would jump out and go after that person. But when the woman would turn to me, my excitement would turn to disappointment, because it was never Cheryl.

The month of April brought erratic temperatures. Some days were warm enough to tempt impatient women into their shorts. The nights brought back the cold temperatures, though, sometimes even below freezing. April 18, 1973 was a cold rainy day. My birthday. I stayed home, hoping Cheryl would remember and come home. But she didn't. Roger and I celebrated alone.

Ten days later, it was the same kind of dismal day. The winds started early in the afternoon, first in short bursts as if gathering momentum for the gales that would follow. It had drizzled off and on for the previous several days. Since it was a Saturday, Roger and I had been out combing the city, more specifically, the hotels. We'd even gone to all the hotels along Main Street. The rain began to fall more and more heavily as the day wore on, and the wind had also picked up. Late in the afternoon, we decided to call it quits after I had rushed out into the rain, thinking a stranger had been Cheryl.

When we got to my place, I was still soaked to the bone. I felt so discouraged. While I changed, Roger made us coffee. Then we sat silently in the living room, just listening to the steady pelting of the rain against the windows. I wondered what Roger was thinking. Maybe he thought I wasn't worth all the trouble and aggravation. Maybe he wanted to call it quits with me but not at this time, because of Cheryl. I sighed.

"What's the matter?" he asked.

"Oh nothing. Just wondering about all the trouble I've put you to."

"Well, it's not enough and won't be until we find Cheryl."

"You really and truly don't mind?"

"In spite of her current problems, I think Cheryl is quite a person, and she is your sister."

206

I lay my head on his lap, reassured. It felt so good to be near Roger. It seemed hard to believe I had held him away for so long. I would have been completely content, except for Cheryl.

Suddenly, the phone rang, exploding into the stillness of the house. I jumped. By the second ring, I got there and picked up the receiver.

"Hello?"

"Is this April?"

"Yes."

"I don't know if you remember me. It's Nancy. Cheryl has been staying with me."

Nancy's voice sounded shaky.

"I remember you. What about Cheryl? Is she okay?" I said anxiously, shooting out the questions.

"She just left here. I didn't want her to go. She seems okay but in a funny way. I wanted her to stay here. But she said she had to go. She said goodbye to me as if she wasn't going to see me again." Nancy sniffled.

"Do you know where she was going?"

"No. And I couldn't go after her because I've been sick the past couple of days and I'm not dressed. My Mom thinks she's going to do something terrible. My Mom's the one who told me to call you. Maybe you can do something. I'm so worried."

"Oh no."

I leaned against the wall, my voice was barely a whisper. Roger was at my side and then he took the receiver from me.

"What's going on," he asked Nancy. He listened to her for a few minutes and then asked for her address. Then he asked some questions about what Cheryl was wearing. When he hung up, he immediately called the police. He explained the situation and gave them Nancy's address and told them we'd meet them there.

It was still raining, but not as heavily, as we drove to the address on Henry Avenue. There were a number of look-alike, rundown shacks, and we found Nancy's house among them. Nancy opened the door before we could knock. 207

"Anything new?" Roger asked, immediately.

"No. I didn't know how to stop her. I just didn't know how to stop her," Nancy sobbed.

"It's all right, Nancy, don't worry. We called the police and I'm sure everything is going to be okay. Thank you for calling me." What I really wanted to say to her was that she should have called me a lot earlier. But she looked so sorrowful.

"Let's drive around and see if we can spot her," Roger suggested.

We had pulled away when Roger noticed a police car arrive and stop in front of Nancy's house. He braked and put the car in reverse. We both got out and walked back to the car. I was so hopeful they had found her. I looked in the back of the car for Cheryl, but there was no Cheryl. Roger exchanged some words with the officer, who then turned and asked me if I had even the vaguest idea where she might have gone.

"No, I don't. We've been looking for her and looking for her and all this time she was here. If only Nancy had called us before this. Now I just don't know where she could be."

. . . you know what happened to our poor, dear Mother? She jumped of the Louise Bridge, is what she did. Committed suicide. Cheryl's words flashed across my mind.

"She jumped off the Louise Bridge," I said out loud.

"What's that?" Roger asked.

"Our mother. Our mother killed herself by jumping off the Louise Bridge. Didn't I tell you that?"

"No, you just said that she did it, you didn't say... never mind, let's go over there."

208

Roger briefly explained the situation to the officer and he agreed to drive over to the bridge to check it out. Roger and I jumped in the car and followed the police cruiser. It was only a few minutes ride, but it seemed to take a lifetime.

"Why doesn't he put his flashers and siren on, for crying out loud?" I said impatiently as we stopped at a red light on Main Street. My eyes were still combing the sidewalks. Maybe she had stopped for a drink someplace. Maybe she had gone back home. Maybe her goodbye to Nancy meant she was going to move back home. Oh, I'd give her such a big hug if that's what she had done.

Finally, we reached the Louise Bridge. I could see some figures on the bridge waving towards the police car. Roger parked behind the cruiser. I jumped out into the rain, now coming down in torrents, and ran to where the police officer was talking to the two strangers on the bridge.

" ...not five minutes ago," one of them was saying, "she just stood up on the railing, I tell you, and jumped off. Ask Stan here. He was with me. We both saw it. We tried to stop it, officer. We slammed on the brakes, but we couldn't get there in time. Christ, one minute she was standing there, balancing, and the next, nothing. Why would she want to do a thing like that? Those Indians are always killing themselves. If they aren't shooting each other on the reserves, it's this. Holy jumpin' Jesus Christ. What a night this has been. And now this. I tell you it's unbelievable."

I was looking down at the waters, looking for the body. It was too dark to see anything, too murky. The man's word rang in my ears. "She was my sister, mister," I said. What did he know? Someday, maybe, I could explain to people like him why they did it. Roger had placed his arm around me. The man mumbled an apology, said he didn't know. I was crying. My tears were mixed with the rain, and they dropped down to where Cheryl was, in that murky water I had once loved to watch. Now I watched, hoping that Cheryl was somewhere down there, alive. But I knew there was no hope. Not for

209

Cheryl. Not anymore. I ached inside. I wanted to let loose with my tears. I felt like sobbing, screaming, wailing. But I just stood there, using the railing for support. Hiding the agony I felt. The agony of being too late, always too late.

After answering some questions for the police officer, Roger and I drove back to Nancy's house. When she opened the door, she saw right away from my expression that the worst had happened. She burst into tears. Her mother saw Nancy begin to cry and walked over and put her arms around her and hugged her. Then she came over to me, a complete stranger, and also gave me a comforting hug. Roger quickly and briefly explained what had happened.

While Nancy's mother busied herself making tea, she said, "Cheryl was like a daughter, you know? She was such a good person. She helped Nancy, you know."

"Yeah, whenever I needed help, she was there." Nancy started sobbing again, but between sobs she continued. "Sometimes, when we needed money, Cheryl would give it to us. She never made us feel like we owed her, you know? When I would get depressed, Cheryl would cheer me up, make me laugh."

"Cheryl would buy groceries," Nancy's mother said, "and she would always joke that they ate them all up anyways."

Nancy and her mother exchanged looks.

Then Nancy said, "I'm not the only one Cheryl helped. She did a lot for other girls, too. Especially at the Centre. She had these big plans, you know. And she used to organize lots of things at the Centre for young people. Then she quit. She changed real sudden, but I never knew why. Oh, she'd still help people, but she wouldn't go out of her way anymore. And then she met that creep, and he moved in with us, so I moved back home 'cause Dad left."

I appreciated them comforting me. I sat in silence because I could think of nothing to say to comfort them in return. We sat in silence for awhile before Nancy's mother said, "Well, enough for tonight. You're probably tired. You go home and get yourself some sleep."

"Thanks for coming back to tell us about Cheryl." Nancy came over to where I was standing and hugged me. Then she said, "Cheryl left some things for us to take care of. Like the

210

typewriter you sent for one of her birthdays. She didn't want Mark selling it on her. And the other is, well, you come back when you're feeling better. Tonight is not the right time. You will come back?"

It seemed very important to Nancy that I return so I promised I would.

When we were back in the car, I said to Roger, "Imagine that, they're so poor and yet they kept that typewriter for Cheryl all that time, when they could have sold it. And the way they talked about her, like they really did love her. They give out such a family feeling. Cheryl must have liked that a lot. No wonder she felt more at home with them than she did with me."

"I think you should come over to my place tonight, all right?"

"All right. I'd like that. Cheryl hasn't been home for a long time but somehow the house would feel much more empty tonight."

When I finally got to sleep, it was past midnight. I dreamt of Cheryl. I could hear her laughter, but I couldn't find her. I looked and looked, but all I could hear was Cheryl laughing. When I did find her, she was in some kind of quicksand. I put my arm out to reach her, to help her, but she wouldn't take my hand. She just kept laughing and sinking down, deeper and deeper. I begged her and begged her to take my hand, and I began crying uncontrollably. When I woke up, I was still crying, and Roger was hugging me. When I had quieted down, I lay my head on his chest, and listened to his heartbeat. A couple of times, the leftover sobs would shake my whole body, and Roger would hold me a little tighter. Gradually, I went back to sleep.

The next morning, the police called and asked if we could identify the body they had pulled out of the river. When we returned a few hours later, I was in more of a daze than I had been before. It was final. It had been Cheryl.

Roger did almost everything for me the next few days. I was mostly silent, pondering the why of Cheryl's death. Once in awhile, I would talk about Cheryl to Roger. Roger helped me with the funeral arrangements. Actually, he did almost everything. After some hesitation, I phoned the Steindalls. I had a long talk with Mrs. Steindall, telling her of Cheryl's death and explaining the absence of our visits. She was very understanding, very sympathetic. That same evening, the night before the funeral, they came to Roger's place to see me.

The funeral service was small and simple. Most of the people who came were Indian or Métis. They had heard about Cheryl's death through Nancy and her mother. They gave me an insight into Cheryl's past by the glowing remarks they made about her. Again, I wanted to cry for the waste of such a beautiful life. But I didn't. I remained outwardly emotionless. Nancy asked me again to come over to their place in the near future, and I promised I would.

When it was all over, and Cheryl was buried, I knew it was time to return to the house, alone. Roger seemed to understand my need and drove me back. He didn't come in with me. Before he left, he said, "Take as much time as you need, April. Then call me. I'll be waiting for you."

"Roger, thank you for everything. I love you."

Roger smiled, "I love you too, April." 212

Chapter
Seventeen

I walked into the house which now seemed so empty, so cold. I decided I would pack all of Cheryl's things away in a big trunk, even her clothes. That way I'd always have a part of her. And being able to touch her belongings would strengthen that feeling.

I opened the door to Cheryl's room and the first thing I noticed was that empty whiskey bottle. I hadn't really noticed it before when I had gone into her room. But there it stood on Cheryl's dresser, mocking me. Suddenly, I was filled with a deep hatred of what it had once contained. I grabbed it by the neck, raised it high, and brought it down and smashed it against the edge of the dresser. Again and again. I brought it down, until it was smashed into a million pieces. I was screaming, "I HATE YOU! I HATE YOU! I HATE YOU!"

My tears came flooding out, and I continued screaming, "I hate you for what you've done to my sister! I hate you for what you've done to my parents! I hate you for what you've done to my people!"

I threw myself on Cheryl's bed, letting all my pent-up tears pour out. I pounded my fists into the bed, allowing my emotions to tumble out. I felt a frenzied rage at how alcohol had torn our lives apart, had torn apart the lives of our people. I felt angry for having done so many wrong things at so many wrong times. And I felt self-pity because I would no longer have Cheryl with me.

"Oh, Cheryl, why did you have to go and kill yourself? All those people at the funeral, they loved you so much. Didn't that count? I loved you so much. Didn't that count? Didn't it matter to you? You had so much going for you. You didn't have to kill yourself, Cheryl! Why? Why?"

I writhed on the bed as if I was in physical pain. I was. At times I would become still, but not for long. Stronger emotions would come crashing down on me and I would toss and turn again, trying to exorcise the painful anguish from within. I pounded my fists into the bed, again and again, in frustration. "If only... " Those words repeated themselves over and over in my head. But it was too late. Cheryl's death was final.

When I had spent the last of my tears, I sat on the edge of the bed and surveyed the mess I had made in the room. The floor had scattered fragments of the whiskey bottle all over it. Cheryl's pillow was soaked with my tears. I looked again at the floor. If only I could smash the problem of alcoholism as easily as I had that bottle.

Temporarily void of all emotion, I systematically began to clean the room. I put the Kleenex tissues into the garbage container. I began picking up the larger pieces of glass. I grabbed one piece a little too savagely and it cut my hand. I looked at the blood oozing out in a thin red line. "Still after more blood, are you? Well, you cut down my sister, my parents, my people. But no more. I'll see to it. Somehow. Some way."

When I had finished cleaning Cheryl's room, I sat down again on Cheryl's bed. I wondered where to start packing, not wanting to start. Then I remembered all of Cheryl's papers, the journals she had kept. There were two boxes under her bed and I began going through them. The first was full of newspaper clippings, but I wanted her journals. They were in the other box.

I began looking through them. The last entry she had made was in January 1972. That was the month I had been raped. I looked for a 1970 journal. It was this one that I was most interested in because that was when I had first lost touch with Cheryl.

The entries for January indicated she had started the search for our parents. February had occasional references to her continued search. There was more in March.

214

I see more and more of what April sees, broken people with broken houses and broken furniture. The ones I see on Main Street, the ones who give us our public image, the ones I see puking all over public sidewalks, battling it out with each other, their blood smearing up city-owned property, women selling what's left of themselves for a cheap bottle of wine. No wonder April ran. She was horrified that this was her legacy. She disowned it, and now she's trapped in that life of glitter and tinsel, still going nowhere. Charitable organizations! What a load of crap. Surrounded by a lot of people, business-wise but empty. Just like the Main Street bums.

The more I see of these streets, the more I wonder if April isn't right. Just maybe. Better to live that empty life than live out on the streets. What if I do find our parents? Sometimes I can't help it, I feel like April does, I despise these people, these gutter-creatures. They are losers. But there is a reason why they are that way. Everything they once had has been taken from them. And the white bureaucracy has helped create the image of parasitic natives. But sometimes, I do wonder if these people don't accept defeat too easily, like a dog with his tail between his legs, on his back, his throat forever exposed.

Happy Birthday, April. What do you give the person who has everything? I can give peace of mind with a few lies.

May 1970 *Struck paydirt with a new address on Austin. The place is rented by a woman named Josie Pohequitas. I knock on the door and it is opened by this little, bent, old woman who is stoned out of her mind. But happy as hell. I have figured out now it's better to see these people at certain times of the day. You have to be late enough so they can start getting over last night's drunk, and early enough so they're not whacked out of it yet. I ask if she knows Henry or Alice Raintree.*

"Henri, Henri Raintree?" she says in a French-type accent.

"Yes, I'm his daughter and I've been looking for him," I say in a pleasant voice. What else can I say?

"Ah, yeah, mais oui, we're good friends, you know. Come in. Here, sit down, here. He comes to our place when the snows are gone. He goes north for winters. He is welcome here. He stays. Sometimes, we have big party. Sometimes, we have big

215

fight. Then he goes. But he always come back, Henri does. He will come back. You come back in couple of weeks. You will see. He will be here then."

I'm tickled a deeper shade of brown, you might say. I tell the toothless woman with her toothless smile that I will be back.

June 1970 I knock at this door again, having been here a few times with no luck and expecting none this time.

"Ah, Cheryl, it's you again. Come in, come in," her face lights up into a big grin, still toothless.

216

"Henri, Henri, come out here and see the surprise that is here for you. Hurry up, Henri," her voice is high-pitched and squeaky.

An old, grey-haired man comes walking out of the kitchen. He is trying to keep his balance, curiosity is piercing through his drunken haze. I assume that Josie has told him about me, but still, it's a few minutes before he realizes it's me.

My smile disappears but a smile slowly appears on that leathery, unshaven face.

"No, no, it can't be. Not my little daughter, Cheryl. My little baby. You're all grown up now."

He chuckles and staggers a little closer to me. He makes a visible effort to draw himself up, but he has drunk too much already and the feat is beyond him. His clothes are worn, dirty, and dishevelled. Tears of happiness and perhaps awakened guilt pour from his watery eyes.

The woman, Josie, is beaming with pride as if this "joyful" reunion were all her doing.

"It's like a miracle. It is like a miracle," she cackles over and over again, watching father and daughter facing each other. I am rooted to the very spot, absorbing the true picture of my father. I make no effort to move towards him. This goes unnoticed and the old man approaches me.

"I cannot believe that we are standing here, face to face, at long last. At long, long last," the decrepit, old man says.

I stand quietly, hiding the horror which is boiling inside of me. I hadn't known what to expect. But it wasn't this, this bent, wasted human form in front of me. My father! I am horrified and repulsed: by him; by the cackling, prune-faced woman; by the others who have crawled out of the kitchen to watch all this "happiness," all of them with stupid grins on their faces; by the surrounding decay; by the hopelessness. The cancer from the houses I've been to has spread into this house, too. To destroy.

All my dreams to rebuild the spirit of a once proud nation are destroyed in this instant. I study the pitiful creature in front of me. My father! A gutter-creature!

The imagination of my childhood has played a horrible, rotten trick on me. All these years, until this very moment, I envisioned him as a tall, straight, handsome man. In the olden days, he would have been a warrior if he had been all Indian. I had made something out of him that he wasn't, never was. Now I just want to turn and run away, pretend this isn't happening, that I had never laid eyes on him. Pretend I was an orphan. I should have listened to April.

Awkwardly he hugs me. I smell the foul stink of liquor on him. Hell, he probably sweats liquor out of his pores. I close my eyes so no one will see what's in them. I hold my breath against the gutter smell. Seems like ages before he releases me. When he does, he turns to the others and says, "Don't just stand there, bring her a drink. Now we have something to celebrate. I found my little girl after all these years. Tell me, Cheryl, where is your sister? Where is April? I missed you both so much. Ah, here we are."

He hands me a beer and wipes his tears and runny nose on the sleeve of his shirt. I don't answer. I just think, "April is far away from you and she'll never know what you are, you gutter-creature!"

Gratefully, I swallow some beer. Disgust, hatred, shame... yes, for the first time in my life, I feel shame. How do I describe the feeling? I swallow more beer.

I stay for the rest of the day in spite of my desire to flee. I stay because I want to know about Mom. But I want Dad sober when I ask him about Mom. Funny, I can still refer to him as Dad. I drink away the hours and pass the dizzy, nauseous sensations, laughing stupidly with them. Josie puts me to bed, just in time, on the battered couch in the living room.

Next morning. I wait patiently for Dad to get up. It is almost noon. He comes into the kitchen. He looked in rough shape last night but now he looks worse, with his weak, flabby arms showing because he's in a torn, greyish undershirt. His dark-coloured baggy pants are held up by suspenders that are frayed to the breaking point and all twisted. I get coffee for Dad. Josie is busy puttering around the kitchen. No one talks, the only noises come from Dad slurping his coffee.

218

Finally, I ask him, "Dad, could we talk?" Sounds like I'm shouting. I lower my voice. "I want to know about Mom. How is she? Do you see her?"

Dad makes a gesture as if he doesn't want to talk about her right now but I persist. "Please, Dad. Tell me about Mom. Where is she?"

Tears come to his eyes again. He says simply, "She died last July."

"Died? Mom died?" I ask, not believing. I then figure out that Mom was in poor health when we were kids and that's why she died. I wish I could have seen her. Poor, dear mother. Maybe that's why Dad turned to booze. He misses her so much he can't live without her. I can forgive that, retract all the bad thoughts about him.

But Dad speaks again. "I may as well tell you everything." He sighs and lapses into another long silence.

I try to make it shorter by telling him to continue. "Tell me what, Dad?"

"Your mother took her own life. She killed herself," he says at last. "She left a letter for me but I had gone up north early that year. I have a nephew in Dauphin. I stop in there sometimes. They sent the letter there. She jumped off the Louise Bridge last July. I took the letter to the RCMP and they checked with the Winnipeg police. They had found a body, and everything matched your Mama. She was not happy with her life. Once she lost you girls and Anna died, she knew she would never get you girls back again. Those visits were the hardest on her. So she stopped going. She tried to kill herself before, once a long time ago."

219   *I digest what he says... too hard on her? What about*
April and me? In those foster homes? Okay, only one was
real bad and April suffered most of that one. But I suffered
for April. And the other ones? Those people weren't our flesh
and blood. They weren't even our race. I remember now,
those promises you made us, promises we believed, all the
waiting for you to take us back home, all the loyalty we gave
you—all for nothing.

"Who's Anna?" I'm angry but I don't want to fight. I want
information.

Dad looks at me, surprised. "You don't know about Anna?
Oh, of course not, you were just a baby yourself when she died.
April must remember her. Maybe not. She was just little, too,
and Anna wasn't with us very long. She was your baby sister.
But she was a sick baby. They should have kept her in the
hospital longer, but, no, they sent her home too early and she
died. They blamed your Mama and me. That was their excuse
for taking you girls away from us. No, my girl, your Mama
was not a happy woman."

"Why didn't you come to see us when we were kids?" I ask
in a soft voice, afraid of an honest answer.

There is another long pause. "I went up north for a long
time. I was never here to visit you again," he says, as if that's
a good enough reason. "No, your Mama did not want you girls
to see the way she was. She was too ashamed. She couldn't face
you again. They shouldn't have taken you away from us. The
baby was just sick, that's all." Dad drifts off in silence again.

Dad asks me to come back and see him tomorrow. I say I
will. I do. Josie says Dad left that morning to see some friends
of his for a few days. Here I thought he would be patiently
waiting for me. Ha! What a joke!

I sat back on the bed with the journal clutched to me. This
was the second mention of Anna. I'd been thinking of Anna
after Cheryl had told me about her. Baby Anna. I remembered
that's what I had called her. Recollections of my mother
220   rocking a baby had come back, much clearer. I'd always had
vague pictures in mind, but I'd never realized the baby was

our own sister. Baby Anna. She'd been with us for just a fraction of our lives. But she was sick and had to go to the hospital. And now, here, in Cheryl's journal, were Dad's words saying the same thing. Baby Anna. Such a small part of our lives. Yet she had changed our lives the most.

This was exactly how Cheryl felt when she found Dad. After all that he told her, she still went back to see him the next day, she was still loyal to him. How was it she had the natural family instinct? I had instincts only for self-preservation, pushing anyone away from me who might hurt me. I was a loner. Only lately had I let Roger in. Then Nancy and her mother, hugging me that night, giving me all that they had felt for Cheryl. Before Roger, who else besides Cheryl had hugged me and meant it? Well, maybe Mrs. Dion. I remembered wishing many times that I could be as affectionate as Cheryl. That meeting with Dad, maybe it destroyed her self-image. Funny, though, since she had seen that side of native life before. I wondered what sort of image she had built up about our parents? Was it that image of long ago that had sustained her, given her hope?

February 18, 1971 So. A son is born to me. It should have been a very special day for him. A day when his aunt, his grandparents, and all his relatives rejoiced. Instead, it's just him and me. What's that joke I read? If he had known what was going to be in store for him, he would have cried a whole lot louder?

February 22, 1971 Having pondered over what to call you, my sweet child, I've decided on Henry Liberty Raintree. May you grow up to be all your grandfather is not.

March 10, 1971 Nance is babysitting and I'm free for a while. Feels great to be let out. Henry Lee's been so cranky lately. Hell, we've got to move out 'cause kids aren't allowed. Landlord's just a prejudiced bastard. I thought Henry Lee would change my life for the better but I can see I thought wrong. Must say I do feel good about this place. Don't think Nance will mind my coming home late. She'll understand.

221

April 8, 1971 Sure am glad Nancy's Mom is letting Henry Lee stay at her place. I'm not so tied down anymore. She sure gives him some good mothering. I don't think motherhood was meant for me. I'd rather be out partying than sitting at home changing dirty diapers.

June 1971 Nancy's Mom is keeping Henry Lee for me for good now. Do I feel guilty? Only when I'm sober. And I try very hard to see that doesn't happen. I give her money all the time, so I'm sure she doesn't mind. Wish I had a mother like that.

October 1971 Today, Dad says he doesn't know where he is going to stay because he can't pay his rent. I know what he wants so I give him forty bucks. His eyes bulge. Usually, I only give him ten or twenty.

At DeCarlos with Nance. The gang is all here, too. Already we got suckers to pay for our drinks. It's cheap coming here. I give my money to Dad so he can go get tanked, and I come here and get mine free. I have to laugh at dumb jokes, let these guys run their hands up my legs. They think they're going to get more later, but I can avoid that.

Mark DeSoto. Now if all these guys were like Mark... but they're not. Nance says Mark's ol' lady, Sylvia, is going to have it in for me if I hang around with Mark. He's over there at another table. He comes to say hello. I ignore him. He was supposed to call during the weekend and didn't. The suckers at my table are really playing up to me tonight. Got to go to the john.

I'm walking back to my table and I hear this shrill voice. "Hey, squaw, I don't share my man with no one. You hear me, bitch? Especially no squaw."

Sylvia comes into my path and stops. I stop. I look her in the eye. "If I'm a squaw, honey, what's Mark? He's as much an Indian as I am." I feel ridiculous and powerful at the same time. I know what I'm capable of. I give her my coldest stare. I know I've won this round. She can't match my gaze. The "blonde bombshell" jabs a finger into my shoulder, telling me what she's going to do to me. I twist around slightly and bring my fist into the side of her face, not real hard but hard enough

222

to back her off. The dumb broad trips over a chair and sprawls on the floor. Everyone laughs, hoping for a fight. I step over her and continue on my way.

"You're going to pay for this, Cheryl Raintree."

"Yeah? Well you better give it your best shot, Sylvia."

Mark struts over to my table. My precious companions scatter. He sits down and grins. "So you're my prize," I say to him, sarcastically. But the evening ends with Mark in my bed.

Mark moves in. Nance moves out. Landlord requests that we remove ourselves after the first party. I find a cheap place on Elgin.

November 1971 I'm working. Mark is working the streets. We're always broke. I sell all the furniture, except the typewriter. I wonder why April gave it to me? She's the one with the writing talent. I give it to Nance for safekeeping so Mark won't sell it.

We're stone broke. Mark owes everyone so we can't hit anyone up for a loan. Mark says to me, "You know that guy who comes to Neptune's and he always looks the chicks over. Well he's loaded and sometimes I sit and talk to him."

"I know who you mean. What about him? You're going to borrow some money from him?"

"He never lends money. But sometimes he sees a chick he likes and asks me if I can arrange a meeting. So, I go to her, and if she's interested, we share the money he pays, see?"

"You mean you're some kind of pimp?"

"Not a pimp, Cheryl. I just do two people a favour and I get some money out of it. We need money now, bad, and I know he's got the hots for you. I just thought you might consider it, just this once."

"You're asking me to go to bed with another man?"

"Well, it's not like there's any feelings between you. Just think of it as a business transaction. I told him you were a very special girl, and he's willing to pay more for you. Come on, Cheryl, one hour's work and you could make fifty bucks. I'll try to get more."

"Forget it." I'm bloody mad. "I'm no fucking prostitute." I storm out of the house.

223

*A week later. We're still broke. I'm drinking at Neptune's.
I'm almost drunk. Mark comes over. This sucker who's been
buying me drinks leaves quickly. Funny the power Mark has.
"Cheryl, please, we gotta get some money. The landlord said
today he'd give us another twenty-four hours and no more."*

"Is he kinky?" I'm just dirt. Who cares if he's kinky.

*Later. I'm back at Neptune's. I have a drink. Another one.
Another one. My parents deserted me, April has left me,
Mark... is a-no-goddamned-good-fucking-son-of-a-bitch. I
have another drink. And another one. Let Mark use me. I don't
care. Let April sit in her fancy white palace. I just don't give a
damn!*

January 1972 *I'm an old pro now. I'm working the streets full
time. I avoid the pigs by picking johns that are obviously not
pigs. Well, pigs in another way. Mark arranges a lot of
meetings, too. I've gotten into other things I bet Mrs. Semple
never even heard of in her old "syndrome speech." I'm still
broke. First thing when I see Dad, he says, "Cheryl, I need a
twenty for groceries."*

"I don't have any."

*He goes into a rage. "What do ya mean, you don't have any?
You got enough to go drinking but you can't spare your poor Pa
any? Did that bum you're shacked up with tell you not to give
me anymore? You're just as bad as your ol' lady was, you know
that? A lazy no good for nothing. Running around all the time,
living with bums. I need some money. I need groceries and I got
to pay the rent. Now I got nothing, just 'cause you couldn't
hang onto a simple job."*

*I tell him he's worse. I swear at him. I tell him what I think
of him, that he's a parasite, a gutter-creature. I tell him it's his
fault Mom killed herself. The tears spring to his eyes. I leave
him. Let him stew in his guilt. I sure as hell stew in mine.*

*At home. Mark comes in. I'm angry and still brooding.
Mark is angry. I'm supposed to be at Neptune's. We need money
real bad. He yells. I yell. He beats me. I'm used to it. He avoids
hitting my face. He has learned it's not good for business.
He leaves.*

I walk along Main Street. This is where I belong. With the other gutter-creatures. I'm my father's daughter. My body aches. I enter a hotel. I don't know which one. The word 'Beverage' is all I see. I need a drink. A couple of drinks. The depression is bitterly deep. The booze doesn't help this time. I'm back on the street. I'm drunk. I want to run in front of a car. The guy who was buying my drinks comes with me. What a creep. We head to my place on Elgin. We take a short cut down a lane. The creep wants to fondle me and kiss me. He can't wait. "Back off, you ugly old man. I'm no whore, you know?" I don't know why I say that, but I repeat it. I can scarcely keep my balance. It's like there's two of me, one watching, one doing.

"I wanna kiss you. I know what you are. So don't pretend with me. I paid for you."

"You stink. Leave me alone, you filthy pig!" I slur the words. He gives me a push. I slam into the wall and fall into a sitting position. My legs have given out. I close my eyes. I like the sensation of everything spinning around at full speed. I open my eyes. I smile dumbly up at the man. He slams his fist into my face.

I wake up. I'm lying on the sidewalk. My legs are sprawled out in front of me. I notice the garbage cans and garbage bags on either side of me. "Hello there!" I say to them. "I've come home at long, long last." I chuckle to myself. I think in the morning the garbagemen will take us all away, me and my friends. I giggle. I try to get up. I can't. So I stay put. Every once in a while I chuckle to myself. I hum a tuneless song.

I wake up. April is holding my hand. I can't see her but it's April. I squeeze her hand.

I felt anger and bewilderment. Not at Cheryl or anyone else. Mostly, I guess the anger was for me. For being the way I was. Because it had caused Cheryl to feel so alienated from me that she couldn't share the most important event in her life with me. Cheryl's baby. Henry Liberty Raintree. Then I smiled. A part of Cheryl still lived. I looked at my watch. And sighed. It was four a.m. I'd have to wait until morning. I paced around the room and finally returned to the journals. I put them back

in the box and set them on the floor. Then I laid on Cheryl's
bed, on top of the covers, still fully clothed. With my hands
under my head, I stared up at the ceiling. The clock
downstairs was abnormally loud and so, so slow. A few hours
more and I could be on my way to Nancy's place to Henry Lee.

For the moment, I thought of Cheryl. The memories of her
voice, the memory of her reciting her powerful message at the
powwow. Why, oh why didn't she talk to me? Why couldn't we
have talked to each other? And would it have helped? At times
I was overwhelmed with memories of her, and tears would
trickle down the sides of my face.

The next morning I woke up, dismayed that I had fallen
asleep. Then I was dismayed to find it was still too early to
go to Nancy's place. The sun, a golden orange ball of fire,
was just beginning to rise. I went downstairs to make coffee
and freshen up. My eyes felt swollen. Again the house
seemed so empty, cold, lifeless. With my cup of coffee in
hand, I opened the front door and stood looking out at the
still empty street. The birds were just beginning to sing
their morning praises to their Creator. It had rained during
the night. Everything was wet. The smell of wet earth was
invigorating. So clean. I stood there breathing deeply when
I noticed there was a letter in the mailbox. I thought of
leaving it for the moment, but didn't. The moment I saw it
was Cheryl's handwriting, my heart started to pound. I tore
it open and sat down, heedless of the damp step.

Dear April,

By the time you get this, I will have done what I had to do.
I have said my goodbye to my son, Henry Liberty. I couldn't
bring myself to tell you about him before. Now I know you will
do what is right where he is concerned. I also know that Mary
and Nancy will do as you wish. They're taking care of Henry
Lee. All my life, I wanted for us to be a real family, together,
normal. I couldn't even mother my own baby!

Do not feel sorrow or guilt over my death. Man thinks he
can control nature. Man is wrong. The Great Spirit has made
nature stronger than man by putting into each of us a part of

nature. We all have the instinct to survive. If that instinct is gone, then we die.

April, there should be at least a little joy in living, and when there is no joy, then we become the living dead. And I can't live this living death any longer. To drink myself to sleep day in and day out.

April, you have strength. Dream my dreams for me. Make them come true for me. Be proud of what you are, of what you and Henry Lee are. I belong with our Mother.

Love to you and Henry Lee,

Cheryl

An hour later I was at Nancy's place once again. She opened the door for me as if she had been expecting me right at that particular moment. I followed her down the hall to the kitchen. Sitting at the table was a small boy eating some cereal. He looked up at me as I walked into the room. He smiled, the same kind of smile I had seen a long time before on his mother's face when she was that age, the age of innocence.

Nancy began explaining but I stopped her. I told her I understood everything. As I stared at Henry Lee, I remembered that during the night I had used the words "MY PEOPLE, OUR PEOPLE" and meant them. The denial had been lifted from my spirit. It was tragic that it had taken Cheryl's death to bring me to accept my identity. But no, Cheryl had once said, "All life dies to give new life." Cheryl had died. But for Henry Lee and me, there would be a tomorrow. And it would be better. I would strive for it. For my sister and her son. For my parents. For my people.

Critical Essays

Deploying Identity in the Face of Racism
Margery Fee

Racism is a major theme in First Nations writing, including systemic and institutional racism directed against whole groups, and personal racism directed against individuals by individuals. First Nations writers do not depict racism simplistically as a unidirectional system of oppression. The discourse of "race" (see Gates) is complex and multifaceted, and it tears groups, families, and individuals apart. First Nations writing elucidates this complexity, examining how racism is internalized and how it circulates. April, the narrator of Beatrice Culleton's *In Search of April Raintree*, recounts a process of identification where she moves from Métis to white to Métis. In her quest to be white, she disavows her parents and Cheryl, the sister she both loves and admires. In fact, since she and Cheryl "could have been almost identical twins, except for our skin-colouring" (106), she is disavowing the part of her that might be seen as Native, a disavowal also reflected in her fear of being a mother of "brown-skinned babies" (117). By the end of the novel, she has identified as Métis and has embraced the privilege of raising her "brown-skinned" nephew. Helen Hoy's "'Nothing But the Truth': Discursive Transparency in Beatrice Culleton"[†] examines the issue of identity in the novel, commenting that April's "final claim to have accepted her identity has less to do with some essence she discovers in herself (or other Métis or Native people) than with her mobilization of the relations, historic and present, in which she finds herself. She begins to deploy positively connections she has hitherto resisted" (177). I want to build on Hoy's insights into the way identification

---

† The references to Helen Hoy's essay refers to the original essay published in "Critical Visions: Contemporary North American Native Writing." ARIEL 25.1 (1994). An abridged version of the same essay appears in this collection. *Ed.*

works in the novel to examine how April and Cheryl deploy identifications to resist and survive the negative identities imposed on them. This deployment sometimes fails them: April is thrown into a period of turbulent readjustment after she is raped by men who label her "squaw," and Cheryl ultimately kills herself, convinced that she is a worthless drunk who cannot mother her son. As she says in her suicide note, "We all have the instinct to survive. If that instinct is gone, then we die" (207). As someone from a culture where suicide is horrifyingly common, Culleton is clearly asking questions about how the life of someone as bright and promising as Cheryl can be cut short in this way.

Because identity is policed from both outside and inside a minority group, the temptation for Aboriginal people to privilege so-called racial purity is at least as great as the temptation for non-Aboriginal people. When April explains, reluctantly, how she feels about admitting she is Métis, she says, "'It would be better to be a full-blooded Indian or full-blooded Caucasian. But being a half-breed, well, there's just nothing there ... what have the Métis people got? Nothing. Being a half-breed, you feel only the shortcomings of both sides'" (142). April doesn't like either side of the binary she sees herself as caught between. However, the ideology of "full-bloodedness" makes April think that the identity she has best claim to is "nothing," although, in fact, it puts her in a position to make choices. This freedom to choose one's identity or move among a series of identifications is normally reserved for the majority, while members of minorities have identities—negative ones—forced on them with varying degrees of brutality.

Ironically, laws based on notions of "race" that are now discredited scientifically and seen (at least by scholars) to be the creation of imperialism are reinforcing these notions now among those who were the prime victims of racism in the past. Thus, those who lack even just one of the supposed qualifications for "authentic" Aboriginality can be whipsawed between the definitions of Aboriginality of those in the Aboriginal community and those in the mainstream. Further, those with claims to Aboriginality have been similarly whipsawed by changes in the law. As Gerald R. Alfred notes in *Heeding the Voices of Our Ancestors*, a discussion of the Kahnawake Mohawk, problems persist because the Canadian state still controls the definition of "Aboriginal" or "Indian" and attaches benefits to those who meet this definition.

> Communities like Kahnawake have continued to rely upon locally defined racialist criteria [for membership] because they provide the strongest and most clear-cut protections against the formulations proposed by those who would reform or simply benefit from the reserve communities.... The retrenchment of racialist policies is also promoted by the fact that social, economic, and political conditions continue to make the Kahnawake-style membership policy [which relies on bloodlines and the notion of a "blood quantum"] relevant and useful to that community.... Resistance to the concept of independently defined membership criteria can only come from a perspective which does not value the Mohawks' inherent right of self-determination. (176)

Aboriginal people themselves do not control how their identity is defined; this contradicts the liberal principles that prompted changes to the Constitution Act of 1982. The Act defines "aboriginal peoples" as "Indian, Inuit and Métis peoples of Canada" (*Canadian Encyclopedia*, 2nd ed. I: 500), opening the door to a complete redefinition of Aboriginal identity, a redefinition that is still taking place in the courts. The inclusion of Métis in the list of Aboriginal peoples attempts to right a wrong done to a people who for a long time suffered from the same racist discrimination as the other First Peoples, but who were denied their special status. However, this has created a new and somewhat disparate group of people—some who belong to a long-standing historically defined people descended from the Red River colonists, and others who are the children of more recent non-Native/Native unions. Further, the attempt to remove the gender discrimination of the Indian Act, 1951 (which violated the equity provisions in the Constitution Act, 1982) by passing Bill C-31 in 1985 also caused problems in reserve communities. The Indian Act removed status from several categories of people, most commonly from Status women who married Non-Status men, while allowing Status men who married Non-Status women to retain it for both themselves and their families; in returning status to those women deprived of it through marriage and to others deprived of it for a variety of reasons, Bill C-31 shifted many people (approximately 100,000) from one category of identity to another. However, the status that was regained is not exactly the same as the status held by those who never lost it. The children of the woman whose status was removed by marriage regain status, but her grandchildren must marry those with status to retain it for themselves. And this problematic "solution" was also applied to status men:

> Rather than raise Indian women to the same power as men, the federal government chose to place Indian men in a position akin to that of women under the Old Act. From now on, the children of Indian men who married Non-Status as well as those of Indian women who married Non-Status could be denied Indian Status ... Bill C-31 adopts the rule that after two consecutive generations of marrying Non-Status, children of the third generation are not eligible for Status. (Daniels 3)

Paradoxically, then, a change in the law which might be seen as feminist in its inspiration also constrains the freedom of some Aboriginal people to choose a marriage partner.

Alfred points out that this redefinition of status has put pressure on communities like Kahnawake to consider as Mohawk those who formerly were explicitly excluded from membership by state legislation, although this redefinition was not accompanied by new resources to deal with this increased membership. Bill C-31 thus serves to consolidate a regrettable focus on ethnic "purity" that in many other areas of society is declining—for example, in the Constitution Act's redefinition of Aboriginal—as it is one of the strongest underlying principles of racism. Perhaps the most obvious problem is that the state legislates identity in these cases in a fashion that replicates the colonial processes of the past. As Big Bear in Rudy Wiebe's *Temptations of Big Bear* says in response to Governor Morris' point that "the law is the same for red and white": "That may be. But itself, it is only white" (31).

The complexity of the issues of identification foregrounded in these laws and histories is further compounded by the situation of those of mixed ancestry who were taken from their birth families and either incarcerated in residential school for most of the year or adopted or fostered by non-Native families. The difficulties that these people have in identifying as Aboriginal are compounded by a lack of cultural background and by pervasive racism in the surrounding culture. They lack both the "purity" of ancestry and the cultural knowledge that might otherwise support an identification as Aboriginal. When, in *In Search of April Raintree*, Cheryl introduces April to an old woman elder, April later reflects, "If I'd had such a grandmother when I was growing up, maybe I wouldn't have been so mixed up" (159). Further, the split between those people who live on the reserve or in rural or northern communities and those who live in the city also produces cultural dilemmas. Aboriginal people have always fought the "divide and conquer" tactics of the dominant culture, but these differences among those who have a claim to identify as Aboriginal cause trouble in individual lives, literary accounts, and political solidarity.

It is not surprising that these issues arise repeatedly in literary works, several of which deal directly with the identity conflicts that are, in part, behind the epidemic of suicide, addiction, and incarceration in Aboriginal communities. Several literary works, including Thomas King's *Green Grass, Running Water* and Jeannette Armstrong's *Slash*, examine characters who, because of racism, have decided—like April— that it is preferable to be white. This choice, however understandable on the individual level, has far more momentous implications than the decision of a white wannabe to "go Native": every member of a minority group who abandons that group makes it more likely that cultural traditions will vanish. Identity for Native people is not just a personal decision, and the community makes it clear that individuals are responsible for the cultural survival of the group; an elder in *Slash* says to a group of young people, "The next generations, and how we survive as Indians depends on that. It's something that can't be changed by any legislations or politicians" (Armstrong 201).

But some First Nations people who wish to identify themselves as Aboriginal have a different problem. Drew Hayden Taylor's *Funny, You Don't Look Like One* sums up his dilemma as a Status Anishnabe who looks white with the remark, "for a while I debated having my Status card tattooed on my forehead," (10) because his identity has been questioned by both Native and non-Native. Richard Wagamese's *Keeper 'n Me* documents the difficulties of Garnet Raven, of unquestioned Native ancestry and appearance, who was adopted by non-Natives and who returned to his birth family as an adult. The decision of such people to identify as Native is fraught with difficulty. The narrator of Lee Maracle's *Bobbie Lee: Indian Rebel* (an "as-told-to" autobiography) comments, "Of course my situation wasn't simple because my old man was white. But when he got drunk and angry with mom he called her a 'dirty old squaw'" (33–34). Marilyn Dumont's *A Really Good Brown Girl* documents the tension between those Aboriginal people with status and those without in "Leather and Naugahyde":

I say I'm Métis
like it's an apology and he says, 'mmh,' like he forgives me, like
he's got a big heart and mine's pumping diluted blood and his voice
has sounded well fed up to this point, but now it goes thin like
he's across the room taking another look and when he returns he's
got 'this look,' that says he's leather and I'm naugahyde. (58)

Martha Stone in Shirley Sterling's autobiographical novel, *My Name is Seepeetza*, not only undergoes the horrors of residential school and the racism of the nuns, but is also shunned by some of her schoolmates because she looks white, like a "dirty shamah" (20). These examples make it clear that identification is a complicated and dangerous process for First Nations people, whatever their appearance, upbringing, or cultural background. Historical, legal, and political forces beyond any individual's control have meant that the category *Aboriginal* has become fluid and contested.

The longing for an unquestioned and acceptable identity in the face of the refusal of one's community or the wider society to grant this is at the heart of *In Search of April Raintree*. April at one point comments, "It came to me that I had criticized the native people and here I was doing the same thing to white people. Maybe that's what being a half-breed was all about, being a critic-at-large" (114). Culleton's discourse rejects whiteness or Nativeness as simple, clearcut identities, and thus criticizes those on both "imagined" sides who feel that they "have" an identity. April doesn't like either side of the binary stereotypes she sees herself as caught between: a racist, materialist white, or a "'drunken Indian ... on Main Street'" (143). However, Cheryl shows her that the binary itself is a flawed construct.

One of the most striking moments in the novel occurs when Cheryl faces the ignorant and insinuating questions of a guest at a cocktail party held by April's mother-in-law:

> "Oh, I've read about Indians. Beautiful people they are. But you're not exactly Indians are you? What is the proper word for people like you?" one asked.
> "Women," Cheryl replied instantly.
> "No, no, I mean nationality?"
> "Oh, I'm sorry. We're Canadians," Cheryl smiled sweetly. (107)

This party shows Cheryl at her most confident and healthy: this is the period before she finds out that her father is an alcoholic and that her mother has committed suicide. She is working with her community. But when her chosen identity—even one she is proud to assert—threatens to limit her, she resists it. She does not take the bait of the exclusionary question, but asserts that the similarities between her and her racist questioner are as important as the differences, and she demonstrates that identity is a tool to use in negotiating ever-changing social relationships, rather than a trap or a fortress.

April, in contrast, resolves at a young age to be white. She states, "when I got free from being a foster child, then I would live just like a real white person" (47). But she realizes that this decision will never be uncomplicated: "How was I going to pass for a white person when I had a Métis sister? Especially when she was so proud of what she was?" (47). April's appearance allows her to choose a white identity at boarding school, where she says her parents died in a plane crash, and where she "was white as far as the other girls were concerned" (84). Because she believes (quite possibly correctly) that the other girls will reject her if they think she is Native, she resists Cheryl's suggestion that she join April there. Once she graduates, she looks for her parents, and discovers the squalid surroundings in which her father lives. This decides her: "That part of my life was now finished for good. I had a plan to follow, . . . [and] I would stick with it, whether Cheryl agreed with it or not. *It was my only way to survive*" (my italics 91). April herself never talks about the threat identifying as Métis might be to her psychological health, but her passionate negative outbursts about "gutter-people" reveal the anger she still holds against her parents, who she feels abandoned her and her sister.

This resolution to be white exacts a heavy toll on her relationship with her only close family: Cheryl. When she and Cheryl live together in Winnipeg, Cheryl's first boyfriend, Garth, reveals that he is ashamed to introduce her to his white friends, and April, while sympathizing with her sister, comments, "I didn't say anything because I was guilty of that, too. I had never invited Cheryl to come and meet me for lunch because I didn't want anyone at work to see her, to know she was my sister. Even now, I knew this wouldn't change me. I would continue to walk the five blocks or so at lunchtime, so I could meet her where she was already accepted" (94). (Even in this moment of insight, April ends by suggesting she is protecting Cheryl from rejection, rather than protecting herself.) April realizes that she is guilty of prejudice against her own sister, but the more she spends time with Cheryl and her friend Nancy and experiences the racist slights they suffer, the more she is strengthened in her decision to pass as white. She reads interior decorating magazines and books on etiquette, and defends her fantasy of being white and rich to herself by saying "Oh, well, Cheryl once had a fantasy which comforted her, and now I had mine" (98). Cheryl's childhood fantasy is of being reunited with her parents, moving to BC, and living "like olden-day Indians" (83). April realizes that her decision is deluded (just as she knows Cheryl's picture of their parents as "strong" and "beautiful" [83] is deluded), but she also knows she needs it to survive, just as Cheryl, she is convinced, needs the false stories of their parents that April told her when they were suffering as foster children:

> I should tell Cheryl what I already knew about our parents. They were liars, weaklings, and drunkards. But...
> I couldn't tell her that alcohol was more important to our parents than their own daughters. I had given her cherished memories of them. I couldn't take that away now. They were too important for her. Those memories and her too idealistic outlook for the future of native people. Those things helped her and gave her something to live for. (109)

Again the issue of survival, of needing "something to live for," is central. And although April is aware of the danger of lying, she is also quite convinced that without her decision to idealize white culture, and Cheryl's to idealize Native culture, neither will survive. And to some degree, the novel tells us, she is right. Idealizations and identifications can be deployed in ways that are both destructive and productive, deceptive and protective.

When the two sisters run away from a bad foster home, they are caught, and the social worker, Mrs. Semple, gives them a speech on what she calls "the native girl syndrome":

> and you girls are headed in that direction. It starts out with the fighting, the running away, the lies. Next come the accusations that everyone in the world is against you. There are the sullen, uncooperative silences, the feeling sorry for yourselves. And when you go on your own, you get pregnant right away, or you can't find or keep jobs. So you'll start with alcohol and drugs. From there, you get into shoplifting and prostitution, and in and out of jails. You'll live with men who abuse you. And on it goes. (62)

She has, in fact, laid out a life trajectory for them, if they decide to identify as Native. Neither takes it seriously, at first. April decides to be white; Cheryl decides to be a Native social worker. These choices—one typically evasive, the other typically resistant—protect them from identifying as the racist's Other.

In one of the darkest moments of the novel, the rape scene, April is nonetheless forced into this identity, the identity of the "squaw"—a figure created to justify sexual and racial abuse: "I began wondering for the hundredth time why they had kept on calling me squaw. Was it obvious? . . . Except for my long black hair, I really didn't think I could be mistaken as a native person. Mistaken? There's that shame again. Okay, identified" (146). Here it seems that April's "true" identity has been discovered—but in fact, as the reader finds out, the rapists are mistaken. They have mistaken her for her sister, who is, by this time, caught up in the "Native girl syndrome." In court, at one point, April thinks that the attorney for the rapists is attempting to suggest she is a prostitute, and she says, in language significantly parallel to her earlier comment about being mistaken as Native, "I was indignant that I could be mistaken as a prostitute" (165). Then she finds out that Cheryl has been working as a prostitute: "Cheryl stood up then and looked right at me. I saw her face in that split second before I looked away from her. I just couldn't look her straight in the face, not at that moment" (167). When she is raped, she feels degraded and in need of constant ritual baths. (Interestingly, as a child, she admires the clean white children, even though they ignore or insult her, and is proud that her mother keeps her house cleaner than anyone else. She reacts to the dirt in the house of her father's friend by retreating home into the bathtub, and quitting the search for her parents that Cheryl later completes.) However, as soon as she discovers that the men who raped her thought she was Cheryl, she stops having the baths: "Another victim of being native. No matter how hard I tried, I would always be forced into the silly petty things that concerned native life.... For some reason, I didn't feel the urgent need for the ritual bath that night" (167). From April's perspective, "she" was not raped—Cheryl was, and implicitly, deserved it—so April no longer has to accept the imposition of Nativeness on her and can overcome her sense that she somehow deserved this degradation. When she thought that she had been raped because her attackers saw her as Native, she had begun to think of herself differently, at one point even thinking of herself as a Native woman: "What would I and other 'squaws' get out of going to court?" (139). Now there is somewhere else to place the blame: on Cheryl and Nativeness. April's refusal to see herself as either Native or as a prostitute protects her, despite Cheryl, who calls her "'a bigot against [her] own people'" (175), points out that "Indian blood" runs in her veins (152), and says, "'You were so shocked when they said I was a hooker. Well, look at you. How did you buy this house, April? You prostituted yourself when you took Bob's money, that's how. You never loved that man'" (179). April has always felt that she was a "coward" and Cheryl the "fearless" one who "never worried about what other people thought about her" (111). But the novel makes it clear that April's "cowardice" protects her, and that Cheryl's courage falters when she can no longer sustain her fantasy about her parents.

One question *In Search of April Raintree* poses is "Why does Cheryl have to die?" Although Cheryl's suicide seems inevitable, at some levels, it doesn't appear to make sense.

First, in a novel that promotes Métis identity, the good sister who never abandons her identity, who confronts racism head on, ends up killing herself. Cheryl is the loyal sister, the sister who never turns her back on April, who hangs on to the idea that she is Native, who finds her father and refuses to turn her back on him. She is the smart sister who goes to university, becomes politically active, and who has just the right riposte for the racist putdown. April, however, betrays her culture and her sister. During April and Cheryl's last quarrel, Cheryl confides in her sister that it was in part to get money for her father that she turned to prostitution. But the novel has also positioned Cheryl's fantasy about her parents as a necessary illusion. When she discovers that they were what she drunkenly calls "'Bums. Boozers. Gutter-creatures'" (180), it seems that their betrayal is responsible for destroying her, although April also blames herself for not telling Cheryl the truth (185). However, Cheryl's drunken outburst, when she uses the racist language she has always avoided against them, does not obscure the fact that they, like her, had hit the wall constructed by racism. Displaced from a small town to a racist and unwelcoming city by tuberculosis, trying to support two children on welfare, dealing with the death of a sick baby and the apprehension of their other children, the parents' pain and suffering certainly accounts for some of their behaviour. Although April and Cheryl blame their parents, the reader can see that it is not a simple matter of "choice," either for them or for Cheryl. Cheryl no longer can deploy identifications to save herself and sinks into a spiral of depression.

Cheryl's suicide seems explicable at deeper levels, too. It seems a logical reaction to April's betrayal: during the brief period between the rape and the final revelations of the trial when April is tentatively thinking of herself as, if not Native, at least as suffering like one, the sisters bond. April goes to a powwow with Cheryl, is introduced to an elder at the Friendship Centre, and begins to think about "just how I felt about being a Métis" (160). Cheryl starts taking an interest in Native issues again: "the old fire had been rekindled" (157).

Once April finds out that she can blame her rape on Cheryl, her tentative steps toward identification stop abruptly as does their slowly awakening connection. Cheryl, in part, kills herself because April abandons her emotionally: "You heard what they said in court, and I saw what you felt when you avoided looking me in the eye" (175). April has told her sister that she feels shame when she sees "'drunken Indians on Main Street'" (152): to look her sister in the eye would be to bring what she feels should be Cheryl's shame back on to her, where it has been impervious, apparently, to April's attempts to scrub it away.

At yet another level, Cheryl represents April's Nativeness. To own her publicly as a sister is to declare Native ancestry, and yet April says, "I loved her. I could never cut myself off from her completely" (47). When Cheryl kills herself, it is too late to do what April has thought of doing for some time: "I would tell her everything was okay" (168). When April goes into Cheryl's room after the funeral, she finds an empty bottle of whiskey and smashes it, screaming, "'I hate you for what you've done to my sister! I hate you for what you've done to my parents! I hate you for what you've done to my people!'" (194). Then she reads Cheryl's journals and discovers that Cheryl has a son. Early that morning, she finds a suicide note in the mailbox in which Cheryl essentially hands the baby over to her, and when she sees the baby later that day, her identification as Métis is complete:

> As I stared at Henry Lee, I remembered that during the night I had used the words 'MY PEOPLE, OUR PEOPLE' and meant them. The denial had been lifted from my spirit. It was tragic that it had taken Cheryl's death to bring me to accept my identity. But no, Cheryl had once said, "All life dies to give new life." (207)

Why does Cheryl have to die? In part to make the point about suicide. April cannot reach out to her own sister because she believes that Cheryl has become a "gutter creature," the racist stereotype that April has defended herself against for years. To forgive Cheryl would be to say that it was all right that

Cheryl has turned to alcohol and prostitution and to open up a possibility that April might go the same route: they are sisters, after all. At the bridge where April hears a witness saying, "'Why would she want to do a thing like that? Those Indians are always killing themselves. If they aren't shooting each other on the reserves, it's this,'" she publicly acknowledges Cheryl, and thinks, "Someday, maybe, I could explain to people like him why they did it" (190). For the reader, if not for this witness, Cheryl's death makes sense. As for the idea that Cheryl has died to give new life, if Cheryl is April's "Native" side, she isn't dead, and the baby also will always mark April as Métis in the same way Cheryl did.

Finally, it seems unfair that April, who has betrayed her people, her parents, and her sister so persistently, gets the baby. It is unfair, just as it is unfair that some children are born to alcoholics, or with skin colour that marks them as Other. April, through the mere chance of her skin colour, is able to use this privilege to marry up, for money; her rapid success reveals how unearned racial privilege actually works. Through this same chance, she is able to avoid racist slights and comments. Although her marriage has overtones of the romance, the novel rejects romance solutions. The adoptive children finally discover that their parents are just as alcoholic and dysfunctional as the racist stereotype would paint them. April marries a white man who proves unfaithful, having married April "only to get back at his mother" (116). She finally reunites with her sister after a long period of estrangement, only to be raped, something she ends up blaming on her sister's having turned to prostitution. There is no happy ending, except that April gets a second chance, after her sister's suicide, to raise her nephew, whose smile is like the one "on his mother's face when she was that age, the age of innocence" (207).

Still, the reader might have some doubts that April, who behaves like a middle-class white social worker, and her white businessman boyfriend, Roger, will bring up the child as a committed Métis activist. The ending might well also support the notion that Cheryl was too "Native-identified" to successfully bring up a child; April takes the baby from Nancy and her mother, who have clearly helped raise him successfully so far, in what could be soon as a reenactment of the social workers taking April and Cheryl from their parents. However, the novel's ending is interestingly convoluted, with a psychological if not a realist logic. April smashes the bottle and goes through her crisis of identification *before* she finds out, through the journals, that Cheryl has a baby. Only then does she find the letter where Cheryl essentially makes her Henry's guardian. Just as Cheryl's letter speaks from beyond the grave in the present, so does the novel itself provide the evidence that April understands her own problematic identifications. April's mission is to share this understanding: she cuts herself on a piece of the bottle as she is, characteristically, cleaning up the mess she has made of Cheryl's room, and says, "'Still after more blood, are you? Well, you cut down my sister, my parents, my people. But no more. I'll see to it. Somehow. Some way'" (195). The novel's power is its success in explaining why Indians kill each other and themselves and how racism feeds destructive processes of identification that lead to despair and alcohol. April has seen to it.

She has survived to do so because she has been able to accept her identity, even during the horrible turmoil surrounding Cheryl's death, rather than have it imposed on her. When the shameful identity as "squaw," as the racist's Other, was forced on her by rape, her sister's support helped her to begin to come to terms with a positive self-identity as Métis. But when Cheryl is forced into the same corner, revealed to the court as a prostitute, April is too tempted by the chance to escape what she still sees as a negative identification to help Cheryl find a way to identify that avoids the "native girl syndrome." April can't look Cheryl in the eye. And it is this refusal of recognition to someone, the refusal to look someone else in the eye as a fellow human being, that leaves Cheryl with no one she can look to for help in seeing a way to identify herself as a mother and an activist. April, on the other hand, has been

looked in the eye and recognized by White Thunderbird
Woman: "Without speaking a word to me, the woman
imparted her message with her eyes." Thus April is able to
understand that there might be a place for her in Métis
culture that is not one of shame, but one that is "special ...
[and] deserving of ... respect" (159).

Acknowledgments

I would like to thank all the students who have helped me to think
about this novel, particularly those in First Nations Writing at UBC;
I also thank those students who shared their experiences of being
"Bill C-31s" with me. Thanks also to Sneja Gunew for reading this
paper and for allowing me to share her ideas on the link between
identity and recognition.

Works Cited

Alfred, Gerald R. *Heeding the Voices of Our Ancestors: Kahnawake
    Mohawk Politics and the Rise of Native Nationalism*. Toronto:
    Oxford UP, 1995.
Armstrong, Jeannette. *Slash*. Penticton, BC: Theytus, 1985.
Culleton, Beatrice. *In Search of April Raintree*. Winnipeg, MB:
    Pemmican, 1983.
Daniels, Harry W. "Bill C-31: The Abocide Bill." Congress of
    Aboriginal Peoples. 1998. 24 June 1999.
    <http://www.abo-peoples.org/programs/dnlsc-31.html>, 1998. 13pp.
Dumont, Marilyn. *A Really Good Brown Girl*. London, ON: Brick,
    1996.
Gates, Henry Louis, Jr. *"Race," Writing and Difference*. Chicago: U of
    Chicago P, 1986.
Hoy, Helen. "'Nothing but the Truth': Discursive Transparency in
    Beatrice Culleton." *ARIEL* 25.1 (1994): 155–84.
King, Thomas. *Green Grass, Running Water*. Toronto: HarperCollins,
    1994.
Maracle, Lee. *Bobbi Lee: Indian Rebel*. Toronto: Women's Press, 1990.
Sterling, Shirley. *My Name is Seepeetza*. Vancouver: Dougas &
    McIntyre, Groundwood, 1992.
Taylor, Drew Hayden. *Funny, You Don't Look Like One: Observations
    from a Blue-Eyed Ojibway*. Penticton: Theytus, 1996.
Wagamese, Richard. *Keeper'n Me*. Toronto: Doubleday, 1994.
Wiebe, Rudy. *The Temptations of Big Bear*. New Canadian Library.

The Problem of "Searching" For April Raintree

Janice Acoose

Although the Métis are literally the only Indigenous people who grew out of the Canadian nation, few non-Métis people know our history or culture. Inevitably, readers may come to texts like Beatrice Culleton's *In Search of April Raintree* eager to learn something about the Métis, for as Kelly Griffith suggests in *Writing Essays About Literature: A Guide and Style Sheet*, literature puts us in touch with "events, places, and people that many of us will never experience in real life" (19). Jeannette Armstrong in *Looking at the Words of Our People: First Nations Analysis of Literature*, explains that the "questioning which shapes the critical pedagogical voice" must acknowledge and recognize that the Indigeneous "voices coming forward in written English Literature" are culture specific voices (7). In "Says Who" Kateri Damm reminds Indigenous[1] writers that "[w]hen we express ourselves ... we must do so from an informed position so that we do not contribute to the confusion and oppression, but instead, bring into sharper focus who we are" (24). Problemitizing the formation of cultural identity for Indigenous peoples, Damm argues that who we are has been "constructed and defined by Others to the extent that at times we no longer know who we are" (11).

For those Indigenous writers who have taken up the pen to re-construct and re-define cultural identity within their literary productions in English, Jeannette Armstrong's "The Disempowerment of First North American Native Peoples and Empowerment Through Their Writing" advises that "our task ... is two fold. To examine the past and culturally affirm toward a new future" (210). However, as a Métis-Nakhawe teacher and student of Indigenous authored texts, I too am often reminded that when some writers formulate "culture" within their texts, they construct a box wherein they pack a brown blob of "Nativeness," singular and indistinguishable. Beatrice Culleton's *In Search of April Raintree* "preserve[s] Native views, Native realities, and Native forms of telling" (Damm, "Dispelling and Telling" 95), but the term "Native" is problematic because it simultaneously suppresses the Métis culture specific voice of both author and narrator. With its protagonists seduced by popular terms like "Native" and "Halfbreed," and confused by colloquial metaphors such as "mixed-blood" and "part-Indian," the text does not success-fully illustrate the Métis cultural identity.

In the decade which preceded the publication of Culleton's text, publishers were eager to capitalize on "the novelty value of the first wave of books written by Aboriginal people" (Young-Ing 183). Indeed, Penny Petrone in *Native Literature in Canada: From the Oral Tradition to the Present* describes that decade as an era which "heralded phenomenal explosions of creative writing by Indians" (112), while the 1980s fed demands for, and interests in, the rapidly changing "Indian life in Canada" (138). Greg Young-Ing in "Aboriginal People's Estrangement: Marginalization in the Publishing Industry" offers a slightly different interpretation of this period, noting that the late 1970s and 1980s reflected a decrease in publishing of Indigenous authored books. He cites Culleton's text as one of the books that appeared during this period when writers "began to develop styles of writing that would carry the unique Aboriginal Voice into contemporary literature" (183–84).

While some attention must be paid to the historical moment in which Culleton's text was written, other authors such as Emma LaRocque, Howard Adams, and Maria Campbell were writing nationalist Métis narratives at this same time. Emma LaRocque in *Writing the Circle: Native Women of Western Canada* explains that "[p]ower politics in literature . . . controlled the type of material that was published" (xvi-xvii) because numerous Indigenous writers were "articulating our colonized conditions throughout

Canada" (xvi). Influenced by "many white audiences, journalists, and critics [who] resorted to racist techniques of psychologically labelling and blaming us" as bitter and biased against white-Canada (xvii), publishers seldom approached or included Indigenous writers in contemporaneous literatures (xvi). Howard Adams, during the 1970s, began promoting Métis nationalism, despite contemptuous racist ploys to silence him. He explains that "in the 1960s and 1970s ... we were now able to get out of our ghetto and get out of our ghetto-mentality, and get away from the deep subordination of ourselves" (Lutz 136).

While Culleton's text does not create a Métis voice in the way that Métis nationalist writers like Adams, Campbell, and LaRocque do, the author does undertake a different project, one that opens up a space for critical discourse about the formation of identity and the transmission of culture. Her semi-autobiographical novel portrays a young girl of mixed ancestry struggling with identity confusion and cultural oppression while simultaneously trying to understand who she is.

Because the narrator, April Raintree, is not exposed to the necessary influences for cultural transmission, she relies on discourse provided to her by white foster homes. This discourse "boxes" her in because she is fed negative stereotypes, while her sister, Cheryl, feeds off of romantic stereotypes: the culturally specific narrative voice is compromised by popularly seductive terms and the slippery texture of colonial English. Yet, the narrative makes clear that identity and culture are inextricably intertwined in the processes of formation and influenced by numerous mitigating factors. Not unlike the narrator, Culleton struggles to open the boxes that construct identity based on "Nativeness." In an interview with Hartmut Lutz in *Contemporary Challenges: Conversations with Canadian Native Authors*, Culleton candidly admits that the possibilities for cultural inheritance for herself were interrupted by her dis-placement in "white foster homes" (98). Those experiences left her struggling to bring into sharper focus a culture specific voice. As she explains to Lutz, for "Native people growing up in urban Canada today . . . there is a lot of pressure on you to assimilate and forget totally what you are as a person, what your heritage is" (97).

Culleton's semi-autobiographical novel reveals that there are numerous factors that contribute to the dis-eased narrative voice, discouraging possibilities for identity formation and Métis cultural transmission. For example, one of the aforementioned mitigating factors, which interferes with cultural transmission and identity formation, is the father and mother's dis-eased condition. The father, Henry Raintree, represents the creator or originating source of culture. Stricken with TB, he is forced to relocate from the small northern community of Norway House to the large urban city of Winnipeg. The move irrevocably changes their way of life and culture. No longer self-sustaining, the Raintrees become increasingly dependent on welfare handouts and alcohol, which is referred to as "medicine" (12). During one of their "medicine" parties, April's mother becomes pregnant. As a mother, she represents the nurturer of the culture; however her role as mother becomes dis-eased when she is hospitalized for "getting fat" (15). Subsequent to the baby's birth, the so-called nurturing mother is pronounced "ill" by definition of the colonial authorities and therefore unfit to care for her children. Prompted by baby Anna's "sickness" (17), the colonial authorities represented as Manitoba's Children's Aid Society apprehend the children; they take baby Anna to the hospital while April and Cheryl are moved to "a nice clean place" (17).

When the Raintree sisters are removed from their dis-eased family of origin, they become culturally malnourished by being dis-placed into a series of white foster homes. Initially, April is culturally dis-placed with the Dion family in St. Albert, "a small French Catholic town" (24), while Cheryl is culturally mis-placed with the MacAdams who, albeit with good intentions, encourage the belief that she is Métis because "[they]'re part Indian and part white" (43). April is dis-placed because she is dis-located from her culture of origin, while Cheryl is mis-placed with a Métis family whose intentions are good but shaped by the boxed colonial constructs of Native identity. While Cheryl begins to construct an identity by un-packing the antiquated colonial boxes, which contain romantic notions of Indians and Métis, April boxes herself into negative stereotypes, closing herself off to any possibilities for the transmission of heritage. When her sister Cheryl presents her with a book about Louis Riel during a visit, April crinkles her nose in distaste. Although not verbalized, her thoughts are revealed in the narrative:

> I knew all about Riel. He was a rebel who had been hanged for treason. Worse, he had been a crazy half-breed. I had learned about his folly in history. Also, I had read about the Indians and the various methods of tortures they had put the missionaries through. No wonder they were known as savages. So, anything to do with Indians, I despised. And here I was supposed to be part Indian. (42–43)

The narrative does not make clear why April, at such a young age, has become so embittered toward "halfbreeds" and "Indians," but it does reveal how she comes to know cultural shame fostered and nourished by her experiences outside her family of origin. She recalls experiences with a so-called foster "mother," Mrs. DeRosier, who with contemptuous venom names her "halfbreed" (37). The venomous contempt poisons April and mal-nourishes her ideas of heritage. The word "halfbreed," which connotes a product of animal husbandry, is used consistently by Mrs. DeRosier and her children who shamefully dehumanize April. In contrast to April's poisonous environment, Cheryl receives cultural nourishment from Mrs. MacAdams, who is Métis, and intellectual stimulation from Mr. MacAdams, who is a teacher (43). However, Cheryl's formation of cultural identity is constructed by "a lot of books on Indian tribes and how they used to live a long time ago" (43), historical images which packed in the colonial boxed constructs of Native identity. Cheryl's zealous pursuit of information about her heritage marks her journey through childhood to adulthood. Although she clings to romantic stereotypes, Cheryl openly expresses cultural pride that is recorded in a series of letters and copies of speeches she sends to April over the years. They also symbolize her conscious efforts to re-construct her heritage. However, the romantic imagery of "Indian" and "Métis", which people gleaned from non-Indigenous authorities, cannot sustain Cheryl when she opens the box filled with family documentation provided to April by the colonial authorities. As a result, when fantasy meets reality, Cheryl's voice is suppressed. This silence is a form of oppression that starves Cheryl's hunger for information about her cultural heritage.

April, on the other hand, attempts to purge her "Métis" have-not cultural heritage and binges on the stereotypes from white mainstream society, that she believes will nourish the type of life she envisions for herself. Throughout her life, April buys into the white "fairytale" ideal only to realize that she can never be anything but a Cinderella in the DeRosier house. Like Cinderella, she envisions that one day a handsome white prince will rescue her from a life of servitude. He appears years later in the form of Bob Radcliff. Rooted in the white "fairytale" ideal, April's romanticized life of wealth and power with Bob begins to fragment when she realizes that "[a]ll these people lived for one of two things: money or power" (114). Her romantic stereotype fractures even more when she begins to notice the hypocrisy and superficiality surrounding the world she has chosen. Finally, moved from her passive state when she overhears a conversation between her mother-in-law, Mother Radcliff, and her friend, Heather, April becomes "fighting mad," on learning that her husband has been having an affair with her friend (114). She becomes enraged when Bob's mother unknowingly reveals that she "would simply dread being grandmother to a bunch of little half-breeds!" (116). While Mother Radcliff's comments only mirror what April has repressed for so long, the comments force her to confront her own culture shame. Inevitably, she liberates her voice when she is able to say to her so-called friend Heather, "Bob's mother would rather have a person like you, a hyprocrite, an adultress, as her daughter-in-law, rather than risk a few grandchildren who would have Indian blood in them" (116). Like Cheryl, April has survived by clinging to romantic stereotypes, but the stereotypes collapse when confronted with reality and they ultimately set in motion a re-formation of identity and a re-consideration of culture. This process is symbolized by April's move from the closely guarded world of the wealthy into shared accommodations with "artistic types" (119), who represent her journey into a liberated world.

During April's time of transition, she makes efforts to re-connect with her sister Cheryl. Cheryl, however, has become secretive and uncommunicative because she discovers that colonial language will not let her re-cover the reality of "Indian" and "Métis" people. Consequently, Cheryl disconnects from any possibilities for identity formation and cultural transmission, a move which is symbolized by the disconnected phone service and April's returned letter marked "[m]oved—no forwarding address" (119). After she receives a telephone call from the "Health Sciences Centre in Winnipeg, asking if [she] were related to Cheryl Raintree" (120), April subsequently moves away from another romantic stereotype, one that she has fostered in the white world that permitted her to sustain a relationship with her "Métis" sister. As hints of Cheryl's alcoholism come to April's attention, she realized that her sister is no longer the proud or exceptional Métis. However, wanting desperately to believe that Cheryl has not become dis-eased by "Native girl syndrome" (62), April tries to rescue her sister. Ironically, it is April who becomes dis-eased and victimized by the "Native girl syndrome" (62). Believing her to be a prostitute and "fucking squaw" (128), three white men brutally rape April. When she learns that the intended victim was Cheryl, "champion of native causes. A whore?" (166), she becomes critically dis-eased and attempts to cleanse herself with ritualistic baths. Cheryl, too, becomes critically dis-eased, although as a final solution she kills herself and terminates any possibilities for her own cultural transmission.

Cheryl's opting for this final resolution moves April to re-examine the past. After her sister's funeral, she finds a box that contains Cheryl's journals. Reading through the journals, April re-visits the last two years of her sister's life. She learns that not unlike her own lies, which she fed to Cheryl about their parents, her sister has lied to her, too. Instead of giving up the search for their parents, Cheryl had located and made contact with their father. Much to her disappointment, instead of the romanticized noble warrior she had imagined him to be, he appeared as a "bent, wasted human form" (197) of the gutter. From the journals, April also learns that their mother killed herself and that their baby sister Anna died in infancy. The writings document for April the point at which her sister's dis-ease has become terminal. She reads that Cheryl's "dreams to rebuild the spirit of a once proud nation are destroyed" in those few moments when she met her father. Through the writing, she hears Cheryl's oppressed—terminally dis-eased—voice: "I study the pitiful creature in front of me. My father! A gutter-creature! The imagination of my childhood has played a horrible, rotten trick on me. . . . Now I just want to turn and run away. . . . Pretend I was an orphan. I should have listened to April" (198). Something else the journals reveal is that Cheryl has kept hidden from April her son's birth; in fact, she learns that Cheryl has given the son, whom she named Henry Liberty Raintree, to her friend Nancy's mother to raise. Not unlike their own mother, Cheryl's dis-ease requires continuous "medicine" which inevitably interferes with her ability to mother the child. When she goes to Nancy's mother's home to claim her nephew, April realizes the possibilities for new life, and perhaps, cultural transmission. She explains that "[a]s I stared at Henry Lee, I remembered that during the night I had used the words "MY PEOPLE, OUR PEOPLE" and meant them. The denial had been lifted from my spirit. It was tragic that it had taken Cheryl's death to bring me to accept my identity" (207).

Unlike April, who comes away from her reading of Cheryl's journals with an understanding of past events, readers of Culleton's text may not come away from the novel sated with an understanding of Métis culture or history. In fact, journeying through *In Search of April Raintree* may leave readers with mis-informed notions about the Métis. April's father, the creator/originary source of culture, is presented as "mixed blood, a little of this, a little of that, and a whole lot of Indian" (11), and her mother, the nurturer of culture, is referred to as "part Irish and part Ojibway" (11). Assuming that readers may take responsibility and dig up information about colloquial metaphors peculiar to colonial Canada, about Métis history as it is documented by white authorities, and about the voices of the authorities who speak the oral histories of the birth of the Métis nation in the Red River homeland, Culleton's re-presentations of the Métis may not be problematic. Assuming, also, that readers can make a connection between the culturally dis-eased, mal-nourished, and oppressed condition of the Raintree sisters and the text's reflection of that condition, *In Search of April Raintree* becomes an important novel for critical discourse surrounding issues of identity formation and cultural transmission. Moreover, the text becomes an important site for the critical exploration of stereotypical constructs and imposed definitions that are re-constructed through colonial English and through the use of that language. Though the text may appear to be simply another box filled with old and archaic images of the wearisome brown blob of "Nativeness," when it is unpacked and opened up, readers may, if they look outside the text and take responsibility for their own education, come to know something about Métis history and culture.

Acknowledgments

I want to thank Jeanie Wills (MA Candidate, Department of English, University of Saskatchewan) for extensive discussions and editorial assistance with this article. Having a writing partner made journeying less frightening through neighborhoods like "formal academic writing" which both of us are dis-eased from at this moment in our academic careers.

Notes

[1] I use the word Indigenous here and throughout the text because of this word's connotative and denotative possibilities: the word literally signifies that we have grown out of the land and infers that we continue to live closely with it, reminded of our spiritual relationship.

Works Cited

Adams, Howard. Interview by Hartmut Lutz. In *Contemporary Challenges: Conversations with Canadian Native Authors*, edited by Hartmut Lutz. 135–54. Saskatoon, SK: Fifth House, 1991.

Armstrong, Jeannette, ed. *Looking at the Words of Our People: First Nations Analysis of Literature*. Penticton, BC: Theytus, 1993.

_____. "The Disempowerment of First North American Native Peoples and Empowerment Through Their Writing." *An Anthology of Canadian Literature in English*. 2nd ed. Ed. Daniel David Moses and Terry Goldie. Toronto: Oxford UP, 1998. 239–242.

Culleton, Beatrice. *In Search of April Raintree*. Winnipeg, MB: Pemmican, 1983.

_____. Interview with Hartmut Lutz. In *Contemporary Challenges: Conversations with Canadian Native Authors*, edited by Hartmut Lutz. 97–105. Saskatoon, SK: Fifth House, 1991.

Damm, Kateri. "Dispelling and Telling: Speaking Native Realities in Maria Campbell's *Halfbreed* and Beatrice Culleton's *In Search of April Raintree*." Armstrong 93–114.

_____. "Says Who: Colonialism, Identity and Defining Indigenous Literature." Armstrong 9–26.

Dumont, Marilyn. "Popular Images of Nativeness." Armstrong 45–50.

Griffith, Kelly. *Writing Essays About Literature: A Guide and Style Sheet*. Toronto: Harcourt, 1983.

LaRocque, Emma. Preface to *Writing the Circle: Native Women of Western Canada*, Edited by Jeanne Perreault and Sylvia Vance. Edmonton: NeWest Publishers Limited, 1990.

Petrone, Penny. *Native Literature in Canada: From the Oral Tradition to the Present*. Toronto: Oxford UP, 1990.

Young-Ing, Greg. "Aboriginal Peoples' Estrangement: Marginalization in the Publishing Industry." Armstrong 177–187.

Abuse and Violence: April Raintree's Human Rights (if she had any)

Agnes Grant

Beatrice Culleton's novel, *In Search of April Raintree*, was greeted with considerable enthusiasm in 1983, at least by most readers. There were critics, however, who dismissed it because they felt the style was too laboured and the story line too simplistic. They predicted that it would never be accepted into the Canadian literary canon. Time has proven the critics wrong; sixteen years later, it is still a widely read and influential book.

The fact that Culleton is an Aboriginal writer, of course, influences the popularity of the book. There is not a wide selection of novels written by Canadian Aboriginal writers that have the broad appeal of *In Search of April Raintree*. It appeals to Aboriginal readers who have never had the experience of finding their voices in Canadian literature. Only too often, literature portrays Canada as a country without indigenous people, or when their presence is acknowledged they are used as minor supporting characters or in a symbolic way to further the plot or the development of the non-Native characters.

In Search of April Raintree appeals to readers beyond Aboriginal circles, however, which demonstrates that Culleton has moved from her own culture in order to present universal themes, insights, and values. Though the theme of the book deals with cultural identity and renewal, Culleton touches a responsive chord in readers from all cultures. Abuse of women and children is not confined to Aboriginal cultures. Rape of women has long been glorified in literature and popular media. When Culleton wrote this book, the largely white, middle-class feminist movement was beginning to speak of such things frankly and openly. Culleton's book, with

its matter-of-fact, almost˙ dispassionate rendering of the
rape scene, reminded all women that misogyny is
compounded by racism. With profound understatement,
Culleton reminded people everywhere of what it is to be an
Aboriginal woman in Canada.

The book was influenced by events in Culleton's life,
giving it an authenticity which often is mistaken for
autobiography. Culleton was a foster child, she was raped
(though her rapist was never caught) and her sister did
commit suicide.[†] What makes this book unusual is that it not
only documents the abuse of April as an adult, it also goes
back into her childhood and shows how her rights were
violated from the time she was very young. There is no
movement in Canada today, nor has there ever been one, that
examines the rights of children the way feminists have
exposed the abuse of women. When the social workers
removed April and Cheryl from their home, April screamed
frantically, "'Mommy, please don't make us go. Please,
Mommy. We want to stay with you. Please don't make us go.
Oh, Mom, don't!'" (18). This emotional scene has moved many
readers to tears, yet the deplorable situation of poor children
in Canada has steadily worsened since 1983. The situation
has deteriorated to the point where the United Nations has
commented on the inequities, even as they pronounce Canada
one of the best countries of the world in which to live.

Culleton documented this poverty in a heart-wrenching
way as the character of April displayed a maturity and
wisdom far beyond her years. She would barricade the
bedroom door with a toybox to protect Cheryl and herself from
fighting, drinking adults. On bad days, she would pack lunch
for herself and Cheryl and they would spend the day in a park
away from irresponsible adults. They watched the non-
Aboriginal children and would have been happy to play with
them. The other children, however, ignored them so they
played by themselves in a corner of the park. April was six
years old and Cheryl was four and a half.

[†] From a personal communication between the author and Beatrice Culleton
Mosionier. *Ed.*

There were happy family times when the parents were not drinking. When her mother was sober, April recalls, "To prolong that mood in her I would help her with everything, chattering away in desperation, lest my own silences would push her back into her, normal remoteness" (12). But for all of her efforts, April was not able to influence her parents' actions. Culleton does not mince words as she describes the behaviour of April's drunken parents and their friends and relatives. April tells how she found her naked mother in bed with a man who was not her father. As well, she recounts how she watched as a drunken man was playing with his "thing" and then peeing on the floor (14). Most puzzling to her was when a visiting woman and her mother got into a fight and her father found their fighting hugely amusing. He laughed and egged them on while April watched in indignation; finally she helped her mother by kicking the other woman. There were a lot of things about her parents' actions that she could not fathom, and when the social workers apprehended the children, April recalls, "There were a lot of grown up things I didn't understand that day. My mother should have fought with her life to keep us with her. Instead, she handed us over" (18).

When the girls were taken to an orphanage, they suffered the indignity of being examined for lice and having their hair cut. Then they were thoroughly scrubbed. However, the important thing for April was that they were together, and once the supervisors left them alone for the night, they were able to cuddle together in one bed like they had at home. April had the consolation of seeing her father outside the orphanage one day, so she knew that her parents still cared for her, though she also had the anguish of not being able to reach him or talk to him, in spite of her best efforts.

After foster homes were found for the girls, they were separated, and April's anguish increased. She recalls, "I was so sad, so lonely, so confused. Why was all this happening?" (24). But April had already learned many survival skills in the first six years of her life. Most importantly, she learned that she had no autonomy and that the simplest technique was to watch, listen, and adapt to whatever was required of her. Her

first foster home was a good one, and kindly Mrs. Dion
reminded her of her mother. Soon she acquired a place in the
family which contributed greatly to her serenity and positive
self-concept. She came to love both her foster parents. When
visits with her natural parents and Cheryl disrupted her
sense of well-being and increased her yearning for her own
family, her foster family understood her feelings and gave her
love and support. They also instilled in her a deep sense of
religion—a Catholic belief system which had only been
nominal in her life with her parents. But April's sense of
security was only a temporary lull. She was to be wrenched
from this home, too. When Mrs. Dion became terminally ill,
April was transferred to a different foster home even before
her death, depriving April of a necessary mourning period.

April's attitude toward life changed dramatically when
she entered the DeRosier home. Up until that point in her life,
she had trusted the significant adults in her life even though
the things they did were incomprehensible to her. She
understood that she was loved and that it was circumstances
which caused the adults in her life to do things which brought
her pain. She was stoic and optimistic, adapting as best she
could to whatever circumstances had in store for her.

In Mrs. DeRosier, she met a different type of human
being. She was racist, manipulative, exploitive, hypocritical,
displaying a conscience long-buried under a facade which she
projected to the community as kind-hearted, even martyred,
humanity. April did her best to comply with her every
demand. She did not understand that she was a hapless
participant in a power struggle, one she could never win
because the struggle was between a grown woman with all
the power and a mere child. What was more, the woman was
white, and April was Métis, so there was no hope of equity.

April attempted to find solace in the religion Mrs. Dion
had taught her, but Mrs. DeRosier's hypocrisy tested April's
faith severely, especially when they went to church, and Mrs.
DeRosier assumed the role of solicitous foster mother. Unfair
and abusive treatment pushed April to the brink of despair,
and she told God: "'Oh, God, why did you let me be born?

Why? Why was I ever born? Why do you let these bad things happen to Cheryl and me? You're supposed to be loving, protective, and just. But you're full of crap, God! You're just full of crap and I hate you. You hear me? I hate you!'" (45). April knew that she had to comply with all the expectations of her, reasonable or unreasonable, but she did become angry. She says, "Helpless fury built up inside me, but I was alone here, unsure of what my rights were, if I even had any" (40). And, indeed, she had none.

Racism, both covert and overt, was at the root of much of the abuse April suffered. Openly racist comments were common in the DeRosier household; the DeRosier children demonstrated in many ways that they were internalizing the message of racial superiority that their mother was instilling in them. Their father, a shadowy figure, also condoned the racism of his wife and children by his refusal to get involved.

The social worker, too, judged the girls on the basis of racial stereotypes rather than looking for root causes of the girls' unhappiness. Her "Native girl syndrome" harangue was totally baffling to the young girls. In a vain attempt to control some aspect of their lives, the girls ran away when they realized they were to be separated again. When they were found, the social worker asked no questions but immediately began to lecture them, telling them they were headed in the wrong direction and if they did not improve their attitudes they would fall prey to what she termed the "Native girl syndrome." She stated that it was characterized by fighting, running away, feeling persecuted, being stubborn and uncooperative, indulging in self-pity, early pregnancy, inability to hold jobs, reliance on alcohol and drugs, which would lead to shoplifting, prostitution, jails, abusive partners, and welfare (62). Though thoroughly bemused by the verbal onslaught, it did sound rather awful, and April assured Cheryl, "'We are not going to become what they expect of us'" (64). Racial stereotypes were also accepted by one of her teachers when Maggie attempted to discredit April's reputation. Though the teacher and April's friend, Jennifer,

later apologized to April, the terrible hurt they had inflicted
could not be undone. April was so alone and powerless that
she was pathetically grateful for their apologies.

Covert racism, which sanctions dominance over "inferior"
people and is inherent in the systemic treatment of foster
children and their natural parents, permeates the book. One
example of this is Mrs. DeRosier's freedom to punish the girls
for running away by cutting off their hair. April refers to her
hair as her "crowning glory," so readers know Mrs. DeRosier
chose this form of punishment because she knew it would cut
to the heart of April's power of resistance. Tomson Highway,
in his novel *Kiss of the Fur Queen*, tells how the character,
Champion, kept his dignity as they were shearing his long
flowing curls in the residential school—but in the end he
could no longer keep up the brave front: "His hair was now
gone completely; Champion had no more strength left..."
(Highway 54). Hair was a particular preoccupation of
European colonizers; dominant groups have long performed
rituals which involve shearing the hair of subordinates.
Cutting hair is found to be a key part of rituals of cross-
cultural domination all over the world (Grant 17). Although
neither April nor Mrs. DeRosier might have understood the
symbolism of this act, it serves to demonstrate the ultimate
power adults have over children and how misuse of this power
can be exacerbated by race.

Some readers might wonder if Mrs. DeRosier is not,
perhaps, overblown. As an individual, perhaps this is so, but
as a composite picture of foster home care, she is not
necessarily exaggerated. Many Aboriginal high-school
students from northern areas, like Champion in *The Kiss of
the Fur Queen*, used to be placed in foster homes in the city
because their own communities did not provide a high school
education. Many of these students report that in these "warm
and supportive" homes, which received generous allowances
for their young boarders, they were confined to the basement
bedrooms, joining the host families only at mealtime. My own
experiences as a foster mother support the fact that few
allowances were made for the trauma the children had

suffered. Foster parents were given no information that might help the children through this difficult adjustment period. Foster parents were forbiddon to contact the natural parents of the children or allow them to visit the children. My foster daughter's aunt was a student in one of my university classes and in that way found her lost niece again. She was willing and able to give her niece a home, but the Children's Aid Society would not pay an Aboriginal family to provide foster care. If a child was being cared for well, its life was not disrupted, but the Aboriginal family was expected to do it for free, in spite of the usually impoverished circumstances. It was to be years before Aboriginal families were considered capable of providing good homes for foster children. When another foster mother pointed her finger at my daughter's face and asked, "Does she have any brains?," I contained my anger; when another foster mother hugged me and said, "We have to do our Christian duty, don't we?", I cringed; and when store clerks held whispered consultations before they would fill my daughter's prescription to make sure I was not abusing the system, I complained to the management. Most distressing was the teacher who said, "And your foster daughter is so clean!" It was then that I realized that my daughter's chances of growing up as a confident Aboriginal person, secure in her cultural identity, were very slim indeed.

April's marriage to Bob Radcliff reinforced her low self-concept as she was constantly overshadowed by her domineering mother-in-law. When Mother Radcliff confided in a friend, "I would simply dread being grandmother to a bunch of little half-breeds!" (116), April was hardly surprised. The marriage ended quickly with a generous monetary settlement, not because of any regard for April's rights, but to sever the relationship as quickly and expeditiously as possible. In keeping with her survival instinct of making as few waves as possible and seizing whatever good the moment might have to offer, April accepted the settlement and relocated to Winnipeg.

Though April achieved financial independence after her divorce from Bob, this was not enough to shield her from abuse and violence motivated by racism. The documentation of the rape she experienced is one of the most graphic rape scenes in English literature and leaves nothing to readers' imaginations. It does not thrill or titillate; readers share April's horror and disgust through every indignity and pain she suffers. Though she documents the aftermath of the rape and describes reactions of rape victims accurately, it is done in such a detached manner that it appears understated.

On the other hand, April's childhood experiences had trained her well for whatever indignity society might offer. Since early childhood, society had violated her basic human rights repeatedly and she had survived, angry and bitter, but she had survived. The indignity and pain of the rape was an extension of her previous life. She had been raised knowing that if she had rights, she did not know what they were. People had power over her, and when they wished to exercise this power to fulfill their own warped needs, she was the hapless victim. She knew what she had to do to survive. She had to comply so the consequences would not be more serious than what was already happening to her. She knew she had to make herself as inconspicuous as possible. She had to fight for life and sanity, but she had to use tactics that were non-threatening to her aggressors. She had to suppress her feelings until she was absolutely certain there was no one to see her crumble.

April's account of the aftermath of the rape can be contrasted with the victim statement of a recent rape trial in Winnipeg. The woman stated, "I have lost myself, the real me, the person I used to be" which the judge found to be a "powerful and compelling" statement (Bray A6). April's self had long been lost; though physically more traumatic, the rape was a further episode where her rights were violated and she had to cope as best she could. She coped because she had to; there never had been anyone in her life who had not betrayed her trust when she most needed help. Victim impact statements have come to be an important part of Canada's justice system, and one can only hope that there are people in the system who are sensitive enough to know that there are some members of society who have been so damaged they are unable to formulate impact statements. They have been trained from early childhood to accept and survive, and it may not even occur to them that they are being victimized because what they experience is part of daily living. This is not to say that they do not hurt as much as women who can verbalize their hurt, but like April, they wait until they are safely locked in their bathrooms to let the tears flow (164).

Reporting the rape was April's first move toward reclaiming her self. The trial was traumatic for her, but she had already mustered the courage to charge the rapist and she had survived the insensitive attitudes of some of the medical staff who had examined her. She knew she would survive the trial, even though she was required to tell her story with all the lurid details over and over again. She never had experienced the luxury of privacy in her life before and did not expect it in adulthood. During her formative years, she had become accustomed to being critically scrutinized by people who, at best, took an impersonal interest in her. She had delicately honed skills which allowed her to maintain an inner dignity and integrity in any situation, however humiliating. Above all, she refused to become a helpless victim.

The relentless barrage of dehumanizing treatment was exacerbated by the fact that April was Métis. Though neglect, violence, and abuse are strangers to no culture, Culleton dramatically portrays how Aboriginals, and especially Aboriginal women, are particularly vulnerable. Society in general has viewed this violence as part of Aboriginal culture, and consequently, Aboriginal people often believe it themselves. George Manuel, the first president of the National Indian Brotherhood, states: "The symbols that point to discrimination and low esteem become absorbed into the daily custom and life style of the wretched of the earth, until we come to believe what is said about us" (Manuel and Posluns 102).

Vicki English Currie, a Blackfoot scholar and educator, supports Manuel's statement. She talks about alcoholism and violence which plague many Aboriginal communities and points out, "Many Indian people who are experiencing inner conflict are under the impression that we are born with this anguish and that it is part of an Indian lifestyle. We seem to accept this self-concept, with all its negativity" (Currie 58).

April Raintree subscribed to this belief about Aboriginal people, though she did not consciously apply it to herself. Readers despair as her attitude persists, knowing that the "search" cannot ever come to fruition until April accepts the fact that she is Aboriginal and that Aboriginals are no better and no worse than any other culture group.

Her moments of vindication are few and far between. She finally convinced the social workers to remove her from the DeRosier home, she sued for divorce and got a comfortable settlement, and the rapist was successfully prosecuted. Vindication, however, does not appear to have been a strong motivation in April's life; Cheryl's survival, and consequently, her own were uppermost in her mind. With agonizing slowness, April's attitude toward her culture was changing, but the shock of Cheryl's suicide jolted her into facing reality.

Culleton chose a happy ending for her book. As April set out to raise Henry Lee with the help of Cheryl's friend Nancy and Nancy's mother, readers feel that the search is finally over. There will be love, peace, and serenity in April's life, and that, too, is part of Aboriginal culture.

Works Cited

Bray, Allison. "Rapist jailed for 'evil' assault on doughnut shop employee." *Winnipeg Free Press* 1 APR:1999:A6.

Culleton, Beatrice. *In Search of April Raintree*. Winnipeg, MB: Pemmican Publications, 1983.

Currie, Vicki English. "The Need for Re-evaluation in Native Education." *Writing the Circle: Native Women of Western Canada*. Ed. Jeanne Perreault and Sylvia Vance. Edmonton, AB: NeWest Publishers, 1990.

Grant, Agnes. *No End of Grief: Indian Residential Schools in Canada*. Winnipeg, MB: Pemmican Publications, 1996.

Highway, Tomson. *Kiss of the Fur Queen*. Toronto: Doubleday, 1998.

Manuel, George, and Michael Posluns. *The Fourth World: An Indian Reality*. New York: Free Press, 1974.

The Special Time

Beatrice Culleton Mosionier

My Dad died in 1997. He was eighty-seven so while I was prepared for his death, it still hit me hard.

Around ten years ago, I took him to St. Norbert thinking that he would have a nice visit with my foster father, Mr. Roy. (I had lived with the Roys from age four to fifteen.) Having retired, they sold their house and moved into a very nice, spacious apartment, overlooking the Red River. Their apartment is comfortably furnished and filled with luscious green plants. Framed pictures of relatives—children, grandchildren, brothers, sisters, nieces, and nephews—cover their walls and they show that the people who live here have long-term stability in their lives with close family ties.

As Mr. Roy was showing us albums of yet more pictures, and talking enthusiastically as he usually did, I caught a look on my Dad's face. He had been quietly listening, quietly looking about, and it occurred to me that perhaps he saw in this place what he could have had in his life had he been a white man. I think I saw that in my Dad's eyes. And I don't think he wanted it for himself. I think he wanted it for his children.

As for the Roys, I could have stayed at their home until I graduated from high school and was discharged from Children's Aid. I could have, but I didn't. After my sister Vivian's death in 1964, my oldest sister, Kathy, and I began to exchange letters, and she asked if I wanted to come live with her in Scarborough, Ontario. Oh yes, of course I wanted to live with my real sister! I'd only been waiting since I was three to go back home, so living with my real sister was just as good.

I guess Children's Aid decided no, and they left it to Mrs. Roy to tell me. Angry and sad, I decided that if I couldn't go live with my real sister, I didn't want to stay in any foster home to pretend that I was a part of a family. The previous year, one of my other foster sisters had gone to St. Charles Academy, a school for girls which took in boarders, so I insisted on going there, too.

On that Sunday evening, just before Mr. Roy took me to the boarding school, I went down to the basement where Mrs. Roy was sorting through laundry, preparing for the Monday morning wash. Awkwardly, I said goodbye. She didn't say much to me and she didn't look at me. I thought she was really angry with me for having chosen to leave them. Later, much later, I thought maybe she wasn't angry with me. Maybe she was very sad that I was leaving. Maybe in spite of all that I'd put her through, maybe she really liked me.

When *In Search of April Raintree* first came out, people read that it was autobiographical and thought April's real parents and foster parents were like mine in real life. That part really disturbed me because unless I could explain what I meant by autobiographical, some would unfairly judge the people I admire and cherish.

When I was eleven or twelve years old, I believed that if I took the time—it had to be special time—and I concentrated really, really hard, I could figure out solutions to all the problems of the world. I don't know if it was my natural flair for being a procrastinator, but I never did find that time.

Vivian committed suicide in January 1964.

Kathy committed suicide in October 1980.

In April 1981, I narrowed my goal from finding solutions to world problems to trying to find answers to questions relating to my own family. Writing *In Search of April Raintree* was, for me, therapeutic. Unfortunately, I still know of people who might have benefited by reading this book and others like it, but didn't. I know of people who should have talked, but didn't. I know of people who should have listened. And didn't. In spite of my writings, I think I am one of those who let their guard down and didn't listen enough.

Of the two sisters, Cheryl Raintree was the character whom I most wanted readers to love. I intended it that way so that when she died we would be so very sorry at the loss of her potential. Both of my sisters were beautiful and special, and they had so much promise, as Cheryl did, and as do too many others who commit suicide. At the end of last year, my nephew committed suicide. Today, I no longer search for an answer on how to prevent suicide, because I don't have, nor do I want control over other people. The answer, if there is one, lies in doing away with the pains that make people turn to thoughts of suicide.

In Search of April Raintree allows non-Native people to feel what it's like to be a Métis in an emotional way, and many have also told me, "This is *my* story!" Others focus on the issue of racism, asking me if I would write some more about it. Readers have asked me how to get rid of racism, and I thought that we can't get rid of it, we can only prepare the receiving end for it, so that the hurt is not so deep.

Then a couple of years ago, I was flicking channels and stopped on a PBS program already in progress. What I saw of the documentary filled me with that excitement a scientist must feel when she's discovered an important solution, but I was also dismayed that this incredible exercise was not well known and widely used. Using the Internet, I learned that the documentary I watched was called, *Eye of the Storm*, and was featured on *Frontline*. The documentary was about an exercise now known as the "Blue-eyed/Brown-eyed" exercise, a practice in which people are divided up according to eye colour with the brown-eyed designated superior and the blue-eyed inferior. The blue-eyed are isolated in uncomfortable conditions and then brought into the room and treated by the brown-eyed according to negative stereotypes commonly assigned to people of colour, women and other "outsiders" in our society (Lester 1). The exercise was developed by Jane Elliot, a third-grade teacher and "pioneer in racism awareness training, inspired to take action by the assassination of Dr. Martin Luther King, Jr., in 1968" (Lester 1).

"The purpose of the exercise is to give white people an opportunity to find out how it feels to be something other than white" (Lester 1).

Having read more information on these workshops, it seemed that Jane Elliot had found that special time. She had looked at racism from all angles; she'd seen its effects on all those involved; and she came up with a way to heal it. Jane Elliot's exercise won't work for everyone. In our world society, there are dominant groups, followers, and loners, and always, there are those of us who are different. And that's natural. We don't have to be bigots. We can give each other respect and dignity without losing anything at all. Like many medicines, Jane Elliot's medicine can be hard for some to swallow, but from what I saw, her medicine is powerful and effective.

Works Cited

Culleton, Beatrice. *In Search of April Raintree*. Winnipeg: Pemmican, 1983.

Lester, Nora. "A Blue Eyed: A Guide to Use in Organizations." *California Newsreel*. 9 July 1999
<http://www.newsreel.org/ guides/blueeyed.htm>

"What Constitutes a Meaningful Life?": Identity Quesl(ion)s In *In Search of April Raintree*

Michael Creal

In Search of April Raintree is becoming an increasingly important novel in the landscape of Canadian fiction. More and more readers have come to see that the story of April and her sister Cheryl gives flesh and blood to an aspect of Canadian history that many Canadians, past and present, have failed to confront or prefer to ignore.

The novel reveals through a simple, powerful narrative, the enormity of the problems facing huge numbers of aboriginal Canadians. The story of April and Cheryl is particular, of course. It is set in Winnipeg and is about two Métis sisters who, at an early age, are "rescued" from their alcoholic parents by the Children's Aid and placed in foster homes in rural Manitoba. In one case, the outcome of the story is tragic, and in the other, hopeful, but the obstacles which both face are cruel and punishing. These problems are the product of a long history: white settlement and conquest, nineteenth century treaty arrangements between the First Nations and the British Crown (a fresh look at this is instructive), the missionary work of the churches, the Indian Act of 1876, and the residential school system. The overall effect of that history has been deeply destructive of the cultures of First Nations. "Indian Reservations" might have seemed a reasonable arrangement in the last century, but some visitors to Canada from other continents have been struck by its similarity to South Africa's notorious system of *apartheid*. Many aboriginal Canadians who moved into towns and cities and others of mixed blood (including Métis like the parents of April and Cheryl Raintree) found themselves between two worlds. On the one hand, there was the world of their old communities and cultures from which they had been torn but which was still a part of them. On the other, there was the world of the "white man" who often seemed to have little use for "Indians" and "half breeds" who did not measure up to the work ethic of Protestantism (and capitalism) and other values of the dominant European and North American culture. For such people, there was a deep and troubling "identity" crisis.

In Search of April Raintree can be read from a number of perspectives, and in this brief analysis, there will be two lines of enquiry. How did April and Cheryl deal with this question of identity; how did they view their heritage? And what did each look forward to as they approached the end of high school and the time when they would no longer be wards of the Children's Aid; what was their *quest*? The two questions are closely related, and in what follows, that inter-relationship will be kept in mind, but the two questions will be dealt with separately.

The Question of Identity

In his books *Sources of the Self* and *The Malaise of Modernity*, the Canadian philosopher Charles Taylor makes clear that one's identity or sense of self is worked out in a kind of "dialogue" with those to whom one is closest and with those whom one regards as most important. These are not always one and the same as we can see in the case of April Raintree. This "dialogue" is not always easy or agreeable. Often, it involves struggle and even rebellion, as we know from personal experience. We are by nature social creatures, and who we become as individual persons is the outcome of a social process. We aren't *determined* by that process; we *do* have a measure of freedom in the choices we make, but we don't make these choices in a social vacuum.

How did Cheryl and April approach this question of identity?

As April came to understand, through the taunts of the white children in her second foster home, that her parents were, in fact, alcoholic; and as she digested the fact, in the schoolyard and from early experience, that Métis and

"Indians" were commonly treated with contempt; she gradually came to a decision. Because she was light-skinned and could pass as white, she decided she was going to *be* white and reject everything that had to do with being Métis. She would invent her own identity and escape the prejudice which had made her life at the DeRosiers' so lonely and miserable. In April's case, she had had no "dialogue" or meaningful conversation with her family or other Métis (except for Cheryl whom we will consider in a moment), and what she had learned from her years at the DeRosiers' was that being Métis held no promise. The only obstacle in this path was her sister Cheryl whom April dearly loved and who was unmistakably aboriginal in her skin colour and appearance. For April, the "white" world and all its material benefits was what she longed for.

When April was sent to St. Bernadette's Academy to finish high school, she had the opportunity to begin creating her new identity. Other students in the Academy knew nothing of her background, so she made up a story about her parents having died in a plane crash. The whole thing seemed to work. She began to distance herself from Cheryl, which caused her some guilt, but when at the law office where she was employed after graduation, she met a wealthy Torontonian named Bob Radcliff, another chapter in her new life began. She married Bob Radcliff, moved to Toronto, and entered a very affluent level of white society.

What April learned in Toronto, however, was that her past could not really be left behind. It became evident that her mother-in-law did not want a grandchild who was part Indian, and her husband, April discovered, was having an affair. The breakdown of her marriage and the satisfactory divorce settlement meant that she was free to return to Winnipeg and make a "fresh" start. There would be yet another April Raintree because April was, indeed, in "search" of her real identity.

The traumas she experienced soon after she went back to Winnipeg drove that search to a deeper level. Her brutal rape scarred her to the depths of her being and severely limited the relationship with her new friend, and old acquaintance, Roger. (At that point, any real intimacy with a man seemed impossible for April.) The realization during the course of the painful rape trial that her sister was, in fact, a prostitute was a devastation that April didn't really know how to handle. After that discovery, her attempts to rebuild a relationship with Cheryl were angrily rejected by Cheryl who was now in a dark hole of despair, and couldn't endure what she felt and believed was April's contempt for her.

By the time Cheryl leapt to her death from the Louise Bridge, April's relationship with her friend Roger had moved to a level of trust (this was a year after the rape), and Roger's support was important in helping April deal with Cheryl's suicide. Reading Cheryl's journals after her death gave April the full account of Cheryl's activities during April's time in Toronto. They recounted Cheryl's search for her father which ended in her discovery that he was a hopeless and pathetic drunk. This revelation was shattering for Cheryl and eventually led Cheryl herself into a life of alcoholism and prostitution. Cheryl's suicide note to April asked April to take care of her one-year-old son Henry Lee and help him find what his mother had longed for but never achieved. The novel ends on that note of hope. April *finds* herself as she unconsciously refers to "MY PEOPLE OUR PEOPLE." She realizes that a kind of denial has been lifted from her spirit and that she can now seek to live out her life with an identity that has continuity with her past, but is open to a future with new possibilities for herself and Henry Lee. It is not a romantic ending; there is every reason to believe that there will be struggle ahead, but good grounds to believe that April can now look at her life honestly and in a positive and hopeful way. As a woman, she has lived through one of the most brutal and degrading experiences possible, but in "dialogue" with Roger (to use Charles Taylor's language), she can find it possible to affirm her sexuality and identity as a woman. Similarly, as a Métis, she has learned through the best of her long years of experience with Cheryl, and through her reading of Cheryl's diary, that she can identify with "her" people. The "search" will go on, but a crucial milestone has been passed.

Cheryl's story is a contrast to April's. She had good experiences in her foster homes (apart from the terrible period with April at the DeRosiers) and was actually encouraged to celebrate her Métis background. She was a spirited young girl, quite fearless in rejecting the official "white" account of Louis Riel. Cheryl's response to that account is a good example of an important issue in historical interpretation. History is generally written by the "victors," but Cheryl believed the "counter (historical) narrative," which sees Riel defending the rights of his people against their "conquerors." The dominant narrative learned in school presented Riel as "a crazy half breed," a "rebel hanged for treason." This is an account which April had simply accepted. Cheryl, in other words, had no questions about her own identity, and what she learned about the old ways of Indians as skilled and courageous hunters, proud and independent in their ways, led her to imagine her parents in light of that picture. She had never been told the truth about her parents (April was reluctant to disabuse Cheryl of her illusions about them), so her sense of herself was very much bound up with this idealised image of her father and mother; she thought that in the olden days her father might have been a chief or warrior, and her mother, she imagined as being as beautiful as an Indian princess.

Cheryl's plan after graduating from high school was to train as a social worker and work among her people. (She had already begun volunteering at the Friendship Centre.) She was unimpressed with April's decision to marry Bob Radcliff and saddened by the distance that had developed between herself and April, but it wasn't until she returned to Winnipeg after a devastating visit with April in Toronto that she embarked on a serious search for her parents. It was the total contradiction between the idealized picture of her parents that she created in her mind, and the reality she eventually confronted, that shook Cheryl to the core of her being. The image of her parents that she had identified with so deeply proved to be nothing more than wishful thinking. What had given her life meaning to that point simply evaporated. The combination of a destructive relationship with Mark DeSoto, and her need to provide money for her father, led her into prostitution and alcoholism. Her sense of self-worth steadily diminished and the fact that she had inadvertently been part of the reason for April's rape didn't help. There was no joy left in her life, and when she decided that she could no longer live with this "living death," she committed suicide.

If one thinks of one's identity being formed in "dialogue" with those around one, as Taylor suggests, it is possible to see a constructive content in Cheryl's "dialogue" with the MacAdams and the Steindalls and in her early years with April. Even her struggle to tell the "truth" about her people in the face of physical punishment at school reinforced her convictions. But she had invested so much in the picture she had created of her parents that the actual communication with her real father, which she had anticipated with such hope and longing, contained nothing that could sustain a positive sense of her Métis identity. As Cheryl herself put it, her instinct to survive vanished (207).

The Quests of April and Cheryl

Up to this point, the accent has been on April's and Cheryl's *Métis* identity, and that point, of course, is fundamental to the novel. But the story of *anyone* (or *everyman*) can be looked upon as a quest for what fulfils, a quest for what is *good* in life as that person understands it. And, indeed, the quest for identity is actually tied up with what one regards as good, with what one can affirm as having value, with what one, in the end, regards as fulfilling, and wants to be identified with.

In North American culture, there is a huge emphasis on the importance of individuality. In fact, this emphasis is usually regarded as one of the notable achievements of the Western tradition. Each person is seen as unique and that uniqueness properly merits respect and calls for celebration. There is a long history behind this high valuation placed on the individual, a history that goes back at least to the Greek and Biblical traditions where individual civic and moral responsibility was stressed as much as individual freedom. In more recent times, the focus has been predominantly on individual *freedom*, and in North American society, this value is often translated in terms of individuals "doing their own thing." This sort of freedom is contrasted to behaviour that conforms to social expectations. In other words, there is a strong tendency in our society to place the individual in a pre-eminent position and to regard society (or community) as secondary. Probably in every society, there is some tension between the aspirations or longings of the individual and the social expectations which surround the individual. We commonly speak of the process of socialization as the way in which that tension is reconciled for good or for ill. But in our era of individualism, the bias favours the individual, and this places our individualism in contrast to the more communal orientation of most other societies and cultures, including the First Nations of Canada. This point needs to be recognized in our further explorations of the "quests" of April and Cheryl.

In his book *The Courage To Be* written almost half a century ago, the philosopher and theologian Paul Tillich talked about how a person may affirm herself, i.e. seek to find her identity as an "individual," or affirm herself as a "participant" in a group or community. The distinction isn't absolute—a person can move back and forth between those poles—but it can be instructive in considering the stories of April and Cheryl. For instance, April can be seen either as affirming herself as an individual (in rejecting her Métis background) or affirming herself as a "participant" in *white* society and culture. This example indicates nicely that every individual has to belong *somewhere* and makes clear that there is often a lot more conformity among those professing individualism than they would like to admit. In Cheryl's case, she can be seen as affirming herself as an individual in defiance of the dominant views of those around her—for example, the teachers and children in her school—but also as affirming herself as a participant in, or member of, Métis or Indian society and culture. In Cheryl's case, that self-affirmation as a Métis was so deep that when she lost all confidence in the life of the community, in its demoralized form, she had nothing meaningful left to affirm, nothing left to live for.

Both Paul Tillich and Charles Taylor (along with many others) see the question of meaning—what constitutes a meaningful life?—as the central spiritual issue of our time. It is an issue that actually arises out of that very insistence that each individual should create for herself a unique individual identity. It is an issue that many in "mainstream" Western and North American culture confront, and it finds expression in a good deal of modern and post-modern literature, art, and film. But the problem of meaning takes on a particular urgency in the case of cultures like those of Canadian First Nations that have been severely disrupted as a "conquering" (or "imperial") culture undermines their very foundations. For Cheryl—initially, at least—building self-respect in the Métis community in the face of that cultural disruption was itself a meaningful, if very challenging, task. It was a "good" to be worked towards, the very centre and focus of her own personal quest. It was, perhaps, because she had so totally imagined that good as being embodied in her parents, that she was completely undone when the truth turned out to be so different. In April's case, the struggle to find the good was difficult, but she was able to move on when she discovered that what she thought was the object of her quest, an affluent married life in white society, for instance, turned out to be only a shadow of what she really wanted. Although she thought a kind of partnership with Cheryl would be the answer, that was probably unrealistic, and the idea never really got off the ground. It took the crisis of Cheryl's death, along with the beginning of an understanding of the good that Cheryl struggled towards but failed to reach, to set April on a new course. The novel suggests that Henry Lee will become a central focus, and if all worked out, Roger will become her partner and an important source of support. At the point when the novel ends, April is just in her early twenties, so there is a long path ahead. In actual fact, however, the quest for the "good," for what really fulfils, is a lifelong enterprise. For some, it might be much more challenging than for others, and this might well be the case for April. On the other hand, she has achieved a clarity as to what she is about, a clarity that many never achieve, so this is very much to her advantage. At any rate, another philosopher, Alasdair MacIntyre, who has written on this subject, has argued that *the good life for humans is a life spent searching for the good life for humans* (my emphasis 219). The direction may be clear—as it appears to be for April—but the actual search is a lifelong task. And MacIntyre makes a further point which is relevant to our consideration of Beatrice Culleton's novel. He argues that our search, our story, is always embedded in the story of those communities and traditions from which we have come. We may rebel against the community or tradition, or we may seek to change or reform it, or we may be willing simply to affirm it as it is. Whatever our stance with reference to those communities and traditions that have in some measure shaped us, our individual stories and our particular quests can only be understood in the light of the larger stories of those communities and their traditions.

To return to the beginning: while the stories of Cheryl and April are powerful in their own right, they invite—if not *require*—us to consider the larger story of Canada's First Nations. That story continues, and the response of other Canadians will affect the shape of that story in the twenty-first century. We will affect it—for good or for ill—and we will be affected by it. So while *In Search of April Raintree* raises many interesting questions about its two central characters, it also raises enormously important questions for all of us about our own country and its First Nations.

Works Cited

Culleton, Beatrice. *In Search of April Raintree.* Winnipeg, MB: Pemmican, 1983.

MacIntyre, Alasdair. *After Virtue.* Notre Dame, IN: U of Notre Dame P, 1984.

Taylor, Charles. *The Malaise of Modernity.* Concord, ON: Anansi, 1991.

_____. *Sources of the Self.* Cambridge: Harvard UP, 1989.

Tillich, Paul. *The Courage To Be.* New Haven: Yale UP, 1952.

In Search of Cheryl Raintree, and Her Mother

Jeanne Perreault

> The contributing factors such as sexual abuse, family violence, alcohol and drug abuse, solvent abuse ... etcetera are only the symptoms of a bigger and more devastating cycle of oppression and deprivation.
>
> —Sarah McKay, talking about suicide,
> Shibogama First Nations Council.
> December. 1992: qtd in *Choosing Life* 18

> Though it is premature to put forth a comprehensive plan of social intervention one thing is clear ... unless there is a genuine transformation of social, political and economic institutions and attitudes of White [sic] society, toward including Native Indians fully, equally, democratically, and fraternally, we cannot expect a meaningful reduction in this needless waste of valuable life.
>
> —Jarvis and Boldt 22

When a student suggested that Beatrice Culleton was making use of a clever literary device to get Henry Raintree and his family out of the northern community of Norway House and into the city, I was taken aback. The literary device my analytic student had identified was tuberculosis. I took the opportunity in that class to add some statistics to the usual class discussions about the interaction of material realities with the shaping of narrative. Readers need to be aware of the social and physical realities facing many people of Native heritage that Culleton brings to the surface of *In Search of April Raintree*. Included in this list are illness, infant mortality, foster care, alcoholism, rape, domestic violence against women, prostitution, and suicide. Representing these violations against her characters is not only (and I do not mean "merely") an aesthetic choice for Culleton. It is essential to the informing discourse of the novel. Race and racism are not inflections upon these issues. They play an integral part in making the following statistics intelligible. I am not trained as a sociologist,[1] but I was dismayed to discover how little information is available and some of it, as you will see, is inconsistent or even contradictory. Beatrice Culleton makes us feel the cruelty of a racist society. The figures below allow readers to move outside the specific anguish of the Raintree family and require us to know the society we have made.

Population

Canadian Panel on Violence Against Women (Aboriginal Panel), Final Report, 1993, provides the following information about the number of Aboriginal people estimated to be in Canada:

> There are approximately 511,791 Aboriginal people with "Status" rights as defined by the Indian Act, of whom 300,000 live on reserves. The 1991 Census indicates that approximately 135,265 people identify themselves as Métis; people who identify as Métis are most likely to live in Manitoba, Saskatchewan and Alberta; and, seven out of ten Aboriginal people live west of Ontario, compared with 29 percent of the total population. The 1991 Statistics Canada Aboriginal Peoples Survey found that almost three-quarters of the Aboriginal population of Canada is under the age of 35. (149)

Every source that I investigated commented on the difficulty of getting accurate figures and comprehensive information about First Nations peoples. Those who were not registered as "status" or "treaty" Indians often were not acknowledged to be Native at all.[2] David Long and Terry Fox, in "Circles of Healing: Illness, Healing, and Health among Aboriginal People in Canada," assert that Native peoples argue that if Métis and Non-Status people are included in the calculations, approximately two million Aboriginal people live in Canada (129). Doctors Waldram, Herring and Young support this view, noting some of the problems of getting accurate figures:

Databases of utilization of hospital and physician care from universal health insurance plans ... do not provide "ethnic identification" though some special identifiers of registered Indians are provided in some Western provinces. (73)

Aboriginal peoples who do not reside on reserves are "not even included [in the Canadian Mortality Database]. Data on the Métis are practically non-existent" (Waldram, Herring, Young 71). For registered Indians, there are two sources of population data: the Indian Register operated by the Department of Indian Affairs and Northern Development and the census conducted by Statistics Canada. Since the census is based on self-report of ethnic origin, it is the only source of information on Non-Status Indians, Métis, and Inuit. Further complicating the issue, as Waldram, Herring and Young comment, "non-cooperation of a large number of Indian bands with Statistics Canada during recent censuses has resulted in incomplete enumeration" (71).[3]

With these cautionary observations in mind, I offer the following information.

Health

Infant mortality on reserves is much higher than it is for the general population: in 1960 the rate was 82 per 100,000; in 1986 it was 16.5; it has now decreased to 10.2. Nevertheless the newer rate still represents nearly double the national standard (Long and Fox 132). Meningitis is a frequent cause of death among Aboriginal infants: a study of the years 1976–83 in five provinces shows that the risk of death was four times that of all Canadians during the post neonatal period (Waldram, Herring, Young 79–80). Pneumonia and infections of the respiratory tract in rural Southwest Ontario afflict 46 percent of Indian infants compared to 18 percent of non-Indians in the first year of life. A study in Southwest Ontario showed that diarrheal disease or gastro-enteritis in infants appeared at a rate of three times the number of episodes, 24 times the number of hospitalizations than that of the general population (Waldram, Herring, Young 79–80).

Long and Fox assert that "[f]or specific age groups, such as those aged five to nineteen, the mortality rate of status Indians is four times the national rate" (132).

Disparity in the rate of tuberculosis between Aboriginal and non-Aboriginal Canadians remains great, with the former having an incidence as much as ten times higher (Waldram, Herring, Young 75).

George Jarvis and Menno Boldt found that in the 1970s "[b]etween ages 30 and 39 the death rate for Natives [was] seven times that of the rest of the population" (8). The statistics are as follows: among Natives, 32.4 percent of deaths were due to accidents while in the general population 8.6 percent of deaths were due to accidents. Natives are 27 times more likely than non-Natives to die by fire, almost 50 percent on Saturday night; motor vehicle accidents account for 10 percent of Native deaths, and 4.2 percent for the general population (11–13). They conclude, "Our informed estimate is that over 40 percent of all Native deaths are directly attributable to the misuse of alcoholic beverages" (20).[4]

Foster Care

Suzanne Fournier and Ernie Crey's analysis of foster care and renewal in Aboriginal communities provides an historical frame for understanding the Raintree family. They note that "by the late 1940s four or five generations [of Native people] had returned from residential schools as poorly educated, angry, abused strangers who had no experience in parenting" (82). With the Amendments to Section 88 of the Federal Indian Act in 1951, Ottawa delegated responsibility for Aboriginal education, welfare, and social services to the provinces. Provinces could negotiate for the amount they would receive for delivery of services. In 1959, only one percent of all children in care were Native. By the end of the 1960s, 30–40 percent of all legal wards were Aboriginal children, though Natives were only four percent of the national population (82). Fournier and Crey say that "by the late 1970s, one in four status Indian children could expect to be separated from his or her parents for all or part of childhood. If non-status and Métis children, on whom statistics were not maintained, are included, the statistics show that one in three, or in some provinces every other Aboriginal child spent part of his or her childhood as a legal ward of the state (88).[5]

A 1990 survey of Aboriginal prisoners in Prince Albert, Saskatchewan, found that over 95 percent came from either a group home or a foster home (Fournier and Crey 90).

Edwin Kimelman, in *No Quiet Place: Review Committee on Indian and Métis Adoptions and Placements*, 1985, distinguishes between Status/Treaty and Non-Status including Métis. In 1981, Kimelman finds that 61 percent of children in care are Native, which includes Status and Non-Status (139). In 1984, the total number of children in care in Manitoba was 2,879. Of this number, 38 percent are Native, and of that, 25 percent are Non-Status (223–24). Many Canadian children were surrendered for adoption to out-of-province or out-of-country families. Of children placed outside of the province, 86 percent were Native (Status/Non-Status); in 1981, 53 percent of all children in care were sent to the USA; 86 percent of that 53 percent were Native (57–58)[6] *Aboriginal Health in Canada* asserts that "in 1981 the proportion of Indian children living on reserves who were 'in care' was more than 5 percent. This slowly declined to 3 percent by 1987, still 3 times the national average" (Waldram, Herring, Young 90).

The Royal Commission study observes that "early separation from family and emotional deprivation generally are prime risk factors for self harm" (*Choosing Life* 23).

Alcohol

While figures and perspectives vary, all researchers comment on the destructive effects of alcohol abuse on Aboriginal people.

Fournier and Crey quote a 1991 federal survey that showed 60 percent of Aboriginal teens aged 12 to 15 admitted to drinking alcohol regularly, a figure that goes to 80 percent in the 16–20 year olds (174). They further note that alcohol psychosis occurs among Aboriginal people at five times the national average and that 20 percent of hospital admissions for alcohol-related illness are Aboriginal persons (174). Information from Indian Affairs and from medical services shows that nearly 60 percent of status Indian illnesses and deaths are alcohol related (Long and Fox 132).

The National Native Association of Treatment Directors estimates that 80 percent of Aboriginal people in Canada are affected by alcoholism, either through being addicted or through the addiction of a close family member (Fournier and Crey 174).

Waldram, Herring and Young argue that "alcoholism should be seen as a disease which affects *individuals*; the fact that some Aboriginal communities appear to disproportionately experience the negative effects of alcohol abuse is not suggestive of a cultural or biological problem, but rather of the fairly uniform negative effects of poverty, racism, and marginalization stemming from colonization" (emphasis in original, 269).

Violence Against Women, Family

Long and Fox report that "a study in British Columbia indicated that 86 percent of Native respondents had experienced family violence" (249). In a study carried out by the Ontario Native Women's Association (1989), 84 percent of respondents indicated that family violence occurred in their communities and a further 80 percent indicated that they had personally experienced family violence (18–20). This account, however, does not tell us how many subjects were interviewed.

The Canadian government's two-volume study (1985) of prostitution and pornography[7] provides no information based on ethnic or racial background.[8] A rough estimate given by a former Native prostitute in Vancouver is that "75 percent were Native girls and women" (*Choosing Life* 29).

Paul Whitehead and Michael Hayes's discussion of alcohol and social problems in Aboriginal communities estimates that offenders had been drinking in 34 percent of rapes (45) In the general population of Canada, 40 percent of women (in a study of 420 women) reported at least one experience of rape (Women's Safety Project).[9] This study likely elicited more forthcoming information from respondents. Usual estimates are that one rape in ten in the general population is reported.

Suicide

The profound importance of suicide among Aboriginal people is underscored by the fact that members of the Royal Commission on Aboriginal People published a separate volume on the issue, titled *Choosing Life: Special report on suicide among Aboriginal people.* Their analysis includes extensive discussion of community response to suicide, which I do not include here.[10]

Waldram, Herring and Young argue that epidemiological data on Aboriginal suicides and homicides are extremely variable in quality. Between 1984 and 1988 the age-standard suicide rates among male residents of Indian reserves were three times and female residents two times that of all other Canadians (90). For every successful suicide "there are many more suicide attempts (also called para-suicide). These may or may not result in any contact with the health and social service systems, and their true magnitude is thus difficult to estimate" (90).

Jarvis and Boldt also discuss suicide: one in every ten (10.4 percent) Native deaths is a suicide, five times higher than the general population's suicide rate (13–14).

In 1980, George Jarvis's study *The Probability of Suicide: Identification of Canadian Population Segments at High Risk* observes that

Canadian native [sic] peoples also appear to have very high rates of suicide despite probable underreporting of this cause of death. Additional difficulties are introduced by the fact that Indian suicides among other

than treaty and registered Indians are not listed as
occurring to Indians. . . . At present we have no way of
estimating suicide rates for the large numbers of non-
status Indians and Métis. (11)

Jarvis finds that the suicide rate among Native people in
1970–72 is "27.9 per 100,000, 116 percent higher than the
national rate for 1971. . . . Unofficial reports indicate that
actual rates of suicide are at least five times as high as these
official reports" (11). Jarvis found that "among Indians and
Eskimos [sic] aged 10–19 there are almost seven times as
many suicides as among all Canadians of the same age. For
females of the same age, rates of suicide are almost eleven
times as high for native peoples as for all female Canadians
aged 10–19" (13). Based on data from 1987–89, researchers
found that an Indian adolescent (10–19 years) is 5.1 times
more likely to die from suicide than a non-Indian adolescent.
Girls of Aboriginal heritage are eight times more vulnerable
than non-Aboriginal girls (*Choosing Life* 13).

The authors of the Royal Commission document assert
that true rates are likely to be higher than official rates
because estimates are that up to 25 percent of accidental
deaths among Aboriginal people are really unreported
suicides. In British Columbia a recent analysis of coroners'
files uncovered 1) a significant number of Aboriginal suicide
victims unclassified as Aboriginal; and 2) a significant
number of probable suicides counted as accidental or
unclassifiable deaths. As others have noted, they are aware
that systemic data collection is limited and that suicide
reporting is suspect. Figures are also skewed because suicide
attempts produce medical complications that may later lead
to death (*Choosing Life* 17).

The Royal Commission study found that among non-
Aboriginal people who attempted or completed suicide,
22–65 percent showed alcohol in the bloodstream. Among
Aboriginal people, 74 percent in British Columbia and
80–90 percent in Alberta have alcohol in the bloodstream
(*Choosing Life* 23).

The Royal Commission's list of systemic attacks on Aboriginal identity that play a part in the high rate of suicide among Aboriginal people reads like a distillation of the experiences of the Raintree family. *Choosing Life* isolates the following identity issues:

- neglect or misrepresentation of Aboriginal history and culture in school curriculum and mass media
- belittling or racist images of Aboriginal people and their behaviour
- loss of land, languages, cultures, and spiritual grounding
- general domination of public discourse and policy by 'European' norms and values
- individual experience of ridicule, stereotyping, discrimination and racism. (29)

Like that list, the Communities that met with the Royal Commission on Aboriginal Peoples have formulated plans for suicide prevention that seem uncannily similar to the conclusion of Culleton's novel:

- cultural and spiritual revitalization
- strengthen bonds of family and community
- focus on children and youth
- holism[11]
- whole community involvement
- partnership
- community control. (*Choosing Life* 83–84)

Conclusion

The number of serious critical articles on *In Search of April Raintree* and the intense response of students, as well as senior scholars to this novel, attest to its literary power. The brutal facts named here reflect the systemic violence of poverty, illness, and despair, and the effects of a history of cultural genocide.

Sociologist, Cora Voyageur has argued that

by speaking on their own behalf, Indian women can pursue their own priorities and concerns. For example family violence is of great concern to Indian women.... If the Indian communities cannot address Indian women's concerns, then women must advocate on their own behalf. They [women] initiate and sustain many community programs and services. They are prepared to deal with societal problems such as family violence, child abuse, unemployment and alcohol abuse. They do not want these issues to be swept under the rug. (110)

In Search of April Raintree lifts the rug, showing the struggles and the strength of Métis women. Voyageur's assertions refer to the activism of Native women in their communities and on behalf of their people. Beatrice Culleton's novel, as well as being an effective character study, a moving plot, and a splendidly-structured narrative, is another mode of activism and a powerful advocate of Native women's rights.

Notes

[1] My thanks to Professor Cora Voyageur, Department of Sociology, University of Calgary, for making her extensive library available to me and to Cheryl Suzack for her careful attention to the editing of this piece.

[2] This problem was not just statistical, but one of constitutional rights. The Aboriginal Panel notes that it was not until 1982 that Métis were included as Aboriginal people under the Canadian constitution:

In 1981, Aboriginal peoples in Canada fought and won the entrenchment of their rights within the Canadian Constitution. Section 35 of the 1982 *Canada Act* confirms that the Aboriginal people of Canada include those individuals with Status resulting from the *Indian Act*, the Métis, and Inuit. (Canadian Panel 149. Information is footnoted as from Department of Indian Affairs and Northern Development. *Basic Departmental Data–1992* Ottawa, 1992).

[3] The Aboriginal Peoples Survey (1991) is "the most comprehensive national survey of Aboriginal peoples with a significant health and social component. It included ... for the first time, Métis' (Waldram, Herring, Young 74).

[4] While it does not take up questions of health as such, *Death Styles Among Canada's Indians*, a sociology "Discussion Paper" published in 1980, shows thoughtfulness in its approach (despite the

title) and includes information that is focused on Western Canada. Jarvis and Boldt's study investigated 35 Indian and Métis communities, reserves, and colonies between Oct 1, 1976 and Sept 30, 1977. They included investigation of official sources, such as Regional Indian Affairs Branch Offices, Provincial Medical Examiners' Offices and so on, and non-official sources, including obituary columns and local mortuaries (Jarvis and Boldt 4–5). Caseworkers, who were all Native Indians, usually known to the families, conducted interviews with family members (Jarvis and Boldt 5). This study found that Natives experience the highest morbity rates, the highest infant mortality rates, and the lowest life expectancies when compared with non-Natives. The authors say, "Extreme economic and social deprivation was evident among the subjects of our study" (Jarvis and Boldt 6).

[5] Fournier and Crey do not provide a source for this figure.

[6] Fournier and Crey discuss this extensively, giving accounts of many people who are seeking birth families and communities.

[7] I place this information in this category as I consider pornography and prostitution a violence against persons.

[8] This study asserts that prostitution pays much less than most people assume: "the best estimate puts net income of a female prostitute at $12–15,000 a year" (385).

[9] Thanks to Professor Barbara Crow, University of Calgary Women's Studies Program, for this information.

[10] For example, their discussion includes observations such as, "Many Native caregivers are critical of approaches to mental health and illness based on categories of medically defined disorders... Some prefer to talk in terms of imbalance or disharmony in the circle of mind body emotions spirit that defines a healthy person and a healthy community according to most Aboriginal traditions" (*Choosing Life* 20). They assert that the "profile of mental disorders among Aboriginal people is primarily a by-product of our colonial past with its layered assaults on Aboriginal cultures and personal identity, and that the psychobiological traits linked to suicidal and self-destructive behavior among Aboriginal people cannot be understood except in that context" (*Choosing Life* 21).

[11] As Aboriginal people use the term, "holism" means "sensitivity to the inter-connectedness of people and nature . . . people and community, and within person of mind body emotion and spirit" (*Choosing Life* 83).

Works Cited

Canadian Panel on Violence Against Women (Aboriginal Panel), Final Report, Ottawa, 1993.

Choosing Life: Special report on suicide among Aboriginal people. Royal Commission on Aboriginal Peoples, 1995.

Fournier, Suzanne, and Ernie Crey. Stolen from our Embrace: The Abduction of First Nations Children and the Restoration of Aboriginal Communities. Vancouver: Douglas and McIntyre, 1997.

Jarvis, George K., and Menno Boldt. Death Styles among Canada's Indians. Discussion Paper No. 24. Population Research Laboratory, Department of Sociology, The University of Alberta, Edmonton, Dec. 1980.

Jarvis, George K. The Probability of Suicide: Identification of Canadian Population Segments at High Risk. Discussion Paper No. 20. Department of Sociology, The University of Alberta, Edmonton, May 1980.

Kimelman, Edwin C. No Quiet Place: Review Committee on Indian and Metis Adoptions and Placements. 2 vols. Winnipeg: Manitoba Community Services, 1985.

Long, David Alan, and Olive Patricia Dickason. eds. Visions of the Heart: Canadian Aboriginal Issues. Toronto: Harcourt Brace, 1996.

Pornography and Prostitution: Report of the Special Committee on Pornography and Prostitution. Vol. 2. Ottawa: Canadian Government Publishing Centre, 1985.

Voyageur, Cora J. "Contemporary Indian Women." Long and Dickason 93–116.

Waldram, James B., Ann D.Herring, and T. Kue Young. Aboriginal Health in Canada: Historical, Cultural, and Epidemiological Perspectives. Toronto: U of Toronto P, 1995.

Whitehead, Paul C., and Michael J. Hayes. The Insanity of Alcohol: Social Problems in Canadian First Nations Communities. Toronto: Canadian Scholars' Press, 1998.

"Nothing but the Truth": Discursive Transparency in Beatrice Culleton

Helen Hoy

Early critical responses to Canadian Métis writer Beatrice Culleton's *In Search of April Raintree*, situating the novel in terms of its simplicity, honesty, authenticity, and artlessness, implicitly bifurcate testimonial immediacy and artistic craft, assigning uncrafted testimony to the "Native informant."[1] Several reviews paradoxically locate the novel's art precisely in its artlessness: "an earnest, artless journal-cum-fiction that is all the more powerful for its simplicity" (Moher 50) and "irritatingly naive at times, but a more sophisticated style would rob it of its authenticity, which is its greatest asset" (Francis 20). Or they inadvertently imply an art ostensibly not contained within traditional aesthetic parameters: "What the book lacks in literary polish is more than made up for in compassion, understanding and *beautifully controlled emotion*" (Sigurdson 43; emphasis mine). At best, they evince a difficulty in devising an aesthetic language to account for the text's emotional power; at worst, condescension and nostalgia for the unmediated authenticity of the speaking "Other."

"'Trembling, but honest,'" is the Crown attorney's characterization of April Raintree's testimony at the rape trial where she witnesses to the assault upon herself. "'Not once did she waver between truth and fiction,'" he avers (168).[2] In a novel in which the telling of untruths and half-truths proliferates both socially and personally, in which "lies, secrets, and silence" are both inflicted upon April and her sister Cheryl by foster parents, social workers, and history books, and prove to be a destructive component of their own interactions "'I lie to protect her and she lies to protect me, and we both lose out'" (186), "honesty" and "truth" seem to

function as talismans. Certainly they do so for reviewers. Ray
Torgrud, selected to promote the novel on the back cover,
refers to Gertrude Stein's maxim "'Write the truest sentence
that you know'" and, describing the book as autobiographical
fiction, notes its "unflinching honesty." The immediacy of her
truth-telling becomes Culleton's guarantor of literary power.
Judith Russell, speculating that Culleton has "invented the
odd experience," concludes that, "in those cases, the story
loses impact through distance" (193).

In a recent graduate course I taught, explicitly directed to
Canadian literatures "on the margins," it was *In Search of
April Raintree* (along with Jovette Marchessault's *Lesbian
Triptych* for quite different reasons) which sparked the most
heated discussion about issues of literary merit and literary
elitism, about the politics of guilt and the status of the truth
claim, about visceral responses and intellectual ones, about
literary author-ity and literary audience(s). As far as one
student was concerned, the book—so simplistic and poorly
written he wouldn't have chosen to finish reading it—was on
the course only because it was written by a Métis writer. This
same dedicated student, for the first time, failed to appear for
the subsequent class on Culleton and, later, to the Freudian
quips of fellow students, confessed somewhat wryly to having
lost his copy of the text. By contrast, another student,
attributing reader discomfiture to the book's "naked,"
"unembellished" visceral appeal, described being distraught
and off-kilter for twenty-four hours after reading it, without
being able to pinpoint the source of her distress for some time.
The flash-point in what had hitherto in the term been a
decorous class came in reaction to a student suggestion that
the novel served to provide Métis readers with a recognizable
reality. Why then, someone shot back, as disconcerting in his
abrupt anger as in the rawness of his formulation, did
Culleton not simply distribute the book to her friends in local
bars. Other students rose to this at once, equally passionately,
with countercharges of literary snobbery (though not,
interestingly enough, of racism). Clearly even to students
versed in notions of hegemony and counter-discursive

production, the presence of a book like *In Search of April Raintree* on the syllabus was fraught and disquieting. As with reviewers, subsequent discussion that day tended to oddly around the idea that Culleton had said what she meant and meant what she said (one student's phrase), and the question of whether, from a literary standpoint, such Horton-like faithfulness sufficed.

Interplaited with the notion of authenticity in *In Search of April Raintree* is the question of identity, both authorial and fictive. April and Cheryl come into maturity as Métis women, in the face of racist-sexist affronts to that identity, most blatantly represented by the "native girl' [sic] syndrome" detailed by their social worker (62). The story of that process is sustained, for most reviewers, by Culleton's own identity as a Métis woman. "Beatrice Culleton set out to tell a story—her own story—in the plainest available language. Nothing else is needed," says Judith Russell (192).[3] Just as Culleton's writing can be read as the straightforward documentation of eclipsed facts of social reality, with her personal experience of racism, foster care, poverty, alcoholism, and sibling suicide warranting the truth status of the novel's representations,[4] so the characters' struggle with identity can be read as a quest for the true self. In particular, April's story can be taken as a dis-covery of an intrinsic selfhood persistently denigrated by others, a sloughing off of false personae ("Only at the end does April realize her mistake of trying to become a white person" [Holman 11]), and a final embracing of an authentic self ("The real April Raintree, the April Raintree she tucked away for safe-keeping, begins to emerge" [Keeshig-Tobias 58]). Paul Wilson who also treats the issue of April's identity as transparent—"April determines at last to embrace her real heritage"—does admittedly go on at least to nuance that heritage, proposing that April's initial pursuit of a white identity is "as faithful to a part of her heritage" as Cheryl's identification with their Native background (30).

Such readings, of the author's and characters' breaking through to a reality and a given identity which have been obscured—historically and personally—by inaccurate representations, are the literary equivalents of recent directions in history. The tendency in history is one which Joan Scott identifies (and subsequently goes on to interrogate): "The challenge to normative history has been described . . . as an enlargement of the picture, a correction to oversights resulting from inaccurate or incomplete vision, and it has rested its claim to legitimacy on the authority of experience," with experiential evidence perceived referentially as simply "a reflection of the real" (776). Such readings treat the novel's medium as transparent, identity as immanent, experience as self-evident, and Culleton as the trembling but honest truth-teller.

In Search of April Raintree is not a seamless, unitary narrative. At the simplest level, it contains two voices, April as narrator and the interpolated voice of her sister Cheryl. The latter voice is represented in a variety of discourses: the stumbling (and unlikely) letters of a pre-schooler; subsequent letters; academic speeches and essays on Métis history; oratory written for a university newspaper but in the end delivered orally and privately to her sister at a powwow; dialogue, most centrally; and, posthumously, diary entries. In addition, the novel either represents or addresses a range of other discourses, including social work and foster care tutelage, classroom history lessons, Native-produced history, ecclesiastical infallibility, the rhetoric of misogynist/racist violence, legal testimony and courtroom summation, the romance of home and fashion magazines, the eloquence of the literary Indian, and the visual/tactile communication of a Native elder. What the characters "experience" is a series of representations, and, especially in the first half of the novel, conflicting and incompatible representations, and outright falsehoods, sufficient to induce in them a certain exegetical wariness. What the characters impart is likewise a series of contingent, partial (in the sense both of incomplete and of partisan), and discordant renderings conducive to the same kind of caution in the reader.

In one of Cheryl's letters to April, mourning JFK's assassination, Cheryl concludes, after a brief tribute to the

Kennedys' youth and energy, not with the man himself nor his political and legislative accomplishments. Instead she gestures towards his speeches and, curioser yet, towards his speech-writers, expressing the hope that Robert Kennedy will keep the same writers. In preparing to teach *In Search of April Raintree*, I was struck most forcibly by this passage, as a key to reading the novel. The president is dead; long live his discourse. Admittedly, in part the passage represents a narrative nod towards Cheryl's developing literary and oratorical strategies, merely a stroke of characterization. But I was startled by the nonchalance of the acknowledgment, the affirmation even, of crafted (and stirring, politically effective) speech that stands in place of the person himself, does not require the authenticating impress of immediate inner emotion, is not necessarily the outer manifestation of an intrinsic self. Impervious to the romance of authenticity, Culleton takes for granted the notion of performance and our dependence on representations. And this from the point of view of a child, presumably more susceptible to naive notions of spontaneous self-expression; in the context of a political administration sustained more than many by personal charisma and so by imperatives of sincerity and authenticity; and regarding an earlier period somewhat less proficient in and cynical about manipulation of the political image than the present.

In one of the rare critical references to the text's discursive self-consciousness, Margery Fee concludes, "Both [*In Search of April Raintree* and Jeannette Armstrong's *Slash*] show how the dominant discourse functions so clearly that some readers may find the demonstration too 'obvious' or explicit to be aesthetically pleasing" (177). Certainly the novel's attention to the hegemonic construction of Native reality is relentless. Cheryl's teacher's vapid assertion "'They're not lies; this is history'" (53) marks but one of the narrative's many moments of irony and confutation. But its examination of what Michel Foucault calls the "political economy" of truth (*Power/Knowledge* 131) and our embeddedness in systems of meaning-making is more far-ranging than that. In the opening pages of the novel, five-year-old April's capacity to apprehend her circumstances is complicated both by apparent mystifications—the word "medicine" for alcohol—and by the constraints of her own experience—her perception of a masturbating man as "peeing" or her mother's childbirth as a hospitalization brought on by obesity. The text is an intricate choreography of (mis)representations, the relationship of the two sisters being no less fraught with the complications of self-construction (and -invention) than are the versions of themselves and their history that they are fed by a racist society. Mrs. Dion's simple instruction that telling the truth is always easier and better than lying, which earlier on seems a touchstone against which the adult hypocrisies surrounding the children can be measured, becomes less compelling over the course of the book. The entire plot of the novel turns on the considerable impediments to truth-telling. The merit of truth-telling remains more imponderable. Most unsettling, though, truth itself becomes less self-evident. Is Cheryl's final, bitter, and self-destroying conviction that she is confronting "the true picture of my father" (197) any less misleading than April's similar callow conclusion as a youngster that "I knew the truth about them [my parents]" (50)?

The acuity and persistence with which the novel registers how the effects of truth are produced render suspect those readings that present the text as a straightforward corrective telling-it-like-it-is. In fact, Culleton rehearses many poststructuralist conclusions about reality as constituted rather than given. In April's inability to take back dishonest words making her an orphan and in Cheryl's suggestion that April's pretense of not caring seems to be turning into reality, Culleton records the power and autonomy of even second-order discursive constructions. In Mrs. DeRosier's precluding of her husband corroborating April's complaint of mistreatment, poisoning the well with lies about a flirtation, the text documents the control of the discursive means of production. Mrs. Semple's dismissive

"'Don't try to tell me that you walked all that way'" (61) and Cheryl's wry surmise that her very resentment at the prejudicial paradigm of the Native Girls' Syndrome marks her as a likely instance of the syndrome both display the Catch-22 scope of pre-emptive discourses. In Mrs. Semple's presumption that the DeRosier mother and daughter "have no reason to lie about who did what" (61), we have the familiar "objectivity" of the hegemonic position and dubious "interestedness" of counterdiscourse. The situatedness of knowledge is given quite literal illustration in April's discovery, regarding an otherwise familiar conversation with her sister about their Native background, that "sitting there in our tent, surrounded by proud Indians, everything seemed different" (153). April's capacity to draw contrary conclusions from Cheryl's inspirational pieces on Riel—"Knowing the other side, the Métis side . . . just reinforced my belief that if I could assimilate myself into white society, I wouldn't have to live like this for the rest of my life" (78) and "White superiority had conquered in the end" (87)—like her capacity to see watery eyes and leathery skin where Cheryl sees quiet beauty, conveys the multivalence, the indeterminacy of the text they are both reading.

At the rape trial, the inhibiting instructions about legal evidence and the constraints on inference—"One could testify to what was directly known," April has been cautioned (149)—are shown to discredit and deflate April's testimony:

"Now, would you say the defendant was intoxicated?"
"I don't know."
"Didn't you state that you smelled liquor on his breath?"
(163)

Besides again highlighting disparities in entitlement to (self)representation, the passage provides ironic (and metafictional) commentary on narrow, disempowering definitions of what constitutes experience,[5] on the simple testimonial's vulnerability to appropriation, and on the suspect division of labour between informant (transparent channel for authentic "raw" data) and specialist (responsible

for interpretive elaborations and artistic transformations).
Just as April tells a fuller story than her legal role allows, the
novel resists the confinement of the witness box.

Identity. Shape-shifting. Vigilant against being named
into Otherness, Cheryl multiplies identities:

> "But you're not exactly Indians are you? What is the
> proper word for people like you?" one asked.
> "Women," Cheryl replied instantly.
> "No, no, I mean nationality?"
> "Oh, I'm sorry. We're Canadians." (107)

"Apple" to her little sister, "Ape" to her vindictive foster
sister, April Raintree/Raintry/Radcliff too eludes definition,
with various selves glinting into and out of sight. Locating
herself inconsistently, she can fantasize of "passing," of living
"just like a real *white* person" at one point, yet later puzzle
over racial slurs wielded by her rapists, surprised she should
be "*mistaken* as a native person" (47, 146; emphases mine).
With one identity unreal and its alternative mistaken, she
challenges assumptions of a fundamental self, a true north
against which other positions are measured as self-betraying
defections. By acceding to neither designation, locating
herself nowhere, she disrupts the binarism that naturalizes
such identities.

When Cheryl assures April that at the Roseau powwow
she'll finally meet "real Indians," April cannot determine
whether her sister is being enthusiastic or sarcastic. The
novel is similarly equivocal on such matters. Cheryl notes
ruefully that her poetic turns of phrase derive from Indian
books, that "'most Indians today don't talk like that at all'"
(159). At the same time, she is re-investing this rhetorical
tradition with significance, having appropriated it from the
discursive archive out of which she fashions herself. Where
does authenticity lie, when a self-defined Native, in the very
course of describing her white-identified sibling as a sister in
blood but not in vision, is estranged from her own example,
acknowledges herself as unnatural? Suggestively, the space
that is opened in the novel for a revelation about Native

existence remains emblematically empty, a stubborn lacuna, as the two white men issuing the invitation pre-empt Cheryl's voice and substitute their own convictions.[6] Given that April comes to Métis identity at the moment that Cheryl abandons it and that the itinerary of April's Nativeness is the inverse of her sister's, can the narrative be said to posit any fundamental Métis reality? Can the search for April Raintree be said to end with the book's conclusion?

The doubling of protagonists further confounds the question of identity. Polar opposites, the two sisters are illustrations of antipathetic extremes—of gratification in and repudiation of their Native heritage. Simultaneously, they are said to be, except for skin-colouring, like enough to be identical twins, so much so that April characterizes her praise for Cheryl's beauty as oblique self-admiration. In place of the bounded and unitary self, *In Search of April Raintree* creates permeable and melded selves. The narrative voice is fluid and inclusive, neither hermetically singular nor neatly bifurcated. (In early third-person drafts, Culleton felt the necessity to represent Cheryl's perspective more equally [Bridgeman 45; Garrod 90]). Rather April's narrative voice is deflected and expanded by, required to make room for aspects of Cheryl's vision. The framework of the novel is chiastic (the double helix provides an apt model), with the dual storylines intersecting and reversing direction, protagonists exchanging roles. Structurally, the critical moment of cross-over is the rape scene, with the interchange between protagonists enacted physically, as it will thereafter be enacted psychologically and politically. April takes on Cheryl's body, is raped as Cheryl, and thereafter, in narrative time if not chronological time, the sisters trade places regarding Métis pride, Cheryl taking on April's shame, her secretiveness, and her superior knowledge of their parents; April Cheryl's resilience, her allegiance to community, and, finally, her son.

Julia Emberley argues that unhappily the ending marks a reclaiming of "'identity' over difference ... a new synthesis of the split narratives of subjectivity constituted in Cheryl and April ... a new order of unification and reconciliation in which

the 'Indianness' of Cheryl is absorbed into the 'whiteness' of
April" (162). By contrast with reviewers, Emberley protests
what she sees as a reinstating of authenticity in the figure of
the Métis. But the narrative has been one of unstable (and
even exchanged) subject positions, positions repeatedly
renegotiated in response to social and discursive practices.
The troubled history of Cheryl's Métis affiliation forestalls
conclusiveness in April's move onto the same ground. The self
constructed in the novel is multiple, provisional,
discontinuous, and shared. To the demand for a "proper word"
to identify people like Cheryl and like April, *In Search of April
Raintree* withholds an answer.

A reading of the novel as spontaneous, cathartic truth-
telling, the laying bare of shocking but revealing realities, is
complicated too by the publication, one year after the initial
text, of an expurgated/adapted version, entitled *April
Raintree*. Culleton produced this school edition, attenuating
or deleting obscene language and the explicit details relating
to sexuality in particular, at the behest of the Native
Education Branch of Manitoba Education.[7] With the presence
of this sister text, Culleton's "truth" immediately becomes
double, duplicitous. The revision acts as a reminder, at the
level of dissemination, of precisely the social, economic, and
institutional (specifically educational) constraints on what
can be said and heard, on how it can be said, that Culleton
conveys within the novel. Culleton though has also
demonstrated her commitment to getting Native materials
into the schools, to transforming the discourse of Nativeness
in practical ways ("Images" 48–51; Bridgeman 49). To the
extent that her cooperation with Manitoba Education is more
than a coerced concession to necessity, the textual twinning
marks a recognition of the plurality and particularities of
places of discursive practice. Oral storytelling, to use another
instance, is not fixed but varies with occasion, season,
audience, function, and time.

April Raintree, furthermore, is not just a bowdlerized,
diminished version of the original. In addition to meeting the
requirements of Manitoba Education, Culleton has

extensively reworked other aspects of the text. She has corrected matters of fact, like the name of a Winnipeg bridge.[8] She has improved verisimilitude, making Cheryl's preschool spelling more phonetic and more plausible, for example.[9] She has added explanatory detail, on how April remains ignorant of her fiancé's resources or how she comes to overhear her mother-in-law and her husband's lover. She has toned down potential melodrama, making the assault on Cheryl by a disgruntled aspiring customer less deliberate and prolonged, and eliminating April's revelation to the indignant witness of Cheryl's suicide, "'She was my sister, mister'" (*Search* 190, *April* 169). She has revised wording to reflect the participant's rather than an observer's perspective.[10] She has made scenes less static. Cheryl's report of her confrontation with school authorities is contextualized within dialogue with April and April's friend Jennifer. April's solitary readings of Cheryl's letters are dramatized as communications with the dog Rebel, with Rebel's inattentiveness permitting more irony and indirection than April's original temporary enthusiasm. With rare exceptions, Culleton has revised in the direction of reducing rather than increasing editorializing, letting scenes speak for themselves.[11] She has replaced statement with illustration and dialogue.[12] In particular, she has expanded scenes between April and Roger, eliminating his sometimes-ponderous condemnations of "game-playing," reducing his knowing comments on Cheryl, and providing engaging, playful banter instead. In these scenes and elsewhere, she invests April with added traces of strength and initiative.[13] Whether in particulars of paragraphing and diction or larger matters of tone and characterization, almost every page of *April Raintree* attests to the existence of an/other version of Culleton's story, and one that has been crafted so.[14]

Neither edition therefore can stand as the definitive text of this narrative, each offering details and exhibiting merits which the other lacks. By their divergent existences—with the full story, the "true" story, flickering into view now in one text, now in the other—*In Search of April Raintree* and *April Raintree* testify against the presumption of artless, raw honesty. Taken as a single, internally discrepant document, (*In Search of*) *April Raintree* conveys the simultaneity, the layered heterogeneity of the ways the fictions of experience, self, and truth can be composed.

But what is going on here? In reading Culleton as resisting the naturalization of reality, experience, and self, am I co-opting *In Search of April Raintree* into the contemporary crisis of epistemological legitimation? Insisting on applying to the text the "linguistic turn" in critical theory? Imposing a postmodern / poststructuralist master narrative of polyvocality, instability, and indeterminacy on a (relatively) coherent, realist narrative? Am I simply substituting for authenticity a new value, the capacity for sophisticated discursive critique, to compensate, like the reviewers, for perceived inadequacies of craft?

Certainly, *In Search of April Raintree* provides a number of passages seeming to resist my reading and to warrant treating the novel as an empiricist reflection of reality. Cheryl expresses a schoolgirl conviction that "history should be an unbiased representation of the facts. And if they show one side, they ought to show the other side equally" (78) and resolves to transform the Native image so as to give April pride. April's Christmas essay both articulates and implements her wish for someone to listen to and hear her, and as an adult she hopes that someday she may be able to explain to others why Native people kill themselves. In such moments, one can read self-referential glosses on the novel's positivist undertaking, emphasizing the necessity for *different* representations rather than for the *problematizing* of representation. Speaking of Pemmican's educational mandate and of the wrong ideas about Native people held by many teachers (Bridgeman 49), Culleton seems persuaded of the possibility of replacing a "clouded" vision with a "clear" one, to use Cheryl's formulation (159). April's closing words, that it has taken her sister's death to "bring me to accept my identity" (207), seem to affirm identity as immanent, as does Culleton's concurrence with interviewer Andrew Garrod's suggestion that April earlier isn't being true to herself (85).

Then too what about the pleasures of narrative, of storytelling? Does my approach evade or even obscure the origins of the novel's appeal to numerous readers, interjecting intellectual complexity into a text I am incapable of appreciating on its own terms because the intellectual is the only (academic) way I know to approach stories? The classes of Native students who, by report, identify most strongly with this novel as a powerful confirmation of their experiences,[15] are presumably not identifying primarily with the way the text implicates itself in the deconstruction of discursive singularity or the way it establishes April's newly achieved identity as provisional. What about the nine-year-olds Culleton mentions who helped inspire her rewriting of the book, children who have never read before but who are reading *In Search of April Raintree* (Cahill 62)? What about my Women's Studies students who describe crying several times while reading the novel?[16] The book is on my syllabi, after all, in part because of my desire to learn more from and about writing that moves and speaks to many, that serves needs that may differ from my own or the academy's.

To argue that Culleton is attentive to the politics of representation, though, may not necessarily be to co-opt her writing into a chic critical movement. Native traditions are notable for their respect for the power of language and their sensitivity to the dangers of its misuse. To cite only one example, Douglas Cardinal (Métis) speaks of the human potential to shape reality through language, in ways reminiscent of contemporary Western theory but deriving from an entirely different cultural tradition: "The essence of creativity in all things is what makes the universe shift. It is to cause something to become from nothing. The word in that way is powerful. When we speak a word we declare something. We create it and then it can be" (89).

Culleton, whose upbringing was largely outside Métis communities, may not be shaped in obvious ways by this discourse. But her own interpellation as "Native" into a variety of incompatible and antipathetic signifying systems inevitably produces a parallel awareness. Several of her essays, "What a Shame" and "Images of Native People and their Effects" in particular, surveying her painful and impossible negotiation of the constructions of Nativeness, suggest that epistemological wariness arises readily from such a position and need not wait on the trends of academic theory. Such wariness lends itself naturally to the highly political question of who gets to tell the stories, but does not preclude the proposing of more plausible stories, however provisional all must be considered to be. Cheryl's final undoing, for instance, can be read as deriving alternatively from a risky reliance on undependable narratives, like the edited story of her parents' merit, or from the exclusion from public discourse of positive narratives of the Native present, such as the one hinted at in the story of her friend Nancy.

To argue that self and racial identity are constructed, moreover, is not to argue that they have no reality, where that reality is constituted precisely through their effects (see Butler 32). To cite a familiar, rueful quip, knowing that race is constructed does nothing to help a black academic hail a cab in New York during rush hour. Nor does the recognition of self/ves and racial identity/ies as constructs preclude agency. Neither acquiescing in the hegemonic "felicitous self-naturalization" (Judith Butler's term, 33) of constructs like race nor removing herself to some impossible position outside discourses, April ultimately treats identity as verb not noun, as action not condition, as performative not inherent—and as communal not individual. Her final claim to have accepted her identity has less to do with some essence she discovers in herself (or other Métis or Native people) than with her mobilization of the relations, historic and present, in which she finds herself. She begins to deploy positively connections she has hitherto resisted. Her speaking of the words "MY PEOPLE, OUR PEOPLE" (207) enacts a political affiliation, an involvement with others in the hopeful shaping of the future.

With some other Native texts like Jeannette Armstrong's *Slash*, I sense that I am ignorant of the cultural traditions out of which they are written and so I refrain from premature judgement. With *In Search of April Raintree*, part of the problem with my aesthetic appreciation of the text may arise because I assume that I am familiar with its genre, the realist novel, and with the book's limitations according to the standards of that genre, and fail to consider the uses to which it is being put. My concern about formulaic characterization and plotting, wooden dialogue, flat, recapitulative narration, sensationalizing, and stylistic blandness (in most of which I echo the reviewers I have critiqued) draws on the norms of high (bourgeois) realism, with its focus on the individualizing of experience, refinements of self-understanding, aptness of detail, originality of language. I am requiring the satisfactions of subtlety, indirection, complexity, values that creep into my summary of the revisions to Culleton's second edition. Yet quite other genres—romance, for example—and quite other pleasures are possible. What about the satisfactions of clarity—moral and otherwise—narrative familiarity, emotional heightening, rapport with a commonplace narrator,[17] pathos?

Wendy Rose differentiates the values subtending Native art and Euro-American art, describing the latter as "special, elite (much of it requires formal training in 'appreciation'), non-utilitarian, self-expressive, solitary, ego-identified, self-validating, innovative ('to make it new'), unique, and—in its highest forms—without rules" (18–19). While noting the limitations of pan-Indian generalizations, she stresses the place, in Native art, of the ordinary, community-oriented, useful, familiar, co-operatively produced, and communally integrated. Functionality and beauty in this art, she argues, are interdependent.

Culleton has spoken of being influenced by "what they call the trash books" (note her implicit reservation about that label) and by movies and television shows, all popular genres (Garrod 87, 95; Lutz 104).[18] She has expressed surprise at finding her book taught in university classes when she had directed it towards the general reader (Bridgeman 47). The rhetorical conventions that her plain-speaking, expository narrative voice invokes are less those of fiction or even of dramatized story-telling than of family history or the everyday recounting of personal experience, aligning her rhetorically with thousands of unofficial, daily chroniclers. Like the Native art that Rose describes and like the proletarian American novels of the depression era (where the formulaic or generic was also taken to gainsay literary merit), Culleton's writing fuses pragmatic and artistic ends, and grows out of the consciousness of a community. Like the proletarian novels also, her book writes beyond the ending of the classic domestic novel or the romance quest, opening up beyond individual self-development into a vision of collective action (see Rabinowitz 77,70). If novelty, authorial self-expression, and originality of execution give way in Culleton's aesthetic credo to instrumental and communal values, then her writing may require different methods of evaluation recognizing these as also artistic achievements.

Within a modernist Western criticism, writing like Culleton's that does not "distinguish" itself and by extension its author (as different, as superior), writing that speaks with the voice of everyday, has its craft rendered invisible.[19] "Honest" and "earnest" are, after all, rather odd recom-mendations for a fiction. Such writing becomes artless, art-less. Transparent. With the author function, the dimension of discursive production, erased from the text, the writer is restored ironically, not as author but as anthropological site, source of authentic life experience, that which is being viewed. Such a critical stance lends itself further to an epistemology in which not only the text but the reality it purportedly transmits so directly, a reality that can somehow be separated from its textual rendering, is no longer a matter of discursive consensus, but remains unmediated, singular, unproblematic. Clarity of language and form threatens to generalize to other critical perceptions, so that first other dimensions of the text and eventually experience itself are understood as equally simple, manifest, and unequivocal.

With its rhetoric of the commonplace, its democracy of manner, *In Search of April Raintree* does admittedly allow an

eliding of its status as artefact, for a focus on the experiences
it reveals. That illusion of transparency is one of its
accomplishments. But only one of its accomplishments. My
concern has been to restore some of the density, the craft-
iness, of that transparency, the density and craft-iness both of
the medium and of the experiences that are constituted
within it. *In Search of April Raintree* is a duplicitous (a
multiplicitous?) book. It both invites *and* disrupts notions of
the real and of the self, of authenticity and of identity, of truth.

Notes

[1] See, for example, "understated tragedy and relentless honesty"
(Norrie 63), "a novel of documentary realism" (Sand 22), "written in
a raw, unsentimental style . . . a powerful story which has been
welling up inside of her for quite some time" (Sigurdson 43), "honest,
poignant account" (Turner 266), "one of the rawest, most tragedy-
laden, saddest, most violent books" (Krotz 64), "a raw, honest
portrayal of the experience, not shaped by any particular political
viewpoint" (Wiebe 50–51), "almost artlessly told" (Wilson 30), "a
book that comes from the heart and from the guts . . . full of honesty,
commitment, and love" (Cameron 165, 166). Margaret Clarke, in her
1986 review of the revised edition, has noted a similar tendency
among reviewers: "The book was considered the product of an
unsophisticated artistic talent, an author who knows her subject
matter, and often instinctively makes good stylistic choices, but who
generally is unaware of the subtleties of literary technique" (136).

[2] Unless specified, references are to the unrevised edition,
In Search of April Raintree.

[3] See also the letter from Maria Campbell, appended to the text:
"How many of those papers [on the fostering and adopting of Native
children] were written by people who have lived through such an
experience?" (viii). For references to the autobiographical (or "highly
autobiographical") nature of the book, see Barton 14, Ferguson 41,
Krotz 63, Moher 50, Morris 113, Petrone 140, Purcell 35, Sigurdson
43, and Turner 266.

[4] Rape is another narrative component rooted in Culleton's own
life (Garrod 90), but since it was not included in the biography
appended to the text, reviewers do not allude to it in their
authenticating of the text.

[5] Since a younger April would have smelled "medicine" on the
assailant's breath, even this, like any "raw" evidence, is not

unmediated. The passage ironically anticipates reviewer Russell's disparagement when Culleton purportedly deviates from direct experience (193).

[6] Julia Emberley would probably insist that it is specifically Indianness as difference, not Nativeness, which remains unrepresented (Cheryl is asked what being Indian is like) and which is finally effaced in the novel, with the sacrifice of Cheryl (Emberley 162). Though often positioned as Indian by others and sometimes conflating Indian and Métis politically and culturally, however, Cheryl repeatedly situates herself as Métis in history and identification.

[7] Details of the mother's nakedness and the masturbating man disappear from an early scene, for example (*Search* 14, *April* 4). Instances of non-marital sexual activity, Cheryl's prostitution, and substantial portions of the rape remain. In the latter instance, specifics of breast, crotch, and penis disappear; "As he prepared to actually rape me" replaces more explicit details; the anal rape becomes implicit only, with the deletion of April's being turned over; and feigned vomiting precludes the forced oral sex and urination (*Search* 133–132, *April* 112–14). Clarke has analysed the unfortunate diminution entailed in the deletion of misogynist invective and of the anal and oral assaults from this scene (Clarke 140–42). In other cases the sanitizing seems more *pro forma*, as in the substitution of "scumbags" for "bastards" (*Search* 164, *April* 145). April's internalized racism is not expurgated, with the exception of one reference to "bloodthirsty savages" and that deletion seems to be more a matter of fine-tuning (*Search* 72, *April* 57). Other passages, though, with the potential to hurt children, like April's shame that her clothes make her look "worse than a Hutterite," are deleted (*Search* 66, *April* 52).

[8] Nairn Bridge is changed to Disraeli Bridge (*Search* 183, *April* 162).

[9] "[C]uld" becomes "kood," and "wuz" becomes "was," for instance (*Search* 31–32, *April* 21).

[10] As random examples, "I was very grateful for their acceptance" becomes "I was grateful to be one of them," April's detached comment on her self-pity at the prospect of seven more years with the DeRosiers becomes the more immediate "I wondered how I was going to ride them out," and her gratitude for the ban on trial publicity becomes the more implicit "I would still have my privacy" (*Search* 25, *April* 14; *Search* 50, *April* 37; *Search* 151, *April* 133).

[11] Examples of such deletions include the dropping of "I suppose the speech would have been okay if I had been guilty of any

wrongdoing" and "I knew that she had liked them [the MacAdams] a lot and that they were real nice people" (*Search* 73, *April* 58; *Search* 51, *April* 39). An exception is the addition of commentary on the paternalism greeting Cheryl at the Radcliff New Year party: "it was the fact that they felt they had to say something accommodating, that was the most annoying" (*Search* 107, *April* 91).

[12] Cheryl's "two cents worth" about April's lifestyle becomes "'You like associating with these rich snobs?'" (*Search* 188, *April* 92). The lighter tone with which April is said to ask Cheryl for help after snapping at her following the rape finds expression with the addition of "'You available?'" (*Search* 135, *April* 118).

[13] April is forthright about her own interest in Roger, for instance, rather than simply speculating about his implied attraction to her without the "gumption" to inquire (*Search* 140, *April* 123). Her more successful intervention during the rape, feigning vomiting to secure her rapists' license number, is the most salient example of such revisions.

[14] Both Clarke and Cameron note evidence that Culleton has attended to matters of craft in making her revisions, Clarke examining specifically the deletions following Cheryl's oratorical address to the White Man (Clarke 136, Cameron 165).

[15] Conversation with Agnes Grant, 14 March 1985.

[16] Lutz too describes students crying or becoming outraged while reading the novel (103).

[17] One reason for Culleton's immediacy, for her inspiring simultaneously identification and aesthetic reservations, is her familiar, low-key narrative voice with its reliance on exposition, sequential unfolding, and editorializing: "That summer and the following summer, we all went to a Catholic camp at Albert Beach on Lake Winnipeg," or "If I'd had such a grandmother when I was growing up, maybe I wouldn't have been so mixed up" (34, 159).

[18] Culleton's appreciation of Margaret Laurence's skill in revealing how others think despite Laurence's omission of the big climaxes or epiphanies of soap operas, suggests an inversion of the conventional aesthetic hierarchy (Garrod 95). Like Culleton's desire to exalt Cheryl so as to make her death more tragic (Garrod 95; Lutz 102), her regard for soap operas reveals a valuing of the strong effects her critics tend to deplore.

[19] Yet the creation of this voice was quite self-conscious. "The style of *In Search of April Raintree* was supposed to be somewhat clumsy," Culleton indicated in conversation with me, 8 March 1994. "It wasn't supposed to be the style of a writer."

Works Cited

Armstrong, Jeannette. *Slash*. Penticton, BC: Theytus, 1988.

Barton, Marie. "Write the Wrong." *Canadian Author & Bookman* 61.1 (Fall 1985): 14.

Bridgeman, J. M. "'This Was Her Story': An Interview with Beatrice Culleton." *Prairie Fire* 4.5 (Jul.-Aug. 1983): 42–49.

Butler, Judith. *Gender Trouble: Feminism and the Subversion of Identity*. New York: Routledge, 1990.

Cahill, Linda, with Peter Giffen. "Adolescent Fiction Comes of Age." *Maclean's* 21 Apr. 1986: 62–64.

Cameron, Anne. Rev. of *April Raintree*. *Canadian Literature* 108 (Spr. 1986): 164–66.

Cardinal, Douglas, and Jeannette Armstrong. *The Native Creative Process*. Penticton, BC: Theytus, 1991.

Clarke, Margaret. "Revisioning April Raintree." *Prairie Fire* 7.3 (Aut. 1986): 136–42.

Culleton, Beatrice. *April Raintree*. 1984. Winnipeg: Peguis, 1992.

———. "Images of Native People and Their Effects." *School Libraries in Canada* Spr. 1987: 47-52.

———. *In Search of April Raintree*. Winnipeg, MB: Pemmican, 1983.

———. "The Pain and Pleasure of That First Novel." *Pemmican Journal* Wint. 1981: 7-10.

———. [A Proud Métis Woman]. "What a Shame!" *Pemmican Journal* Wint. 1981: 22-25.

———. Interview by Hartmut Lutz. In *Contemporary Challenges: Conversations with Canadian Native Authors*, edited by Hartmut Lutz. Saskatoon, SK: Fifth House, 1991. 97–105.

Emberley, Julia V. *Thresholds of Difference: Feminist Critique, Native Women's Writings, Postcolonial Theory*. Toronto: U of Toronto P, 1993.

Engel, Marian. Rev. of *In Search of April Raintree*. *Sunday Star* (Toronto) 3 Jul. 1983: G8.

Fee, Margery. "Upsetting Fake Ideas: Jeannette Armstrong's *Slash* and Beatrice Culleton's *April Raintree*." *Canadian Literature* 124–25 (Spr.-Sum. 1990): 168–80.

Ferguson, Rob. "'Native Girls' Syndrome.'" *City Magazine* (Winnipeg) Fall 1985: 4142.

Foucault, Michel. *Power/Knowledge: Selected Interviews and Other Writings, 1972–77*. Ed. Colin Gordon. Trans. Colin Gordon and others. New York: Pantheon, 1980.

Francis, Anne. Rev. of *In Search of April Raintree*. *Quill & Quire* 49.11 (1983): 20.

Garrod, Andrew, ed. "Beatrice Culleton." *Speaking for Myself: Canadian Writers in Interview*, St. John's, NF: Breakwater Books, 1986. 79–95.

Holman, John. "An Agonizing Tale of Two Métis Foster Children." *Windspeaker* 6 Jul. 1990: 11.

Keeshig-Tobias, Lenore. Rev. of *April Raintree. Resources for Feminist Research* 15.1 (Mar. 1986): 58.

Krotz, Larry. Rev. of *In Search of April Raintree. United Church Observer* Nov. 1983: 63–4.

Krupat, Arnold. *The Voice in the Margin: Native American Literature and the Canon*. Berkeley: U of California P, 1989.

Moher, Frank. "April in the Métis Netherworld." *Alberta Report* 10 Oct. 1983: 50.

Morris, Roberta. Rev. of *April Raintree. Waves* 14.1–2 (Fall 1985): 112-13.

Norrie, Helen. Rev. of *April Raintree. Winnipeg Free Press* 11 May 1985: 63.

Petrone, Penny. *Native Literature in Canada: From the Oral Tradition to the Present*. Toronto: Oxford UP, 1990.

Purcell, Jeanne. Rev. of *April Raintree. Humanist in Canada* 18.3 (Fall 1985): 35–36.

Rabinowitz, Paula. *Labor and Desire: Women's Revolutionary Fiction in Depression America*. Chapel Hill: U of North Carolina P, 1991.

Rose, Wendy. "Just What's All This Fuss about Whiteshamanism Anyway?" *Coyote Was Here: Essays on Contemporary Native American Literary and Political Mobilization*. Ed. Bo Schöler. Aarhus, Denmark: Seklos, 1984. 13–24.

Russell, Judith. Rev. of *April Raintree. Queen's Quarterly* 94.1 (Spr. 1987): 191–93.

Sand, Cy-Thea. Rev. of *In Search of April Raintree. Kinesis* Dec. 1983: 22.

Scott, Joan W. "The Evidence of Experience." *Critical Inquiry* 17 (Sum. 1991): 773–797.

Sigurdson, Norman. "Métis Novel Overwhelming." *Winnipeg Free Press* 30 Jul. 1983: 43.

Turner, Lillian M. Rev. of *April Raintree. Canadian Materials for Schools and Libraries* 13.6 (Nov. 1985): 266–67.

Wiebe, Armin. Rev. of *In Search of April Raintree. Prairie Fire* 4.5 (Jul.–Aug. 1983): 49–51.

Wilson, Paul. Rev. of *In Search of April Raintree. Books in Canada* 13 (Feb. 1984): 30.

The Effect of Readers' Responses on the Development of Aboriginal Literature in Canada: A Study of Maria Campbell's *Halfbreed*, Beatrice Culleton's *In Search of April Raintree*, and Richard Wagamese's *Keeper'n Me*

Jo-Ann Thom

Many Canadian Aboriginal writers claim that Beatrice Culleton's *In Search of April Raintree* (1983) has influenced their literary development more than any other work of literature with the exception of Maria Campbell's *Halfbreed* (1973).[1] Campbell showed Aboriginal people that literature could be used as a tool for political change by exposing the racism that exists in Canada and the devastating consequences it has had on the lives of Aboriginal people. As an eyewitness to the events she recounts, Campbell possesses the narrative authority needed to persuade readers—especially those from mainstream Canada—that she tells "the truth." Her strategy is an effective one as evidenced by *Halfbreed's* rise to best-seller status in the early 1970s. Following Campbell's example, many other Aboriginal people wrote their life stories, although none achieved the same success as she did.[2]

Beatrice Culleton employs a different literary strategy although, like Campbell, she writes to expose "the truth." Based not only on her own story but on the stories of her siblings and of the other foster children with whom she lived, Culleton's *In Search of April Raintree* showed would-be Aboriginal writers that they could work in the medium of fiction to create narratives that do not claim to tell a true story but that nevertheless reveal "truths." The authority Culleton claims is that of the communal voice in so far as the story she tells is shared by many Aboriginal people.[3] Culleton's use of imaginative fiction, rather than factual reporting, makes *In Search of April Raintree* an important novel in the embryonic canon of Canadian Aboriginal literature.

As an English professor teaching contemporary
Aboriginal literature, I introduce students first to Campbell
and then to Culleton to show how our literature has
transformed from an account of the author's life to a work of
fiction based on many lives. I also think it is important to
show young students what life was like a relatively short time
ago. I believe, like April Raintree, that "it's best to go back in
my life before I go forward" (Culleton 11). Culleton and
Campbell take me back to a time in my past and the past of
Aboriginal Canadians that was difficult to experience but
must be understood and remembered. The class that I teach
is a survey of works of contemporary Aboriginal literature,
and the students' responses to these works interest and
surprise me. The class is usually comprised of equal numbers
of, usually young, Aboriginal and Euro-Canadian students,
and I've observed that reading these early works is traumatic
for both groups of students but for different reasons. That is
not to say that *In Search of April Raintree* and *Halfbreed* are
not still very popular. What I am saying is that my students
are disturbed by the information revealed in them and are
consistently relieved to move on to later works, such as
Richard Wagamese's *Keeper'n Me*. A comparison of Campbell
and Culleton's early works with Wagamese's novel will
illustrate that recent developments in Aboriginal literature
are linked, in part, to readers' responses.

Steeped in the mythology that Canada was settled, for the
most part, by peaceful negotiation and that Canadians are, as
a whole, polite, considerate, and a trifle boring, my white
students—and I think many white readers—are startled to
see themselves through Métis eyes and to hear their
behaviour analyzed from a Métis point of view. For many
readers, Campbell's autobiography gives them their first
opportunity to hear a genuine Métis voice. Campbell tells
them that the Métis of her childhood existed in a virtual state
of siege because of the horrors perpetrated on them by their
white neighbours and the agents of white institutions—"the
relief people and the wardens and the Mounties" (94). With
few exceptions, the white characters in *Halfbreed* are

unpalatable, leaving white readers unable to situate themselves comfortably within the text and without characters with whom they would chose to align themselves. Margaret Atwood, in her discussion of mixed-blood writer Thomas King's short stories, argues that "the comfortable thing about a people who do not have a literary voice, or at least not one you can hear or understand, is that you never have to listen to what they are saying about *you*" (emphasis in original 244). In *Halfbreed* (1973), white readers hear over and over again what the Métis say about them, and they do not like it. It is ironic that most consider Campbell's grandmother, Cheechum, the most congenial character in *Halfbreed* even though it is white people whom Cheechum despises. Cheechum teaches Campbell that the "white man" is the real villain of their world because she believes that—and the text provides no evidence to contradict her—he strives to divide the Métis by encouraging them to hate themselves as a people. Campbell's revelations of a racist conspiracy are very traumatic for my white students and many white readers.

Although Culleton, like Campbell, is Métis, the world that she reveals in her novel *In Search of April Raintree* differs radically from the road allowance community depicted in *Halfbreed*. Culleton turns to fiction to write about Métis people who belong to the generation that follows Campbell's. Belonging to the same generation as Campbell's children, the Raintree sisters are urban Métis who have lost their language and culture, and who are alienated from their community. It is no surprise that April, with no Cheechum to guide her, accepts completely the racist beliefs that engulf her. Most white readers are shocked to hear that April learns racist attitudes from her foster family and from her social worker, Mrs. Semple, who teaches her that, because of her Métis ancestry, she is likely to fall victim to what the social worker calls "the native girl syndrome" (62), which will condemn her to a life of crime, prostitution, and abuse. As a social worker, Mrs. Semple is responsible for April's well-being, yet she teaches April to fear and despise her very identity by telling her that, "'if [she doesn't] smarten up, [she'll] end up in the same place [the other Native girls] do. Skid row!'" (62). In both *Halfbreed* and *In Search of April Raintree*, white readers learn that racism in this country is not just the practice of a few isolated individuals; it is a significant part of Canadian culture.

Although many Aboriginal readers can identify with the first part of *Halfbreed*—the story of Campbell's community— a large number respond negatively to Campbell's personal story which contains her confessions of prostitution and drug addiction. In her introduction, Campbell maintains that she writes to tell "what it is like to be a Halfbreed woman in our country" (2). Although these words are the most quoted in the text, for some Aboriginal readers they are problematic. Understandably, many critics infer that Campbell is speaking to white readers on behalf of all Métis women.[4] Her words invest the narrative with the authority of the communal voice. Ironically, when she was writing, Campbell felt alienated from her community, believing that she was the only one who had experienced the trauma she had.[5] At that time, her greatest fear was that her people would reject and abandon her when her years of prostitution and drug abuse were revealed. Her fears were not groundless. Even today, her words anger many Aboriginal readers because they believe that, when considered in the context of her confessions, these words substantiate the very stereotypes that plague Aboriginal women in this country. As Métis poet Marilyn Dumont points out in her "Squaw Poems," many Aboriginal women believe that, to avoid being stereotyped as a "squaw," they must adhere to a more rigid standard of behaviour than white women. Because of this belief, they learn to "[avoid] red lipstick, never [wear their] skirts too short/or too tight, never [choose] shoes that [look] the least/'hooker-like'" and act "so god-damned respectable that white people/. . . feel slovenly in [their] presence" (Dumont 18). The many Aboriginal women who remember and live by these lessons feel that Campbell's words betray them.

In much the same way, many Aboriginal readers feel betrayed by Cheryl Raintree's transformation from a proud

Métis into a "gutter-creature" who is the embodiment of every negative stereotype they encounter. As a girl, Cheryl is the most sympathetic character in the text, much more so than her sister April, because she is proud of her heritage in the face of extreme adversity. But her identity is built on a "fragile foundation" (Lutz 100) because she acquires it from books and has little contact with real-life Métis until she approaches adulthood. She spends her life dreaming that she will find her father and imagines him to be "a tall, straight, handsome man. [Who] in the olden days, would have been a warrior if he had been all Indian" (Culleton 198). When reality crushes her and she surrenders to Mrs. Semple's "native girl syndrome," many Aboriginal readers are angered because they expect better from someone who was always so proud of her Métis identity.

In the end, neither *Halfbreed* nor *In Search of April Raintree* offer readers much hope of healing from the trauma of racism or hope of reconciliation between Métis and white. This should come as no surprise considering the historical settings of both books. *Halfbreed* ends in 1966 with Cheechum's death, and at that time Campbell stops "being the idealistic, shiny-eyed young woman [she] once was" (184). She becomes a pragmatist who sees reconciliation coming at some distant time, not because of any moral or spiritual awakening, but as the result of tolerance brought about by need. In *Halfbreed*, Campbell does not call for the return to Métis tradition and culture that was Cheechum's goal in life—she does this much later in her 1994 book *Stories of the Road Allowance People*. In 1966, Campbell's only hope lies in political change.

In Search of April Raintree ends in 1972 with Cheryl's death, which prompts April to reassess her life and look to the future in much the same way as Campbell does after Cheechum's death. However, after a life of pragmatism, April seems to transform herself into the "idealistic, shiny-eyed young woman" (Campbell 184) whom Campbell left behind. Like Cheryl, who thought that her son "Henry Lee would change [her] life for the better" (Culleton 201), April invests her hope for the future in her sister's little boy and in her people, even though she is not sure who her people really are. April knows she is "part-Indian," but her only knowledge of the Métis comes from Cheryl's schoolgirl speeches and essays. Still, like Cheryl, she dreams of making the world better for the Métis whom she now calls "MY PEOPLE, OUR PEOPLE" (207). Because "the memory of [Cheryl] reciting her powerful message at the powwow" haunts her, April begins to romanticize the heritage that she spent her life denying (206). And although readers are encouraged by her sudden interest in her people and her culture, her sudden conversion to Métis-ness seems to be built on as fragile a foundation as Cheryl's was, and more trauma seems to be in the offing.

Nevertheless, Culleton opens the door for later writers, such as Richard Wagamese, by showing them that it is possible to use fiction to imagine a better life. Wagamese, in his novel *Keeper'n Me* (1994), takes up the theme of cultural reclamation with which Culleton leaves her readers. Published eleven years after Culleton's novel, *Keeper'n Me* thematically resembles *In Search of April Raintree* in that the Children's Aid Society removes its protagonist, Garnet Raven, from his family and places him in a series of white foster homes. Like April, Garnet grows up having no knowledge of his identity as an Aboriginal person other than the negative stereotypes that he learns from his foster families. At the end of Culleton's novel, April can only intuit that she must return to her people to secure a better future. Wagamese's novel moves to the next step. He transforms the novel into a healing narrative in which he uses imagination to detail how Garnet Raven relearns his culture and reclaims his identity as an *Anishanabe* man thereby erasing the scars of racism and cultural alienation.

Keeper'n Me differs from *In Search of April Raintree* in that Wagamese spends only twenty of its 214 pages dealing with the trauma Garnet experiences as a result of his forced integration into mainstream society. Instead of dwelling on the Raven family's victimization, *Keeper'n Me* concentrates on Garnet's personal healing that occurs while he learns to be

Anishanabe, not "a brown white guy" (12). Readers of all backgrounds gain a better understanding of the contemporary *Anishanabe* world because they learn as Garnet learns. Still, the twenty pages that describe Garnet's life in mainstream society and his alienation from his identity are important because they build the foundation for a relationship with the readers. In the same way that readers align themselves with April Raintree when Mrs. DeRosier abuses her, readers align themselves with Garnet when, as a little boy in a white foster home, he runs home traumatized after being typecast as the "itchybum" in a game of "cowboys and itchybums . . . [c]ause [he didn't] know how to be an Indian" (13). Although readers may come from disparate backgrounds, all were children and, as children, all were at one time hurt. Wagamese uses the image of a child lost and alone to draw on this commonality, so that readers empathize first with Garnet as a lost little boy and later with Garnet as a man.

Wagamese differs from Culleton in that he uses humour to persuade readers to listen to Garnet's story. Like April, Garnet tries to hide his identity, and before being reunited with his family, Garnet experiments with a number of different identities to avoid being who he really is. Ultimately, after he is befriended by Lonnie Flowers, a black man, Garnet decides to be black too. Although readers can sympathize with Garnet's search for an identity, they find themselves laughing at his incongruous appearance when he arrives back on the White Dog Reserve in Northern Ontario in the late 1970s. Expecting to feel out of place, Garnet dresses in what he believes is the image of a cool black man from the big city complete with a permed Afro, brightly coloured clothing, platform shoes, and gold chains. The White Dog residents respond with the humour that Garnet soon learns is characteristic of the people of his home:

> "Ho-lee!"...
> "Wow!"
> "Sure he's a Raven?... Looks like a walkin' fishin' lure or somethin'!"

"Yeah, that hair's a good reminder to the kids 'bout
foolin' round with the electrical!"...
"Damndest-lookin' Indyun I ever saw! Looks kinda
like that singer we seen on TV that time... We got us one
James Brown-lookin' Indian here!" (Wagamese 35)

With these comments Garnet's *Anishanabe* education begins.
Rather than trying to hurt him or make him feel unwelcome,
the community gives him his first lesson. They teach him that
he must learn to be himself by letting him know what his self
is not.

The humour that permeates *Keeper'n Me* serves multiple
functions in the novel. Like Thomas King's humour,
Wagamese's is subversive, but his subversion is more
conciliatory than King's. Atwood points out that King's stories
"ambush the reader. They get the knife in, not by wacking you
over the head with their own moral righteousness, but by
being funny" (244). Although funny, Wagamese does not quite
ambush readers. Instead, he cajoles them. Rather than
assaulting them with harsh realities or biting humour, he
teaches them in much the same way that the people of White
Dog teach Garnet. The humour in *Keeper'n Me* is reminiscent
of the humour in Algonquian oral stories in that it is used to
teach the people to behave without alienating them from the
circle of the community.

Keeper, Garnet's teacher and the other narrator of the
novel, uses humour to instruct and relieve tension. Keeper
addresses the readers directly to teach them about the effects
of European colonization on Aboriginal people. He explains
how the Christian missionaries taught the people "that all
[they] hadta do was believe in the Great Book and all the
problems of the world would disappear":

Get on your knees an' pray, they said. So those Indyuns
back then they got on their knees outta respect for their
visitor's ways. Us we do that. And they prayed and they
prayed and they prayed ... When they looked up from all
that prayin' they discovered all their land was gone. Up to
then us Indyns never figured the land was a problem but

accordin' to the Great Book it musta been on accounta it was the first thing to disappear Salvation and real estate been workin' hand in hand ever since that time. (75)

Keeper's criticism of the missionaries and their "Great Book" could easily offend many readers. To diffuse any tension and encourage readers to stay within the circle of the text, Keeper follows his criticism with a quick apology and dismisses his own words as a joke: "Sorry. Don't mind me. Get goin' kinda always wanna throw in a funny" (76). In addition to allowing readers to save face, Keeper's humourous disclaimer prevents his lesson from turning into a ponderous lecture and acts as a mnemonic device to inspire readers to remember his words.

Whether one likes it or not, to identify ones self as an Aboriginal person in Canada is to make a political statement. Contemporary Aboriginal writing reflects this reality in that almost all contemporary Canadian Aboriginal literature contains some kind of political agenda, usually one that corrects the inaccurate depictions of Aboriginal people in mainstream literature and works to advance social change. Because this political agenda originates in the margins of Canadian society, its authors must always be cognizant of their audience and its responses if they hope to achieve their goals. In *Halfbreed*, the political agenda is overt. By writing the stories of her community, family, and self—stories that many Aboriginal people share—Campbell subverts the mainstream historical narrative which has excluded Aboriginal voices. Many readers, especially ones in academia, complain that *Halfbreed* is not sufficiently "literary," but perhaps "literariness" was never Campbell's point. Nevertheless, her use of an autobiographical narrative rather than a historical one, as a means to further political ends, has been very effective in that it provides its readers with an eyewitness account of history. Following Campbell, Culleton writes to effect personal healing and social change, but her work is more literary in that she chooses fiction, rather than autobiography, as her vehicle. She shows the writers that follow her that fiction can be used to give voice to many stories—not just those of the author—and that the imagination can be a powerful healing tool. Wagamese, and many Aboriginal writers who follow Campbell and Culleton, have quickly become cognizant of readers' low tolerance for seeing Aboriginal people portrayed as victims and white people as victimizers, even though those are the positions that each has historically occupied. Influenced by readers' responses to their predecessors' works, this generation of writers experiments with literary strategies designed to make their texts more congenial to readers and to make their subversion more covert. Although their literary strategies have changed significantly from those that Campbell and Culleton employed in earlier years, this generation of writers' political agendas have changed very little. Perhaps this tells us much about the social situation in Canada at the brink of the millennium.

Notes

[1] Adapted from Jo-Ann Thom, "Only As Sick as Our Secrets: Memories, Trauma, and Cultural Healing in Maria Campbell's *Halfbreed*, Beatrice Culleton's *In Search of April Raintree*, and Richard Wagamese's *Keeper'n Me*." A.C.C.U.T.E. Conference, U of Ottawa, 30 May 1998.

[2] Lee Maracle's *Bobbi Lee: Indian Rebel* (New ed. Toronto: Women's Press, 1990) is the most well-known of these, but there are many others. These autobiographical accounts are still being published, some by vanity presses.

[3] See Susan Sniader Lanser's theory of communal voice in *Fictions of Authority: Women Writers and Narrative Voice* (Ithaca, NY: Cornell UP, 1992).

[4] Many critics have interpreted Campbell in this manner. See for example, Agnes Grant, "Contemporary Native Women's Voices in Literature," *Canadian Literature*, 124–125 (Spring-Summer 1990): 124–131, and Kate Vangen, "Making Faces: Defiance and Humor in Campbell's *Halfbreed* and Welch's *Winter in the Blood*," *The Native in Literature*, ed. T. King, C. Calver, and H. Hoy (Oakville: ECW, 1987) 188–205.

[5] In *Fictions of Authority* (see note 3), Susan Sniader Lanser uses this term to describe "a practice in which narrative authority is

invested in a definable community and textually inscribed either through multiple, mutually authorizing voices or through the voice of a single individual who is manifestly authorized by a community" (21).

⁶ I will be referring throughout to a telephone conversation I had with Maria Campbell on 25 March 1998.

Works Cited

Atwood, Margaret. "A Double-Bladed Knife: Subversive Laughter in Two Stories by Thomas King." *Native Writers and Canadian Writing.* Ed. W.H. New. Vancouver: UBC Press, 1990. 243–250.

Campbell, Maria. *Halfbreed.* Halifax: Goodread Biographies, 1973.

_____. *Stories of the Road Allowance People.* Penticton, BC: Theytus, 1995.

Culleton, Beatrice. *In Search of April Raintree.* Winnipeg, MB: Pemmican, 1983.

Dumont, Marilyn. *A Really Good Brown Girl.* London, ON: Brick Books, 1996.

Lutz, Hartmut, ed. "Beatrice Culleton." *Contemporary Challenges: Conversations with Canadian Native Authors.* Saskatoon, SK: Fifth House, 1991. 97–105.

Wagamese, Richard. *Keeper'n Me.* Toronto: Doubleday, 1994.

"The Only Dirty Book":
The Rape of *April Raintree*

Peter Cumming

> We need the books that ... grieve us deeply, like the death of
> someone we loved more than ourselves, ... like a suicide. A book
> must be the axe for the frozen sea inside us.
> > —Franz Kafka, Letter to Oskar Pollak,
> > January 27, 1904, qtd. in Bartlett 651
>
> The dirtiest book in all the world is the expurgated book. ...
> > —Walt Whitman, qtd. in Blodgett 29

Beatrice Culleton's *In Search of April Raintree* (1983) is a
moving, well-crafted, politically powerful novel. Beatrice
Culleton's *April Raintree* (1984), a revised version requested
by the Native Education Branch of the Manitoba Department
of Education, is not. However well-intentioned (by educators,
author, editors, and publisher), *April* is a travesty, a
depoliticized echo of *Search*. Created to protect young readers
from obscenities, *April Raintree's* bowdlerization introduces a
new obscenity: dishonesty.

Not everyone would agree that *April* is a mistake.
Culleton apparently welcomed the chance to rewrite *Search*
for a younger audience, noting "there's parts in it that if I'd
known young kids would read it I would have written it
maybe differently" (Silvera 314). Anne Cameron suggests—
though she offers no substantiation—that there is
"improvement in writing skill" from *Search* to *April* (165).
Dawn Thompson makes the dubious claim that "the second
novel [is] more collective than the first, in that it was
commissioned by the representative of the collective, the
government..." (100). Although Margaret Clarke laments "the
way in which Culleton, or her editor, has undercut the power
of the rape scene" (140), she nonetheless welcomes the revised

version because it "will make the novel available to schools" (136). And Helen Hoy argues that *April* is much more than "just a bowdlerized, diminished version of the original" (170–71).

To my mind, critics who have attempted to justify the changes in *April* have "protested too much": the "losses" in this "translation" far outweigh any "gains." *April* is not, as Hartmut Lutz suggests, "a slightly edited school edition" (Culleton, "Beatrice" 97): the changes from *Search* to *April* are substantial and significant. Many deletions and additions in *April* are changes for the worse; improvements that might have been made in the revised version—notably in the character of the white, Harlequin romance figure, Roger Maddison are not. In fact, Roger's problematic role in the novel is exacerbated in *April*. Moreover, the most significant changes—in the representation of April's rape—seriously compromise the integrity of the revised novel. Indeed, *April* fails—aesthetically and, therefore, politically—precisely because of some of the changes made to *Search*.

Purportedly, most of the changes are to make *April* appropriate for young readers. However, the target age group for *April* is ill-defined. Hoy invokes "the nine-year-olds Culleton mentions who helped inspire her rewriting of the book (Cahill 62)" (175), but clearly *April* is not for children, but for young adults. In her Acknowledgment, Culleton suggests that *April* has been adapted to be "suitable for high school study" (iv). *Canadian Materials* claims that while *Search* is suitable for "Grades 11 and up / Ages 16 and up" (Mountford), *April* is suitable for "Grades 10 and up / Ages 15 and up" (Turner). Yet, given the exposure of young people to strong language and overt sexuality and violence in media, newscasts, and their own lives, whether the extent or kinds of revision in *April* are justified for any high school / adolescent audience is highly debatable.[1]

Based on assumptions about what is "suitable" for young people, the principles of revision of *April* are as obvious as they are conservative. Jim Frey, a language development consultant for the Manitoba Native Education Branch, worried that *Search*'s "graphic descriptions of a rape scene and its strong language *might have* alarmed parents . . . so the version for schools is being toned down" (qtd. in Bird; my emphasis). Thus, *April* obsessively sanitizes the overt sexuality and violence and swearing that provide both verisimilitude and power in *Search*. Along with these changes, however, is a whole grab bag of revisions that collectively lessen the impact of *Search*: grammatical "corrections" that weaken the authenticity of the voice of the narrator and other characters; new or repeated copyediting errors; a loss of verisimilitude resulting from a rewriting of direct perception as general, stated observation; overwriting; superfluous exposition and character development; cuts which depoliticize the novel through a softening of its characters and events; and a general move away from the dialogical toward a monologic mode.[2]

When swearing and even mild expletives are obsessively removed or replaced with euphemisms, *April* loses both verisimilitude and the political edge that so distinguish *Search*. Thus, *April* attacks God not by telling Him He is "full of crap" (*Search* 45), but by calling Him a "phoney" (*April* 32). *April*'s rapists are no longer "lousy dirty bastards" (*Search* 164) but "lousy dirty scumbags" (*April* 145). Instead of Mark, Cheryl's pimp, being "a-no-goddamned-good-fucking-son-of-a-bitch" (*Search* 204) he is "a good for nothing woman user" (*April* 181). Cheryl's accusations that April is "'a superior white bitch'" who knows "'fuck-all'" (*Search* 180) become accusations that *April* is "'a superior white madam'" who knows "'zilch'" (*April* 159). The sanitizing of language in *April* goes to a nonsensical extreme: Cheryl's "Got to go to the john" (*Search* 202) becomes "Got to go say hi to Marie" (*April* 180); Cheryl's "'Well, I don't need your goddamned pity'" (*Search* 178) becomes "'Well, I don't need your factitious pity'" (*April* 178); the onlooker who sees Cheryl commit suicide doesn't say, "'Holy jumpin' Jesus Christ'" (*Search* 190) but "'Holy jumpin' Jupiter!'" (*April* 169); the new rage among children even changes from "sniffing glue" (*Search* 97) to "sniffing up" (*April* 82).

Along with sanitization of language, *April* suffers a general depoliticization. When Mrs. DeRosier vindictively chops off Cheryl's hair, April's "'What did you do to my sister?'" (*April* 42) fails to carry the same political implications as "'Why did you scalp my sister?'" (*Search* 55). The shift of blame from "all the crap white people gave" (*Search* 47) to "what kids like the [cruel, racist] DeRosiers gave" (*April* 35) softens Culleton's anger against systemic racism into mere vilification of individuals. Similarly, Culleton's change of *April*'s conclusion about the Native derelicts she sees while seeking her parents from "They are a disgusting people" (*Search* 110) to "They were disgusting people" (*April* 94) transforms *April*'s internalized racism and self-hatred into a mere repulsion for individuals. Even Cheryl's militant pride in her Aboriginal heritage is reduced from political insight into personal subjectivity. Cheryl's specific naming of *Canada: the New Nation* as the textbook that contains a "load of crap" about white-native relations (*Search* 78) is watered down to a nameless "textbook" containing "rubbish" in *April* (63). Cheryl's defence of her essay about Riel, "if they show one side, they ought to show the other side equally. Anyways, that's why I'm writing the Métis side of things" (*Search* 78) is radically undercut with additions in *April*: "*(Unfortunately, I'm not unbiased but fortunately, I don't plan on writing a history book.) . . . Anyways, I'm writing the Metis side of things but just for myself. And you*" (63; emphasis added).

If any aspect of *Search* might have benefitted from revision, it is the troubling role of the initially hostile but ultimately sympathetic white lawyer, Roger Maddison. Hoy points out that there are "expanded scenes between April and Roger" in *April* (170–71), but does not point out that these changes serve to exacerbate Roger's problematic role in the novel. In both texts, when Roger is first introduced, a new genre (one which does not sit totally comfortably with the social realism of the rest of the text) is invoked: that of the Harlequin romance.[3] If April's fairy tale romance with the Toronto socialite Bob Radcliff is exposed for the sham it is, her Harlequin romance with Roger, despite its disturbing contradictions, is never adequately deconstructed. Through April's eyes, Roger is introduced as the handsome, yet disdainful, Harlequin hunk: "When I first saw Roger Maddison, I thought to myself, 'Now there is somebody I wouldn't mind spending the rest of my life with'. . . . [H]is rugged looks were the kind one could look at forever . . . [b]ut . . . [h]e was a perfectionist and when I made my first small mistake, he tore into me" (*April* 77). Though Roger's "[tearing] into April" should give a reader pause, given the role of rape in the text, Roger later miraculously reappears in April's life as "[t]his gentle, concerned . . . Roger . . . I hadn't seen before" (123). Before he knows that April has been raped, Roger's attempt to comfort her trivializes what she is going through: "'April, April, April. What am I going to do with you?'" (142). When they disagree about April's inability to get over the rape, they both apologize, but April takes most of the blame upon herself: "[W]e both knew we were equally at fault. Well, maybe I was more at fault" (154). A white lawyer with a little too much time on his hands, Roger overflows with vague advice for April and Cheryl's mixed up Native lives: "'April, I'm sure Cheryl could have given you something that is very important. Right now, I don't know exactly. But something to do with your attitudes about yourselves'" (165). After Cheryl's suicide, Roger disturbingly takes over April's agency: "Roger did almost everything for me the next few days . . . Roger helped me with the funeral arrangements. Actually, he did almost everything" (171). In this world of Harlequin emotions, the paradox of love initially looking a lot like hate is simplistically resolved:

> "Roger, how come you were so nasty to me when I worked there?"
>
> "I liked you," he smiled. That made me feel good. (124)

Most disturbingly, in texts so centrally about truth and lying and about relations between women and men and Natives and non-Natives, Roger tells an outlandish lie—he has an adopted Indian brother—and claims he was going to tell another—that he has a sister who was raped—only to have April (and Culleton?) pass this all off as a lover's game: "'Were you really? You don't have any scruples, do you?' . . . By this time, I was fully relaxed and comfortable with Roger in every way" (156). From a woman who has struggled with her racial identity and fought to overcome a brutal gang rape, this easy banter and facile understanding with Roger, extended rather than curtailed in *April*, not only strains one's credulity but also offends one's sensibilties. Yet strangely, even here, Hoy attempts to recuperate the unrecuperable in Culleton's revised text:

> Even the novel's apparent endorsement of Roger's lie about an Ojibway brother Joe (which I find offensive... but which seems to serve its purpose ultimately in creating a playful intimacy between the two suitors) may function to disrupt the moral economy in the novel of wholesome truths and pernicious lies. It confounds not only simplistic judgements but, given Roger's Ojibway friend Joe, the ostensible binarism of truth and falsehood itself, being neither simply one nor the other. (162–63)

Perhaps Ockham's razor, the scientific and philosophical principle that, all things being equal, the simplest explanation is the best one, might be applied to literary criticism here: the simplest explanation is that Roger Maddison is a mistake in *Search* and a bigger mistake in *April*.

If the sanitization of swearing and sexuality results in a general depoliticization of *Search* in *April*, and if Culleton's problematic construction of Roger Maddison as Harlequin hero trivializes her important subject matter even more in *April* than in *Search*, these pale beside the effect of the bowdlerization of the pivotal rape scene in the novel. When April Raintree, having denied the Native side of her Métis heritage throughout her life, is mistaken for her proudly Native sister Cheryl, who has unfortunately degenerated into what a social worker has labelled the "native girl syndrome" (*April* 48), April becomes the unfortunate victim of a brutal gang rape. In *Search*, this rape is presented from April's point of view, in a grimly realistic manner, in an extremely graphic and disturbing fashion, and with complexity (April shows some sympathy for one of the men involved in the rape). The rape is multiple and prolonged: April is raped vaginally, anally, orally; a rapist urinates in her mouth; then, after several pages of vivid narration, she vomits and escapes with her life (*Search* 127–132).

In *April*, by contrast, the obscene language, identification of body—and even clothing—parts, much of the detail of the rape, and most of the logic behind April's vomiting are all excised (111–15). The desire to edit out most of the disturbing details of the grisly rape scene is perfectly understandable; it is also, I think, most unfortunate. Culleton indicates how hard the scene was to write: "I was reluctant to swear in it.... I was reluctant to use the words the rapist uses and [April] uses to describe the rape in detail" (Silvera 314). And many readers have discovered how difficult the scene in *Search* is to read.[1] Norman Sigurdson writes: *Search* "is not always an easy book to read, and it must have been a very difficult book to write"; Grant writes: "[r]eaders cringe with revulsion as the rapist yanks April's hair and commands, 'I said suck'" (131). Yet C. H. Mountford's argument that Culleton's "piling of horror upon horror weakens rather than strengthens the impact of her story" is exactly wrong. The rape scene, as originally written, is painful. Yet it is painful for a reason; it performs a crucial function in the novel that the expurgated scene in *April* cannot duplicate. Indeed, the rape scene in *April* is not merely a pale imitation, but a travesty, of the original. And this scene is so essential to April's discovery of her identity that its failure represents a failure of *April* as a whole.

Both Clarke and Hoy acknowledge the centrality of the rape scene and some unfortunate ramifications of its revision in *April*. While declaring her understanding for the reasons behind the cuts in the revised edition, Clarke states, "[S]peaking as a critic of a work of art, I believe that work of art is *violated* at a profound level by the excision" (140–41; emphasis added). I agree entirely—*Search* is "raped" by the savage cuts to the rape scene in *April*—yet I also feel that

Clarke misses some of the crucial significance of the rape scene when she concludes: "[t]hese excisions and substitutions may make the book easier for some, but they severely compromise the story's relevance to *the violence against females* which is at its core" (141; emphasis added). April's rape is about her rape as an individual and as a woman; however, it is more centrally about her rape as a Native person—and through her, I believe, about the "rape" of all Native peoples. Or, more correctly, as Clarke goes on to say, "In Culleton's original version, April's Metis identity is firmly joined in the men's language to her female identity... I suspect that for Culleton the two experiences are inseparable; they certainly are for her heroine" (141).

In *Search*, what exactly is the function of this graphic, disturbing, multiple, seemingly interminable gang rape? And why does the expurgated version in *April* fall so far short of offering its readers—even, or especially, its young adult readers—the "truth" about rape, about (some) men and women, and about relations between Native and non-Native peoples? In brief, this rape scene represents the politicization of April Raintree: the rape is both her death (of her attempts to "pass" as white) and her birth as a person capable of accepting her identity as Métis. Although April says at the end of the novel that "It was tragic that it had taken Cheryl's death to bring me to accept my identity" (*Search* 207), it is really her being raped as a Native woman—her disempowerment as both Native and woman painfully conjoined in the doubly pejorative word "squaw" (*Search* 128)—that ultimately brings her to a recognition of "MY PEOPLE, OUR PEOPLE" (*Search* 207). As Hoy points out,

> structurally, the critical moment of cross-over [between April and Cheryl] is the rape scene, with the interchange between protagonists enacted physically, as it will thereafter be enacted psychologically and politically. April takes on Cheryl's body, is raped as Cheryl, and thereafter, in narrative time if not in chronological time, the sisters trade places ... April [taking on] Cheryl's resilience, her allegiance to community, and, finally, her son. (168)

However disturbing the rape of an individual woman, the rape of April Raintree is about that and even more—it is about the rape of a Native woman. Moreover, the rape is not "only" about April as an individual, as a woman, or as an individual Métis coming to terms with her identity; it is also about what white Europeans have done to Aboriginal peoples during the history of their contact. As a result, the disturbing graphic detail and the prolongation of the scene become the rape and politicization not only of April but also of the reader. The scene is disturbing because it is meant to be disturbing. The scene is excessive because it must be so. Reader identification with April and the raw power of April's narration of her rape ensure that the reader (perhaps particularly the non-Native reader) is politicized—is raped— along with April. Culleton writes of Cheryl: "I wanted people really to get involved with her . . . so that they'd really feel the pain when she died" (Culleton, "Beatrice" 102); Culleton does the same thing with April—she builds reader identification so that readers really feel the pain when April is raped.[5]

April's vomiting is key to a broader interpretation of the significance of the rape scene. April vomits at three points in *Search*: when she is first taken away from her parents, when she is raped, and when she is forced to retell the rape in court. The first time she vomits is when she is forcibly taken from her family and her home (from her culture) by social workers and force fed porridge by nuns:

> To my horror, I threw up just then. . . . I was bathed and put to bed, and by then, I was feverish. . . . I dreamt my parents were on the other side of a large, bottomless hole . . . I glanced up at their faces again. The faces had changed. They weren't my parents. They were the two social workers who had taken us away . . . When I was awake, a new kind of terror came to me. . . . I would see this huge, white, doughy thing, kind of like a dumpling, and it would come at me, nearer and nearer and nearer. . . . and I felt that if it ever touched me it would engulf me, and that would be the end of me. (*Search* 21–22)

Clearly, the young April's dreams are about her identity, particularly about the relationship between her parents and the "whites" who have taken her from them. Her horror, vomiting, and delirium brought on by the representatives of "white" power—the social workers and nuns—prefigure her loss of control and brutalization by white men in the rape. Her fear that the "huge, white, doughy thing" might engulf her "and that would be the end of me" surely represents the threat of white hegemony to her identity. The final time April vomits is when she is forced to recount her rape in court: "[A]lthough I loathed going over those words that told the story of that night . . . I couldn't just say I had been raped. I had to describe the act itself" (*April* 132). After she is allowed off the stand, April "headed straight for the washroom. Once there, I threw up" (*Search* 150; *April* 133). Again, April's vomiting symbolizes her reaction not only to her rapists but to her helplessness in the face of the representatives of white hegemony, the courts.

The central vomiting scene, though, is during and after April's rape; however, the differences between her vomiting in *Search* and in *April* are critical. In *Search*, there are logical, psychological, and physical reasons for April's vomiting—she has been raped vaginally, anally, orally, and one of the rapists has urinated in her mouth. However, in *April*, the vomiting is reduced to being a conscious strategy to avoid being raped:

> I raked [sic] my mind desperately for thoughts on how to put a stop to all of this but my mind was jumbled up. Then one idea came. I put it into action. I began to pretend to vomit. . . . I continued with the pretense of wretching [sic]. . . . I didn't let up on my pretense. (*April* 114–15)

The pretence of retching in *April* completely fails to have the emotional power of the enforced retching of *Search*. In *Search*, April vomits as a direct result of the indignities forced on her by both individuals and her society; her vomiting after the rape connects with her vomiting as a child when she was taken by social workers and the church away from her family, home, and culture. Both incidents connect with her vomiting after being forced to retell the details of the rape in the court. Curiously, though, Hoy goes to pains to valorize the revised version of the vomiting: "April uses her scripted role of helplessness and victimization strategically, feigning vomiting to secure the rapists' license plate number and ultimately their arrest and conviction" (164).

If the rape scene functions to politicize April and the reader, if the combination of the graphic sexual detail, shouted obscenities, multiple indignities, intersection of sexual and racial slurs, and protracted length of the scene all work together to "rape" April and the reader and to expose to April and the reader the parameters of power within which they live, what happens when Culleton rewrites the scene in *April*? As elsewhere in the novel, all swearing, explicit body parts, and sexual references are excised, what was specific becomes vague, and what was brutal becomes banal. The hatred against women in "bitch," "fucking," "cunt," "goddamned cunt,' "cocksucker," "whore" evaporates as the rape in *April* becomes a sort of "No Name" rape. The body and clothing parts of "breast," "crotch of my jeans," "zipper," "jeans," disappear into generalities. Euphemism reigns: "'I like my fucking rough'" (*Search* 128) becomes—with no apparent irony— "'I like my loving rough'" (*April* 111); "'You goddamned cunt!', he yelled in rage" (*Search* 129) becomes the limp "This enraged him and he swore" (*April* 113); "He undid his zipper and pulled down his jeans. Then he forced me to lay the full length of the car seat. When he prepared to come down on me . . ." (*Search* 130) becomes "As he prepared to actually rape me" (*April* 113); "Suddenly, he shoved his penis into me so violently that when I felt the pain of his thrust tear into my body . . ." (*Search* 130) becomes "Suddenly, I felt the pain of his thrust tear into my body" (*April* 113); "The second rapist made me turn on my stomach, but I was beyond caring" (*Search* 131) becomes "The rape by the second man inflicted a whole new pain" (*April* 114); "'You're going to fuck this bitch, dummy'" (*Search* 131) becomes "'You're going to, dummy'" (*April* 114).

Curiously, considering the role of the Native Education branch of the Manitoba Department of Education, the taboo against sexual swearing and against naming body and clothing parts is not extended to racist slurs. Indeed, there is a displacement of sexual epithets onto racist ones in *April*. Thus, "ungrateful bitch" (*Search* 129) becomes "ungrateful squaw" (*April* 112); "you little cunt" (*Search* 129), "you little Indian" (*April* 112); "you fucking little savage" (*Search* 130), "you little savage" (*April* 113); "you little cocksucker" (*Search* 131), "you little squaw" (*April* 114). The effect of this phenomenon—a rape in which gender-related obscenities are abjured while race-related ones are not—is contradictory to what one might expect. While using racist terms exclusively might be expected to intensify the racist component, which I am arguing is essential to an understanding of the role of the rape scene in the novel, its effect is precisely the opposite. As Thompson rightly observes, "virtually every reference to April's body is censored, and thus her gender is deleted from the scene; only her race remains. . . . Thus for a non-Native reader, much of the violence disappears in part because the violent words against all women's bodies disappear..." (98).

Clarke describes the "real terror" a reader feels when reading the rape scene in *Search*: "For the first time in my experience as a reader, this ultimate symbol of female victimization was portrayed with complete openness and without the sly and subtle romanticization of male violence that one finds in too many rape accounts" (140–41). Similarly, Grant commends the unflinching presentation of rape in Culleton's original: "Fully seven pages are devoted to straightforward description. The scene totally lacks coy allusions, titillation, or sexual excitement . . . Readers owe Culleton a considerable debt for dispassionately and competently handling a topic that is too often romanticized by writers. . . ." (128–29). Yes, Culleton's representation of rape in *Search* is remarkable. However, this is not "only" the representation of a rape; this is a rape which is also a metaphor for non-Native/Native relations.

By contrast, the rape in *April* is not a rape at all—because the hatred, violence, obscenities, body parts, and gender differences which would make it a rape have all been erased. If April's rape—in addition to being about the rape of an individual Métis woman about whom readers care—is also an extended metaphor for non-Native/Native relations, what happens when the vehicle of this metaphor (the rape itself) is bowdlerized? With no vehicle, the tenor of the metaphor (relations between non-Natives and Natives) is not illuminated at all: the metaphor loses its figurative power. Because the rape in *April* has been emptied, the experience of reading that scene does not fulfill the function that reading that scene in *Search* does. And that makes *April Raintree* dishonest.

Understandably, Beatrice Culleton had difficulty writing *In Search of April Raintree*: "Sometimes I wish I hadn't had to write it . . ." (Silvera 321). In particular, she had difficulty writing the rape scene in *Search*: though she "had to stop and think about" the language she would use in that scene, ultimately she "decided to go with reality" (Silvera 314). Fortunately, Culleton had the courage to follow her instincts as a writer: she did write the novel and she did go with "reality" in it. Unfortunately, faced with the opportunity for wider distribution for this novel, Culleton and her publishers went on to produce a "version" of the novel that they and educators thought would be more "suitable" for young people. In doing so, they created a less honest work of art: they lied about "reality"—about rape, relations between women and men, relations between Native and non-Native peoples, about that "huge, white, doughy thing, kind of like a dumpling . . . [that] I felt . . . if it ever touched me it would engulf me, and that would be the end of me" (*Search* 22).

In one of the epigraphs with which I begin this argument, Walt Whitman, regretting his concession to have his work expurgated as "an evil decision growing out of the best of intentions," claims that "[t]he dirtiest book in all the world is the expurgated book" (qtd. in Blodgett 29), and Jessamyn West says that there is only one kind of dirty book, and that is a book that falsifies life (qtd. in Sayers 124). On both counts,

it is not *In Search of April Raintree* that is a "dirty book" in
need of being cleaned up; rather, *April Raintree* is a "dirty
book" that—in stopping short of and mystifying the "truth"—
does a disservice to readers both young and old.

Notes

¹ Critics seem to assume that the changes in *April* are *necessary*
if young readers are to read the novel, without problematizing the
assumptions about children and young adults which those changes
expose. See Perry Nodelman's astute challenges to such widely-held
assumptions in *The Pleasures of Children's Literature* (72–90). My
own teaching experiences with *Search*—first, with Aboriginal
students (Inuit young adults in the eastern Arctic), and secondly,
with non-Aboriginal undergraduate classes in children's and young
adult literature—leads me to be skeptical about whether most of
these changes are desirable for either Native or non-Native readers.
Some teachers, students, and other readers may be more
"comfortable" with the revised version; however, my contention, as
reflected in the Kafka epigraph with which I begin my argument, is
that this is not a text with which any reader should be
"comfortable"—rather, this is a novel which "must be the axe for the
frozen sea inside us."

² The move from dialogic to monologic modes may be an
occupational hazard of "translating" adult books into children's and
young adult books. A similar diminution seems to occur in Joy
Kogawa's adaptation of her complex, dialogical novel *Obasan* into
her much less dialogical children's book *Naomi's Road.*

³ In describing her writing of *Search*, Culleton notes that
"I started off in the third person and [the novel] sounded really
like a Harlequin—not a romance but it had that quality to it"
(Silvera 312).

⁴ Some of my (female) undergraduate students choose not to
read the scene, an option I respect and for which I have sympathy,
though I argue that the scene is a productively painful one to read.
In informal, anonymous surveys I conduct about which texts have
meant the most to my students, a very few students put Search at
the bottom of their lists—presumably because the text has been too
disturbing for them to read—while the vast majority place *Search* at
the very top of their lists (right up with *Anne of Green Gables* and
Charlotte's Web).

[5] Margery Fee assumes Native readers for the novel, Clarke assumes female readers (138), Hoy speaks of Native and female readers (175), and Culleton assumed, as she wrote the novel, that her readers would be adult and female though she also expressed surprise that a lot of men have read it (Silvera 314). Thompson suggests that the rape scene "constructs its reader as female; she is thus asked to identify with both subject and object. However to what extent male readers have the necessary preparation for such a "double identification" ([De Lauretis] 144) and can thus identify with April, is a complex question that, for now, I must leave unanswered" (97). My own sense is that the full horror of this scene as presented in *Search* can "rape" Native and non-Native, female and male readers because of the strong reader identification Culleton creates for April. As with Patrick Lane's poem, "Wet Cotton," (in which a group of young men bond by raping a drugged girl with a sausage— and "retch" as part of their bonding), men's readings may be complicated by their physical bodies seeming to be forced to be made complicit with the male perpetrators of this rape, while their emotional identifications are clearly with April the victim and survivor of this rape.

Works Cited

Bartlett, John. *Familiar Quotations*. Ed. Justin Kaplan. 16th ed. Boston: Little, Brown & Company, 1992.

Bird, Bradley. "Canada's Only Metis Publisher: Winnipeg's Beatrice Culleton." *Winnipeg Free Press* 8 Dec. 1984: 21.

Blodgett, Harold. *Walt Whitman in England*. Ithaca, NY: Cornell UP, 1934.

Cameron, Anne. "Metis Heart." Rev. of *April Raintree* and *Spirit of the White Bison*, by Beatrice Culleton. *Canadian Literature* 108 (1986): 164–66.

Clarke, Margaret. "Revisioning *April Raintree*." *Prairie Fire* 7.3 (1986): 136–42.

Culleton, Beatrice. *April Raintree*. Winnipeg, MB: Pemmican, 1984.

Culleton, Beatrice. *In Search of April Raintree*. Winnipeg, MB: Pemmican, 1983.

_____. Interview with Hartmut Lutz. In *Contemporary Challenges: Conversations with Canadian Native Authors*, edited by Hartmut Lutz. 135–54. Saskatoon, SK: Fifth House, 1991.

_____. Interview with Makeda Silvera. In *The Other Woman: Women of Colour in Contemporary Canadian Literature*, edited by Makeda Silvera. 310–331. Toronto: Sister Vision, 1995.

Fee, Margery. "Upsetting Fake Ideas: Jeannette Armstrong's *Slash* and Beatrice Culleton's *April Raintree*" *Canadian Literature* 124–125 (1990): 168–80.

Grant, Agnes. "Contemporary Native Women's Voices in Literature." *Canadian Literature* 124–125 (1990): 124–32.

Hoy, Helen. "'Nothing but the Truth': Discursive Transparency in Beatrice Culleton." *Ariel:* 25.1 (1994): 155–84.

Hulan, Renée "Some Thoughts on 'Integrity and Intent' and Teaching Native Literature." *Essays on Canadian Writing* 63 (1998): 210–30.

Kogawa, Joy. *Naomi's Road.* Drawings by Matt Gould. Toronto: Oxford UP, 1986.

——. *Obasan.* Toronto: Lester & Orpen Dennys, 1981.

Lane, Patrick. "Wet Cotton." *Mortal Remains.* Toronto: Exile, 1991. 32.

Mountford, C.H. Rev. of *In Search of April Raintree. CM Archive Book Review* 12.1 (1984). 17 September 1998 <http://www.umanitoba.ca/cm/cmarchive/vol12no1/search aprilraintree.html>

Nodelman, Perry. *The Pleasures of Children's Literature.* 2nd ed. White Plains, NY: Longman, 1996.

Sayers, Frances Clarke. "Walt Disney Accused." *Children and Literature: Views and Reviews.* Ed. Virginia Haviland. New York: Lothrop, Lee & Shepard, 1973. 116–25.

Sigurdson, Norman. "Metis Novel Overwhelming." *Winnipeg Free Press* 30 July 1983: 43.

Thompson, Dawn. "Typewriter as Trickster: Revisions of Beatrice Culleton's *In Search of April Raintree." Intersexions: Issues of Race and Gender in Canadian Women's Writing.* Ed. Coomi S. Vevaina and Barbara Godard. Creative New Literatures Series—07. New Delhi: Creative Books, 1996. 90–105.

Turner, Lillian M. Rev. *of April Raintree. CM Archive Book Review* 13.6 (1985). 17 September 1998 <http://www.umanitoba.ca/outreach/cm/cmarchive/vol13n o6/aprilraintree.html>

The Limits of Sisterhood

Heather Zwicker

In her afterword to *The Bluest Eye*, Toni Morrison distinguishes between stories that are "touching" and those that are "moving."[1] "Touching" novels make their readers feel strong emotions, but only fleetingly. Stories that are "moving," on the other hand, result in some sort of change: certainly a change of consciousness in the individual reader, but also often larger social reform as a result of the wake-up call delivered by a novel using the language of strong emotion. These terms chart out a useful spectrum for evaluating *In Search of April Raintree*, a novel that undoes me every time I read it. I find the story of two sisters losing track of one another in the mess of systemic racism, foster care, alcoholism, sexual assault, and its virtual recapitulation in the legal system harrowing. To judge from the comments students make when I teach the book, my response to the novel is not unique: students report that the novel leaves them feeling sad, helpless, angry, and despairing. Is there a usefulness to these feelings? Is there a way to read the novel that makes it "moving" rather than merely "touching"? This essay attempts to answer these questions by attending to the relationship between the sisters and to the metaphorical implications of sisterhood in *In Search of April Raintree*.

In her groundbreaking essay on Culleton, Helen Hoy astutely points out the dangers of criticism that oversimplifies the novel by recognizing only its "discursive transparency." While Hoy's warning is well taken, I think it's important to acknowledge that the novel—though complicated—works in the first instance through the simplicity of its literal story, the story of sisters. Having lost home and parents, subject to the uncaring vagaries of Children's Aid, April and Cheryl nonetheless always have each other. April protects Cheryl, remembering her birthday with gifts during family visits; Cheryl seeks April's advice, shares her essays with her, and gives April a reason to dare run away from the DeRosier residence. The letters the girls write to each other sustain them in their separate foster homes, standing in for the family denied them. Arguably, the only thing that doesn't get taken away from April and Cheryl is the fact that they are sisters. Just as it sustains the characters themselves, so does their relationship give us as readers a way to navigate and mitigate the horrors unfolded by the narrative. We, too, hope that the girls can make good—together—on April's assertion that, "'When we're old enough, we'll be free. We'll live together. We're going to make it. Do you understand me? *We are going to make it*. We are not going to become what they expect of us'" (64).

But the trope of "sisters" works in less literal ways, too. Taken metaphorically, "sisterhood" describes a well known—and fraught—trope for feminism. Having galvanized the women's liberation movement of the 1960s and 1970s, the concept of sisterhood (loosely defined as women of all classes, races, cultures, nations, and sexualities acting as one to overthrow the patriarchy), started to fracture in the 1980s and 1990s as differences among women stubbornly refused to be willed away by a cozy, familial metaphor. Although a wide range of recent work suggests that "sisterhood" remains a generative trope for feminist scholarship, significant critiques, especially by women of colour, have demanded that we rethink some of its conceptual assumptions.[2] As a result, contemporary feminisms face the problem of how to hold onto the best parts of "sisterhood" without capitulating to its more problematic implications—how, that is, to conceptualize community among women without asserting similarities or identities where there are none, how to capitalize on and celebrate difference without giving up on the possibility of solidarity. *In Search of April Raintree* shows us how and why this work matters. The novel resonates with the metaphoric implications of sisterhood, demonstrating that even within a relationship as close as literal sisters' there exist irreducible differences between women that make community a vexed and difficult, but nonetheless crucial, venture.[3]

Of principal importance to the novel's conceptualization of sisterhood is the fact that April and Cheryl are not alike. The novel explicitly articulates the sisters' differences from one another as an issue under debate when April wonders, "What was it that made her like she was and me like I was?" (102). Much more than a tired old nature/nurture debate is at stake here; the moment asks us to consider questions like, what does it mean for two women to be sisters, to be deeply joined to one another, even mistaken for one another, and yet not at all the same as one another? How can women structure community around differences rather than identities? Is dialogue across difference possible? What might it look like? These are not questions that Culleton answers for us. Rather, the disintegration of the relationship between April and Cheryl as the novel unfolds, serves to demonstrate the inevitable disintegration of a feminism that fails to respond to the need for a community founded on mutual responsibility and recognition of difference.

In the early parts of the novel, the sisters' dissimilarities are not so pointed. While April and Cheryl obviously have distinct personalities even as children, it is only as they grow up that their differences from one another acquire social, political, and material consequence. The novel shows us the process by which putatively personal characteristics can become politically charged. For example, even in the early parts of the novel, Cheryl is far more outspoken than is April. As the narrative advances, Cheryl's directness gets reconfigured as Métis pride, just as April's shyness turns into shame and political quiescence. In fact, it is April's shame about being Métis, measured against Cheryl's respect for it, that constitutes the earliest recognition of irreducible difference between the girls. Put more abstractly, race becomes a constitutive element of their gendered identity early on, and their different identifications are particularly charged because they are articulated in a systemically racist society. Whereas Cheryl embraces her Métis identity wholeheartedly, conducting research into Louis Riel's life and traditional Indian practices to counter the lies she encounters in school, April believes that being Métis

> meant being poor and dirty. It meant being weak and having to drink. It meant being ugly and stupid. It meant living off white people. And giving your children to white people to look after. It meant having to take all the crap white people gave. Well, I wasn't going to live like a half-breed. When I got free of this place, when I got free from being a foster child, then I would live just like a real white person. (47)

April's belittling of Métis identity is immediately followed by the problem of Cheryl: "What about Cheryl? How was I going to pass for a white person when I had a Métis sister? Especially when she was so proud of what she was?" (47). This is the first rift between them, and although April leaves it unresolved for the moment—"Well, I had a long time to figure that one out," she adds—it nonetheless articulates the ongoing problem of difference between the two girls (47). From this point on, April is coded as the "white" sister, Cheryl as the "brown" one.

Characteristics that follow from this early recognition continue to mark April and Cheryl as politically incompatible. April adopts an assimilationist stance, choosing to pass as white (although she never gets rid of the fear that she will be outed as a Native person). April seeks independence while Cheryl idolizes community; Cheryl looks to the past while April looks to the future. April pretends that her parents are dead while Cheryl volunteers at the Native Friendship Centre. These are not merely personal differences, but ideological ones: they articulate distinct political perspectives that can be readily mapped onto familiar feminist paradigms. April's insistence on determining her own identity is deeply liberal in political orientation. Moreover, she articulates this world view in contradistinction to Cheryl's perspective: it is immediately after reading one of Cheryl's letters about her work on Riel that April decides on a career for herself, saying, "Riel and Dumont, they were men of the past. Why dwell on it? What concerned me was my future" (87). Cheryl vs. April, history vs. the future, Métis heroes vs. "my" future: April's renunciation of history and community in the drive to be a self-made woman in white society marks her as a quintessentially liberal subject.

Cheryl, on the other hand, adopts identity politics articulated around a clear and uncompromising self-representation, insisting that mainstream society come to terms with her indigeneity. Her political and personal yearnings articulate perfectly with one another, as the dream she confesses to April demonstrates:

> 'I used to think that when Mom and Dad got better and took us back, we could move to the B.C. Rockies and live like olden day Indians. We'd live near a lake and we'd build our own log cabin with a big fireplace. And we wouldn't have electricity probably. We'd have lots and lots of books. We'd have dogs and horses and we'd make friends with the wild animals. We'd go fishing and hunting, grow our own garden and chop our wood for winter. And we wouldn't meet people who were always trying to put us down. We'd be so happy. Do you think that would ever be possible, April?' (83)

Although Cheryl recognizes the improbability of this dream (hence her use of the conditional mood), it captures an image of the life she wants. Significantly, however, it is based on an idealization of the traditional past—life of "olden day Indians" that might somehow be lived in the present. Such an idealistic vision of Indian life and identity fuels both her work at the Native Friendship Centre and her search for her own parents, equally. The personal is deeply political in Cheryl's formulation of identity politics.

Neither April nor Cheryl's politics proves adequate to the challenges they face. Cheryl cannot connect the past she dreams about to the present she inhabits. Nowhere is this more telling than at the moment she meets her father, whom

she had idolized as an Indian warrior: in the very "instant"
she meets her alcoholic father, her "dreams to rebuild the
spirit of a once proud nation are destroyed" (198). With no
space to mediate between "identity" and "politics," Cheryl's
intensely personal political vision falters, resulting eventually
in the most cataclysmic and most painful event in the
narrative, Cheryl's suicide. I contend that feminist readers of
the late 1990s find Cheryl's death intensely painful to read,
not simply because it means the loss of an individual
character, but because as feminists we desperately want
Cheryl's uncompromising political vision to triumph over
April's liberal quiescence. Cheryl as a character would seem
to have learned the lessons of feminist difference well: she can
hold onto both gender and race as constituent elements of her
subjectivity, and she can turn that subjectivity into a radical
political platform that intimately links the personal to the
political, the communal, the social, and the historical. We
want her—and her politics—to triumph; her death seems so
wrong in part because her politics seems so right.

Feminist readers, I would also argue, have a much easier
time seeing the inadequacy of April's politics: produced as
critics by the lessons of difference from the 1980s and 1990s,
we come to the novel suspicious of assimilative politics.
Whereas our feminism sides with the political route Cheryl
takes, resuscitating and valuing the components of
traditional life that colonialism forcibly erases, we assume
that April ought to learn the limits of liberalism. The novel
nicely sides with us on this score. April's liberal vision of self-
determination is constantly quashed by systemic racism:
neither her close friends nor her husband's family ever allow
her to forget that she is Métis, and in spite of the careful way
that April distinguishes herself from Cheryl, her sexual
assault rests on her being actually mistaken for her sister. In
this moment, the distinction between the two women is
instantly collapsed, not only reintroducing the question of
difference in extremely urgent form (April's earlier question,
"What was it that made her like she was and me like I was?,"
must echo here), but also rendering impossible any easy

pluralist solution to the feminist question of difference within community.

Let me explain. If the primary issue contemporary feminisms have come up against concerns the irreducibility of difference between women, then one obvious solution would seem to be that women should simply acknowledge the differences between them and get on with their independent lives. Dovetailing perfectly with April's commitment to self-determination, such an approach offers a liberal solution to an intractable social problem. However, the novel insistently demonstrates the inadequacy of April's live-and-let-live politics by insisting that April and Cheryl, as women, are responsible for each other's well-being. Community may be difficult to construct, *In Search of April Raintree* argues, but it's absolutely crucial. For all that April might like to believe herself an independent individual, she is forcibly denied that vision in the rape scene, where her assailants position her as a Native woman (Fee "Upsetting Fake Ideas" 176). In addition to the obvious damage to body and mind, this sexual assault damages April's politics, too—though it takes the character the rest of the book to notice. Even as the trial scenes that follow reinforce the lessons of the rape, April finds herself "indignant that [she] could be mistaken as a prostitute" (165). Although April does not see it, what this scene means to readers is that April has to negotiate her relationship to a woman, a sister, a self-identified Native person that is at once like her and utterly unlike her. Succinctly put, April and Cheryl have to figure out what it means to be sisters.

The latter part of *In Search of April Raintree* demonstrates how very difficult a prospect arriving at meaningful sisterhood can be. The novel contains several examples of the limits of sisterhood: it is a sister, after all (Sylvia Gurnan), who initiates the attack on Cheryl/April. Nicole, the Dion daughter, is obviously a foil to Maggie DeRosier, suggesting that sisterly relationships are not given, but made. Building a positive relationship proves to be necessary for biologically-related sisters, too, and April and Cheryl don't always do a very good job of it. To point to some

obvious examples, April neglects to invite Cheryl to visit her
when she first moves to Winnipeg, and their relationship is
further strained by the racist confines of the Radcliff family.
For her part, Cheryl withholds from April the huge changes in
her life: the fact that she has quit school, moved in with Mark,
traded sex for money, and borne a son. These examples make
it appear as though the problem between the sisters is
another instance of the many secrets and lies that run
throughout the novel (Hoy "Nothing But the Truth" 156). But
as the most damaging moment in their relationship
demonstrates, the problem does not have so much to do with
disclosure as it does with a radical inability to conceive of the
differences between them.[4]

The trial scene and its aftermath constitute the pinnacle
moment in the feminist problematic that the novel addresses.
The recognition of difference between the sisters is at its most
intense and its most insoluble at that point—as is the need for
community between them. During the trial scene, April
discovers that Cheryl has been working as a prostitute. At the
moment of this revelation, Cheryl silently pleads for
understanding, but April rebuffs her. This moment
reverberates through the remainder of the novel because it is
the moment that brings to the fore both Cheryl's inability to
articulate the actual conditions of her life and April's inability
to comprehend the gulf between them. That this moment
constitutes a recognition of incommensurability that
resonates well beyond the trial is evident from the way April
reflects on it after the fact:

> I kept thinking of the look she had given me that
> afternoon. The look I had so coldly turned away from. As
> if I had judged her guilty. Still, she was my sister, my flesh
> and blood, and when she returned, I would tell her
> everything was okay. It really wouldn't be okay, but I
> decided I would try my best to forgive and forget.
> (167–168)

The passage is telling because it articulates the problem
between the two sisters as not merely a matter of difference,
but as a nearly total incongruity, an incommensurability,

that April can see no way around. The only option she can see is to ignore the difference between them, trying to adopt an ethos of forgiving and forgetting that does not allow for narratives of pain and betrayal to be admitted and worked out. Such an ethos is utterly at odds with a feminist politics dedicated to grappling with difference. As for Cheryl: her inability or unwillingness to describe her life to her sister suggests that she faces the same crippling sense of divergence between them.[5]

While *In Search of April Raintree* efficiently articulates the problem of meaningful sisterhood, it does not provide easy models for achieving it. Dialogue and honesty, the obvious antidotes to secrecy and lies, prove utterly inadequate solutions to incommensurability. From the trial scene on, dialogue between April and Cheryl is so vitriolic as to undermine the possibility that differences can be resolved by talking, and honesty is similarly inadequate. When Cheryl does return home after the trial scene, she responds to April's forgive-and-forget resolve by telling the truth, but not in a way that produces greater understanding between them: "'Oh? You think things should return to normal, do you? Well, good luck!'" (173). Her statement recognizes the enormity of the misunderstanding between the sisters, but in a way that forecloses the possibility of recovering that lost ground. Similarly, Cheryl speaks honestly when she diagnoses, "'It's pretty bad in this stinking world when you can't even trust your own sister'" (175). Again, though, merely pointing to the absence of trust between them—and perhaps even its impossibility—is not enough to move beyond the impasse formed by radical incommensurability. The point is not merely that the sisters treat each other badly, but that the historical, material, and discursive conditions of systemic racism that make April and Cheryl intelligible in the ways they are—April as the good girl, Cheryl as the bad girl—are never located outside their relationship with one another. Instead, these conditions actively *produce* the relationship between the two sisters. Guilt and shame, for instance—

quintessential social feelings—run through their relationship as Cheryl charges April with condescending to her, which April feels guilty about, while at the same time Cheryl is ashamed of the things she's done that get April into trouble in the first place. There is no way to brush over or brush aside social, historical, and material contexts in order to assert a sisterliness between the two women, and talking honestly cannot will away their incommensurability.

The novel forces us to the most brutal recognition of the inadequacy of honesty and dialogue in the form of Cheryl's death. By the time she commits suicide, Cheryl has abandoned not only her conversations with April, but also her journal writing: her diaries end with April showing up at the hospital. April comes close to understanding the limits of dialogue herself in reading Cheryl's diary. Toward the end of reading the journals, April asks a series of questions that grow in intensity: "Why, oh why didn't she talk to me? Why couldn't we have talked to each other? And would it have helped?" (206). Far from merely rhetorical questions, these are serious questions that the narrative works inexorably toward: to take them seriously is to understand a good deal of the intellectual work *In Search of April Raintree* assays. What matters is not just to figure out what kind of a language can traverse the differences between women, but rather to attempt to understand why dialogue on its own may not be enough to overcome incommensurability. What makes the articulation of experience in language possible at all? What enables an interlocutor to hear and understand another's experiences? What produces silence, and what might different silences mean? When is dialogue helpful, and what are its limits? What are the underlying conditions for pursuing alliances among women? Although the novel raises these questions, it does not—to Culleton's credit—attempt to give them simple answers. Reverberating throughout the ending and beyond, questions like these, I contend, are what make the novel particularly poignant—they are what make it "moving" rather than merely "touching." *Why couldn't we have talked to each other? And would it have helped?* Feminists have to attend to questions like these in order to begin building community on the basis of difference.

When I discussed *In Search of April Raintree* in an earlier essay, I made much of the ending of the novel. Celebrating the novel's move away from the nuclear family toward a family unit reconstructed around chosen connections, such as April has with Cheryl's son, I argued that "the psychic and familial chaos wrought by Cheryl's suicide is healed by the promise of Liberty born as the next generation" (152). Parts of my earlier reading I still stand by. I still believe, for instance, that the chosen family is more important than the natal family, and that—as I have been arguing—it is in turning a biological given into a meaningful community that "sisterhood" becomes most significant. Similarly, I continue to see as significant April's rising political consciousness toward the end of the novel. But on reconsidering my earlier argument, I am unhappy with the way it glides over Cheryl's death. The community encoded in the final pages of the novel may well figure a reconstructed family, one organized along lines of affiliation rather than mere filiation, but it is also a community founded on the unresolvable absence of Cheryl. Although her voice has been filtered through April's consciousness throughout the novel, Cheryl's story only really begins to emerge after she has died, through the disembodied text of her journals and April's recollections. More uncomfortably, for a feminist reader, it is the white-identified April who gets to take care of her "brown" sister's child and move on.

This absence of Cheryl cannot conscionably be glossed over. The implications of the argument I am making here, in this essay, require seeing the community figured at the end of *In Search of April Raintree* as deeply compromised, so seriously flawed that it cannot be recuperated by the classically comedic ending that introduces the next generation as the means of soothing political discord. For rather than demonstrating the possibility of a workable feminist community that has managed to get beyond incommensurability, the death of Cheryl marks the sisters' failure to turn biological connection into meaningful sisterhood. In order for the novel's incipient feminist vision to be realized, both connections need to be present.[6]

Granted, there is an insistent optimism in the novel's closing lines that wants to obliterate the most awful aspects of what went before: the parents' alcoholism, the children's removal into social care, the horror of April's foster situation, Cheryl's alcoholism and death. To will these things away in the service of an optimistic reading of the text appears to me dangerous, however. Culleton doesn't give us any answers: sisterhood raises more problems than it solves; dialogue isn't enough; honesty isn't always possible or necessarily helpful. But the absence of answers, I believe, is what makes the novel so very productive. The most useful way to read *In Search of April Raintree* is to take away from the novel the questions that it raises: How have we as feminists gone wrong? Where do we go from here? What might a meaningful and responsible sisterhood look like? How might we talk to one another? And will that be enough?

Acknowledgments

I would like to acknowledge the generous and attentive readings given this essay by Julie Rak and Cheryl Suzack. Dave Watt provided expert bibliographic assistance, too. My gratitude to all.

Notes

[1] Morrison's afterword is quite critical of *The Bluest Eye*; in her analysis of its strengths and weaknesses, she comments that "many readers remain touched but not moved" (211).

[2] The archive on feminist understandings of "sisterhood" is enormous. Robin Morgan is widely credited with circulating the most problematic understanding of the term. Major critics of such usage who theorize difference among women include bell hooks (especially "Third World Diva Girls: The Politics of Feminist Solidarity" in *Yearning*, "Where is the Love: Political Bonding

Between Black and White Women" in *Killing Rage*, and "Sisterhood: Political Solidarity Between Women" in *Feminist Theory*); Audre Lorde (especially the pamphlet *I Am Your Sister* and "Age, Race, Class, and Sex: Women Redefining Difference" in *Sister Outsider*); Trinh T. Minh-ha (especially "Not You/Like You" in *When the Moon Waxes Red*); Hazel Carby; and Frankenburg and Mani. For a useful Canadian perspective, see Himani Bannerji. For evidence that the trope of sisterhood remains an enabling—if troubling—one for a wide range of feminist work, see Fleischner and Weisser; Nnaemeka; and Ang-Lygate et al.

[3] As I hope the following discussion will make clear, it is certainly not my intention to argue that feminism today should go back to the good old days of second-wave sisterhood. However, this essay is occasioned in part by a certain dismay I feel at the sense that, in the name of both well-earned critique and anti-feminist backlash, we feminists are in danger of losing our ability to conceptualize *community* in a meaningful way.

[4] At some moments in the novel, and to a certain degree, the sisters are cognizant of their differences. For instance, at the end of Cheryl's visit to April in Toronto, April says, "This time when Cheryl and I parted at the airport, I knew it was more realistic to acknowledge there would never be complete honesty between us" (111). Cheryl, too, recognizes their incompatibility: "I told [White Thunderbird] that you were my sister but in blood only. I told her your vision was clouded but that when your vision cleared, you would be a good person for the Métis people" (159). But while instances like these suggest the recognition of a certain divergence in their lives, they can't grapple with what I would call the deeper incommensurability between them.

[5] We know less about Cheryl, of course, because the narrative is filtered through April.

[6] Return, for a moment, to Cheryl's hopeful statement to White Thunderbird: "I told her that you were my sister but in blood only. I told her your vision was clouded but that when your vision cleared, you would be a good person for the Métis people" (159). April's vision does clear, but because April's political awakening is dependent on Cheryl's death, by the time April comes to be "a good person for the Métis people," she is no longer Cheryl's sister in the most literal sense.

Works Cited

Ang-Lygate, Magdalene, Chris Corrin, and Millsom S. Henry, ed. *Desperately Seeking Sisterhood: Still Challenging and Building*. London: Taylor & Francis, 1997.

Bannerji, Himani. *Thinking Through: Essays on Feminism, Marxism and Anti-Racism*. Toronto: Women's Press, 1995.

_____, ed. *Returning the Gaze: Essays on Racism, Feminism and Politics*. Toronto: Sister Vision Press, 1993.

Carby, Hazel. "White Woman Listen! Black Feminism and the Boundaries of Sisterhood." *Black British Feminism: A Reader*. Ed. Heidi Safia Mirza. London: Routledge, 1997.

Culleton, Beatrice. *In Search of April Raintree*. Winnipeg, MB: Pemmican, 1983.

Fee, Margery. "Upsetting Fake Ideas: Jeannette Armstrong's *Slash* and Beatrice Culleton's *In Search of April Raintree*." *Canadian Literature* 124–125 (Spring-Summer 1990): 168–180.

Fleischner, Jennifer, and Susan Ostrov Weisser. *Feminist Nightmares, Women at Odds: Feminism and the Problem of Sisterhood*. New York: New York University Press, 1994.

Frankenburg, Ruth, and Lata Mani. "Crosscurrents, Crosstalk: Race, 'Postcoloniality' and the Politics of Location." *Cultural Studies* 7:2 (1993): 292–310.

hooks, bell. *Feminist Theory From Margin to Center*. Boston: South End Press, 1984.

_____. *Yearning: Race, Gender, and Cultural Politics*. Toronto: Between the Lines Press, 1992.

_____. *Killing Rage: Ending Racism*. New York: Henry Holt & Co., 1995.

Hoy, Helen. "'Nothing but the Truth': Discursive Transparency in Beatrice Culleton." *ARIEL:* 25:1 (1994): 155–184.

Lorde, Audre. *Sister Outsider*. Trumansburg, NY: The Crossing Press, 1984.

_____. *I Am Your Sister: Black Women Organizing Across Sexualities*. New York: Kitchen Table/Women of Color Press, 1985.

Morgan, Robin, ed. *Sisterhood is Powerful: An Anthology of Writings from the Women's Liberation Movement*. New York: Random House, 1970.

_____. *Sisterhood is Global: The International Women's Movement Anthology*. Garden City, NY: Anchor Press, 1984.

Morrison, Toni. *The Bluest Eye*. New York: Plume Book, 1994.

Nnnaemeka, Obioma, ed. *Sisterhood, Feminisms and Power: From Africa to the Diaspora.* Trenton, NJ: Africa World Press, 1998.

Trinh T. Minh-ha. "Not You/Like You: Postcolonial Women and the Interlocking Questions of Identity and Difference." *When the Moon Waxes Red.* New York: Routledge, 1991.

Zwicker, Heather. "Canadian Women of Color in the New World Order: Marlene Nourbese Philip, Joy Kogawa, and Beatrice Culleton Fight Their Way Home." *Canadian Women Writing Fiction.* Ed. Mickey Pearlman. Jackson: UP of Mississippi, 1993. 142–154.

Contributors

Janice Acoose is of Métis/Saulteaux inheritance from the Sakimay-Saulteaux First Nations and the Marvil Métis community in Saskatchewan. She is the author of *Iskwewak Kah' Ki Yaw Ni Wahkomakanak: Neither Indian Princesses Nor Easy Squaws* (Women's Press, 1995). In addition to her work as a scriptwriter and co-producer for Katip Ayim Media Productions and CBC Radio, she has published articles on Maria Campbell, Indian residential schools, and contemporary First Nations women's issues. Her articles have appeared in *Looking at the Words of Our People: First Nations Analysis of Literature* (ed. Jeannette Armstrong, Theytus, 1993), *Gatherings* (1994), and *Residential Schools: The Stolen Years* (ed. Linda Jaine, Extension Division Press, 1993). Currently, she is an associate professor of English at Saskatchewan Indian Federated College, and a doctoral candidate in English at the University of Saskatchewan.

Michael Creal is professor emeritus of humanities at York University. In addition to publications on Voltaire, the French Revolution, and modern optimism, he has served as chair of humanities from 1967 to 1974 and as Master of Vanier College from 1974 to 1982. He has edited and written an introduction to *In the Eye of the Catholic Storm: The Church Since Vatican II* (HarperCollins, 1992), and contributed to the collection *Moral Expertise: Studies in Practical and Professional Ethics* (ed. Don MacNiven, Routledge, 1990). His current teaching interests have made extensive use of fiction in the areas of social ethics and contemporary moral issues.

Peter Cumming is a children's author and playwright who lived for six years in Inuit communities in the eastern Arctic. His children's books include *A Horse Called Farmer* (Ragweed Press), *Mogul and Me* (Ragweed Press), and *Out on the Ice in the Middle of the Bay* (Annick Press). His plays include *Ti-Jean* and *Snowdreams*, both published through the Playwrights Union of Canada. In 1994, he was awarded the George Wicken Prize in Canadian Literature for his essay, "'The Prick and Its Vagaries': Men, Reading, Kroetsch" (*Essays on Canadian Writing,* 1995). His teaching interests include profeminist masculinities in contemporary Canadian fiction, First Nations literatures, and pedagogical issues arising from new technologies. Currently, he teaches children's and young adult literature at the University of Western Ontario and the University of Guelph.

Margery Fee teaches postcolonial literatures, Canadian literature, and First Nations writing at the University of British Columbia. Her recent publications include "Aboriginal Writing in Canada and the Anthology as Commodity" (*Native North America: Critical and Cultural Perspectives*, ed. Renée Hulan, ECW Press, 1999), and "Who Can Write as Other?" (*The Postcolonial Studies Reader*, eds. Bill Ashcroft, Gareth Griffiths, and Helen Tiffin, Routledge, 1995). She has published on Indigenous writers Jeannette Armstrong, Beatrice Culleton, Keri Hulme, and Mudrooroo Narogin, and has just completed editing a special double issue of *Canadian Literature* on Thomas King.

Agnes Grant is the author of *No End of Grief: Canadian Indian Residential Schools* (1996) and *James McKay: A Métis Builder of Canada* (1994). She coauthored *Joining the Circle: A Practitioner's Guide to Responsive Education for Native Students* (1993) with LaVina Gillespie, and edited *Our Bit of Truth: An Anthology of Canadian Native Literature* (1990). She teaches Native Studies education courses at Brandon University for the Brandon University

Northern Teacher Education Program (BUNTEP) and Program for Educating Native Teachers (PENT). She has written numerous articles on Native literature and Native educational issues. Her most recent publications include "'Great Stories Are Told': Canadian Native Novelists" (*Native North America: Critical and Cultural Perspectives*, ed. Renée Hulan, ECW Press, 1999).

Helen Hoy is associate professor of English and women's studies at the University of Guelph. In addition to teaching at the universities of Toronto, Manitoba, Lethbridge, Guelph, and Minnesota, she has served as chair of the Department of English at the University of Lethbridge (1989–90), and director of graduate studies for the Institute for Advanced Feminist Studies at the University of Minnesota (1991–93). She is the author of *Modern English Canadian Prose* (Gale, 1983), and coeditor, with Thomas King and Cheryl Calver, of *The Native in Literature* (ECW, 1987). She has published articles on Canadian fiction, including Hugh MacLennan, Gabrielle Roy, Robertson Davies, and Alice Munro, and on Native Canadian women writers, including Jeannette Armstrong, Maria Campbell, Beverly Hungry Wolf, and Lee Maracle. Currently, she is completing a book entitled, *How Should I Eat These? Reading Native Women Writers in Canada.*

Beatrice Culleton Mosionier is author of several books including *Spirit of the White Bison* (Peguis, 1985) and *Christopher's Folly* (Pemmican, 1996). Beatrice has acted as the playwright-in-residence for Native Earth Performing Arts; worked for the Royal Commission on Aboriginal Peoples; and travelled extensively to fulfill reading and speaking engagements for a wide range of audiences. She is currently working on a new novel.

Jeanne Perreault is professor of English at the University of Calgary. She is coeditor (with Sylvia Vance) of *Writing the Circle: Native Women of Western Canada* (1990), and coeditor (with Joseph Bruchac) of *Critical Visions: Contemporary North American Native Writing*, a special issue of Ariel (1994). She is the author of *Writing Selves: Contemporary Feminist Autography* (1995). Other publications include "Memory Alive: An Inquiry into the Uses of Memory in Marilyn Dumont, Jeannette Armstrong, Louise Halfe, and Joy Harjo" *(Native North America: Critical and Cultural Perspectives*, ed. Renée Hulan, ECW Press, 1999), and "Writing Whiteness: Linda Griffith's Raced Subjectivity in *The Book of Jessica" (Essays on Canadian Writing*, 1996*)*. Currently, she is examining the racializing of whiteness in white women's texts.

Cheryl Suzack is a Ph.D. candidate in English at the University of Alberta and a member of the Batchewana First Nations of Ojibways. She is currently working on a dissertation entitled, "Strategies for Cross-Cultural Exchange: Native North American Women's Writing and the Politics of Location."

Jo-Ann Thom is a Métis woman who was born in Manitoba. She holds a B.A. with Distinction and an Honours Certificate from Saskatchewan Indian Federated College and an M.A. in English from the University of Regina. She has served as head of the English department at Saskatchewan Indian Federated College (1976–78), and since 1978, as dean of academics. Her article "When Good Guys Don't Wear White: Narrative Voice, Discursive Authority and Ideology in Leslie Marmon Silko's *Almanac of the Dead*" appeared in *Native North America: Critical and Cultural Perspectives* (ed. Renée Hulan, ECW Press, 1999). Her teaching and research interests include the development of Aboriginal literature in Canada and Canadian Aboriginal poetry.

Heather Zwicker is associate professor of English at the University of Alberta. She locates her work at the crossroads of postcolonialism and cultural studies, with a particular focus on queer theory and feminisms. Her teaching interests include postcolonial theory and fiction, queer theory, feminist studies, and contemporary African, Canadian, and Northern Irish literature. Some of her recent publications include "Between Mater and Matter: Radical Novels by Republican Women" (*Reclaiming Gender: Transgressive Identities in Modern Ireland.* ed. Marilyn Cohen and Nancy Curtin, St. Martin's Press, 1999), "Homosexuality in Zimbabwe" (Encyclopedia of Lesbian and Gay Histories and Cultures. ed. George Haggerty, Garland Publishing, forthcoming), and "Gendered Troubles: Refiguring 'Woman' in Northern Ireland" (*Genders*, 1994).